*LIFE'S GATEWAY TO HAPPINESS*
*BOOK 2 in the SHOW ME SERIES*
Published by Anne Stone

Copyright © 2016 by Judith A Seligstein Living Trust
ISBN:978-0-9970691-5-0

Edited by: Mosaic Editing
Printed in the USA.

Cover Design and Interior Format

# Life's

## GATEWAY TO HAPPINESS

*The Show-Me Series*

BOOK 2

# Anne Stone

*To my family and best friend Cynthia Farrar.*
*You are always there cheering me on.*
*And, as always, to you Dad.*

# Prologue

KELLY SAMUELS WAS SHOCKED BEYOND her wildest dreams. She didn't know how she had made it back to her condo but she had. She glanced at the clock as she stumbled through the door—it was well past eight o'clock. She had no idea what had happened in the last four hours since she'd heard the words that she still couldn't fathom.

She'd been fired. Fired from the job that she'd given her heart and soul to for the last year and a half. Out of nowhere, Bill had called her into his office and fired her due to poor work performance. Poor work performance? She'd worked in the information technology department of Lattice Works since she'd obtained her graduate degree from Atlanta's Emory University. Lattice Works was a company that developed software in the medical field. She was the company's senior software development tester for newly developed programs.

She was stunned to say the least. How could this have happened to her? She'd flown up through the ranks in her short employment with the company. She'd worked eighteen-hour days *for what*, she thought. For being humiliated for something she had nothing to do with. Bill had accused her of poor job performance, and he hadn't let her speak at all during their five minute discussion. *Discussion*, she thought with a sneer. What discussion? It had all been one-sided and, before she knew it, she was being escorted back to her desk by a security guard. She was given five minutes to pack up her things, and then she was walked directly to the front door and practically thrown out. The last thing she heard was, "Don't ever come back here."

Kelly rehashed everything. She remembered how she felt walking down the hallway to Bill's office. Her hands were clammy; her heart was pounding against her chest—thinking back, she guessed her senses had taken over. Fearing the worst, yet when she'd been called to his office she hadn't a clue as to why he'd asked to see her.

She recalled sitting stiffly in the uncomfortable chair that he'd held for her. She'd glanced around the room as she entered his office and noticed the head of human resources was already seated at the table.

She'd known then that the meeting was not going to have a positive outcome.

Kelly watched Bill as he sat in his chair. He was all business and, within seconds of him beginning his speech, she heard the words, "You're fired. Gather your personal belongings and immediately vacate the premises. Your last check will be direct deposited at the end of the month. You haven't been with the company long enough for a severance package."

Kelly was stunned. She didn't recall even opening her mouth. Bill stood and opened the door. As she left his office, a security guard followed her to her office. A box had already been placed on her desk for her personal belongings.

She grabbed her photographs of her family, a plant, her coffee mug, daily planner, radio, and pen set that her parents had given her as a graduation present. She threw it all into the box. She reached for her purse, slamming closed the desk drawer. Throwing her purse into the box with the remainder of her personal items, she threw her coat on and, with head held high, picked up her box and headed for the front door.

The security guard didn't say a word to her until she reached the front door. And then, the words that kept reverberating through her mind were said, "Don't ever come back here."

Bill had no idea what was truly going on at his company, and she didn't know what to do. She sat on the couch in her family room until the wee hours of the morning and then realized she needed to go home—back to St. Louis and back to her family. She could regroup there and then decide what to do.

Kelly ran to her room and threw open her closet door. On the back of the door was her full length mirror. She looked at herself. She was a sight. Her long, light brown hair stuck out at odd angles as a result of her running her fingers continually through it as she'd replayed her day. Her brown eyes were red-rimmed from crying—her mascara had run down her face. *So much for water proof,* she thought. She compared herself to a clown with a bright red nose, and she was almost as pale as one, too.

She couldn't do anything about her appearance except wipe the mascara from her face. She grabbed her face cleanser and headed off to the bathroom where she removed her old makeup and the tear-strewn mascara.

She returned to her closet, grabbed her suitcases and started filling them with anything she could lay her hands on. By the time she'd packed her car and placed a forwarding order for her mail in her mailbox, it was almost three in the morning. Kelly had kept extra temporary forwarding orders in case she was ever sent out of town on business for an extended period of time. Clearly she would not need them anymore.

By her estimates, if she drove straight through from Knoxville, Tennessee, maybe exceeding the speed limit a little bit, she'd be in St. Louis around ten in the morning. She was sure her sister, Angelina, would be up in the next couple of hours.

Angelina was married, and she and her husband Alejandro had adopted a little boy within the last year. Matthew would be turning eight soon. They also had a three-month-old daughter, Angelina-Maria. Kelly knew how busy Angelina was with the children. Alejandro was often gone, either at the hospital where he worked as a doctor or away giving talks. *I can help her with the kids,* Kelly thought as she finished packing her car. She'd call Angelina around seven and tell her she was coming home for a visit. Kelly knew she'd be up with the baby and getting Matthew off to school. Yes, she'd go to Angelina's.

Kelly had three additional siblings, none of them nearly as reliable. Her younger siblings, Colleen and Wyatt, still lived at home while her brother James lived in an apartment. Kelly didn't want to return to her parents' home as she could never explain to them what really happened at Lattice Works. She would take refuge at Angelina's. Her house was huge and she could easily help her with Matthew and Angel while she looked for another job. With her decision firmly in place, she jumped into her car and pointed it towards home.

# Chapter One

"SHH, ANGEL.  GO TO SLEEP.  That's right, close your pretty eyes and go to sleep."

Angelina was exhausted.  She'd been pacing around her house for what seemed like hours trying to calm her three-month old baby.  Alejandro had been called back to the hospital during the night, and she'd been up with the baby ever since the garage door went up.  To top it all off, she still had to get Matthew off to school.  She didn't know how she was going to get through the day.

Angel finally drifted off to sleep.   Angelina was getting ready to sit down on the couch, when she looked up and saw Matthew heading her way.  He was dressed and ready to go to school.

Matthew was her adopted son.  His parents had been killed in an automobile accident.  Alejandro had been his doctor as he was undergoing dialysis and preparing for a kidney transplant.  Immediately, Angelina had fallen in love with him and they agreed to adopt him.  He was a bright little boy and knew that his mother was stressed with his little sister.  He'd heard her cries all through the night, and knew he had to help his mother.

"Mom, is everything alright with Angel?  I heard her crying. Where's Dad?"

"Honey, she's tired. Just a little cranky, that's all. Your dad got called back to the hospital during the night."

"I hope the person's okay. I remember when he used to come and see me during the night when I was at the hospital."

"He did. I remember."

"I remember you coming to see me, too."

Angelina nodded, remembering those days well. She also remembered Alejandro visiting her when she had been in the hospital. Gosh, that seemed so long ago and, at times, it seemed just like yesterday.

"Mom, don't be mad at me, but I called Gabby."

"When?"

"A few minutes ago. She's going to take me to school."

Before Angelina could open her mouth, she heard a faint knock at the door. Matthew rushed to the door and opened it. There stood her sister-in-law and best friend, Gabriella. They had gone to college together and had taught together at St. Margaret's before she had Angel and became a full-time mom. Angelina still called her Gabriella, but most everyone shortened it to Gabby.

"Gabby, let me get my book bag."

"Bad night?" Gabriella asked her friend.

"You could say that. She was sleeping soundly until she heard Alejandro leave at two. She's been crying ever since he left."

"She misses her daddy."

"Not sure about that, but I can say that I certainly do. He can always get her to calm down and go back to sleep. He's got that special touch." Angelina yawned and closed her eyes. "Thanks, Gabriella. I appreciate it. I wasn't sure how I was going to get him to school. I thought I'd take him in at lunch time if Angel cooperated and slept for a few hours."

"Matthew's quite the little boy. He was so cute when I answered the phone. He was whispering—I couldn't understand a word he was saying. I made out that he wanted me to pick him up for school, that Angel had been crying for a loooong time, and Alejandro wasn't home."

"Thanks, I really appreciate it."

"Let me get him out of your hair. I'll bring him home, so you don't have to worry about that. You get some rest, too."

Gabriella reached down and hugged Angelina goodbye. Matthew waved and, in a whisper, told her and Angel to have a good day. And then, they were out the door. She took a deep breath. Hopefully she'd be able to catch a few winks before the baby woke.

The next thing Angelina knew, her cell phone was ringing. Following promptly after, the baby started crying again. "I can't catch a break," she said to herself. Reaching over, she grabbed her cell phone from the coffee table. She glanced at the clock as she answered. Surprisingly, she'd caught almost two hours of sleep. With the baby screaming in the background, she answered her phone.

"Angelina?"

"Kelly? Is that you?"

"Yeah," she answered tiredly. "I've got a problem."

"What's wrong?"

"Well, I decided to make an impromptu visit home. I tried calling you a little while ago, but your cell just rang."

"Oh, I guess I didn't hear it. I was napping. Angel's been a little fussy this morning."

"I'm sorry to hear that. Well, I don't want to bother you, then."

"Kel, what's wrong?"

"I've had a little accident."

"Are you okay?"

"I am, but I need some help. I'm about twenty minutes from your house and, well, I almost hit a deer. I swerved to avoid it and ended up in a ditch. I can't get enough traction on my rear tires, and I'm just plain stuck!"

"Did you call for a tow truck?"

"I don't have any numbers with me and thought maybe you could help."

"Where exactly are you?"

Angelina lived in a rural section of the suburbs. Alejandro had bought his home when he returned to St. Louis from Wisconsin. He had neighbors, but they were all spread out within the subdivision. It was like driving through rural Missouri when anyone visited.

"I'm near that abandoned farmhouse by the highway. You know the one where the man used to cut his grass with his walker perched precariously on top of his riding mower. I always worried that he would lose it and not be able to get off his lawn mower."

"I know where you are. I'll call for a tow truck. You sit tight and stay warm."

"I'm not going anywhere."

☙

Kelly disconnected the call and closed her eyes. It was the middle of February and she knew it would be a while before a tow truck appeared. Temperatures were hovering at the freezing mark, and she was starting to get cold. She'd turned off her motor because, with the way her car was situated in the snow, she knew her exhaust pipes were buried.

Kelly was exhausted—she was crashing from her high. She was still in shock and couldn't believe where she was... Sitting in her car in a ditch in Missouri. She should be back in

Knoxville, sitting behind a computer, and performing user-acceptance testing on a new program that was getting ready to roll out to medical clinics all throughout the country. Behind her closed eyes, she could still see Bill basically calling her an incompetent employee. As his words rolled through her mind, her exhaustion took over and she began to cry. She was furious with herself. At least six weeks ago she should have taken things into her own hands and sought out Bill when all hell had started breaking lose between her and her boss, Ken Jones. She hadn't wanted to ruffle feathers—instead, she'd wanted to keep everything under the radar. She had thought everything would pass in time. She would see the project to the end, and then go to human resources and ask for a transfer. Her decision to not act on this situation cost her the job that meant everything to her. Her indecision to act would have consequences that she would never be able to expunge from her record. She'd been fired, and how did one cover that up on a résumé? She definitely couldn't seek out Lattice Works for a letter of recommendation that was for sure. Her life was in utter chaos, and she had no idea how to remedy it.

Tears were streaming down her face. She hadn't heard back from Angelina and guessed she was still trying to locate a tow truck driver. She was startled back to reality though when she heard a loud banging against her window. She was surprised to see a man whose face was covered by the hood of his coat—all she could see was his dark brown hair sticking out from under the hood. Thankfully, her doors were locked. She hadn't considered that someone might attack her. Her heart started to beat faster—she didn't know what to do. Would this man help or hurt her? Then, she heard the voice and her name.

"Kelly, it's me, Alec. Alejandro's brother."

Kelly took a deep, relieved breath and unlocked her door.

Alec pulled open the door and noticed the dried tears on her face. "Are you hurt?" he asked. He whipped off his gloves and reached for her hand to check her pulse.

"I'm okay, really. I just slid off the road when I tried to avoid a deer. It darted out in front of me."

"You should've hit it."

"Seriously? Why would I want to do that?"

"To avoid being in the ditch."

"But the deer... My car..."

"That's what we're told. Hit the deer and avoid an accident. More people are killed or seriously injured when trying to avoid a deer. Now, are you sure you're not injured?"

"Nothing but my pride."

"Let's get your things, and I'll take you to the house. We'll call for a tow truck there. By the way, what are you doing here? I had no idea you were in town."

"Just got here. I drove in this morning."

"Must have left Knoxville pretty early."

"You could say that." Kelly grabbed her purse and laptop from the trunk. She'd get the remainder of her things once she was out of the ditch. Alec grabbed her bag put it in his backseat and held his car door open for her. She assumed that she was headed to Angelina's, but Alec pulled off the road a few miles before Angelina's house.

"Where are you taking me?"

"To my house."

"I thought Angelina had sent you. I was headed to her house."

"Well, we can go there, but first I need to drop by my house and let Chancey out. I was called into the hospital early last night and was just headed home to let him out."

"Chancey. What a name."

"Yeah, and he's had way too many chances to stay. He gets

into more trouble than Matthew could ever think of getting into. I'm sure we'll go home to some type of mess."

And sure to his reputation, Chancey had gotten into trouble yet again. They were greeted with a mess when they walked through the door. Trash was strewn about the kitchen. Alec glanced back at Kelly and noticed that she was shivering.

"How long were you stuck in that ditch?"

"Not too long."

"What do you call 'not too long?'"

"Okay, a while. I lost track of time."

"First, let me call Angelina and let her know that you're okay and that you're with me. Then I'm getting you something hot to drink. You look like you're freezing."

A shiver wracked through her body and she nodded in agreement.

Alec called Angelina, and Kelly listened as she sat down on the couch.

"Angelina, it's Alec. I've got Kelly with me. We'll be by shortly… We'll tell you when we get there. Have you called for a tow truck? Don't worry about it, I'll handle it. You just get that little one to calm down."

Thankfully, Alec had a single-serve coffee maker. He quickly made her a hot cup of coffee while he contacted a neighbor who had a towing service. He arranged to meet him within the hour at Kelly's car. Kelly was very thankful for Alec's help after the hell that was the past twenty-four hours. Hopefully this was a sign that things would start getting better.

# Chapter Two

A LEC DECIDED TO MAKE A cup of coffee for himself as
he watched Kelly drink hers. While she waited for her
coffee, she wrapped herself in a blanket. She was still shivering when Alec handed her the cup of hot coffee. "Tell me the
truth. How long were you sitting in that snowbank?"

"I guess it was a little longer than I thought. I'd already
spoken with Angelina, and she was going to call a tow truck,
but I guess she got busy with the baby."

"Well, we have to get you warm before we head out again.
Why don't you drink your coffee, and then take a hot shower.
That should warm you up. I'm going to call Ralph and tell
him to hold off on meeting us. Once I'm convinced you're
warm enough, then I'll let him know and we can meet him."

"We can't do that. I'm sure he's busy."

"Don't worry about it. We need to get you warm. Ralph
will think nothing of it. Now, let's get you to that shower."

"Okay. That sounds like a good idea."

Alec led her to one of his spare bedrooms and went in
search of some towels for her.

☽

Kelly walked into the bathroom and was pleasantly surprised with what she discovered. Shower gel and lotion from

one of her favorite stores was on the counter, along with a spare toothbrush and toothpaste. She wondered if he had a lady friend that often stayed over, but she wasn't going to let herself judge him. He was Alejandro's brother, and he was entitled to live any way that he wanted. She wouldn't question whether he had a live-in girlfriend—it just wasn't her business.

"Here you go," he said as he walked into the room, handing her the towels he'd retrieved from the linen closet. "I also brought you one of my sweatshirts. It's a little warmer than what you're wearing. In all honestly, I don't know why you didn't dress warmer."

She'd left her house so quickly that she really hadn't stopped to think about what the temperatures were like in St. Louis versus Knoxville. It was definitely colder in St. Louis—she knew that. "I left in a hurry and didn't really think about the temperature difference. Thanks for the sweatshirt. I'll give it back to you at Angelina's."

"Don't worry about it. I'm just worried about how cold you are. Take your shower and hopefully you'll warm up." With that, Alec turned and walked from the room, closing the door on his way out.

Kelly had forgotten how much Alec resembled Alejandro. He was dark-skinned, had dark hair and dark brown eyes. His hair was cut short just like his brother's. Kelly raised his sweatshirt to her nose. She inhaled it deeply and decided it smelled just like Alec. She loved the scent of his aftershave.

She placed the sweatshirt on the bed, and headed into the bathroom. She turned the shower on as hot as possible and waited for the water to warm. She removed her clothes, hopped in, and waited for the water to warm her. She closed her eyes—all she could think about was everything that had happened to her in the last twenty-four hours. Yesterday, at this time, she'd been working diligently in Knoxville and, less than twenty-four hours later, she was standing in Alejandro's brother's house taking a hot shower.

Kelly stepped out the shower and felt much better. She put her clothes back on and threw his sweatshirt over her head. Kelly opened the bathroom door and was surprised Alec standing there with his hand raised.

"Oh, hi," he said. "I was just coming to check on you. Feeling better?"

"Yes, I am. Thank you, and thank you for your sweatshirt."

"I just got off the phone with Ralph. He said he'd meet us at your car in the next few minutes. Ready?"

Kelly nodded and followed him from the bedroom. He reached for her coat and helped her put it on. She grabbed her purse and laptop, and they headed out the door.

❦

In a matter of no time, Ralph had pulled her car from the snowbank. He gave her the same advice Alec had, "Next time, hit the deer. You'll be safer that way."

"I just don't understand the logic behind that," she said, shaking her head. "How will I be safer? But okay, whatever you say." Kelly reached into her purse to retrieve her checkbook to pay Ralph, but he just waved her on.

"On the house this time," Ralph said as he got into his truck and drove off.

"Come on. Let's head over to Alejandro's. I'd like to check on Angel. She was still crying when I spoke with Angelina."

Kelly hopped into her newly-freed car, and Alec got into his—he followed her as she drove to Angelina's. They had a huge driveway, so Kelly and Alec parked off to the side. Kelly got out of the car and noticed that Alec was still in his front seat—he had just taken a phone call. She grabbed her purse and laptop from the backseat of her own car and headed to the front door.

Kelly hadn't even had the chance to walk up to the door when it was flung open. Angelina stood there with a crying Angel in her arms. Kelly hurried up the sidewalk. She didn't want the baby getting cold, so she quickly crossed the threshold into the house and closed the door behind her. Angelina looked worn out. She had dark circles under her eyes and an upset baby clinging to her neck.

Kelly reached for Angel, but Angelina refused to give her up. Alec came bustling through the door and stopped abruptly. Placing his hands on his narrow hips, he looked at both mother and daughter. "I could hear her all the way out to the car."

"Alec, she's been like this since Alejandro left at two this morning. She took a brief nap, woke up screaming again, and hasn't stopped since. I've tried everything. She's not hungry, doesn't need a change of diaper… Here, maybe you have the magic touch like your brother does."

Angelina handed over her daughter and grabbed Kelly into a tight embrace. "Are you okay? Were you hurt when you slid off the road?"

"I'm fine. Thankfully Alec appeared out of nowhere. I was just a little cold, and Alec took care of me." Angelina looked questioningly at her brother-in-law. "He fixed me a cup of coffee, and I took a shower to warm up. I'm fine now."

"Angelina, I don't know what got into your sister, but she drove here in just a t-shirt. A t-shirt! Can you believe that? It's winter!"

"I told you! I just started driving and didn't think about the temperatures. It was much warmer in Knoxville."

Alec just shook his head while he continued to calm Angel. He held her securely in his arms and started walking about the house with his niece.

❧

Alec had taken Angel into the nursery, and Angelina led Kelly into the family room where she flopped down on the couch. "Would you like something to drink?" she asked tiredly.

"No, Angelina. I'm fine," Kelly said as she sat beside her sister. Sighing deeply, she closed her eyes and threw her head against the back of the couch. "I guess you're wondering why I'm here."

Angelina looked at her sister, nodded, and said, "I am. Let's talk after Alec leaves, okay?" Kelly nodded her head in agreement. Angelina was still surprised by Kelly's presence. The last time she'd talked to her, Kelly hadn't even mentioned a trip home. It came out of nowhere, but she decided she wasn't going to pressure Kelly as to why she was there. She'd let her tell her in her own way.

Alec had been with Angel for only a few minutes when he walked casually into the family room. "I've done my good deed for the day."

"Alec, thank you. I really appreciate it," Kelly said.

"I'm not talking about you, Kelly. I'm talking about Angel." With a winsome smile on his face, he turned to Angelina, "I have the magic hands. Your daughter is fast asleep." He raised his hands and wiggled his fingers.

Angelina gaped at him. "What did you do? She's been upset all day."

"I guess it's the pediatrician in me. As soon as I walked into the nursery, she started sucking her thumb and went to sleep. I didn't do anything."

"She thought you were Alejandro, that's what I think."

"Maybe? I don't know." Turning to Kelly he said, "Are

you okay now?"

"Yeah, I'm fine. I am finally warm."

"Okay, then. Well, I've gotta head into the office. Joe called just as I was pulling into the driveway, and he said the office is packed with sick children. I wish I could stay longer and chat, but duty calls."

"I understand." Angelina walked over and hugged Alec. "Thanks for calming Angel. I'll call you the next time Alejandro isn't around and Uncle Alec can come to her rescue."

"You're going to give me a big head," he chuckled as he headed to the front door.

"Nonsense. What's true is true. Thanks again," Angelina said as she followed him out of the room.

Kelly got up and walked over to the windows. She looked out across the expansive backyard. Angelina approached her sister and put her arm around her waist, hugging her closely.

"Whatchya thinkin'?"

"I was just remembering the Fourth of July picnic when you and Alejandro sprung your engagement on us. That was a special day."

"Indeed, it was." Angelina paused, "Kelly, what's wrong? Why are you here?"

Walking away from Angelina, Kelly wiped her hand across the bar. Turning back to her sister, she said, "I can't go home. I just can't go to Mom and Dad's."

Kelly didn't look at her sister as she waited for her to explain.

"Kelly, what happened? What caused you to drive home, out of the blue, without warning? And at three in the morning. Tell me. I can help you."

"You can help me by letting me stay here. Please, Angelina. I'll help you with Matthew and Angel. I'll be your housekeeper. Anything. Just let me stay. I can't go home."

Angelina walked towards her, reached for her hand, and led her back to the couch.

"Kelly, just calm down for a minute and tell me what happened," she said as she sat back down on the couch. Kelly continued standing. She was nervous. Anxious. Kelly started fidgeting with the hem of Alec's sweatshirt. She didn't want to disappoint Angelina, but she knew her sister wasn't going to give up without an explanation.

"Kel, just tell me what's wrong. I won't tell anyone unless you tell me it's alright. You can stay here. Don't think twice about it. We have plenty of room, and the kids would love to see more of their aunt. Come on now…" Angelina reached for Kelly's hand again and drew her down to the couch.

"I'm just so embarrassed. I don't know how to say this."

"Just… out with it, alright?"

Sighing deeply, she said, "I got fired."

"Fired?"

"Yeah, fired."

"What happened? I thought you were doing so well at Lattice Works. You've had how many promotions?"

"Three."

"Three in a year and a half. I'd say you were a star employee…"

"Well, Bill didn't think so. He fired me for poor job performance."

"Did you just say job performance?"

Nodding her head, Kelly closed her eyes and scrunched her forehead. She bit down on her lip to prevent the tears from forming.

"How can that be?"

"Your guess is as good as mine. Now do you understand why I don't want to go home?"

"Yes and no. It's your choice, but you'll have to tell Mom

and Dad eventually."

"I know. I just can't right now. I'll call them and let them know that I'm in town and staying with you, but that's it. Can we keep it just between us?"

"I can't lie to Alejandro, Kelly. He's going to want to know why I didn't tell him you were coming to stay. I have to tell him why you appeared out of nowhere. You have to understand that."

"He can't tell anyone. Promise me!"

"I'll tell him he has to keep quiet about your visit, but I can't promise that he will."

"I understand."

Standing abruptly, Kelly headed for the front door. "I'm going to get my luggage and bring it in. I'd like to take a nap, if that's okay with you. I've haven't slept in a day and a half, and I'm exhausted."

"Go get your bag, and I'll get you fresh towels."

"Thank you, Angelina. You're the best."

Kelly walked out the door and Angelina headed off to one of the guest rooms. Her day had gone from bad to... not terrible. She knew that Angelina wanted more of an explanation, but she didn't have one. She also knew that she'd have to eventually tell her parents why she was in town, but that was a problem for another day. Right now, she just wanted to rest.

&#x1F66F;

Alec was tired. He hadn't slept in what seemed like forever. He felt like he was back doing his residency. The last month had been exhausting, and he needed a vacation. Being a pediatrician, especially during the winter, his office hours were packed during the day and then his evenings were spent rounding at the hospital, checking on all of the children that were hospitalized. And to top it off, today he'd had to deal with having Kelly's car pulled out of a snowbank. He really wanted to start the day over.

He got to his office and it was well past noon. He walked through the door and his brother caught him as he walked into his office.

"Good morning, or is it afternoon?" Joe joked as he sat in the chair in front of Alec's desk.

Alec did everything he could, but he just couldn't suppress his yawn.

"Rough day?"

"Rough day? How about rough day and night."

"What's up? I know you were called into the hospital last night, but you can't be just getting back."

"Yes and no." Yawning again, he said, "How's the waiting room? Are we behind?"

"Don't worry about that. I took care of it, and we're back on schedule. Tell me what's going on with you."

"I was headed home from the hospital to shower and change, and I found a car stuck in a snowbank. It was just down the road from my home. You know, where the abandoned farm is?"

"Yeah, okay. Was the person injured?"

"No, she was fine, but you'll never guess who it was."

Joe just looked on, "I have no idea."

"Kelly."

"Kelly? Kelly who?"

"You know Kelly. Angelina's sister."

"What was she doing here in a snowbank? Doesn't she live in Atlanta?"

"No, Knoxville."

"Okay, so why is she here and not there? Alejandro didn't tell me she was visiting."

"I don't think he knew. I'm not sure why she's here, just

that she is. In fact, I don't think Angelina knew she was coming either. She just seemed… I don't know, I just think she
was surprised, too."

At that moment, Ashton walked in the room, flopping
down in the chair next to Joe, "It's nice of you to join us on
this bright and busy day. It's been hell here. Where have you
been?"

"Nice to see you, too, Ashton." Alec said as he yawned.
"I've been helping a stranded woman out of snowbank."

"Sounds interesting."

"Yeah, well, it ended up being Angelina's sister. She'd just
driven in from Knoxville, and she swerved to avoid a deer and
ended up off the road."

"I don't know why people just don't hit 'em. More people are injured in accidents trying to avoid the deer than just
hitting them," Ashton said.

"I know, I told her the same thing. Anyway, I went by
the house and Angel was crying her head off. Angelina said
she'd been crying since Alejandro left for the hospital early
this morning. Can you believe that as soon as I held her, she
calmed down?"

"Yeah, right. I find that hard to believe."

"It's true, Joe. Ask Angelina. She said she was going to
call Uncle Alec to calm her when Alejandro wasn't around. I
guess he has the magic hands, too." Alec yawned again.

"Why don't you go home? I know you didn't get any
sleep last night. Ashton and I can handle the rest of the day.
Unless we have some last minute emergencies, I'm sure we
can handle the load."

"You sure?"

"Yeah," Ashton said. "You look beat. Go home and get
some rest."

Alec yawned again. "Thanks. I'm glad we added you to

the practice. It sure helps out on days like today."

"You mean I'm only good for that," Ashton said, kidding.

"No, you know what I mean. Thanks again," Alec said as he stood to leave for the day.

Alec walked out of the office while Joe and Ashton looked on.

"He sure does look beat," Ashton said.

"Yeah, he does," said Joe. "He's been burning the candle at both ends lately." Joe stood up and said, "Now, let's take care of our patients. Maybe we can get out of here a little early."

Both men stood and headed off to their own offices to prepare for their afternoon office hours. Joe was worried about his brother and made a mental note to keep his eye on him.

# Chapter Three

A LEJANDRO WALKED THROUGH THE DOOR earlier than Angelina expected—Kelly was still napping. Gabriella had just brought Matthew home and was getting ready to leave when Alejandro joined them in the family room.

"What are you doing here?" Alejandro asked Gabriella. "I was surprised when I saw your car in the driveway."

"I brought Matthew home from school. And I could also ask you the same thing," Gabriella smirked.

"Yeah, well I haven't had sleep in what seems like days. I went into the hospital early—"

"Yeah, yeah, yeah," Gabriella interrupted as she reached up and placed a kiss on her brother's cheek. "That's why I'm here. I was helping Angelina out."

"You were?" He turned to Angelina, "Honey, is everything alright?"

"Ask your daughter that question," she said over her shoulder as she walked Gabriella to the door. "I'll talk to you later, Gabriella. Thanks again for the save today. It meant a lot, especially with Kelly showing up out of nowhere."

"Yeah, what's up with that?" Angelina just gave her friend "the look" and Gabriella knew not to question her further.

"Love you," Gabriella said as she walked out of the house.

Angelina closed the door, turned around, and ran directly into her husband.

"Whose car is that?" Alejandro asked as he placed his arm around Angelina's waist and walked her back to the family room.

They sat down on the couch and she answered, "Kelly's."

"Kelly? As in your sister Kelly?"

"You got it."

"I didn't know she was coming to town."

"I didn't either," Angelina whispered as she snuggled closer to Alejandro.

"Why are you whispering?" Alejandro whispered back.

"Because Kelly is sleeping and, if she wakes, I don't want her to hear us."

"Angelina, what is going on here?"

"Well, I'll tell you. My day started at about the same time yours did at two this morning." Alejandro raised his eyebrows. "Your daughter started crying as soon as the garage door went up and didn't stop until Alec came by."

"Alec? What was he doing here? Between Gabriella and Kelly showing up, on top of Alec… This is getting stranger by the minute."

"You're telling me. Anyway, Gabriella took Matthew to school for me. I've got to say, Matthew is one hell of a big brother. He called Gabriella this morning when I couldn't calm Angel and asked her to take him to school."

"He did?"

"Yep, and when your daughter finally settled down, Kelly called. She tried to avoid a deer on the road and ended up in a snowbank over near the abandoned farm. She called me and I was going to call a tow, but Angel started in again and I completely forgot about her."

"How does Alec play into the mix?"

"Well, he was coming home from the hospital and saw her car stuck in the snow. He went to see if the occupant was okay when he discovered it was Kelly."

"I'm sure he was surprised by that."

"He was. I don't know how long she'd been there, but he took her to his house and called Ralph. She was pretty cold, so he warmed her up and then they had her car towed out. He came by because he heard Angel crying in the background."

"Is she okay now?"

"She's been perfect since Alec came by. I swear there's something in the Alvarez blood. He held her for about two seconds, calmed her, and had her to sleep. I told him that I'm calling him whenever you're not around. Between the two of you…"

"We've got the magic touch."

"You do," Angelina said as she snuggled even closer. "Now, about Kelly."

Alejandro tightened his hold on her and kissed her brow.

"She's going to stay with us for a while."

"Okaaaay," he said. "You know I love your family, but why doesn't she want to go home to your parents."

"She has her reasons." Sighing she went on, "You need to promise me you won't tell anyone what I am going to tell you. You promise?"

"Is she pregnant?"

"Alejandro!" she cried as she slapped his chest. "I can't believe you! No, she's not pregnant!"

She paused a moment and added, "At least, I don't think so…" She pulled away from him slightly, "Now promise me, please?"

"I promise. Now tell me what's going on."

Angelina told him about Kelly's phone call and her story

about being fired. "I think there's more there than she's telling us. I just have a feeling. I've never seen her like this... She's really upset. Not that she shouldn't be, but I'm worried about her. I hope she'll tell us the truth, but for now we have to believe that's all it is."

"Why was she fired?"

"Supposedly job performance."

"Job performance?" Alejandro asked incredulously.

Angelina nodded.

"I don't understand. I thought she was working her way up through the ranks."

"She was."

"How can that be then? It just doesn't make sense. If she's been receiving promotions..."

"Three in a year and a half."

"That's the thing... I can understand your skepticism. I agree there has to be another cause here."

"I don't want to question her too much. When she got here, she was truly frazzled with her long drive and then sliding off the road. I'm going to give her some distance and hope that she will be honest with me. We just have to be patient."

"What about your parents?"

"I'm not sure if she's called them or not. I'm sure she's embarrassed after having excelled in graduate school to have been fired from her first real job. I'll talk to her later and see when she plans on telling Mom and Dad. Please promise me you'll go easy on her."

"Sweetheart, you don't have to ask me—you know I will. Maybe she'll open up to me. We have a pretty good relationship. At least, I think we do."

"No, you do. I know she likes you and feels comfortable around you, or she wouldn't have asked to stay with us."

Angelina put her head down on his shoulder and sighed. "I could take a nap. I'm exhausted."

"Well, why don't you? I'll watch Matthew and Angel."

"You're tired, too."

"Don't worry about me. I'm used to it. Take a nap, and I'll worry about dinner."

"You're sure?"

"Don't ask twice." He kissed her cheek and got up from the sofa. "I'm going to change real fast, and then I've got some reading to do. I'll be in my office."

Angelina watched her husband leave the room. She often wondered how she'd been so lucky to find Alejandro. It had taken them a while to fall into their relationship, and they'd experienced more than most couples had in a lifetime, but things were really good now.


Kelly woke from her nap and was greeted by an extremely quiet house. She got out of bed and checked on Matthew, who was playing in his room. "Hi there, Matthew."

"Hi, Aunt Kelly. What are you doing here? When did you get here? How come—"

"One question at a time! I got here earlier today. I'm going to stay with you for a while."

"Cool! That's great," he said as he ran over to her and threw his arms around her thighs, hugging them as tightly as he could. Kelly squatted down and hugged him in return.

"Maybe you can help me with my homework. Mom usually does, but I know she's resting now that Angel is sleeping. And Dad is busy in his office."

"Your father's home?"

"Yeah. He got home right after I did. He's in his office reading."

"Oh, okay. Thanks. If it's okay with you, I'm going to say

hi to him, and then I'll be back to help you. Why don't you get started?"

Matthew ran over to his desk and pulled his homework out of his backpack.

Kelly took her time walking down the hallway towards Alejandro's office. She didn't know what she was going to say to him. She was the one who was valedictorian of her class when she'd gotten her advanced degree. Everyone thought she was so bright. Smart. How could she explain to Alejandro that she'd gotten fired? She was the one that was supposed to shine, excel in whatever she chose to do.

As she approached Alejandro's office, she noticed the door was partially closed. A glimmer of light from his desk lamp illuminated the hallway. She peeked in, and he was sitting with his back to the room, looking out towards the backyard. His hand was perched on the side of his head and he appeared to be deep in thought. She rapped her knuckles on the six-paneled oak door, but he didn't even flinch. She knocked louder and stuck her head through the doorway. He turned around in his chair, looked her directly in the eyes, and smiled.

"Kelly," he said as he started to stand. "Come on in."

Kelly approached the desk, and he came around the front and pulled her into a hug. "Have a seat," he said as he pulled out the wing-backed chair that sat in front of his desk. She sat while he joined her in the adjacent chair.

She just stared at him—she didn't know what to say or how to start.

He spoke first, trying to ease her into their conversation, "Angelina's resting."

"I know. Matthew told me when I went in and checked on him. He's conned me into helping him with his homework."

"He's good at that," he chuckled. "Matthew's a bright boy.

We go through this every night with him. He generally finishes his homework without any help, he just likes one of us there to review it with him. That's all." He smiled at her and paused before he continued, "Angelina told me you're going to be staying with us for a while."

"That's okay with you, isn't it? If it's not—" she rambled.

"Kelly, stop," he said, raising his hand. "It's fine with me. We have this huge house and plenty of room for you."

She smiled shyly at him.

"I want you to be comfortable around here. And with my crazy schedule, maybe you can help Angelina with the kids. I know she was a little overwhelmed today with Angel. From what I hear, Alec and Gabriella helped her out. I wish I could be here more, but with my schedule and all…"

"I'm more than happy to help her. I just appreciate you letting me stay here." Taking a deep breath, she continued, "I guess she told you why I'm here."

"She did."

"And?"

"I'm not going to prejudge you. I'm sure there is a perfect explanation for your firing. From what I hear, though, your performance was exemplary, especially with receiving three promotions in the last year and a half. There's got to be something else going on here—job performance doesn't make sense to me. Maybe you misunderstood Bill."

"You know him?"

"Yeah, I do. So do Alec and Joe. I met with him and my brothers when they were interviewing him about Lattice Works' software. Alec and Joe are looking at upgrading the computer software at the clinic, and they asked me to join in with them on the presentation."

"Huh, I didn't know that." Shrugging her shoulders, she added, "Well, I know what I heard, and that's what he told me.

I met with him for about five minutes, and then I was escorted out of the building like a convicted felon." She looked
down at the floor and started ringing her hands in her lap.

Alejandro noticed her nervousness, but didn't say anything.
He had to agree with Angelina—something wasn't right here,
and there had to be more to the story. Alejandro felt that Kelly had become comfortable discussing her situation with him,
so he asked, "Have you told your parents yet?"

Kelly looked at him with round, shocked yes, her hands
freezing in place. She looked away, not wanting to tell him
the truth. A chill went through the room, and he noticed her
shoulders begin to shake—she was trying her best not to cry.
He looked at her hands which were now clutched to the arms
of the chair, her knuckles white. He reached for her hand and
pulled it from the arm of the chair. Holding it between the
two of his, he noticed how cold her hands were. He rubbed
them and said, "Kelly, everything is going to be okay. You can
tell them whenever you're comfortable with it. I know this
happened less than twenty-four hours ago and that you're still
getting used to the idea. Take your time. Angelina and I are
here whenever you need to talk. Got it?"

She smiled at him and nodded shakily.

"Kelly, if you need anything just let me know. I'll do
whatever I can to help you."

"Thank you," she whispered as she tried to keep her tears
at bay. "I know you will. Now, I'd better go check on Matthew." She slowly got up from the chair, turned, and placed a
kiss on his cheek, "I'm just thankful I have you for a brother-
in-law." With that, she walked from the room.

Alejandro stared after her, going over in his head the way
Kelly had reacted to their conversation. She was nervous and
maybe even scared about something that happened with this
firing. He decided he was going to do his own investigation.

He'd hopefully find the answer to this mystery.

# Chapter Four

A LEJANDRO HAD BEEN EXTREMELY BUSY of late. He'd been working directly at the hospital the last couple of weeks and was headed out of town for a conference where he was giving a presentation.

The day before he was scheduled to leave town, he called Ashton Holder, Matthew's pediatrician. Matthew was scheduled for a regular office visit while he was out of town. Typically Alejandro accompanied Angelina when he went in, but unfortunately this time he was traveling. Alejandro, being the concerned father, wanted to make sure Ashton ran a series of specific tests on his son. Prior to Alejandro and Angelina adopting him, Alejandro had been Matthew's doctor as he waited for his kidney transplant.

"Ashton, hi. It's Alejandro."

"Hi there. How are you?"

"Exhausted, but fine otherwise. I'm calling because Matthew's scheduled to see you this week and I'm traveling. I want to make sure that—"

"Alejandro, don't worry. I've got it taken care of."

"I know, but—"

"Alejandro, stop worrying. This is just a check-up. I'm sure he's just fine."

"But—"

Ashton was tired of this behavior. Every time that Matthew was scheduled to see him, Alejandro called to make sure that he was on board to run specific tests. In fact, he never had to run the tests, but did so anyway to calm Alejandro's concerns. Ashton knew about Alejandro's first wife and son dying in a flash flood. He knew that Alejandro was still dealing with his grief, but this whole situation was getting old. He was going to talk to Alec and Joe about their brother.

Ashton told Alejandro not to worry—he would deal with it and would send him the test results as soon as they were available. Alejandro calmed down and thanked him as they ended their conversation.

Ashton immediately headed to Alec's office. Office hours had just ended and he was wrapping up his dictations for the day before leaving. Alec's door was opened, so Ashton walked in unannounced and flung himself into the chair that sat directly in front of Alec's desk.

"Something troubling you?" asked Alec.

"Yeah, you could say that," he said as he brushed his hand through his hair. "You could say my trouble is your brother."

"Joe?"

"No, Alejandro."

Alec smirked. "I guess Matthew's coming in for a visit."

"Indeed he is, and Alejandro's not going to be here."

"That's right… He's giving a presentation at a conference this week. I think he's leaving tomorrow, maybe?"

"Alec, we have to do something here. He's like this every time I see Matthew. Even on those occasions when he's an emergency visit for a cold or the flu."

"I know. He can get a little uptight."

"Uptight? That's what you call it? I feel for Angelina."

"Don't worry about her. She can deal with him." Glancing down at the calendar, Alec realized just what was troubling his brother. The anniversary of Tammy and Michael's deaths was fast approaching. He was sure that was the cause of Alejandro's concerns. He made a mental note to pay his sister-in-law a visit while Alejandro was on his trip.

"Ash, they've been through an awful lot together as couple. Between Matthew, Angelina, and Alejandro's own issues—"

He didn't get a chance to finish his thought as Joe walked in.

"Did I miss the invitation to the party?" asked Joe as he strode over to a chair.

"Party? If you call dealing with your brother a party," Ashton said.

"Alec, what did you do now?"

Both Alec and Ashton spoke in unison, "Alejandro."

Joe smiled and sat down. "Is Matthew coming in soon?"

"Wow. Both of you really know your brother."

"We do, and we know what he's been through in the last four years. I personally don't know how he kept it together like he has. He's had his moments, and I'm sure he's going to be rehashing the memories again in a few short weeks, but who wouldn't? Grief is tough to deal with. It can rear its ugly head at any time, whether expected or not. We need to put ourselves in our patients' lives sometimes and be the one on the receiving end of the diagnosis or be the one hearing the unfortunate words that your loved one has died. Alejandro's done that so often as a physician, but when he had to experience it on the reverse side, it really hit him hard. It caused him to put into perspective how precious life truly is."

"I guess you're right, Alec. He's been through a lot, but he just needs to relax a little."

"I don't disagree with you. He's pretty high-strung at times, but Angelina's really helped calm him these last couple of years. Having her and Matthew, and now little Angel, he's starting to relax somewhat. Personally, I would be on pins and needles just like he is. Alejandro is too aware, and being a specialist in his field gives him even more fuel to worry about Matthew. Any little illness would cause me to question whether he was rejecting his kidney. As a doctor, I know I shouldn't be like that, but how could you not as a parent?"

Joe and Ashton nodded in understanding.

Alec continued, "Joe, I'm going to run by Alejandro's on my way home now. I'll call you after."

Joe raised his hand as he walked from the room. "Go easy on him," Joe called as he walked down the hallway. Joe always left Alec to deal with Alejandro when it came to their family. Alec just had a way with their brother that always seemed to bring him back to reality.

☾

It was just past the dinner hour when Alec rang the door-bell at Alejandro's. He was taken aback when Kelly answered the door.

"Oh, hi there, Alec. Come on in."

Alec strolled through the door with his coat in hand. It looked like he planned on staying a while. Kelly reached for his coat and hung it in the coat closet. "If you're looking for Alejandro and Angelina, they're not here. They're at some school thing with Matthew."

"Oh, I wasn't aware of that. Well, then I won't keep you," he made to turn around.

"Oh no, come on in and keep me company. Angel's here and you need to visit with your niece." She led him into the family room where Angel was contentedly sitting in her bouncy seat.

Kelly started to reach for her, but Alec stopped her before

she could unfasten the restraints holding the baby in place.

"Leave her. She looks happy just where she is. Let's sit and talk and, if she gets crabby, I'll hold her. My motto is to leave them alone when they're content." He seated himself on the couch while Kelly sat at the opposite end from him. "So what's new with you?"

"Not much. I've been helping Angelina with the kids and the house. Were Alejandro and Angelina expecting you?"

"No, I just wanted to come by and check on Alejandro before he goes out of town."

"Well, I know he's been working non-stop since I got here. I hardly ever see him, and I think he's leaving for a conference tomorrow. From what I understand, he's going to be gone a few days."

"Yeah, he is. I just wanted to touch base with him, that's all."

"I think Matthew has a doctor's appointment in the next couple of days with your partner, Ashton Holder?"

"Yeah, that's him."

"I'm going with Angelina when she takes Matthew in. She didn't want to go alone in case she'd miss something he had to say. Usually Alejandro goes with her. At least, I think he does."

"Yep, he certainly does."

Kelly raised her eyebrows. "Are you being sarcastic there or what?"

"Yes… no. Alejandro just gets a little worked up about Matthew and his doctor's appointments."

"I can understand that."

"Yeah, I guess I do, too. It's just that he—"

"Come on now, Alec. Think about what you're saying, and why he gets that way."

"I know, I do." He stopped and looked down at the floor,

then changed the subject. "Enough about that. What else have you been up to besides helping Angelina?" Alejandro had told Alec the evening of her arrival that she'd lost her job and was staying with them until she got her feet back underneath her. He felt he should know especially after coming to her rescue. Alec promised not to say anything to Kelly as he'd wait for her to tell him.

"Not much really. Taking it easy."

The next question flew out of Alec's mouth before he had time to think, "Would you like to go out sometime? I mean, get away from the kids and go out to dinner and a movie with me?"

Alec began to immediately second guess himself before Kelly responded. *Did I just ask her out on a date?*

"You know, that sounds like fun. I haven't been to dinner or a movie with friends in a long time. I used to work such ungodly hours that I never had time for myself to do anything fun. So, if you're serious, I say yes. I'd love to go out with you."

"Great," he said, relieved. "Just let me know what evening works best for you and we'll make it a date." He decided he'd question her a little more about what she did working for Lattice Works on their date.

"Thanks, Alec. That sounds like fun."

Just then, they heard a noise and Matthew came running into the room, throwing himself into Alec's arms. Apparently the rest of the family was back from the school function.

"Uncle Alec," he yelled excitedly. "What are you doing here?"

"I came to see you."

"Really? You came to see me?"

"Yes. You, your mother, your father, your sister, and aunt."

Angelina walked into the room, "Matthew, it's getting late.

Go get dressed for bed, and I'm sure your Uncle Alec will put you to bed and read you a story."

"I'd love to do that," Alec said as he put Matthew down. "Okay, buddy. Go get your pajamas on, and I'll meet you in a few minutes."

Matthew hurried off to his bedroom.

"Alec, what are you doing here?" asked Angelina as she placed a welcoming kiss on his cheek.

"I came by, as I said, to see everyone."

"I think I know better than that," she said. "Did Alejandro call you?"

"Not me, but Ash."

"I see," she said just as Alejandro finally walked in the room. "What are you doing here, Alec?"

"Do I have to explain a third time?" he said, laughing. "I already told Matthew, Angelina, and now you that I came by to see everyone."

"Uh, huh," Alejandro said as he headed for the bar. "Drink anyone?"

Alejandro knew why his brother showed up out of the blue, and it had everything to do with the conversation he had with Ashton earlier in the day.

"Well, you know I don't want one," said Angelina. "Kelly, Alec, would you like a glass of wine or something harder?"

"No thanks," they both responded while they all watched Alejandro pour himself a glass of wine.

"I'm going to head off and make sure Matthew's getting his PJs on. You know how he can linger and not get ready for bed," Angelina said.

"I think that's all kids. Bedtime is a hard concept to get ahold of. They think they can stay up just as late as we do," added Alec.

"Well, on that note," Kelly said, getting up, "I think I'm

going to head off to bed myself. Alec, call me and we'll set up a time to go out."

"Sounds good," he said as Angelina and Kelly walked from the room together.

Angelina leaned into her sister and whispered, "What's this? You and Alec are going out?  On a date?"

"He just asked me to dinner, that's all.  Nothing big there."

"I don't agree with you.  This is a big thing for Alec—he never goes out.  He pretty much works or goes home, and when he's home he's usually working out. Remember, he is a confirmed bachelor."  Kelly did not need a reminder. At Angelina and Alejandro's wedding, Kelly had caught the bouquet and Alec caught the garter.  Kelly remembered how Alejandro joked with Alec, wondering who would be the next married one in the family.  Alec politely reminded him that it wouldn't be him.

"You don't have to remind me.  I do have the lovely photo of the two of us at your wedding."

Angelina laughed.  She remembered that photo very well. Angelina had made Kelly sit on Alec's lap, showcasing the bouquet and the garter that they'd each caught.

"This so-called date doesn't mean anything to me.  It's just dinner and a movie, nothing else."

"Huh, well I guess we'll see about that," Angelina said as she walked into Matthew's room.  Kelly continued into her bedroom and closed the door.  Leaning against the door, she pondered what Angelina had just said.  Was this more than dinner and a movie to Alec?  Was it a true date?  *Nah*, she thought.  They were just friends and he was a bachelor.

*

"Did I hear you correctly, Alec?  Are you taking Kelly out on a date?"

"I'm taking her out to dinner and a movie. That's all. It's not a date."

"Really, now? It sounds like a date to me. Remember what I told you—you're going to be the next one married in the family. How can you forget my wedding?"

"I didn't forget that scene at your wedding. How could I? Angelina framed that photo of me and Kelly and it sits proudly in my family room," said Alec sarcastically.

Alejandro laughed. He remembered how Angelina had insisted on where Alec should keep it.

"This is not a date, so get that idea out of your head."

Alejandro watched his brother. He thought back to how he had fought against dating Angelina, and maybe that's what Alec was doing—fighting with himself about dating Kelly.

Changing the subject, Alec asked Alejandro about his upcoming trip and presentation at the conference. He was trying to take his time leading into why he was actually there. He watched Alejandro sip his wine.

Alejandro sat down on the couch and brushed his hand across his forehead and down the side of his face. Slowly raising his eyes, he glanced at his brother. Alec knew what was coming next and waited for it. Alejandro took another sip of his wine and placed the glass down on the end table next to the couch. Turning back to his brother, he started in, "I know why you're here Alec, and don't pretend otherwise. It's about my conversation with Ashton, isn't it?"

Alec continued watching his brother's movements. Alejandro stood and began to pace about the room, a normal gesture on his part. When Alejandro had to think something through, he either sat in his office chair, looking out the window across the backyard, or he paced. Alec watched him silently.

Alejandro turned towards his brother and said, "Yes, I did

call Ashton, and yes, I did request a battery of tests for Matthew. What's new? I do it every time Matthew visits the office. So anything else? It's not like this is new for him. Why did you invite him into the practice anyway?"

Alec had been waiting for Alejandro's barrage. It wasn't anything new to him or Joe. What was new was him questioning both their and their father's decision on hiring Ashton. He'd joined the practice in the last year, filling the gap their father made when he pretty much retired. Even though their father still came into the office, it was irregular and he no longer had a patient load dedicated solely to him. John Alvarez filled in when one of them took vacation or when they were busy performing school check-ups right before school started.

Alec knew Alejandro. He was an exceptional doctor, and he wondered if, this time specifically, he had a reason for requesting this specific round of tests. "Alejandro, what's going on? You're questioning our decision—and mind you that includes Dad's decision—on hiring him. You know he comes highly recommended. He's added a lot to the practice, and I have no second thoughts with hiring him."

Alejandro sat down and threw his head back against the couch. He closed his eyes momentarily and then looked Alec squarely in the eyes again. Breathing deeply, with anguish in his voice, he said, "This is the first doctor's appointment that I'll miss since Matthew had his transplant. I'm just being cautious, that's all."

"Cautious? You're like this every time he comes in, whether you're with him or not. What gives?"

"Nothing. I'm sure he's fine… Now let's get back to you and Kelly."

"Let's say we did, and not. I'm going to go read Matthew a story and then head out. I'll see you when you return from your conference. I hope you're in a better mood then."

Alejandro laughed off Alec's comments as he left the room. He finished his glass of wine and headed off to his office to finish the last minute changes he wanted to make to his presentation. *Nothing is wrong with Matthew,* he thought to himself. *I'm just being me and being overly cautious. Just like I should have been with Angelina when I misdiagnosed her condition.* Alejandro still hadn't forgiven himself for misdiagnosing her infertility, thus causing her the turmoil she endured for over a year. He wanted to be on his game and make sure his family stayed safe and healthy.

Alec joined Angelina and Matthew in his bedroom. By the time Alec appeared, surprisingly, Matthew had fallen asleep. Instead of staying in his room to talk, Angelina led him into the living room, knowing that Alejandro was ensconced in his office. "Okay, out with it, Alec. Why are you really here?"

"I just wanted to check on everyone."

"Good story, but I want to hear the real reason, and I can only guess what it is. Did Alejandro call you or Joe about Matthew's appointment?"

"No, he didn't call one of us—he called Ashton directly."

"I see. And the problem is…"

"No problem."

"Come on now, Alec. I think I know you a little better than that. Is he worried about Matthew?"

Alec stared at Angelina. He knew she was a strong woman after experiencing all that she had in the last two years. He truly loved her as though she were his own sister. He'd known her since she and Gabriella had been freshmen in college. He couldn't get anything past her, so he finally told her about Alejandro's call and the tests he requested.

"I know, Alec. I knew he'd be calling one of you, especially when he realized he was going to miss Matthew's appointment. Alec, that's just him. You have to get past it. He wants to be in control, but can't be in this case. He's no longer Matthew's doctor, and I don't care what he says—he's had a hard time turning over his case to someone else. The anniversary of Tammy and Michael's deaths is just around the corner. Just cut him some slack. You should know by now how he gets this time of year. He becomes increasingly protective of those he loves. You included."

"Okay, okay, I hear you. I'm going to head on out now."

"Just you hold it right there, mister. What's this with you taking Kelly out on a date?"

"It's not a date."

"Sure seems like one to me."

"It's just dinner and a movie. I thought it would be good for her to get out, start socializing. Has she even started looking for another job yet? Has she told your parents that she's basically living around the corner from their house?" He paused briefly and, pointing a finger at her, added, "You need to forget about that photo from your wedding. Alejandro reminded me of it, and I'm sure you haven't forgotten about it either."

She definitely had not forgotten about that photograph. She looked at him, smiled, and went on with what she wanted to say, "No and no. She talks to Mom and Dad, but I'm sure she hasn't told them she's actually living down the street from them—Mom thinks she's still in Knoxville. Alec, I don't know what really happened to her, but I'm guessing there's more to the story. I want to help her, but she has to first acknowledge to herself that she's truly lost her job, and then she has to tell my parents. Until then, I don't think I can help her."

"Well, maybe I can. I'll see what I can do." Alec knew Bill quite well. In time, after he truly got to the bottom of

Kelly's predicament and fully understood what happened in the last moments of her employment with Lattice Works, he might intervene and contact Bill. Alec turned and hugged Angelina, kissing her on the cheek. "You take care now. Call if you need anything while Alejandro's out of town. I'm just down the street."

"Yeah, right."

"Just around the corner."

"And down the road quite a piece," she chuckled. "Don't worry. I'll be calling at two in the morning when Angel can't get back to sleep."

"I'll be waiting," he said as he walked down the sidewalk to his car.

# Chapter Five

KELLY SPENT AS MUCH TIME as she could with Matthew and Angel. She made it her priority to help Matthew with his homework while Alejandro was out of town. That way, Angelina could focus on the baby and not be too stressed out. Thursday was upon them and Matthew's doctor's appointment was that afternoon. Kelly was in the kitchen when Angelina took a call on her cell. Kelly could tell by the way Angelina was talking that it had to be Alejandro on the other end.

"Yes, I'm picking him up from school after he eats lunch... Yes, I know what you told me... Yes, Alejandro, I will make sure that Ashton calls you immediately once his examination is over." Sighing deeply, she continued, "Yes, I will make sure that he runs that extensive battery of tests that you requested... Yes, I did receive your email with the specific tests that you want to be run."

Kelly had zoned out during the first thirty seconds of the conversation, but she perked up when she heard Angelina finally speak from her heart.

"Alejandro, please stop. You're rambling. Take a deep breath."

There was silence in the room, then Angelina started

speaking again, "Better now? Alejandro, you need to calm down. Everything's fine. Kelly is going with me as a second set of ears. I promise I'll write down everything that he says, and I will call you when I leave the office. Don't be surprised if Ashton doesn't call you right away—I think you've kind of pissed him off with your expectations of him and your over-protectiveness."

Kelly heard another silent pause as Angelina listened to her husband speak. "Okay, now. I've gotta go change Angel before I pick Matthew up from school. Just relax and I'll call you later... I love you, too."

Kelly had no idea that Alejandro got this worked up. She walked into Angel's nursery as Angelina was changing her outfit. "You okay?"

"Why wouldn't I be?"

"I heard your conversation with Alejandro. I had no idea he got this worked up."

Angelina finished dressing her daughter, picked her up, and turned towards Kelly. "Yeah, he does... Normally, I just listen to him rant, and then eventually he gets the picture and calms down. But today... today was different. Alejandro is pretty intuitive. I hope he hasn't seen something with Mat-thew that's he hasn't shared with me. I don't think so, but then again he did try and shield me from his condition right before the transplant."

Angelina turned and walked from the nursery. Kelly fol-lowed.

"Alejandro gets worked up any time Matthew goes to the doctor. In many ways, I think he still feels as though he's his physician. He wants to make sure that he stays on top of ev-erything, and I mean everything. He takes it to the extreme, which is what he's doing right now, especially since he's not here. Kelly, this is the first time he's missed any type of doctor's appointment Matthew's had since his transplant. He's being Alejandro, the concerned parent… I expect it from him, especially since the anniversary of Tammy's death is just around the corner. He gets this way all the time. I just deal with it." Angelina paused and finished dressing Angel. "Now, let's gets this little one into her pumpkin seat, and then we can head out and pick up Matthew."

Kelly placed her hand on Angelina's arm, stopping her momentarily. "Angelina, does Alejandro still have his night-mares?"

"No. At least, not that I've noticed recently. I don't want you to get a bad impression of him. I love him so much that at times my heart aches. This is just a phase that he goes through, and I've become accustomed to his antics. He loves us all dearly but he still grieves over Tammy and Michael, and I don't expect that to ever change. Now, that's enough said about my husband. Let's go get Matthew."

*C*

Angelina went into St. Margaret's to pick up Matthew while Kelly sat in the car with Angel. She had no idea that Alejandro was so protective. Living with him certainly opened her eyes to her brother-in-law's deep love of his family.

Matthew jumped in the car, reached over, and kissed his sister's forehead. "Hi, Aunt Kelly."

"Hi, yourself. How was school?"

"It was great. Hey Mom, are we going to see Uncle Alec and Uncle Joe?"

"I don't know, sweetheart. Your appointment is with Dr. Holder. If they have time, maybe we can say hello. How does that sound?"

"Awesome. I love seeing them. I wish they'd come over more often," Matthew added as Angelina drove in the direction of the clinic.

Angelina parked the car, then she and Kelly got out of it. Matthew opened his door, got out of the car, and headed towards Kelly's side where she grabbed ahold of his hand while Angelina pulled Angel's car seat from the car. Thankfully, Angel had fallen asleep on the drive over. Angelina just prayed she stayed that way during Matthew's office visit. When Matthew's name was called, Nurse Sadie Eberle led them to the examining room. She'd been on the staff since Alejandro's father had started the practice, and she remembered both Angelina and Kelly from when they used to see Alejandro's father when they were children.

"Oh my gosh, is that you, Kelly?" she said as she led them down the hallway.

"Yeah, it's me Sadie. How are you?"

"I'm just great. I had no idea you were back in town."

"I'm just visiting," Kelly said as they walked into the examining room. Angelina set Angel's car seat on the floor, then sat down in a chair with Matthew perching himself on her lap. Kelly stood chatting with Sadie for a few moments and then they were left alone.

"Dr. Holder will be in shortly."

Turning quickly to Angelina, Kelly leaned in closely to her face and whispered, "I hope that Wyatt or Colleen don't have appointments with Dr. A soon. I don't want Sadie saying anything to Mom about me being in town."

Angelina said evenly, "Well, I guess you better start thinking fast because I think they do have appointments with either Alec or Joe in the next week or so. Did you forget that Dr. A retired, or semi-retired? And knowing Sadie, she will say something to Mom about seeing you. You're going to have to tell them what happened soon."

Sighing, Kelly turned and said, "I know. I will."

Ashton knocked softly on the door, announcing his presence, and walked into the room.

Matthew was cautious around him—he hadn't completely warmed up to him since he took over for Alejandro's father. He started acting shyly. Angelina thought it was strange as he clutched his arms around her neck.

Angelina introduced him to Kelly and indicated that she was there as a second set of ears in Alejandro's absence. Ashton reached down and started talking to Angel. He thought the interaction with Matthew's sister may calm him, which in fact did. Matthew began commenting on Ashton's comments made to the baby.

"She's really growing. Pretty soon she'll be as big as you, Matthew."

"I don't think so. She's got a long way to go."

"I guess you're right," Ashton replied as he watched Matthew and his sister.

"Dr. Holder, when will Angel start to walk?"

"Oh that won't be for a while. Why?"

"Because I can't wait to take her in the backyard and play. I just love my little sister."

"I know you do," Ashton said, turning to Angelina. Matthew crawled out of Angelina's arms and sat beside his sister.

Ashton watched Matthew's interaction with his sister. He began asking Angelina the routine questions that any pediatrician would ask his patient.

"How's Matthew like school?"

"He loves it," replied Angelina.

"Does he have many friends?"

"He does. I can't keep up with all of the names. I think he's really adjusted to St. Margaret's. Last year he was in the public schools because there were no openings for him at St. Margaret's. All in all, I think he's transitioning well."

"Good grades?"

"All A's."

"Matthew," Ashton called his name, and he looked up from playing with Angel. "Your mom tells me you have all A's. That's awesome."

Matthew smiled. "Yeah, it's been easy. I love my new school."

Ashton turned back to Angelina. "How's his appetite?"

"Well, you know kids. One day they like something and the next day they can't stand it." Ashton nodded as he listened and made notes in Matthew's file. Just as Ashton was ready to ask his next series of questions, Angelina reached into her purse and pulled out a sheet of paper. She presented it to Ashton. He knew what it was.

"I take it this is from your husband."

"Yes, it is. He wants to make sure you run these specific tests."

"I know about them. I spoke with him last week."

"I know, but he just wants to make sure—"

"I understand, but come on now. He's got to relax a little, give up his controlling influence as a doctor. He's no longer Matthew's doctor. I am. I will run these tests, but I'm not sure they're really needed. "

"I have to believe that Alejandro has Matthew's best interest at heart. If he feels they're needed, then they are," said Angelina.

With that, Matthew chimed in. "Yeah, Daddy does need to relax sometimes. He's always watching me, always asking me if I'm feeling okay."

Angelina listened to her son. She had no idea Alejandro did this as much as Matthew led on that he did. She knew he was protective, but maybe he was going a little too far.

"Is he like this all of the time?" Ashton asked Matthew.

"No, just recently. I think it's because he can't be here today. He's giving some sort of... what do you call it, Mom?"

"It's called a presentation, Matthew."

"Yeah, presentation. My dad always comes to the doctor with me. He has since before I was adopted. I'm sad that he's not here today."

"Sweetheart, you know he would have been here if he could."

"I know."

Ashton wrote down Matthew's concern about his father's protectiveness. He'd have to address that again sometime, especially if it was causing Matthew to become upset or anxious.

Ashton examined Matthew and scheduled the series of tests that Alejandro had requested. He left the room and Sadie returned to draw the various samples needed for the tests. Matthew was used to needles and didn't flinch once. Ashton returned to the room and indicated that all seemed well. They'd hear from him soon regarding the test results. Angelina thanked him, and just as he was about to leave the room, she asked if Alec and Joe were around.

"Joe's in his office, and I think Alec's with a patient. You're more than welcome to check on Joe. In fact, I think he's expecting you."

Angelina picked up Angel's car seat and grabbed Matthew's hand. Kelly asked for directions to the restroom and said she'd meet them in Joe's office shortly.

Kelly went to the ladies room and, as she made her way down the hallway towards Joe's office, became distracted and blindly crashed into something. Next she felt a pair of hands grab her to steady her forward movement. Once she got her bearings, she looked up at a smiling Alec.

"Hey there, are you in a hurry or something?"

"Oh, hi Alec… No I'm in no hurry, just heading back to Joe's office. Angelina and the kids are visiting with him since we've completed Matthew's visit with Ashton."

"Oh, I see. How did it go?"

"You have to ask Angelina that question."

"I will," he said as he guided her down the hallway. Upon entering Joe's office, Matthew couldn't contain himself. He ran to Alec and threw himself into his arms.

"Hey there, buddy. How'd it go with Dr. Holder?"

Matthew looked up at him and scrunched his nose. "I don't like him."

"You don't?"

"No. I don't think he likes Daddy either."

"I see," Alec said as he looked over Matthew's head at both his brother and Angelina. Quickly changing the subject, he said, "Well… Hey, Matthew I still need to read that book I promised you the other night. If you can stay awake, how about I come over tonight and I can help put you to bed?"

"That sounds great," Matthew said as he turned to Kelly. He needed to use the restroom, too, so Kelly took him while Angelina stayed back talking to Joe and Alec.

"Well?" asked Joe.

"I have to agree with Matthew. I don't think Ashton particularly cares for Alejandro. He made a comment about the tests Alejandro requested that caused Matthew to agree with him about Alejandro needing to relax. I don't know…"

"We know how he can be this time of year. I'll talk to Ashton again and put his concerns to rest," Joe said.

"You know how he is. Alejandro loves us so much that he can't fathom us being injured or sick. He's a wonderful father and husband. I just get concerned that he's going to go too far, letting the grief consume him again."

"Don't worry Angelina. I'll talk to him again. I promise

Joe and I will not let that happen."

"Thanks."

"Now, what did he say about Matthew?"

"All's well until the test results come back. I don't think he has any concerns. I'd better get going now, though. I promised Alejandro I would call him when we were done." Angelina reached down and picked up Angel's carrier. "Thanks again for letting me vent. Love you both," she said as she walked out of Joe's office.

Angelina met Kelly and Matthew in the hallway. Alec caught her eye and came running out of Joe's office.

"Kelly, do you have a sec?" Alec asked as Angelina continued down the hallway.

"Ah, sure. Angelina?"

"Go ahead. We'll meet you in the car."

Kelly turned back to Alec as he approached. He grabbed her hand and held it loosely between them. "I'm going to come by tonight since I promised Matthew I'd read him that story. I know it will be a late when we're done, so would you care to go out for a coffee after I finish my story?"

"Reneging on your dinner invitation?"

"No, of course not! I still plan on taking you to dinner. I just thought it would be a nice treat for you since you helped Angelina out today, that's all."

"I'll go if you promise me dessert, too."

"Of course. Then it's a date."

Kelly smiled as he squeezed her hand.

"You better go since Angelina's waiting for you."

"Yep, okay then. I'll see you tonight." Kelly walked away.

Turning around in the hallway, Joe caught Alec's eye. "Did I hear you correctly? Did I just hear you ask Kelly out on a date?"

"Well, it's not really a date. It's just in appreciation of her helping Angelina out today. It's just for coffee."

"And dessert, too. If I heard correctly."

"Yeah, dessert too," Alec said as Joe chuckled, returning to his office. He also remembered that photograph of the two of them from Alejandro's wedding. Yep, Alec had done it—asked Kelly out on a date.

&

Kelly opened the car door and was greeted with Angelina's huge smile. She settled herself into her seat all the while Angelina couldn't wait to ask her the question that had been on her mind the entire way to the car.

"So?" she asked excitedly.

"So, what?" Kelly replied.

"Did he ask you out on another date?"

Kelly just smiled at her.

"He did, didn't he?"

"Well, if you call coffee and dessert tonight a date, then I guess so."

"Yes," Angelina said as she pumped her fist into the air. Kelly smiled at her. "I'm so happy for you. Alec is just a really nice—"

"Angelina, stop right there," Kelly said as Angel started fussing in the backseat. "Don't get your hopes up. It's just a casual outing and nothing more. Now, let's get these kids home. I think I hear your daughter getting ready to start in."

Angelina nodded in agreement and pulled away from the clinic. She couldn't wait to tell Alejandro about the latest developments between her sister and his brother.

# Chapter Six

IT WAS ALMOST FOUR O'CLOCK when they walked in the door. She suggested that Kelly help Matthew with his homework while she fed and changed Angel. Instead of taking Angel into the nursery, though, she took her into her bedroom and closed the door. She quickly changed Angel and laid her down on the bed while she called Alejandro to fill him in on Matthew's appointment and her sister's date with Alec. She lay down on the bed beside Angel—she was so excited she couldn't wait to share her news with him.

Alejandro answered on the first ring, "Well?"

"You're not going to believe this—"

"Is Matthew okay?"

"Yeah, he is, but Alec asked Kelly out again."

"Angelina, first things first. I know you're excited, but what about Matthew?"

Angelina tickled Angel's feet. "Did you hear that? Angel just laughed."

"Yes, I did. Now what about Matthew?"

"Alejandro, don't you want to hear what I have to say?"

"Yes, dear, I do. All in good time. But please tell me about our son."

"You know, you just need to calm down. Stop being so

overprotective."

"Angelina, not now. Please…"

"Alright… I was just trying to rile you up that's all. I know you want to hear about his appointment." Angelina told him everything, including Ashton's concern about his protectiveness. Alejandro ignored the comment and asked about the tests. "He's going to call you. I told him you would be anxiously awaiting his call. Now onto your brother, Alec."

"He asked Kelly out again?"

"Yes, isn't that exciting? They're going for coffee and dessert tonight after he reads to Matthew."

"Huh, that's so unlike him."

"I know. He said he wanted to reward her for going along to Matthew's appointment."

"Don't get too excited, Angelina. Alec doesn't have relationships. Don't pressure him. He's too focused on his career and doesn't want anything to interfere with it."

"I know. Can't I hope? I love Alec and Joe just as must as I love my sister. I want to see everyone as happy as we are. Aren't you the one that told him he was going to be the next one married in the family?"

"I did," he said. "Now, sweetheart, you need to stay out of this. If Alec wants to get involved, he's the one that needs to make that decision. Not you. Not me. Right now, I just don't see it happening.

Angelina huffed but acquiesced.

"Oh, by the way, I changed my flight. I'm coming in late tonight."

"How come? I thought you had a dinner to attend tonight."

"It got cancelled because the venue had a fire. So instead of waiting around to find out where it had been rescheduled, I decided I wanted to come home and be with my family."

"When should we expect you?"

"Don't wait up, it will be late. I just can't wait to hold you and the kids. I've really missed you, Angelina."

"I always miss you when you're out of town," she said as she told him she loved him and disconnected the call. Now she had to focus on Kelly and Alec's date.

❧

Alec walked through the door as Kelly was rinsing the dishes. Angelina was giving Matthew his bath and putting Angel to bed.

"Where's my main man?" Alec asked as he walked up beside Kelly. "Here, hand me those, and I'll put them into the dishwasher."

Kelly passed the plates and silverware to him and he loaded them into the dishwasher, "Matthew's taking a bath and Angelina is putting Angel to bed."

Kelly was just finishing washing the last cup when a bubble splashed up onto her nose. Alec only noticed it when she started wrinkling her nose and moving it back and forth. Raising his hand, he brushed it aside. Smiling at her, he said, "Better?

"Much better," she laughed.

They finished the dishes and walked over to the table, bumping legs as they sat down. Kelly seemed a tad nervous to him. He didn't say anything, but wondered why she seemed so nervous with their closeness.

Angelina walked in and blurted out, "Guess who's coming home early?"

He didn't have a chance to respond before she was telling them that Alejandro was heading home a day earlier than expected. Alec wondered what was up with that, but Angelina told him about the fire and how his dinner had been cancelled. He thought it was a good enough reason for him to return home sooner than expected—he just hoped there wasn't another reason behind it.

Alec got up and walked into Matthew's room and lay down beside him on his bed to read him his favorite book. By the time he'd finished, Matthew was fast asleep. Alec pulled the covers up around him, kissed him on the forehead, and walked from his room, leaving the door slightly ajar.

Kelly and Angelina were sitting in the family room talking. Kelly's back had been to the door and, as he placed his hands on her shoulders, she jumped, throwing her hands up around her throat. She turned around to look at him with wide eyes, "You scared me."

"I can see that," he chuckled. It looked like he more than scared her. "Are you ready to go?"

"Yeah, just let me get my coat." Kelly stood and headed off to her bedroom. "I'll be just a minute."

Alec sat down while he waited for Kelly to return. "Wow, did I scare her or what?"

"She's been a little jittery lately. I guess she's still trying to come to terms with her job situation."

"I think I'm going to bring that up tonight."

"Thanks, Alec. Alejandro and I think there's more than meets the eye with that whole situation."

Kelly rejoined them in the family room with coat and purse in hand. Alec helped her with her coat and led her outside to his car. He opened the car door for her and helped her into her seat. Closing the door, he looked back at the front window. Angelina, being her nosy self, was watching every move he made. He raised his hand to her so she'd know that she'd been caught and walked around the car to the driver's side. As he got in, he mumbled, "She's something else."

"What did you say?"

He told her about witnessing Angelina at the window, watching them leave.

"Oh, that doesn't surprise me. My mother did the same thing to her and Alejandro when they were dating."

Alec smiled, shook his head, and started the car. He took her to a café that specialized in after-dinner coffees and desserts. Many theatre goers frequented the café since it was open until the early morning.

Alec ordered a sampler plate of various desserts for both of them, as well as Irish coffee. Alec made idle chit chat while they waited for their coffees and dessert. He asked her about what she liked to do in her free time.

"I love to exercise... take long walks... I didn't have too much time to do that while I was in Knoxville because I worked such long hours. But now, I think I'm going to take up jogging again when the weather breaks. I never really enjoyed it, but since Angelina lives in the country I think I'd like running down the country roads, taking in the various farms and such."

"We should run together sometime. That's one of my passions. Between that and lifting—"

Their conversation was interrupted by their waitress delivering their drinks and dessert plate. Kelly was in pure heaven. She thoroughly enjoyed the rich, creamy cheesecake topped with cherries, and the éclair and cream puffs were to die for.

"I feel like I've died and gone to heaven. This is incredible!"

"Yeah, it is pretty heavenly. I don't indulge in desserts very often, but this is pretty spectacular."

They finished their dessert and were enjoying their coffees when Alec changed the direction of their conversation. "So, have you told your parents you're in town?"

Kelly was shocked by the question. She looked away from

him, scrunched her eyes up, and said, "Why'd you have to ruin our evening?"

"I just asked a question." Alec could tell she was extremely bothered by it. "Kelly, I just wanted to know. Your Mom's coming in with Colleen next week. I don't want to say something that I shouldn't."

"I understand," she said.

Alec could tell she was upset. He reached for her hand. He just wanted to let her know he was supporting her, but she withdrew it and clasped it into a fist in her lap. He thought it was an odd gesture, but didn't comment.

"I'll go by and see them this weekend. I just had to come to grips with the downsizing and all." Downsizing slipped out. *Hey, that sounds pretty good,* she thought. Yep, she'd go with that even though she'd told Angelina something completely different.

Alec just looked at her. "Downsizing? What are you talking about?"

"I lost my job because the company downsized."

"Oh, Kelly, I wasn't aware of that. I'm sorry. I didn't know Lattice Works was in a financial bind. We're in the process of purchasing software for the clinic. In fact, Joe, Alejandro, and I met with Bill not too long ago and he never mentioned this. Now I have to wonder if we should continue with our transition… I'm going to have to contact him and maybe put a hold on everything."

Kelly jumped in. He couldn't talk to Bill—she didn't want him to know the real reason for her firing. "No, Alec. Don't do that. You need to go through with the upgrade."

"Not if they're having financial issues. I don't want to upgrade our software only to have a vendor go out of business. This is a major upgrade for us." Alec ran his hand through his hair. "You should have told me about this when you first arrived in town…"

"Alec, please forget I told you about the downsizing. Lattice Works is just going through some growing pains. Please don't do anything." When she first came home, she'd had no idea that Alec knew Bill or was even working with Lattice on upgrading the software at the clinic. If she'd known she wouldn't have said anything about downsizing. Man, she was digging herself into a hole.

Alec looked skeptical but promised her that he would research it further before making a final decision. He could tell he'd upset her, so he called it an early night. "I've got early rounds at the hospital tomorrow, so I guess we should call it a night."

He reached for her coat and, as she slipped it on, he grabbed the collar, adjusting it across her shoulders. He must have really upset her with his questioning of why she hadn't told him about the downsizing. Something was going on with Kelly. He hoped that she'd settle down and be able to tell her parents about her job loss. Maybe then she'd feel comfortable enough to move on with her employment search.

# Chapter Seven

THE NEXT DAY, KELLY WAS in a snit of a mood. She snapped at Matthew when she helped him get ready for school and was just as unpleasant with Angelina. Kelly disappeared into her room when Angelina heard the phone ring.

"Hey, Angelina, it's Gabriella. How are things going over there?"

"Good, except my sister's in a foul mood today."

"I wonder what that's about."

Angelina told Gabriella about the "date" that Kelly had with Alec the night before.

"I wonder what happened. Alec is so easy going. Maybe he said something that upset her. Has she told your parents about what's going on?"

"Not that I'm aware of. Oh, wait a second. Here she comes. Hold on."

Kelly stalked into the room, walking by Angelina without looking at her.

"Where are you off to?"

"I'm just headed out for a bit. Why do you care?"

Angelina frowned. "Well... You know, you go ahead and go out. Don't let the door hit you on the way out, and maybe you'll come back in a better mood," she said as Kelly stormed out the door.

"Wow, was that you, Angelina? I can't believe you talked to her like that."

"She needs someone to knock some sense into her. She's been like this ever since she got back last night. I think I'm going to have Alejandro give Alec a call and find out just what happened last night. They weren't out very late."

They talked a while longer, catching up on things. She told Gabriella about Matthew's doctor's appointment. "I don't think Matthew cares too much for Ashton. I guess time will tell. Now, I'd better go check on the baby. I'll talk to you later."

Gabriella wished her friend well. She'd barely gotten a dial tone when she speed dialed Alec. He answered on the first ring.

"Hey there, sis. How goes it? Don't you have school today?"

"I'm good. And no, I don't have school. I'm headed off to a workshop that doesn't start until ten." She paused briefly and just decided to go all in, "So what's this I hear about you having a date last night? With Kelly?"

Alec growled into the phone, "I gather you talked with Angelina."

"Uh, huh."

"Well, I wouldn't call it a date per say. I just took her out for coffee and dessert. It was in appreciation of her helping Angelina take Matthew to see Ashton."

"Yeah, I heard about that. What's the deal with Ashton? I don't think you've earned any brownie points with that hire with either Matthew or Alejandro. Are you sure you should have hired him?"

"I don't know what I'm going to do with you or Alejandro. Yes, I am confident in his hire. You're only hearing one side to the story, Gabby."

"Well, from what I've seen, I have to agree with our big brother. I just don't like how he approaches things."

"How would you know? Do you have a child that sees him?"

"You know the answer to that. And I, for one, would not send my child to him. He needs to improve on his bedside manner."

"Whatever, Gabby. What's the real reason for your call?"

"As I said, I was just checking on your date. Tell me about it. Alec, Kelly's perfect for you. She's smart, has a good head on her shoulders, she's loyal, a good listener, and she's definitely not too outspoken—an excellent choice to attend all of those hospital functions that you go to." Gabriella laughed, knowing full well that Alec rarely attended social functions at the hospital. "And she's gorgeous! What more could you ask for?"

"Gabby, I don't have time for this. I'm busy right now. I'll call you later," he said as he hung up the phone. He'd heard enough from his sister and didn't want to hear what Gabriella had to say about his so-called date.

℅

Angelina had just hung up the phone with Gabriella when Alejandro walked into the room. "Was that Kelly I heard storming out of here?"

"Indeed, it was."

"What was that about?"

"I haven't a clue, but I think you should ask your brother about it."

"Huh?"

"Their date last night."

"Oh, yeah," Alejandro said as he reached for his phone

and speed dialed Alec. While he waited for Alec to answer, he grabbed Angelina's hand and forced her to sit beside him while he talked with his brother.

"Hello," Alec said gruffly into the phone.

"What's got your panties in a pickle?" Alejandro said as he smiled at Angelina. She chuckled as quietly as she could.

"I take it that this isn't just you calling, but also your wife."

"Ah, you could say that."

"Put me on speaker phone so you won't have to relay what I have to say about her sister."

"Okay," he said. "You're on speaker."

"Hi there, Alec. How goes it?" asked Angelina.

"Angelina? I'm ready to kill you. Between you and Gabriella—"

"Now, what have I done?" Angelina asked incredulously.

"What haven't you done? You told Gabby about my supposed date with your sister."

"Supposed? In my book, a date is a date, and what you went on last night was indeed a date."

"Whatever. Is Kelly there?"

"No, she left a little bit ago."

"Good." Pausing briefly he said, "Just what's up with your sister? What's her story?"

"What do you mean?"

Alec proceeded to tell them about his conversation with Kelly, her comment about the downsizing, and her parents. "All of a sudden, she seemed really nervous. I get the feeling she's not being completely honest… Alejandro?"

"Yeah?"

"Did you get the feeling that Bill Lattice was hiding something from us regarding the financial stability of the company?"

"Ah, no. In fact, I performed a pretty detailed review of

their financials myself. It appears that they're doing really well. Of course, unless they were hiding something from us, I think they're pretty stable."

"It just doesn't make sense to me. Why would Kelly be fired because of downsizing if the company is doing well?"

"Alec, what are you talking about? Kelly told me she was fired for job performance."

"Huh. Something's not right here. She specifically told me she lost her job due to downsizing. I questioned whether we should move forward with our planned upgrade. She told me to go through with our plans as it's just 'growing pains.' I have to wonder what the real story is."

"Alec, you know Bill pretty well, don't you?" asked Alejandro.

"I do, and I know where you're going with this. I'm going to contact him and see if he'll tell me what's up with this picture. Kelly's not being completely honest with any of us."

"That's not like Kelly," said Angelina. "She has seemed a little more nervous lately. I attributed it to her losing her job, but I have to agree there is definitely something else going on with her."

Angel started crying then. They all agreed they'd try to talk with Kelly in their own way to see if she would tell any of them what truly had happened to her when she lost her job.

☾

Kelly took her sweet time driving to her parents' house—she drove around the corner several times before pulling into the driveway. Since it was relatively early on a Friday morning, she expected that both of her parents would still be in the kitchen, lingering over their morning coffee—her dad normally went into the bank late on Fridays.

Kelly didn't even knock. She opened the door and walked

in, taking both of her parents totally by surprise. Her mother jumped up from the table and immediately pulled her daughter into a tight embrace. "Kelly, sweetheart, what are you doing here? Why didn't you call and tell us you were coming into town? I would've cleaned your room."

Kelly hugged her mother and pulled away from her embrace. She walked over to her dad and placed a kiss on his cheek. Before Kelly could say another word, Wyatt and Colleen came running into the room. Colleen threw herself into her sister's arms. "Kel, it's so good to see you. It's been so long since you came home."

Wyatt smiled at his sister, waiting for his turn to welcome her with a warm hug. Kelly hugged him and then walked over to the counter to pour herself a cup of coffee. Everyone was waiting for her explanation as to why she was in St. Louis in the early morning hours of a Friday.

Jackie didn't bother waiting for Kelly's explanation and started questioning her. "When did you leave Knoxville? Was there much traffic? Why'd you decide to visit—there's nothing going on in town. No craft fairs, no outdoor festivals..."

As Kelly listened to her mother, she kept thinking to herself, *This is the reason I didn't want to tell my parents.*

Finally, Kelly had enough. She jumped from her chair and asked if she could speak with her parents alone. Wyatt and Colleen told her they were happy she was home before they headed off to their rooms to finish dressing for school.

"Honey, come sit down and tell us what's wrong. Why are you here without warning? No email or phone call..."

Kelly sat down. She didn't know how to begin to tell her parents the unthinkable. She knew they would be disappointed in her, and that was something she couldn't begin to bare. All through school she'd achieved excellent grades, winning several scholarships and receiving many honors. She had also been a national merit scholar. Although both James and Angelina were older than Kelly, they had both been jealous of her accomplishments. They had worked hard in school, also making the dean's list and honor roles, but their accomplishments still waned in comparison to Kelly's. Wyatt and Colleen were still in high school and were doing just as well as she had. They definitely weren't jealous of her accomplishments, and they often talked of topping the number of scholarships that she had received. She didn't want to disappoint them either.

Her father smiled warmly at his daughter. He reached for her hand. "Kelly, what's wrong? Whatever happened, your mother and I will support you. Don't doubt that for a second."

Kelly jumped up from the table and paced the kitchen floor. Her parents watched her, saying nothing. Kelly got more nervous by the second. She returned to her chair and looked first at her mother, then her father. She found herself clenching and unclenching her firsts. She took a deep breath and found it difficult to swallow. Next, she found it difficult to breathe. She wondered if she were in the beginning throes of a panic attack. Her father again reached for her hand and held it securely in his, just like when she was a little girl and she was upset about something that had gone wrong.

Her father's touch calmed her. She focused on her breathing and stared at her hand securely held by the one man that meant everything to her—her father. Her role model. She knew she was going to disappoint her father especially, but knew she had to tell him the truth. And now was the time. It had come to this.

"Mom, Dad, I don't know how to tell you this," she said as she took another calming breath.

"Honey, just take your time," her mother said. Jackie's mind was racing. What had happened to her daughter? Was she pregnant? Was she in trouble? A myriad of thoughts filled her mind. Jackie looked at her husband Ben while Kelly looked at her hand. "Sweetheart, did you drive all night and just get into town?" Jackie didn't know what to say to her daughter as she smiled at her, trying to make her feel more comfortable with whatever she had to share.

Kelly took a sip of her coffee, swallowed, and began to tell her parents her story. "I don't know how to tell you this, so I'm just going to come right out and say it. I've been in town for a couple of weeks."

Her mother took a sharp breath but said nothing.

"I've been staying at Angelina's—"

Her father interrupted her, "Kelly, are you ill?"

She shook her head no.

"Kelly, honey, just tell us. We'll help you make it better."

"Dad, you can't make it better. I… I lost my job."

Her parents seemed to release a collective sigh of relief, "Sweetheart, that's not the end of the world. You'll find another."

In Kelly's mind, it was like a scarlet A branded on her chest. It was the absolute worst thing that could ever happen to her. She been fired for reasons her family would never know. Yes, she'd told Angelina she was fired because of job performance, but she had decided, while talking with Alec, that she'd change her story. The cause would be downsizing since that's what everyone else was being fired for these days. Her parents wouldn't need to know the real reason. Bill had told her it was job performance, but she knew otherwise. And over time she'd have to come to terms with it.

"Kelly, why didn't you tell us sooner? You know we would have helped you."

"I know, Mom. I'm just too ashamed." Thinking back to that nightmare of an afternoon, she didn't want to relive the shame she felt. The embarrassment of knowing that she'd been fired… Fired because of job performance, downsizing, or whatever else was an embarrassment to her and her family. Word would get out all over their community that the scholar, A-plus student couldn't hold down a job.

Kelly told them about her journey from Knoxville and how she'd ended up in the snowbank near the abandoned farm. She told them how Alec came upon her and rescued her. She told them everything. Everything except what she believed to be the real reason behind her firing.

"Honey, go get your things and come home. I'm sure you're an imposition at Angelina's. I can't believe Alejandro is happy about you staying with them."

Kelly was actually hurt by her mother's comments. She was helping Angelina with the kids. She didn't think Alejandro was upset with her living with them. In fact, she thought he was more than okay with it. He knew how much she was helping his wife. "Mom, I think they're both okay with me living there for now. I've been helping Angelina with the kids and Alejandro welcomed me with open arms. My living with them temporarily is not an issue with either one of them."

"If you say so." Jackie didn't understand why Kelly wouldn't come home, but she knew not to press her daughter any more on the subject.

# Chapter Eight

KELLY LEFT HER PARENTS' HOUSE shortly after telling them about her decision to keep living with Angelina. Her mother seemed particularly upset, but Kelly chalked it all up to her love of ruling her children's lives. She'd tried to do it with Angelina when she and Alejandro were first dating. Kelly wasn't going to allow her the same freedom that Angelina gave their mother. Her situation was a little different since she'd been living on her own for quite some time, whereas Angelina lived at home up until she and Alejandro had gotten married.

Kelly needed to get out and burn off some of her frustration with her mother. Thankfully she had her running shoes on, so she headed to a nearby park. In fact, the park was halfway between her parents' house and Alejandro's. It was a beautiful day and the temperatures had warmed. Snow was still on the ground, but it had melted somewhat over the last week with the temperatures finally getting out of the thirties. The running path was clear, so she stretched and started down the path. She started off walking, then slowly eased into her jogging pace.

Kelly couldn't focus. Her mind kept drifting from the conversation she'd just had with her parents, to her night out with Alec the evening before, all the way back to Bill's last words to her. She felt overwhelmed. She needed to get ahold of her emotions. Off the beaten path, she noticed a large boulder. She parked herself on it, and a smaller rock laid right in front, so she rested her feet on it and wrapped her arms around her knees. She tried to slow her breathing. She was a mess—an absolute mess. She'd always prided herself on her prowess. Now, she'd lost her confidence in herself and wondered how she would go on. How would she recover from the blow of being fired?

As she sat there, draped over her folded knees, she started to cry. She didn't know where the tears came from, but they openly flowed down her face. She tried to brush them aside but they just kept coming.

☾

Alec had a scheduled day off and had decided to take it. He'd been working tirelessly of late and thought he owed himself the day. After experiencing his inquisition from Gabriella, Alejandro, and Angelina, he'd decided to go for a run.

As he crested the rise in the trail, he noticed someone pulled off to the side. They were sitting on the boulder that kids loved to crawl on, pretending they were king of the world. He slowed as he approached and discovered that it was Kelly. She was openly sobbing, her shoulders shaking. He hurried to her side, not knowing if she were injured or not. She didn't hear him approach until he was upon her, calling out her name.

He hunched down next to her and put his hand across her back, but she didn't move. "Kelly, hey there… What's wrong? Are your hurt?"

She didn't respond, unable to stop sobbing. Alec rubbed her back even harder, but she still didn't respond to him. He then put his arms around her, hugging her as closely as possible. "It's going to be okay," he said as she turned into his arms. She threw her arms around his waist, buried her head into his neck, and cried.

Alec wasn't completely convinced that she hadn't fallen and hurt herself. He talked softly to her, trying to soothe her as he kept rubbing her back. He held her for probably only a minute or so before her tears slowed and she loosened her grip on his waist. She wiped the tears from her face and slowly pulled away from him. She tried to avoid eye contact with him, but Alec placed a finger under her chin and slowly applied pressure, raising her chin so their eyes would meet. She tried to avert her eyes, but he placed both of his hands on either side of her face and held her head steady, causing her to look him directly in the eye.

"What's wrong? Why are you so upset?"

She tried to wipe her eyes and her nose with the back of her hand, but his hands prevented it.

"Kelly, are you hurt?"

She shook her head.

"Did you fall?"

Again, she shook her head.

"Then what's wrong? What's got you so upset?"

She pulled away from him and slid off the rock. She spoke with her back to him, but he couldn't understand exactly what she was saying. He approached her from behind and wrapped his left arm across the front of her shoulders, drawing her against him. His right hand snaked around her waist as he pulled her towards him. "You're safe, Kelly. Safe in my arms. Please tell me what's got you so upset."

The tears started again and she dropped her chin so it rested on his forearm. He held her as she cried, whispering that all would be well—he would fix whatever was troubling her.

Out of nowhere, she spun around in his arms, clasped him around the waist, and held on for dear life. They stood like this, wrapped in one another's arms, speechless until her crying waned. Using his thumbs, he wiped the few remaining tears from her cheek, reached for her hand, and pulled her back towards the boulder. He sat down and pulled her into his arms. Her back was facing him and they didn't say a word. He waited for her to share what had upset her so much. Alec held her for several minutes before she was comfortable enough to speak.

"I'm okay now. You can go ahead with your run."

"I'm not leaving you."

"Please, just go," she practically yelled at him. "I'm fine now." She pulled away from him and started towards the trail. He let her take a few steps then jogged up beside her. He grabbed her hand, stopped her forward motion, and stepped in front of her.

"Would you please stop being so stubborn and let me help you?"

She shook her head and tried to move around him, but he wouldn't let her. Alec had had enough of her behavior. "So, is this how you acted at Lattice? When you didn't get your way, you stormed out... Is that what happened? You lost your temper and that caused you to lose your job."

She just looked at him, her face slackening.

"I guess I hit the nail of the head, didn't I? It wasn't down-sizing that cost you to lose your job, it was insubordination."

"You don't know what you're talking about."

"I think I do."

"You have no idea. I told you it was downsizing, and that's what happened."

"Then, explain to me why you told me one thing and my sister-in-law and brother another."

She flinched. "Just leave it alone okay? I'm not your worry."

"Yes, you are."

She glared at him, "No, I'm not!" And with that, she stormed off.

As Alec watched her jog back to her car, he made his decision. He was going to contact Bill and try to get to the bottom of her story. Something just didn't add up, and he was going to try and uncover the true reason behind her firing.

☾

Kelly was more upset when she got to her car than when she'd left it only half an hour ago. She phoned her mother and asked her if she could use the cabin. The Samuels' had a lovely cabin—really a summer home—in the woods in the Missouri Ozarks. It wasn't too long of a drive from St. Louis—one that she could reach in a few short hours.

"Mom, I need some time… Time to myself. I'd like to go out to the cabin and take some time to—"

"Honey, that sounds like a good idea."

"Please don't tell anyone where I am. I'll tell Angelina where I'm going, but I'm going to expect her to keep it a secret. Just you, Daddy, and Angelina can know."

"I promise, honey. Take the time you need to find the answers."

Kelly hung up the phone and headed to Angelina's where she spoke in confidence with her sister.

"Angelina, I'm going to go to the cabin for a few days. I need to take some time and try and find the answers that I'm struggling to put my finger on. You, Mom, and Dad are the only ones that know. If Alejandro wants to know where I am—"

"I'll tell him you've returned to Knoxville for a few days.

He'll believe that." Angelina hated keeping Kelly's where-abouts from Alejandro. She knew she couldn't have lied to him when Kelly had first come back to St. Louis, especially since she was living with them. But now—even though she hated it, she had to do it for her sister. Angelina turned and hugged her sister. She knew she was having a really hard time coming to grips with her firing. She hoped and prayed that she'd find the answers she was looking for in the quiet isola-tion of the cabin.

Kelly threw her things into her suitcase and was walking out the door five minutes later.

Not fifteen minutes after Kelly left, the doorbell rang. Angelina looked out the window before opening the door and noticed Alec's car in the driveway. She opened the door and barely got a hello out of her mouth when Alec stormed through the door.

"Where's Kelly?"

"Ah, she's not here right now. What do you want with her?"

"I'm really worried about her."

Angelina stared at him, shocked, "Why are you worried about her? She's fine."

"From what I saw about a half hour ago, she's a complete mess."

"What are you talking about?"

Alec proceeded to tell Angelina about his run in the park. He told her about finding Kelly in tears, how he'd tried to talk with her and calm her, how it didn't work.

"I accused her of losing her job because she was being insubordinate. I can't believe I said that to her. She's running with two separate stories—I was just trying to find the truth, and I got mad. Insubordination slipped out." He paced in circles, just like his brother was known to do. "I didn't mean anything I said. I know she's hurting, and I'm sure I hurt her even more. Please Angelina, tell me where she is so I can make it right. I don't want to hurt her any more than she's already hurt."

"Alec, I don't know what to say. She's not here right now. You'll have to try and reach her later on."

With that, the baby started crying and Angelina headed off in her direction. Alec watched her depart. He shook his head and walked out of the house. He would give Kelly time… Time to cool off from their conversation and time to deal with her emotions.

☾

Kelly listened to the radio as she took her time driving to the cabin. She stopped on the way and bought supplies. Her parents kept the summer home well stocked with staples, but since it was spring and they hadn't been to the Ozark's since early winter, she had no idea what supplies were on hand.

She purchased milk, bread, and fresh vegetables. Her parents kept the freezer well stocked with meat, so she didn't worry about that. Her mother liked to entertain at the last minute, so barbeques were frequent. She kept the freezer stocked with homemade bratwursts and sausages that could only be purchased at a local shop. Jackie was often envied at her parties because the sausages were so good. Kelly could pick up smaller items, if needed, at the corner grocery in town.

She arrived at the cabin and phoned her mother, letting her know of her safe arrival. She told her mother that she didn't know how long she was going to stay, but she'd try and call her daily. Kelly put all of her groceries away, and then took a hot shower. She hoped the warm water would soothe her and make her feel somewhat better.

Her thoughts proved wrong. She felt worse than she had before her shower. She sat down on the couch in the family room and turned the lamp on. It was turning dark outside, and she didn't want to sit in the complete dark.

She didn't have an appetite. She looked at the four walls. She noticed that one of the pictures hanging on the wall was slightly askew, so she stood and straightened it. She returned to the couch and looked at the other three walls. No additional pictures were out of line. Next, she looked at her hands. They were clenched tightly in her lap. She thought back over the day, how it had started with a trip to her parents, telling them the news she had such difficulty sharing with anyone, most especially them. At least she hadn't told her parents the truth. She'd told them what she wanted them to believe was the truth.

She felt like someone had died. She felt like she had died. She felt only pain—pain of disappointment. She'd disappointed not only herself, but her parents as well. What did they think of her? She was a failure. She was sure they'd lost all confidence in her, just like she'd lost in herself. Time stood still.

Before long, all of the emotions that's she'd experienced for the day caught up with her and she drifted off to a troubled night of dreams—dreams she had wished would never reappear, scenes that she'd experienced and never wanted to experience again. She thought she'd locked those memories away, deep down inside never to reappear again… Unfortunately what she wanted and what her brain wanted her to experience were two very different things. Those memories would never ever leave her, no matter what she did or what she tried. They'd be with her a lifetime.

# Chapter Nine

ALEC WASN'T SURE HOW, BUT he found himself pulling into his garage. He didn't remember driving from Alejandro's. The last thing he remembered was walking out of the house and down the driveway towards his car.

He walked into his house and headed for his home office. He dropped down at his desk and fired up his computer. He needed answers. He logged onto his work computer and started to review all the information he'd gathered on Lattice Works. If they were having financial problems, he was going to unearth them and walk away from the system upgrade that the clinic needed so badly. They could continue on with their software until they could research another vendor.

He worked diligently at his research and, before he knew it, the room had darkened. He looked at the clock and discovered it was well past five o'clock. He'd been sitting at his computer for hours going through the detail of the Lattice Works proposal, along with their financial information. Something didn't add up, but he just couldn't put his finger on it.

He needed a break and decided to call Joe. He answered on the first ring. Alec asked him if he could come by for dinner.

"Sure, I'm not doing anything—just finishing up rounds at the hospital. I'll be there in the next hour."

"Perfect. I'll order pizza, and it should be here when you get here."

Alec hung up the phone, placed the order, and waited as patiently as he could for his brother to arrive. Alec then decided to phone Alejandro. He thought his other brother needed to be there for their discussion.

Alejandro agreed to join them. He was home alone since Angelina had taken the kids over to her parents for game night.

Alejandro made it to Alec's within twenty minutes of taking his call. "Thanks for inviting me. I needed to do something tonight. Angelina's at her parents' house for game night. I had a few things to do and didn't want to go." He'd brought a couple of bottles of wine as his contribution to the meal. Alejandro had barely arrived when Joe came in with pizzas in hand.

"I met the delivery man as I drove in. These sure smell good. Oh, hey Alejandro. I didn't know you were going to be here."

"Alec just invited me."

The men set up house in Alec's office where they were close to all of his files and his computer.

"We need to do this more often," Alejandro said as he took a sip of his wine. "I miss this."

"Yeah, we should. But since you got married, you don't seem to have the time like you used to," Alec said as he took a bite of his pizza.

"Hey. Don't make it sound like I don't have the time to do anything anymore. I do. We just need to make the effort."

"Yeah, yeah. That's what all married men say."

Alejandro laughed, "Angelina wouldn't mind if I spent

time with you. She's always with Gabby and her sisters. We just need to do it and stop talking about it."

They agreed to make the time to get together and just be brothers.

Alec brushed his hand across his jaw. He hadn't had the chance to talk to Alejandro lately about how he was truly doing. Tammy's death always lingered in the back of their minds. Alec was aware that the anniversary of her death was fast approaching and he wanted to know how his brother was faring. "So how goes it, Alejandro?" asked Alec.

"What do you mean? Everything is going really well. Matthew seems to be doing just fine. He's adjusting to the baby." He stopped and thought for a moment. "Angelina's doing as well as can be expected. She's still adjusting to being a first-time mom. She's anxious, especially when she can't get Angel to calm down... You know, Alec. You were there that one day."

"I was. She did seem a little overwhelmed."

"Well Kelly's really helped us an awful lot these last couple of weeks. She gets Matthew up and helps him with his homework. I think that's helped calm Angelina a bit."

"How are you doing with the adjustment?"

"Fine. I just wish I were around more to help Angelina. My schedule has been really hectic of late. When Michael was a baby..." He stopped and took another sip of his wine. Alec saw all expression leave his face. Momentarily, he went into his own little world. Joe and Alec exchanged glances, unsure of how he was really dealing with all of these changes—marrying Angelina, adopting Matthew, and having Angel all within a very short time. Their brother had been through so much. And then, the blank look left his face and he took another bite of his pizza.

"Alejandro, you know we are here for you if you ever need

to just talk."

"I know, and I appreciate it. Don't get me wrong, I'm so happy with my life now. But there's a part of me that will always love Tammy and Michael. Sometimes, I just really miss them."

"We know what you've been through. Don't be too proud to not seek the help you may need to deal with their loss."

"I know, Joe. I will seek the help if I need it. Angelina is a godsend. She understands, really she does. It's just that…"

"We know. Their anniversary is coming up. Just know that we're here if you need us."

"Thanks, I appreciate it. Really, I do." Alejandro cleared his throat, "Now, Alec, why did you call this meeting?"

Alec brought his brothers up to speed on his conversation with Kelly. "I'm concerned that, if she was in fact downsized, Lattice Works is having financial difficulties."

"I thought we vetted the company pretty well," said Joe. "I went through their financials with a fine-tooth comb. We sent it to the accountants and our attorneys. I think they would have seen something if they were having problems."

"I agree, Alec. We would have found something," Alejandro said as he stood and began his pacing. Joe and Alec both watched him move from one end of the room to the other. Finally, he said, "What do you want to do?"

"I'd like to contact Bill and see if I can find out what's really going on here. Why would Kelly tell me one story and you and Angelina a completely different one? From the outset, something just hasn't seemed right here. I'd like to get to the bottom of it before we install Lattice's software. We need to think of the clinic. It needs to be first and foremost here. We can't afford to make this upgrade if it will financially affect us and our patients."

"Agreed," said Joe. "Why don't we sit Kelly down and talk

to her? Maybe she'd shed some light on our situation. Once she understands what's at stake, maybe she'd feel comfortable enough and tell us what actually happened."

"I've tried reaching her all day. She's really unstable."

"What are you talking about, Alec? I saw her briefly this morning and she seemed fine to me," Alejandro said, perplexed.

Alec recounted the encounter he had with Kelly at the park. "She was hysterical. I found her sobbing on a boulder. I did everything I could to calm her, and when she wouldn't tell me what was wrong, I kind of…"

"What?" asked Alejandro.

"Accused her of losing her job due to insubordination."

"You what?" Alejandro asked incredulously. "Are you crazy? Kelly would never be insubordinate. She walks a fine line and never does anything wrong. I know this whole situation has thrown her off her game, but she'll recover and get back on the train."

"I'm not sure about that."

"Let me call Kelly," Alejandro said as he reached for his phone. He dialed her number and waited for her to answer.

"Huh, went straight to voicemail… Let me call Angelina and see if she's with her." Alejandro called Angelina and asked if he could speak with Kelly.

"She's not here."

"I tried her cell and she didn't answer."

"Umm, ah, Alejandro she returned to Knoxville for a couple of days. She needed to take care of a few things."

"Really? Now? When did she leave?"

"This morning. Alejandro, I'm kind of busy right now. Can we talk about this when you get home?"

"Sure, honey. I'll see you in a little while. I love you."

"I love you, too," Angelina said as she disconnected the call.

"Something's not right here, Alec. Angelina was a little too evasive. She said Kelly returned to Knoxville to 'take care of a few things.'"

"Well, that sure came out of nowhere," Joe said as he took another bite of pizza.

"Something just doesn't add up here," Alec said as he stood and headed to his desk where he booted up his computer. Alec pulled up a list of phone numbers, reached for his phone, and dialed.

The phone rang and rang and rang until the answering machine picked up, "Hi, I'm not here right now. Leave a message, and I'll call you back."

"That's strange," Alec said. "Voicemail again."

"Who were you calling?"

"Kelly's home in Knoxville."

"I'll see what Angelina can tell me about her whereabouts." Alejandro got up to leave. "I'll call you later, Alec."

"Yeah, keep us both informed. Once we know where Kelly is, we can talk to her and find out what's really going on at her former employer." Joe said, grabbing another slice of pizza. "For the road," he said as he followed Alejandro out the front door.

This whole situation didn't sit well with Alec. He was worried about Kelly. When she'd first arrived in town and he'd found her in the snowbank, she didn't seem nearly as upset as she did today, and that really bothered him. He liked Kelly and didn't want anything to happen to her. He hoped that she made it safely back to Knoxville. He was concerned about her drive, especially with the state of mind that she'd been in earlier in the day. Something had thrown her over the edge, and he just hoped that he could help her climb back over the precipice.

# Chapter Ten

ALEJANDRO DROVE HOME AS QUICKLY as he could. He couldn't wait to speak with Angelina about Kelly's whereabouts. He didn't believe that she'd returned to Knoxville. With as upset as Alec said that she was, that drastic of a move just wasn't Kelly. He didn't believe that she'd drive that distance in the state of mind that she was in. If he was a betting man, he believed she wasn't far. Angelina wasn't one to keep secrets, especially from him, and he'd get her to confess where her sister was.

❦

Angelina got home a few minutes before Alejandro appeared. Both of the kids had fallen asleep on the short car ride from her parents' house. Thankfully Angelina had the foresight to dress the kids in their pajamas before she'd left their house. Angelina carried Matthew in and put him to bed, removing only his shoes as she tucked him in and placed a kiss on his forehead. She didn't want to disturb Angel, so she left her in her car seat. She would need to be fed in a few hours, and she'd move her to her crib then.

As she had driven home, Angelina pondered her conversation with Alejandro. She couldn't lie to her husband. She would try, but in the end knew she'd cave and tell him where

Kelly was.

☙

Alejandro found Angelina in the family room with two glasses of wine in hand. She kissed him softly on the lips and passed him his glass of wine. "Did you have a good time with your brothers?"

"I did. It was eventful." He swirled his wine in the glass before taking a sip. He reached for her hand and pulled her towards the couch where they sat down. He enveloped her in his arms and held her closely. He asked how her day went and then led into his discussion with his brothers. He shared with her their concern over the upcoming anniversary of Tammy's death. "I know they worry about me. I just wish everyone would try and forget about it."

"We can't. We love you and know how all of this has affected you. We'll always be there for you. You know that, don't you?"

"Of course I do." Alejandro took another sip of wine, "Enough of that—let's move on. Alec informed me that he ran into Kelly at the park today."

"That's what I hear."

"And?"

"And what?" Angelina looked Alejandro in the eyes and said, "She met with my parents today and told them about losing her job."

"That makes sense. It explains why she was so upset when Alec found her."

"Yeah, it does. You know how Mom can be."

"I do. Jackie can be a piece of work when she sets her mind to it. But do you really think Jackie's the problem? I don't. I think there's more than meets the eye going on here. Kelly's keeping something from us. She's telling two different stories about her job loss. Alec is really concerned. He's in the process of working with Bill to upgrade some software at the clinic, and he's worried that Lattice Works is having financial problems. I don't agree with him."

"Why not?"

"I did my own due diligence, and I just don't buy it." Alejandro turned and placed his hand on his wife's cheek. "Honey, be honest with me. Kelly's not in Knoxville, is she?"

Angelina didn't look at him.

He rubbed his thumb across her lips, leaned in, and kissed her. "Where is she Angelina? Is she at the cabin?"

Angelina couldn't believe that he'd guessed where she was so quickly. She jumped from the couch and walked towards the windows. She glanced out across the expansive backyard, wondering if she should break the promise she'd made to Kelly and tell him the truth.

Alejandro approached her and wrapped his arms around her. "Honey, I know she's not in Knoxville. I know you know where she is. Alec is really concerned about her frame of mind. Wherever she is, did she get there safely?"

"Yes," she murmured. She just couldn't break the promise she made to Kelly. Angelina's stomach was in knots. She needed to be faithful to her sister, but if what Alejandro said was true, what state of mind had Kelly actually been in when she'd left that morning? Angelina was confused. She didn't know what to say to her husband. She grabbed ahold of Alejandro's hands and squeezed them tightly. She then turned around in his arms and wrapped her arms around his waist. He felt her shake her head, trying to decide what to do.

She pulled away and looked up into her husband's eyes and then closed hers. She knew that Alejandro didn't believe her. She hated lying to him and, in the end, knew that she couldn't. Sighing deeply, she looked up into his eyes and smiled at him. "You know me too well." She reached for his hand and drew him back to the couch. They sat down and he pulled her close. She laid her head on his shoulder and said, "Yes, you're right. She is at the cabin. But Alejandro, I promised her. I told her that I wouldn't tell you where she was."

"You didn't tell me. I guessed, didn't I?"

"Semantics aside, you know where she is. She'll figure out that I told you."

☾

Alec cleaned up after his brother's left. He was torn. He didn't know if he should drive all the way to Knoxville to find her, or if he should call Bill and confront him with the situation. He was so uncertain as to what he should do. Kelly was proud of her job and her accomplishments, and he knew enough about her personality that he didn't want to cause her any more grief, but he wanted to help her overcome the sense of loss that she was experiencing. His mind drifted. He was clueless. He sat, staring at nothing in particular, when he recognized the ringing of his cell phone.

He looked at the caller ID and answered immediately—it was Alejandro.

"I know where she is."

"Where?"

"I don't know if I should tell you. Angelina is so torn up about this."

"How did you get it out of her?"

"She didn't really tell me. I guessed." Alejandro told him about his conversation with Angelina. "She's at her parents' cabin, and Angelina has no idea when she's planning on returning."

"What do you think we should do?" He paused for a second and said, "I know what I'm going to do. I am going to phone Bill tomorrow and talk to him—see if he'll tell me anything about what transpired with Kelly's firing. More than likely he won't tell me anything, but I can try. And then... And then, I am going to drive out to the cabin and see her. Alejandro, I'm really worried about her. Granted I don't know Kelly all that well, but I've never seen her so emotional, so devastated... It was like someone she knew had just died. It's like something had hit her in the face, and she didn't know how to respond. More than likely this all stemmed from having to tell her parents about her situation. I have to help her. I just do."

"I understand. I'll tell Angelina what you're planning on doing. Why don't you come by here tomorrow morning, and we'll figure something out?"

Alec agreed and ended the call. He threw his hands up, covering his face. He massaged his temples as he noticed a tension headache developing behind his eyes. He sat on his couch until the wee hours of the morning, planning his conversation with both Bill and Kelly. He needed to be prepared for anything that may arise out of either conversation. Deep down, he wanted—no, needed—to help Kelly get through this. He didn't know why, but just knew that he had to.

Alec decided Alejandro should be in on the call made to Bill. He would have included Joe, too, but he'd been called in to the hospital to deal with a six-month old that had been admitted to the pediatric intensive care unit.

Alec called Alejandro on his way over to make sure that he was home. He'd barely had two hours sleep the night before, and he wanted to get this phone call with Bill over with.

☾

Alejandro ended the call. Alec was on his way over to talk to Bill Lattice, so he decided to get some food ready before he got there. Not more than a minute after Alejandro had made his way to the kitchen, there was a knock on the door. He went to the door to discover Alec standing on the threshold. "Well, that was quick."

"Yeah, I called on my way over."

Alejandro led Alec into his office. Angelina was busy giving Angel a bath and didn't know Alec was coming over.

"I thought about this all night. I don't think we should bring Kelly into the conversation—not unless we absolutely have to. I want to see how he reacts to me asking about the financial status of the company."

"I think that's a good call. Let's feel him out, take his temperature, and go from there."

"Any news about Kelly?"

"No, I just know that she made it to the cabin safely. She called Jackie and told her she was there and didn't know when she was coming home."

"Good. I'm glad she made it safely. I was really worried."

"What's going on here, Alec? You seem to have grown quite fond of Kelly in the short time that she's been here."

"It's not that. It's just… I wish you could have seen her yesterday. I'll never forget the way she sobbed and the look on her face when I told her she'd been insubordinate. I don't know where that came from and right now I can't take it back. I can only make amends for it."

Alejandro clasped his brother on the shoulder. "She's gotten under your skin, Alec. I think you're falling for her."

"No, I'm not."

"Yes, you are. You're feeling the same sense of guilt and protectiveness I felt for Angelina. I hope that you can recognize it earlier than I did. We almost broke up, and it took her almost being swept away in that flash flood for me to deal with my memories of Tammy's accident and death. I almost lost her, and I'll always regret the time we lost before we found ourselves again."

Alec just looked at his brother. Maybe he was right. He'd have to think about that later after talking with Bill.

Alec phoned Bill and, surprisingly, he answered his phone. Whenever Alec had phoned Bill in the past either he spoke with his secretary or the call went directly to voicemail. Alec told Bill he was putting him on speaker phone with Alejandro. After making their pleasantries, Alec got to the point. "Bill, I've heard through the grape vine that Lattice Works is downsizing. Is that true?"

"Where did you hear that? Downsizing? It's the complete opposite. We're in a hiring mode. I plan on adding fifty jobs in the next six months."

Both men were taken aback. Five or ten seemed reasonable for a company the size of Lattice, but fifty? Fifty was a lot of jobs to be added to a relatively small company. "Have you advertised these jobs locally?"

"Locally and throughout the country. I'm having a hard time finding someone with the specific skill set that we need. I think we've added about twenty percent of these jobs in the last couple of weeks."

"What areas are you adding these jobs in?"

Bill ticked through the listing of jobs. "I'm adding fifty percent of these jobs to the IT sector of the company. As soon as this phase rolls out, we're working on another upgrade, so I'm in need of programmers and system testers to make sure the upgrades are seamless to our customers."

Alejandro looked at Alec quizzically. That made no sense. Fifty percent job increase in the department that was supposedly downsizing? Alec just shook his head. Nothing made sense. Bill advised them of some additional changes he was making in the company, but nothing suggested that he was financially strapped. Alec informed Bill that he'd be following up with him in the next few days regarding the timeline with their install and ended the call.

Alec paced the room. What was the truth? From everything he knew about Kelly, and now with the discovery that Lattice Works was in a hiring frenzy, he just couldn't wrap his head around what was unfolding before him. He covered his face with his hands, trying to fend off the headache that had returned. He ran his hands through his hair, turned, paced back towards his brother, and said, "Alejandro, your thoughts?"

"I don't know. Maybe she's in a crisis that we just don't know about. Maybe her firing was actually because of job performance. I don't know. I hate to think that."

"I know."

Angelina walked in the room, "Alec, I didn't know you'd arrived."

"Yeah, Alejandro and I just had an interesting phone conversation with Bill."

"You did?" Angelina couldn't read the expression on her husband's face. "So? What did he have to say?"

Alejandro met Angelina halfway across the room and reached for her hand. He didn't know what to say to her, didn't know if he should confess what he thought her sister was going through. So he said what was on his mind, "Do you think Kelly's having some type of breakdown?"

Wide-eyed, Angelina looked at Alejandro. She pulled away from him and sat down on the couch. Glancing between the two brothers she said, "Where did you get that idea? For heaven's sake, no! Kelly is the sanest person I know. Nothing bothers her. Why do you think that?"

Alejandro told her about their conversation with Bill. "They're not in a hiring freeze, they're in a hiring boom. And from Kelly's track record, I find it hard to believe that she lost her job due to her performance."

Alec stopped his pacing and sat down in the chair opposite Angelina.

"Alec, I know my sister. She's not having a mental break-down."

"But you didn't see her yesterday at the park. Maybe, she's been acting and keeping this from you."

"No, I don't think so. Something else is playing into this."

"That's what I think, too. Angelina, I need the directions to the cabin. I'm going to go see her. Make sure that she's alright."

"Alec, no, you can't do that. I promised her. My parents promised her that we wouldn't tell anyone where she was."

"Did you tell me? Did you tell Alejandro?"

"Well, no. Alejandro guessed where she was."

"So there. You didn't tell me or him." Looking between the couple he held out his hand. "Directions, please?"

Alejandro grabbed a piece of paper from his desk and wrote down the directions to the Samuels' cabin. Alec stuffed them into his pocket, stood, and reached for Angelina. He hugged and thanked her. "I'll call you later and let you know how she is."

Angelina kissed him on the cheek, thanking him for want-ing to help her sister. Angelina didn't know what was up with Kelly, but she definitely wasn't having a breakdown. Angelina knew there had to be a good reason why Kelly was telling two different stories. She hoped that her sister found the an-swers that she was looking for at the cabin.

Alec left the house, ran by his home, and packed a quick bag. He didn't know how long he'd be gone. As he headed down the highway, he phoned Joe and told him where he was going. He knew he'd be out of town at least overnight and, depending on Kelly's frame of mind, he may be gone longer.

Joe told him not to worry about the clinic—he'd call in their father since he was their back-up when one of them had to be away. "Find the answers, Alec. It sounds like she needs someone on her side."

Alec ended the call and headed off to hopefully rescue Kelly from her demons.

℡

Alec had barely left the house when Angelina turned to Alejandro. "Alec reminds me a lot of you when we were just getting together."

"He does?"

"Yep. He has that Alvarez sense of protectiveness and guilt. I hope he can help Kelly like you helped me."

"Time will tell," Alejandro said.

"Hopefully it will lead down the same road we travelled."

"I certainly hope you're not planning on turning into a Gabriella."

"Who me? Why would you think I was trying to put those two together?" she chuckled. "I know what I see, just as Gabriella knew what she saw in us. He cares for her, and I think she cares for him. I just hope he didn't ruin their chances when he accused her of insubordination. Alec is what Kelly needs right now. I just hope she sees it, too, and lets him in."

# Chapter Eleven

K ELLY DIDN'T SLEEP AT ALL her first night at the cabin. She tossed and turned the entire night. She didn't know why, but all she could think of was Ken Jones, her direct boss, in her last job at Lattice Works. He was something else. He should never have been a manager. He didn't know how to manage a staff or personnel issues—he passed them on, ignoring them, not wanting to face reality. He often times promoted the weak performers, leaving those who excelled behind to clean up their messes.

He managed through intimidation, not caring what he said or who he hurt along the way. He didn't like it when issues that he should have been aware of were brought to his attention by someone else. In his mind, he was the superior one and everyone else was beneath him. No one should question his authority or the decisions that he made.

Kelly also thought about Ariel Layton. She was Kelly's best friend at Lattice Works. They had both been hired on the same day, and they both had worked under Ken Jones. They were hired into different departments, but over time began working in IT for Ken.

They were in the same orientation class and became fast friends. They held the same interests—they loved to exercise and often jogged the streets of Knoxville together after work before heading home. They enjoyed the same types of music, attending concerts as often as they could. Ariel had even considered moving into Kelly's condo with her, but had moved in with one of her college roommates instead. They lived only blocks away from one another and spent a good amount of time together on the weekends. Kelly thought they were best friends until that fateful day when Ariel betrayed her.

So much had happened leading up to that day. Ariel and Kelly were assigned to the new upgrade that Lattice had been working on for years. They were in the final stages of user-acceptance testing of the software when Kelly noticed some anomalies with the data being reported. Once discovered, Kelly spent several evenings analyzing the test data. It didn't make sense to her. She'd discovered the inconsistencies by accident since she wasn't responsible for the specific phase that this had been tested in. Kelly eventually determined that if a fix wasn't installed prior to the launch of the new software, serious issues would arise. She figured out what was needed to fix the error, and took it directly to Ken.

Ken was furious with Kelly. He didn't like the fact that she discovered this issue, especially since they were well past this phase of testing. She should have brought it to his attention weeks prior when they were in the process. If he stopped to fix what wasn't functioning, it would put the entire project behind and they would never meet their target launch date. That was one thing Ken definitely didn't do—not meet the established target dates for launching new software.

Ken berated her. He cornered her in his office and pushed her up against the bookshelves that lined the walls of his office. She was caught off guard by his behavior and, when she fell against one of the bookcases, several books fell off the shelves causing a loud thud. The door to his office was partially ajar, so when the books crashed to the floor, his secretary came running. Thankfully, this ended his outburst and allowed Kelly the chance to regroup.

She didn't understand why he was so upset with her. She brought the issue to his attention, thinking he'd be elated with the fact that it was discovered prior to implementation. Kelly believed it was better to fix the problem now rather than later.

Taking a deep breath, she turned to Ken. She was going to try and ignore what had just transpired between the two of them. She'd give him the benefit of the doubt and ignore his physical berating—maybe it had been an accident. She wanted to believe that he'd just lost his balance. In the end, she wanted to solve the issue, not have it blow up in their faces. "I'm sorry that I had to bring this to your attention, but this is a major flaw in the program that needs fixing. I didn't just bring you the problem, I also brought the solution on how we can implement the fix, test the fix, and still stay on schedule."

Ken just looked at her. No matter what she said, he didn't hear her. "So you're telling me that you failed in your segment of the test, and now you're trying to cover your own ass with the fix to correct it?"

"I didn't test this."

"Then why are you the one bringing this to my attention?"

Kelly explained that she discovered the flaw by accident while she was reviewing her test results. "Ken, I did the research needed, and did it on my own time to discover a solution to the problem. I'm not trying to blame anyone. I'm just trying to fix it so we can move forward without any issues and make our target date for implementation."

"Kelly, let me go through this information. I have a million other things I have to do, but now I also have to take care of this. I'll be dealing with you later."

"But Ken, I didn't do this part of the testing."

"I find that hard to believe. Why else would you put in personal time for the supposed fix? As I said, I'll deal with you later. Get back to work."

Kelly picked up her files and left his office feeling like she'd just run a marathon. She was exhausted with trying to explain not only the issue, but herself as well. She'd had no part whatsoever in this phase of the testing—Ariel had been responsible for this. But she was her friend and didn't want to throw her under the bus. She'd wanted to address this without bringing her friend into the mix. She was covering for her and would for as long as she could.

Kelly remembered leaving Ken's office and running to the bathroom. She didn't want anyone to see her fall apart. Never in her wildest dreams did she think Ken would blame her on missing this crucial flaw in the program. She was devastated. It took her a few minutes, but she gathered her wits and made her way back to her office, trying to forget what happened in his office.

Kelly hadn't been able to concentrate. She'd had the beginnings of a migraine. She often got migraines when she was stressed, but she hadn't had one since graduating from graduate school. Before she knew it, her head was pounding and she'd barely been able to make it home that night. She called in sick the next day, which thankfully was a Friday. She'd have the weekend to recover.

Monday rolled around and she returned to work. She went about her normal routine, attending all the necessary meetings that were expected of her. Ariel had been out of town and had returned to work on Monday, not knowing what had transpired between her and Ken the Thursday before. Ariel had also been experiencing some personal issues, so she'd missed a significant amount of work, and Ken had been riding her about her attendance. The last time they'd spoken, he threatened to put Ariel on corrective action.

Ariel during this time had not been performing to her ability. Kelly had covered for her several times, discovering flaws with the test scripts that Ariel had created for their user-acceptance testing. Once pointed out, Ariel made the necessary corrections to ensure that they achieved the necessary results.

After experiencing Ken's tirade from the week before, Kelly sought out Ariel to inform her of her discovery. Ariel was already upset when Kelly met up with her. Apparently Ariel had been warned that morning by Ken that she needed to focus on her job and not let personal problems interfere with her work ethic. Kelly showed Ariel what she'd discovered and explained that the specific program had been tested under her watch. Ariel denied that she should have caught the flaw in the program. In fact, she turned the tables on Kelly and accused her of not catching the flaws.

Kelly had the necessary back-up to prove Ariel was at fault, but Ariel continued to deny it. Kelly was shocked and hurt. They were friends. She certainly expected Ariel to own up to her mistakes, but she didn't. Ariel's behavior called into question their friendship. Was Ariel really her friend or was she using her? At that moment, Ken called both of them into his office. He yelled at Kelly but was extremely nice and gentle with Ariel. Kelly was enraged. How could he blame her for the error that she'd discovered while he praised Ariel about the work she was doing? Everyone knew Ariel was making mistakes. It was common knowledge around the department.

Kelly rolled over in bed—she was tired of revisiting that day during her sleepless night. She'd worked herself into such a tizzy that she started to develop another migraine, and this one was worse than the last one she'd experienced. Thankfully, she'd remembered to pack her medicine when she fled from Knoxville to St. Louis. She could barely see while she located her pills in her toiletries bag. She checked the front door to make sure it was locked and headed off to bed. She hoped that she could sleep the migraine off.

Right before she fell asleep, she remembered Ken's sickening laugh and threats he made concerning her job. He accused her of running away from him that Friday when she called in sick with her migraine. He hadn't thought she'd been sick at all—he just thought she was avoiding him and the issue. She'd been placed on corrective action instead of Ariel that day. As she drifted off to sleep, she could hear him snarling at her. She could feel his hot, foul breath on her face. She could feel him trapping her against the desk. And then, her world went dark.

# Chapter Twelve

A LEC DROVE STRAIGHT THROUGH TO the Samuels' cabin. He'd been on the road for almost three hours when his cell phone rang. He was just approaching the turn off to the cabin when he pulled from the road to answer the incoming call. It was Angelina.

"Are you there yet?"

"I'm just pulling into the driveway."

"Is she there?"

"Her car's here."

Angelina kept talking to him, rambling on about nothing while he got out of the car and walked up the front steps. He knocked on the door and waited. Kelly didn't come to the door. It was almost four o'clock in the afternoon and surely she was home—her car was there. "She's not coming to the door."

"There should be a key underneath the flower pot that's sitting underneath the window. See if it's still there."

Alec practically ran to the flower pot and upended it. Taking a deep breath, he said, "I got it. I'm going in—I'll call you right back."

Alec opened the door and called out Kelly's name, slipping his phone in his pocket. No answer. He walked into the room and perused the front of the cabin. He could tell she'd been there as he found her e-reader and laptop computer in what appeared to be the family room, but Kelly was nowhere. He entered the kitchen and found a cup and plate in the sink, so he knew she'd at least eaten something since she'd arrived the day before.

As he walked through the cabin, he noticed how dark it seemed. All of the blinds were closed, along with the curtains. He wondered what was up with that since it was a beautiful day outside. The sun had shone brightly on his drive. He noticed a dim light at the end of the hallway which he headed towards. He passed several closed doors that he assumed were bedrooms. He called out her name again and there was still no answer. He walked into the opened bedroom doorway and saw light coming from what appeared to be the bathroom. The door was slightly ajar. As he approached, he saw a shadow underneath the door. He frantically began to call her name as he neared the door. He tried to push it open but something stopped its path. He eased through the opening and discovered Kelly lying on the floor in a pool of blood. A quick glance at the sink revealed a brown bottle of pills. He reached for it as he knelt beside her.

He could tell she was breathing regularly and the blood on the floor appeared to be from a head wound she'd likely encountered by hitting the side of the vanity as she'd fallen to the floor. He glanced at the pill bottle, concerned that she may have overdosed until he read the drug's name and the instructions for use. He breathed a sigh of relief—she likely had experienced a migraine, and fainted from the side effects of the migraine before she could take her medicine. He called her name again, but she didn't stir.

He scooped her up into his arms, carried her into the bedroom, and laid her on the bed. He returned to the bathroom where he discovered a first aid kit. He examined her head wound and saw that it wasn't as bad as it had first appeared. He cleaned it, applied a bandage, and then called Angelina.

"Did you find her?"

Sighing, he said, "Yeah. I found her collapsed on the floor."

"Oh my God, is she okay?"

"She hasn't woken yet, but does she get migraines?"

"Yes, really bad ones. They're debilitating. Her collapsing makes sense—she often gets dizzy and faints. Alec, I'm glad you're there to take care of her. When she gets these headaches, she's sometimes out of it for several days."

Alec heard Angelina talk to someone else in the background, and then she came back on the line. "Now it makes sense why she was so emotional yesterday. She often gets depressed and irritable right before she gets one. It all makes sense now."

"Yeah, those are the signs in some people who get severe migraines. I'm not sure that's the entire reason why she acted the way she did, but I'm sure it contributed to it."

"Hold on a second…" Angelina handed the phone to Alejandro.

"Alec, what's her condition?"

"I haven't had a chance to take her vitals yet. She has a superficial wound on her head, and I don't think she's been out for long—I'm guessing maybe just a few minutes before I got here." Alec turned to look at Kelly and noticed her stirring. "Wait a minute… I think she's coming around. Hey, I'll call you back."

Alec ended the call and went to her side. Kelly was waking up. She immediately grabbed the side of her head. Scrunching her forehead, she appeared to be trying to open her eyes but the little light in the room caused her additional pain. He quickly ran to close the bathroom door. He'd still have some light to see, but it should reduce the effects on Kelly.

He sat beside her on the bed and called her name. "Kelly, it's me, Alec. What's wrong? Do you have a migraine?"

She murmured a yes and turned her head away from him.

"I'll be right back," he said as he left her to go retrieve his medical bag from the car. He hurried back to her side and noticed that she'd fallen asleep. He took her blood pressure and thankfully it was in the normal range. He breathed deeply, then closed the door to her room and headed out to the kitchen where he got himself a glass of water. He took a few moments to himself before calling back Alejandro. He elected to call him on his cell instead of the house phone to be sure he got Alejandro and not Angelina.

Alejandro didn't even say hello. "Well?"

"First of all, I don't think she has a concussion. When she briefly woke up I asked her if she had a migraine. She said she did, and that's all I could get out of her before she fell asleep. I think she was able to get a dose of her medication, but she was out before I could ask her."

"That's good. I didn't realize she had migraines, or we might have been able to piece together her behavior from yesterday. I asked Angelina about it, and she said that she sometimes gets that way right before she gets a really bad one. Angelina also said she didn't think she'd had a migraine in a long time. According to Angelina, she used to get them a lot when she was in school and stressed all of the time."

"Makes sense. Hopefully I'll be able to get something out of her while I'm here. She was really out of it, and I'm not sure she even realizes that I'm here. I'll call you tomorrow unless something comes up."

Alec checked on her several times before he also drifted off to sleep on the family room sofa. He heard a noise and got up to see Kelly walking down the hall towards the kitchen. Since he wasn't sure if she was aware of his presence, he waited for her to seat herself at the table with a glass of water before approaching her. He softly said her name from the doorway. He startled her, and she jumped in her chair.

"Alec, where did you come from? You practically scared me to death." She reached up to brush the hair out of her eyes and felt the bandage on her forehead. "What's this?"

"You collapsed in the bathroom and must have hit your head on the vanity. While you were out, I cleaned it up and bandaged it. What happened, Kelly? What caused you to collapse?"

"Let me just sit here for a second," she said as she closed her eyes and rubbed her temples. He could tell she still had her headache. She opened her eyes and recalled her day. "I didn't sleep last night. I tossed and turned the entire night. I knew I was getting a headache, but I didn't take my medicine soon enough and, by the time I went to take it, I got really dizzy. That's all I remember."

Alec examined her more thoroughly while she was awake and determined she didn't have a concussion.

"Why are you here? And how did you know I was here? I'm going to kill Angelina."

"She didn't tell me."

"Well, then who did?"

"Alejandro."

"Okay, so she told him."

"No, not really. He figured it out all on his own. She just confirmed it. You know she can't lie to him."

Kelly closed her eyes and put her head on the table.

"How's the head?"

"It's pretty bad. The one I had not long ago was nothing compared to this one. Wow! I haven't had one this bad since I was in school."

Alec reached for her hand, but she shied away from him, withdrawing her hand and placing it in her lap. He thought her action was kind of strange, unlike her. He'd held her hand before, and it had never seemed to bother her. In fact, she had sat in his lap at Alejandro's wedding after she'd caught the bouquet and he the garter. His touch hadn't bothered her then, but it sure did now. "Come on, why don't you get back to bed, and I'll give you a massage. Maybe if you relax, it will go away."

"No, that's okay. I'll be fine," she said as she got up and slowly ambled down the hallway, clutching the side of her head the entire way. He followed closely behind her. He was worried about her, but not as concerned as he was before he'd arrived. He knew how painful migraines were, along with their after-effects. He was going to stay with her until she recovered. Hopefully that would be tomorrow.

# *Chapter Thirteen*

ANGELINA WAS PLEASANTLY SURPRISED WHEN Gabriella appeared at the door. She hadn't seen her in days.

"So what's this I hear about Kelly?"

"It's not as bad as Alec thought. I mean it is, but it isn't. Kelly's having one of her migraines. It sounds like it's a pretty epic one, too."

"Poor thing. I remember her getting them when we were in college. Do you remember that time she was so excited to come up for a visit and at the last minute she couldn't come because of a migraine."

"Yeah, I do. She'd really wanted to visit that weekend, too." Angelina led Gabriella into the kitchen and put the kettle on to boil water for them. "Tea or hot chocolate?"

"Angelina, you should know by now what I favor."

"Just thought I'd ask. I knew you'd choose the hot chocolate," she chuckled. Angelina got out the mix and added it to the mugs. "Marshmallows or whipped cream?"

"Do you even have to ask?"

"No." Angelina got the can of whipped cream from the refrigerator. "Matthew should be done with his bath. Do you want to go check on him?"

"What about Angel?"

"She's napping."

Gabriella went in search of Matthew while Angelina prepared their hot chocolates. Minutes later, Matthew came running into the room asking where his hot chocolate was. Angelina gave him the mug she'd prepared for herself while she decided to make herself a cup of hot tea instead. All three of them sat around the table. Gabriella hadn't seen Matthew for a few days and drew him into a conversation. "So how are things at school?"

"They're good. I got an A on my math test the other day. I was the only A in the class."

"Wow, that's something you should be proud of."

"I am. So is Mom."

"What about your dad?"

"I guess he is. He's been real busy lately and hasn't been in a very good mood." Matthew took a sip of his drink while Gabriella looked over the top of his head at Angelina. She wondered what that comment was all about. Matthew continued talking about school and went into a huge discussion about a science experiment he was involved in. "And my partner and I were the only ones that got the result the teacher wanted."

"Wow, Matthew, you seem to really enjoy science."

"I do. I want to be a doctor like my dad," Matthew said as he drained the last of his hot chocolate from his mug.

Before long, it was time for Matthew to head off to bed—he'd been trying not to nod off for the last ten minutes. Since Gabriella didn't see him too often, she volunteered to tuck him into bed and read a story to him. Twenty minutes later she returned to the kitchen and found Angelina staring into her cup of tea. "So what was that comment all about?"

Angelina knew what she was referring to as she had also

noticed Alejandro's change of mood lately. He usually was always more than happy to help her with the kids and knew when she was at her wits end. He'd step in and handle whatever needed to be taken care of. But lately, his mood seemed darker, and he was more irritable. "Think about it, Gabriella, and you'll have your answer," Angelina said as she took a final swallow of her tea. She walked over to the sink, rinsed out her mug, and placed it into the dishwasher.

"You don't have to tell me, Angelina. I know what it's all about. I had just hoped this year would be different."

Shaking her head, Angelina said, "Not this year. I think it's worse because of Angel. It all started when he couldn't go to Matthew's appointment with Ashton. He demanded a slew of tests be run. He called and basically harassed Ashton, and then Ashton alluded to Alejandro's call during Matthew's appointment."

"How unprofessional is that?" Gabriella replied. "I knew there was a reason why I didn't like him. I don't think they should have hired him. I know my dad thinks the world of him, but there's just something about him. I can't put my finger on it, but I just don't care for his bedside manner."

Angelina just smiled at her. She knew how her husband felt about Ashton and now she knew how Gabriella felt. Clearly, neither cared for him.

❧

Alec woke abruptly when he almost fell out of the chair that he'd placed beside Kelly's bed. He wanted to be near her in case she needed him during the night. It was near midnight now, and he didn't know if she'd wakened or not. He was still exhausted from a sleepless night of worry the night before, his early morning meeting with Alejandro and Bill, and then his drive to the cabin. He replayed the conversation he'd had earlier with Alejandro regarding his relationship with Kelly.

*She's gotten under your skin, Alec. I think you're falling for her... Yes, you are. You're feeling the same sense of guilt and protectiveness I felt for Angelina. I hope that you can recognize it earlier than I did... I almost lost her, and I'll always regret the time we lost before we found ourselves again.*

He watched Kelly sleep. Was he falling for her? He didn't think so... But maybe Alejandro was right. She seemed to capture his every thought. He worried about her, especially since their incident in the park. He needed to get his head together and come to grips with whatever was going on with him... With them, if anything.

Kelly started groaning in her sleep. He slid off the chair and onto the side of her bed. He brushed the hair off her face, and watched as her eyes gradually opened. Something caused her to jump and pull herself away from him.

"Alec, is that you?"

"Yeah. Hey, what's wrong? Are you scared?"

"No, I'm okay," she said as she brushed her bangs out of her eyes and sat up in bed. She scooted back up against the headboard and rubbed her temples.

"Any better?" he asked as he tried to catch her eyes. She shook her head no. She'd been avoiding his eyes and he wondered what that was about. She wouldn't look at him directly and barely acknowledged his presence. "Do you want another dose of your medication?"

"No, I hate taking those pills. I hate the way they make me feel."

"I don't think it's the pills that make you feel that way. I think it's the migraine itself."

"Whatever," she murmured. She took her hands and covered her eyes. He could tell that she was really hurting.

"What can I do for you?"

"Just leave me alone."

"Kelly, no. I'm here for you. I want to help you."

She removed her hands from her eyes and looked at him directly. "Just go, please. Leave me alone. I'll be alright."

"No, I'm staying until I'm sure you're over this."

"I don't care what you do, just leave me be," she said as she lay back down and turned her back to him. Within moments, she was asleep again. Alec just sat there, watching her breathe. He needed to make right with her. He leaned over the bed and placed a soft kiss against her forehead, then left the room.

*☾*

The next morning, Kelly found Alec sound asleep on the couch in the family room. The throw that he'd covered himself with had fallen onto the floor beside him. She reached for it and covered him—there was a slight chill in the air since the heat had yet to turn back on that morning.

Wrapping herself in a blanket, she sat in the chair across from the couch and watched him sleep. She could tell he was dreaming because his eyelids fluttered. Never before had she noticed how long his eyelashes were. What she had noticed was that he was handsome. He had dark hair and brown eyes that, if she thought about it, just took her breath away. He was well toned from his hours spent in the gym lifting weights and running. She'd always thought Alejandro was gorgeous, but Alec? He was off the charts gorgeous in her mind. She wished she would have really gotten to know him when Angelina and Gabriella were in college.

Although, she'd never met the Alvarez family until Angelina and Gabriella had met in college, their families had grown especially close the previous year when Alejandro had performed the lifesaving surgery on her sister, Colleen. Their

families were tied together and even more so now since Alejandro and Angelina had married. Alec and Joe had always
been there on the sidelines when she'd visited Angelina in
college, but she hadn't met Alejandro until Colleen's health
scare.

As she continued watching Alec, she noticed a small scar
on his chin. She wondered where that had come from. She
was lost in thought and didn't realize that he'd awakened and
was staring directly at her. Clearing his throat, he brought her
out of the world she was in.

"Do you like what you see?" he asked, teasing.

"Huh? What did you say?"

He repeated himself as he sat up on the couch.

"I don't know what you're talking about."

"You were staring at me."

"I was? I wasn't aware of it," she said as she stood and left
the room. She was preparing a pot of coffee when he joined
her a few moments later.

"Do you think you should be having caffeine?"

She looked over her shoulder at him, giving him a dirty
look.

"You know too much caffeine can be a trigger for migraines."

"I'm well aware of the effects of caffeine on a migraine.
It can be a trigger, but can also stop one, too," she said as she
continued making her coffee.

"Maybe you need to cut back on the caffeine."

"I know what I need, and right now I need a cup of coffee,
thank you. And why, may I ask, are you here? I didn't invite
you."

"Where the hell did that come from? I came out here, to
the middle of nowhere, to make sure you were okay. I was
worried about you. After your little melt down at the park,

I was just really concerned. Can't a friend be worried about another friend?"

"I didn't realize we were friends."

Alec approached her. His hands were clenched at his sides. He got right in her face and looked her directly in the eyes. She did her best not to flinch or let the tears fall. She turned back to the counter, away from him. He grabbed her upper arms and spun her around.

Placing both hands on her arms, he looked her directly in the eyes. She felt a lone tear fall down her cheek. Reaching up, he brushed the tear aside with his thumb. Almost whispering, Alec said, "Kelly, I want to help you. I want you to know that I am here for you, and I am not going anywhere. You can trust me. I won't hurt you."

With that, she burst into tears. Alec wrapped both of his arms around her and pulled her close, letting her cry.

Alec noticed a different Kelly. She wasn't hysterically sobbing like she'd been at the park. This time she let him really hold her as she cried. When her tears slowed, he pulled slightly away from her and wiped the remaining tears from her face with his thumbs. He grabbed her hand and led her back towards the couch where he held her in his arms. He thought she'd drifted off to sleep, but she hadn't. She'd just finally relaxed... Relaxed for the first time since leaving Knoxville.

Maybe Alec could help her, help her get past what had happened to her. Her mind told her she could trust him, but could her heart? She didn't know if she could allow that to happen. She'd given up on finding someone. She'd pretty much given up on men in general. Lately, she grouped all men in the same category as Ken, even though she knew she shouldn't do that. She also knew that she could trust Alejandro, but could she trust Alec, too?

# Chapter Fourteen

ALEC FELT KELLY FINALLY RELAX in his arms as she drifted off to sleep. He knew sleep was the best thing for her to rid herself of the migraine. He drifted off to sleep as well since he hadn't slept well for worrying about her. The next thing he was aware of, Kelly was nestling herself deeper in his arms. He was holding her when nature called. He eased her out of his arms and laid her on the couch, covering her with the throw he'd used the night before. It was almost noon, and he decided he needed to check in with Alejandro.

Angelina was cleaning up the kitchen when she heard Alejandro's cell phone ring. He was in the basement helping Matthew with his science project. Thinking nothing of it, she answered the phone. It was Alec.

"Angelina, hi!"

"Alec, how's Kelly? How's her migraine?"

"I think she's better. She's resting peacefully."

"I'm glad to hear that. Alec, I'm sorry. I forgot her signs for a migraine. I should have told you that was more than likely what was going on with her."

"That's alright. We're past that now. I'm going to stay with her until I'm sure that she's okay, then I'm going to head on home. It's not fair to Dad to have to cover for me. I know he enjoys interacting with everyone at the clinic, but he's retired now. It's my responsibility."

"Alec, don't worry about it. John's in his element. He loves it. I think he actually wishes he were practicing more than he is. He's always over here talking with Alejandro about some type of medical advancement."

"I know. I just don't want to—"

Angelina interrupted him, "I'm just glad that you were able to find Kelly and treat her."

"I'm sure she would have been fine. Migraines are an animal I've never personally experienced. I can't imagine the pain that she was in. Occasionally, I have a patient that comes in with the symptoms, and I can definitely see the pain they're in." He stopped speaking briefly, sighed, and continued, "Angelina, I'm going to try and find out what really happened to her in Knoxville. I know she's keeping something from us. I just hope she'll feel comfortable enough to trust me."

Alec heard Kelly stirring in the other room. "I'd better go. I think she's waking up."

"Alec, thank you. Please tell her that I love her and hope she feels better."

Alec smiled as he disconnected the call. Kelly had a lot of people who cared about her. He needed to make sure she knew that. Her friends and family would be there to support her with whatever had happened to her.

Alec got up and went in search of Kelly. The door to her bathroom was closed and he could hear the shower. He assumed she was feeling better, so he headed off to the kitchen to make a late lunch.

Alec was sitting at the kitchen table reading a medical journal when he heard her approach and quickly finished reading the article that he was on. She approached the table and pulled the chair out just as he was setting the journal down on the table.

"Feeling better?"

"Much," she said as she glanced about the room. "You made breakfast?"

"Well, it's really lunch time, but yes I made breakfast." He stood and walked over to the stove. Reaching for an oven mitt, he pulled out their plates that had been warming in the oven. He'd made scrambled eggs, bacon, and toast. He poured her a glass of juice and served her.

She reached for her fork then set it down. She looked up from her plate. For once, he noticed a relaxed expression on her face. "Thank you," she said warmly as she reached for her fork again and scooped up some eggs. Looking up into his eyes, she added, "I mean it. Thanks for being here. And I'm sorry, too."

"Sorry?"

"Yeah. For being an emotional mess this morning and the other day. That's not me. I'm normally not emotional or a crier. Now, Angelina, that's another story."

"I know. Alejandro's told me about how she gets," he sheepishly smiled as though he were breaking a confidence. They ate in silence, then Alec set his fork down and looked at her. "It's a gorgeous day. If you're feeling up to it, would you like to take a walk?"

Smiling at him, she said, "That's sounds like a good idea. I'd like that." They finished their lunch or be it breakfast, cleaned up the kitchen, and headed outside. There was a slight chill in the air, so they both grabbed their jackets as they walked out the door. Kelly's sleeve was turned inside out and she had a difficult time getting her arm through. Alec noticed this and stepped in to help her. They both reached for her sleeve at the same time. She didn't know why, but his touch surprised her, causing her to drop her jacket and she yelped in surprise. Alec reached down and picked up her coat from the ground. He righted the sleeve and helped her put it on.

"Sorry about that," he said. "I didn't mean to…"

Alec didn't get a chance to finish his statement as Kelly turned her back to him, zipping her jacket. A moment later, she turned back and headed down the stairs. He looked at her, not sure exactly what had just transpired between them. It was almost as though she were afraid of his touch. He shook his head. He was just imagining it again.

The Samuels had a beautiful piece of property. Off to the side of the house, there was a fully stocked lake containing various types of fish. Kelly said they often had family fishing tournaments. Wyatt, she explained, was quite the fisherman and had even won several of the family tournaments. "Your brother, however, is not a very good fisherman."

"Huh, that doesn't sound like him. He used to fish all the time on Lake Wisconsin. In fact, he and Tammy almost bought a lake house just so he would have a place to store his boat and fish. He loved going up there. It got him out of the city. He could relax and just unwind. Now, I think he just sits in his home office and looks out the window."

"I've seen him do that. It's like he gets lost…"

"Yep, that's my brother. He tunes everything out around him. That's his way of either thinking something through, or just letting go. Alejandro loved Tammy and Michael. It was a love…" He stopped before he could finish his thought. He looked down at the ground, "Sorry about that."

"Don't be. I can only imagine what he went through. Losing not only the love of your life, but your first love…"

"Kelly, he loves Angelina with all of his heart. It's different with her. He's different."

"I'm sure he is. I just wish he didn't have to go through

remembering what happened. I realize the anniversary of their deaths is coming up. I've seen a change in him since I arrived. He's a little more short-tempered with Matthew. He's even moodier. And yes, I've caught him several times deep in thought, staring out the infamous window."

"We've all noticed it. I think he has more on his mind this year, especially since they've had Angel. Last year was bad enough between Matthew's transplant and everything that they went through with Angelina. I just wish we could all forget about that day and move on. We all loved Tammy and Michael—they'll always be a part of our memories—but he's making new ones with Angelina. I just wish he could see that and move on."

"I know grief is an ugly animal. Maybe in time he'll be able to get through this part of year without the painful memories."

"I hope so," he said as he skipped a rock across the lake.

They walked around the lake until the sun began to set and a chilly wind started to blow out of the north. "Shall we call it a day and go inside?"

"That sounds like a good idea. I'm starting to get cold." Alec had wanted to hold her hand while they'd walked along but refrained. She looked cold to him, so he went to her side and tried to put his arm around her waist, but she pulled away from him.

"I'm okay. Let's go make a fire," she said as she left him standing in her tracks.

That was the second time in a day that she rebuffed his advances. He just wanted to help her with her coat and warm her. It bothered him that she pulled away from him. He decided to forget about what appeared to be a fear of him and talk to Angelina about it later on.

With her head start, she made it to the house before he

did. When he walked through the door, he found her bent over the fireplace making a fire. "Here, let me do that. You go find something for dinner." She handed over the kindling that she held in her hand and headed off to the kitchen.

When Alec entered the kitchen after, he found her literally bent over putting a pan in the oven. As she stood, she wavered against the stove. He hurried to her side and tried to steady her. Again, she pulled away from him. The more he thought about it, the more he realized that each and every time he touched her, she pulled away. He decided to ask her about it.

"What's up with that?"

"What are you talking about?"

"Every time that I reach out and try to help you, you pull away."

"I didn't realize it," she said as she turned her back to him. She'd pulled the makings of a salad from the refrigerator and had turned to the sink to wash the vegetables when he approached her side. As he neared, he could see her back stiffen. She was scared of him. *But why?* he wondered. When he reached her side, he pulled the head of lettuce from her hands and set it in the sink. He stilled her hands as she tried to reclaim the lettuce. Her head was bowed. Using his index finger, he gently raised her chin so he could look her directly in the eyes. She tried to look away again, but he didn't allow it. Cupping his hand along the side of her face, he took a deep breath and approached the subject that he originally was going to speak to Angelina about.

"Who hurt you, Kelly?"

On the impact of his words, all of the color drained from her face—she turned as white as a ghost. She reacted immediately and spun away from him, knocking the salad bowl to the floor. Ignoring the loud clang of the bowl as it hit the floor, she hurried from the room.

He stood, baffled, as he watched her run from the room. Running his hand through his hair, he followed her and found her sitting in front of the fireplace. The room was lit only by the glow of the flames. She stared intently at the fire as the flames engulfed the log. He noticed her stiffened back and how she rung her hands back and forth in front of her. He'd hit the nail on the head. Yes, someone had hurt her, whether it be emotionally or physically or both.

"Kelly, we don't have to talk about it if you don't want to. Come on now, let's eat. I'm starved." He thought that by suggesting they eat, she'd come out of her funk and be comfortable with him again. She stared at the fire a few moments longer and then stood and returned to the kitchen. He didn't bring up her change in mood from earlier. The more he was around her, the more he knew that she was hiding something malevolent from her family.

## Chapter Fifteen

THE NEXT MORNING, KELLY SEEMED like her old self. When he ensured that she was no longer suffering from the side effects of her migraine, he informed her that he was returning to St. Louis. At this point in time, he realized he couldn't do anything more for her. He'd decided while lying in bed the night before that he was going to go to the source of where he believed her problems originated… Lattice Works.

"I'm going to head off now. Are you sure you've got everything that you need?" He'd also made up his mind that he wasn't going to inundate her with any more questions about her health. He believed she was well enough to be on her own and he had to leave it at that.

"I'm good," she said as she stood on the threshold as he walked down the stairs to the driveway. "Thanks for taking care of me."

"Sure, anytime," he said as he opened his car door. "I'll talk to you soon," he added as he got into the car. He started the engine and rolled down his window as he pulled away. Waving goodbye, he turned down the driveway, never once looking back. She was on her own, dealing with whatever monsters she was carrying around.

❆

Kelly watched the taillights disappear as he rounded the curve in the driveway. She was alone now. Where she wanted to be, or thought she wanted to be. She closed the door behind her and headed off to the kitchen to put away the dishes. She contemplated returning to St. Louis as well. *Maybe tomorrow*, she said to herself as she emptied the dishwasher, returning the dishes to their respective places.

❆

Alec had barely made it back to the highway when he dialed Alejandro's cell. He told him that he was on his way back to the city. "What's your schedule look like?" he asked his brother.

"I'm good today—pretty open. Why?"

Alec told him about his interactions with Kelly. "Any time I touched her, she shied away—almost as though she were fearful of a man's touch. Maybe I'm imagining it. Maybe she's still upset with me. I don't know. I just know something's not right." Alec didn't want to tell his brother about his discovery until he was able to see him in person.

"Call me when you get closer to the city, and I'll meet you at my office. Dad's got you covered at the clinic. We can fill Joe in later. Until we discover what's going on with Kelly, I don't want Angelina to know about this."

"Agreed," Alec said as he continued on towards St. Louis.

It was nearly one in the afternoon when he called Alejandro and told him he was about a half hour out of the city.

❆

Before leaving the house, Alejandro sat with Angelina while she fed Angel. They talked about Kelly. He wanted to feel her out. "So Kelly hasn't lived at home since graduating from college?"

"That's right. As soon as she graduated, she headed off to Emory for grad school. Then she got her job at Lattice Works and moved to Knoxville."

"I know you didn't date much while you were in school, but did she?"

"She did. She had a couple of steady boyfriends. In fact, we thought she was going to get married when she graduated from Emory, but they broke up. Her boyfriend at the time decided he wanted to travel abroad for a year before entering the workforce. That was so against Kelly's principles that she broke it off."

"Do you think she regretted it?"

"You know, I don't. I think she was okay with the way their relationship ended. She dated someone in Knoxville for a while, but he moved to Arizona to be closer to his family. Why? Do you think she's got boyfriend problems?"

"I don't know, do you?"

"I don't think so. She'd been working such ungodly hours that she didn't have time to date."

Alejandro glanced at his watch. He'd told her he had an early afternoon meeting and had to leave.

"Thanks," she said.

"For what?" He said as he was putting his jacket on.

"For caring about Kelly."

"Why wouldn't I? She's family. When I married you, I told your siblings that I wanted to be there for them just like you were. And that's what I'm doing. I'm hoping to help her get through whatever's troubling her." Alejandro looked at his watch again. "I've gotta go. I love you."

"Love you, too," she said as she watched him walk out the door.

Alejandro didn't want to interrupt their meeting once it started, so he stopped to get sandwiches on his way into the

office. He was sure Alec would be starved. He was just walking through his office door with their lunch in hand when
Alec appeared. He looked beat, like he hadn't slept in days.
"Wow, you're looking pretty scruffy there. You're a sight for
sore eyes."

"Yeah, and I'm feeling that way, too," Alec said as he
plopped down on the couch in Alejandro's office. "I'm pretty
beat. I didn't sleep much while I was gone."

Alejandro handed Alec his sandwich. He'd bought him
the roast beef special that he always enjoyed.

Popping the top on a soda, he took a bite of his sandwich.
"Wow, this sure is good."

Alejandro joined him on the couch. He opened his sandwich and spread it out on the table in front of him. He opened
his chips and started crunching away. He'd just reached for
his iced tea when Alec started in.

"Someone hurt her."

Alejandro stopped, his hand around his drink, "What are
you talking about?"

"Last night she was in the kitchen fixing dinner. When I
went to help her, she seemed to lose her balance, so I rushed
to her side. When I reached for her, she pulled away. I asked
her about it and she said it was nothing. Then I asked her."

"Asked her what?"

"Who hurt her?" Taking a sip of his drink, he went on,
"Alejandro, she turned as white as a sheet and ran from the
room. What I asked freaked her out. Something happened in
Knoxville, and I've got to get to the bottom of it."

"While I was waiting to leave today, I talked to Angelina.
According to her, she's been in several long standing relationships. The last one ended, I would assume, not too long ago.
The guy returned to Arizona to be near family. Angelina
said she hasn't dated anyone recently since she was too busy

working."

"I have to believe that whatever happened to her occurred recently. Maybe it was her last boyfriend. If something happened with him, it might have caused her to lose focus and maybe she really did lose her job because of job performance."

"You could have something there," Alejandro said as he took another bite of his sandwich.

"Or maybe something happened at the office. I just wish we knew more about her job loss."

"I do, too." Alejandro took a drink. "Angelina has no idea what's troubling Kelly. She knows something's not right, but she can't put her finger on it. And I won't dare ask Jackie. She'll just freak out. Remember when Angelina and I told everyone about her infertility? Well, I found out later on that she went ballistic with Ben. She blamed me totally for not diagnosing her peritonitis earlier. She'd wanted to sue me until Ben calmed her down. He made her understand exactly why Angelina held off telling everyone about her condition. Don't get me wrong, I love Angelina's mother, but she can be a firecracker at a moment's notice."

"I understand." Alec stood and wrapped the remainder of his sandwich up. He started pacing.

"You're starting to act like me," Alejandro said, making Alec stop. "Angelina accuses me of pacing when I have something on my mind. I drive her crazy."

"I do have something on my mind," he said as he returned to the couch.

"Did you think about what I said the other day?"

"What exactly was that? You've said an awful lot lately," he said, feigning ignorance as he ran a hand through his hair.

"Do you have feelings for Kelly?"

Alec rubbed his hands across his face. He looked Alejandro directly in the eyes and said, "Yeah, I've thought about it."

"And?"

"God, I don't know. I wasn't looking for anyone. I don't need a relationship right now."

"That's exactly how I felt when Angelina and I got together. I told her we'd be friends only—nothing else because that's all I could give her. And then, it just happened. I fell head over heels in love with her. I tried to fool myself into thinking I cared for her because we were friends, and she was best friends with Gabby. But no, it was something more. I soon found myself thinking about her at the most inopportune times. I couldn't go to sleep without talking to her, and I couldn't start my day without wishing her a good day. I was totally blindsided by it. I still wasn't over Tammy, but she helped me. Helped me heal. I'm not going to say that I don't still miss my family. I do. But when I get down, I look at what I have today. I have a beautiful wife. I have Matthew and Angel. What more could a man want? I'm glad I went for it because I couldn't be happier."

Alec was silent.

"Alec, you've been alone for too long. You've always put your career and the practice ahead of your own needs. You need to stop and look at your future. Would each day be a little brighter with Kelly in it? I think it would and, if I were you, I'd go for it."

"But?"

"But what? We'll find the answers to help her get through whatever she's going through. I know you'll be there every step of the way. She's a fantastic woman. Kelly's smart, sexy, and beautiful. Give it a chance, or I'm afraid you'll regret it. I almost lost Angelina when I wasn't honest with her about Tammy. I can't wish back the time we spent apart, granted it was only a few short weeks, but we lost that time forever. Don't give up on her. She's worth it."

"Your right, she is. But right now she won't let me be close. She won't let me touch her or hold her hand. I'm afraid to think what would happen if I tried to even kiss her. We've got to find out what happened to her, and I know exactly where I'm going to start." Alec stood and started his pacing again. Alejandro watched his brother formulate his plan. He abruptly stopped and turned towards his brother. "Tell Joe I've gone out of town again. I'm out of here."

"Where are you going?"

Alec waved goodbye as he ran out the door. He didn't tell Alejandro what his plans were for fear he'd tell his wife. He knew he couldn't lie to her as was evident when Kelly asked Angelina to cover for her—they couldn't keep secrets from one another. Alejandro was better off not knowing what he was up to. He didn't know if he'd find the answers that he was looking for, but he was going to try everything in his power to get them because he needed to help Kelly overcome whatever was troubling her.

# Chapter Sixteen

A S KELLY TOOK A STROLL around the lake, she thought about her walk with Alec the day before. From the moment they had left the house until they'd reentered it, she'd been on edge. He'd tried to help her with her jacket and she pretty much freaked out when they had barely even touched. And then when she'd started to get cold, he had wanted to put his arm around her and she dodged him and ran away back to the safety of the house. What was wrong with her?

She really liked Alec. He was fun to be around. He was gorgeous. She was lucky that he showed any semblance of interest in her. He had so many of the same characteristics that Alejandro possessed—she knew why Angelina fell in love with him. And, if given the opportunity, she felt she could fall in love with Alec.

From the moment he came to her rescue when she slid off the road, to today when he was leaving her behind, she felt a connection with him. She didn't know what it was, but she knew she wanted to see him more often. Yet every time that he wanted to get near her, she flinched. She needed to get over this feeling of uneasiness, but she didn't know how. The memories were always with her. No matter what she tried to do to forget them, they were still there.

After sitting for most of the morning feeling sorry for her-self, Kelly decided to pack up and head on home. She hoped being around friends and family would bring her out of this funk.   And if Alec appeared, she would do her best to be more open with him—allow his touch and maybe even allow herself to return it.

❧

Alec ran home after leaving Alejandro's office. He took a quick shower and packed an overnight bag. He was going to do everything in his power to find out what happened to Kelly. Alec jumped in the car and programmed his GPS for his destination. He hoped to be there by ten o'clock—it was almost a seven hour drive to Knoxville. He decided that he was going to surprise Bill at the office. If he gave him a heads up to his arrival, he'd possibly figure out why he was visiting and be prepared for his onslaught of questions.

Alec wasn't sure if Bill knew that Kelly was his sister-in-law. He'd met Alejandro when they were going through the due diligence to vet Lattice Works for the clinic. Angelina's last name was Alvarez now—not Samuels—so he might not have put two and two together.

Alec drove straight through and arrived in Knoxville at almost eleven. On his way down, he'd made a reservation at the hotel that was practically across the street from his desti-nation. Bill wouldn't know what hit him come nine o'clock tomorrow morning. Alec was going to get answers. He was going to get to the bottom of Kelly's nightmare.

❧

Alejandro and Angelina were sitting in the family room enjoying a nice quiet evening when they heard the back door open. The kids were fast asleep. When they heard the door close, Angelina looked at Alejandro with a panicked look on her face. "Did you hear that? It sounded like the back door."

"I did. You stay here, and I'll check it out," Alejandro said as he stood and headed off in the direction of the noise. Angelina didn't hear anything after he left. No noise, no voices, nothing. Just as she was about to investigate what was going on, Alejandro walked back into the room with Kelly by his side. "Look what the cat dragged in," Alejandro said as Kelly made her way to her sister.

"Kelly, oh my." Angelina pulled her sister into an embrace. Pulling away, she looked her over. "How are you feeling?"

"I'm doing okay. I feel a lot better than I did before. I forgot how bad those migraines can get. I haven't had one that bad for at least a few months. I am so thankful that Alec came out to check on me."

On the way home, Kelly decided she wasn't going to bring up how Alec had found her. She was just grateful for his presence. Kelly sat down. "I did tell Alec what a poor fisherman you are," she said to Alejandro.

"You what? Where did you get the idea that I am a poor fisherman? I love to fish. Tammy and I used to go up to Lake Wisconsin all of the time. I'd catch enough for us eat while we were there, and often times I brought fish back to share with my colleagues."

"From what I remember, Wyatt out-fished you last summer when we had the fishing tournament at the cabin."

"Oh, that. I purposely didn't do well out there—I wanted Wyatt to win. He follows me around like a lost puppy. I wanted him to think that he could beat me. In fact, I rarely put any bait on my line. No bait, no fish," he chuckled. "And it worked! Wyatt single handedly beat me and your father."

"That he did," chimed in Angelina. "I didn't know you were such the fisherman. We need to go out to the cabin more often so you can fish. It would be a nice trip away from the city so you could relax. It's better than you sitting looking out that window," Angelina said as she pointed to one of the windows that she often found him staring out of.

Alejandro laughed. "That's a good idea. I'd love to do that."

It was getting late and Angelina was doing her best to stifle her yawns.

"I think this momma's sending me a signal. Come on, honey. Let's get you to bed. You had a rough day with Angel and you need to get up early since Matthew goes back to school tomorrow. These long weekends just fly on by." He turned to Kelly, "Don't they?"

Alejandro stood and reached for Angelina's hand. He pulled her off the couch and drew her close to his side. "It's great having you home, Kelly. We'll see you tomorrow."

"Thanks, Alejandro. Angelina, get some sleep and I'll see you both in the morning." She waved at them as they headed off to their room.

Kelly was also tired from her drive back from the cabin. She methodically went through the house turning off lights and making sure the doors were locked. She'd left her suitcase in the kitchen when she came in. She went to retrieve it, but discovered it was gone. Alejandro must have taken it to her room.

Kelly went to her room where she discovered that Alejandro had indeed carried her suitcase to her room. She was tired but not too tired, so she decided to unpack and put her clothes away. She'd do laundry tomorrow and help Angelina get caught up around the house. Then, she decided she needed to look for a job. She'd wasted so much time avoiding the job hunt. The trip to the cabin helped her put some things into perspective, and finding a job was now at the top of her list.

Kelly put her clothes away and sat down on the bed. She also needed to call Alec and thank him for coming to her aide, but she realized she didn't have his phone number. She'd have to call the office. She'd taken one of his business cards when she'd gone to the clinic for Matthew's appointment with Ashton. It was in the bottom of her purse, she was sure of it.

Kelly suddenly became exhausted and decided to head off to bed. She hoped that she'd get a good night's sleep. Lately, she'd been having more and more dreams about Ken and Ariel. She hoped that tonight would be dream-free as they often put her in a bad mood the next day. She fell asleep almost as soon as her head hit the pillow.

*

Alec checked into his hotel room and sat down on the bed. He was tired. The last several days had been a whirlwind. Between Kelly's meltdown at the park, her running away and Alec following her to the cabin, then Kelly's migraine and his decision to return to St. Louis only to turn around and head off to Knoxville... Just thinking about the last several days' events was giving *him* a migraine.

Alec ran his hands through his hair and covered his face with his hands. He tried to suppress a yawn but it didn't work. He decided to head off to bed. Tomorrow was another day, and tomorrow he'd hopefully begin to find the answers to Kelly's mysterious firing and behavior.

Alec was going to do anything in his power to help Kelly return to the happy, cheerful, fun-loving woman that he knew before all of this happened. He'd find a way to bring her back, to bring back the woman he was most assuredly falling in love with.

# Chapter Seventeen

A LEC WOKE FEELING JUST AS tired as when he'd gone to sleep the night before. He thought he'd slept the entire night when he woke. Thinking it must be dawn since his room was bathed in light, he looked at the bedside clock and was disappointed with the time. It was only one in the morning. The light streaming in through the crack in the drapes was from the lights illuminating the parking lot.

Alec tried every single trick he knew that would help him fall back to sleep, but nothing worked. He counted sheep, tensed and relaxed his muscles, even sang the ninety-nine bottles of beer song to himself. Nothing worked. Alec was starting to get frustrated. He heard every noise in his room—the creaking and groaning of the bed as he continually tossed and turned, the ice machine just down the hall clunking ice into the empty bin every ten minutes, the door slamming shut in the room across the hall from him. All of these noises in conjunction with his racing mind prevented him from fall-ing back to sleep. He lay awake the remainder of the night, and when his wake-up call came through at five thirty that morning, he growled at the phone.

He crawled out of bed and headed for the shower. He hoped a nice, long shower would do him good and help fully wake him up. As he stood under the hot water, he closed his eyes and all he could see was Kelly sitting on the boulder in the park, crying her eyes out. He had to find the answers. He wanted to be the one to bring the sadness to an end and put a smile back on her face. He wanted to be the one to make her happy again. He wanted to be the one to hopefully bring focus on them as a couple. He wanted to do it all, to right her and put her on the path to being the fun-loving Kelly that she once used to be. He hoped that he'd find the answers just a short block away from where he currently was.

By the time Alec finished his shower and dressed, it was barely six fifteen in the morning. The breakfast buffet opened at six thirty, so he gathered his files and headed off to grab a hot cup of coffee. He hoped the caffeine jolt would wake him enough to get through the first part of his day.

Alec had not one, but three cups of coffee before eight o'clock in the morning. He read through the files on Lattice Works he'd retrieved from his home office before heading out. He'd just finished rereading the contract when his cell chirped to life. It was an incoming text from Alejandro informing him that Kelly had returned home the night before. Alec didn't think twice—he hit speed dial and, before the phone rang on his side, Alejandro was answering, "I see you got my text?"

"I did. What's up with that?"

"I have no idea. Angelina and I were sitting here and we heard the door open. When I went to check on it, she was standing in the kitchen with her suitcase at her side."

"Really?"

"Yeah, and when she came in to talk, it was like she'd just left a few hours earlier. No mention of why she'd returned, only that she told you I couldn't fish."

"That's right. What's up with that letting a ten-year-old

out-fish you?"

Alejandro laughed, "Wyatt's older than ten, Alec. He idolizes me and follows me everywhere when I'm around him. The trick to losing a fishing derby is no bait."

"No bait?"

"Yeah, you can't fish without putting bait on the line. I chose to just drop my hook, end of story."

"I'll have to remember that trick," Alec said, laughing. "Changing subjects… I'm less than a block away from Lattice Works. I'm going to head over there in a little while—surprise my friend Bill and see where it goes."

Alejandro didn't seem surprised by this in the least. Alec went on to discuss his strategy with his brother. "I would think that if I threaten to pull the contract, he may fess up. He knows I have a lot of contacts and, if I pull my contract, he more than likely will lose additional business from all of my peers that I recommended his software to."

"That might work. Give it a try. If it doesn't work, we'll just have to try something else."

Alec told Alejandro he'd call him when the meeting was over. He returned to his room, retrieved his suit coat, and headed off in the direction of Lattice Works. He had all the confidence in the world that he would get the answers he was searching for by using a certain method of intimidation.

Alec arrived at Bill's office unannounced. In fact, as Alec was walking off the elevator, he ran smack into Bill as he was heading to his office. To say Bill was surprised to see Alec was an understatement. In fact Bill, was so rattled, he could barely get Alec's name out.

"A-Alec?" he said as he reached out to shake Alec's hand. Alec didn't offer his hand immediately, but waited a few seconds to shake Bill's. "What are you doing here?"

"I've got a few things that I need to discuss with you," Alec said as he shifted his briefcase from one hand to the other.

"I wasn't expecting you. Let me check to see if anyone is using the conference room, and we'll set up in there."

Alec followed Bill as they worked their way to his office. Bill checked with his secretary and discovered that the room was open.

Bill led Alec to the conference room and asked if he cared for anything to drink. Alec really didn't need any more caffeine that morning, but he agreed to another cup of coffee. This meeting could run longer than he anticipated, and he wanted to be sharp in case Bill tried to pull a fast one on him. Alec settled into a welcoming chair. It was a leather, high-backed, swivel chair and was extremely cushy. He could fall asleep sitting in it, especially after the night he'd experienced. He decided it would be comfortable enough for the amount of time he planned on being there.

Bill returned to the room, his arms laden with his files. Two of his managers had accompanied him and were also carrying files. They wanted to be prepared to answer any questions that Alec threw at them. They started to sit down when Alec stood, raised his hand, and said, "This meeting is just between the two of us. I thought I made myself clear when I arrived that I am meeting with just you. I'd like to review the contract in detail."

Bill was exasperated. He turned to his managers and asked them to leave. "I've got it. I'll call you if I need anything from either of you." Both men grabbed their files and walked out of the room. Alec could tell that Bill was annoyed with him, especially for expecting him to drop all of his plans for the day to meet with him.

Alec followed the two men as they walked out the door and closed it behind them. Alec decided from the get-go that he was going to remain in charge of this meeting—not Bill, and definitely not the minions who he'd quickly dismissed from the conference room. Alec sat down and watched Bill. He could tell he was nervous, unsure what this meeting was all about. Alec placed his elbows on the table, steepled his fingers in front of his face, resting his fingertips on the bridge of his nose, and carefully watched Bill's movement. One could hear a pin drop—it was that quiet in the large conference room. Bill finally sat down in the chair opposite Alec, and aligned his files on the table in front of him. Alec just observed until Bill looked up at him from his perfectly organized files. Clearing his throat, he looked Alec directly in the eyes. "Would you care to tell me what this is all about? I was under the impression that I'd cleared up any issues you had with Lattice Works. When we spoke, I went into explicit details about our latest hires and job postings, along with what our future plans are. I'm confused as to why you are here. Would you care to enlighten me?"

Alec slowly took his files out of his briefcase and opened them. He'd planned this meeting in its entirety in his head last night. He was going to make Bill squirm, beg him for his business; then, he was going to drop a bomb on him... The bomb that would reveal whether Kelly was fired for job performance or something else.

Alec went through the contract in minute detail with Bill. When he got to the installation and onsite testing of the program prior to full implementation, he knew he had Bill. The contract stipulated that the clinic would have a Lattice Works representative on hand during the entire installation process. This was a huge change for the clinic. Patient records were at stake here as the data integrity was crucial. Alec was going to insist on a complete review of all files and data before the switch was turned on and they were live with the new program.

Alec knew he was making more out of this upgrade than was necessary. They'd performed several upgrades at the clinic over the years and they incurred no issues with the data transfer, and Lattice Works had a reputation that superseded all of their competitors. They were top in their field and neither he, Joe, nor Ashton had any concerns. Their father, along with Alejandro, also went through the entire vetting process. If his father was comfortable with their choice of providers, it was a win-win for all since he hated to make any changes to the clinic, especially when it dealt with patient files.

The implementation was the final section of the contract. Alec couldn't wait to read the article that dealt with testing and implementation.

"So," Bill continued, "we will provide a member from our IT staff to come up to St. Louis for the entire crossover phase. This person will be dedicated to your clinic only and will be responsible for seeing the process through from beginning to end. We will set up a test database with all of your patients' files. We will run the upgrade in our test database and provide as many reports as you need in order to be comfortable that the information will transfer successfully. My employee will also perform all of the onsite training of your staff. They will remain onsite after the install until your employees are comfortable with everything and there are no issues."

Alec listened carefully to Bill's explanation of the process, then he asked the most important question, "So who will be assigned to our clinic?"

"I don't have an answer for that. I have to talk with Ken Jones, the manager of our IT Department. We'll need to see who he has designated for the upgrade."

"Ken Jones?" he said aloud. That was Kelly's direct manager, he was sure of it. He'd heard Angelina mention his name right after Kelly came home after being fired. That was interesting... Now, he was sure his plan would work.

"Yes, Ken Jones. He's been with Lattice for a number of years. He runs a tip-top department. They always meet their deadlines."

Alec raised his eyebrows. Why would Bill comment on how efficiently Ken ran his department and how he always met their deadlines? He'd have to ask a few more questions. "That's fine. I'd like to meet Ken. Also, I'm not sure if you're aware of this or not, but my sister-in-law works for you."

Bill looked mildly surprised. "Really? Who's that?"

"Her name is Kelly Samuels. She's worked for you for the last year or so." After releasing her name to him, Alec knew he'd sucker punched him right between the eyes. Bill's eyes widened and the color immediately drained from his face. He got nervous and fidgety.

"Yes, she does," Bill answered. "In fact, I had no idea she was related to you by marriage. She works directly for Ken. She has an exemplary record. She's quickly moved up through the ranks and is a senior tester for Ken."

Alec knew then that he'd get his way. "I haven't talked to Kelly in a while," Alec said as he watched Bill's expression. Alec wished he had a hidden camera on him—he enjoyed watching Bill squirm. "I'd like to make a few changes to the contract before I approve it."

"What changes would you like to make?"

"I want to name specifically who will be performing the testing."

"Alec, I'm sorry, but I can't do that. It all depends on the work schedule and how Ken has allocated his staff."

"That's going to be a deal-breaker for me."

"That's an unusual request."

"It may be, but I want to know who I am entrusting my patients' data with. I want my sister-in-law, Kelly Samuels, to do the testing, and I want that written into the contract."

"Ah... Alec, I'll have to check with Ken to see if she's available."

"The way I look at it, it's Kelly or no one. She's family and has a vested interest in the success of this upgrade. I trust her and know she'll have my family's interest at heart. She will be thorough and that's who I want." If Alec got his way, he'd be able to keep a close-eye on Kelly, hoping she'd overcome whatever was troubling her as well as determine what had affected her so greatly. While he wanted her to be happy and to have the job back that she loved, he also hoped she'd never discover who was behind her rehiring. He knew she'd never forgive him with his meddling.

Alec could see the wheels spinning. Bill had to figure out a way to rehire Kelly and bring her back specifically for this project. He had to do it without divulging that he'd fired her. He was going to have to act fast or the deal would fall through.

"How long will you be in town for?"

"I plan on leaving tomorrow."

Bill looked at him. He was nervous. His back had stiffened and he was sitting totally erect in the chair. He was clenching his pen tightly in his hand—so tightly that his knuckles were turning white.

"Let me see what I can do, and I'll get back with you."

"That's fine, but we'd better have a deal or I will be looking for a new vendor to perform my upgrade. I don't care how good your software is. I will find someone to do what I want, or I will hire someone to write the code needed to perform my upgrade. Do you understand? Kelly is the deal-breaker here. She will be the one doing the work or no one will. Got it?"

Bill nodded his head. "I'll get back to you by five o'clock

tonight."

Alec gathered his files, returned them to his briefcase, and stood. "I'm glad you see it my way. I'll be waiting for your call." Alec didn't even bother to shake his hand. He opened the door so forcefully that it clanged against the wall.

Bill stood in shock while he watched Alec leave the room. He had to think fast. He couldn't lose this contract. There were too many other deals relying on the successful implementation at Alec's clinic. If word got out that Alec had cancelled his project with Lattice Works, all of his hard work would go down the drain. Alec had a lot of clout in St. Louis and his word could be Lattice's undoing.

Alec couldn't wait to get back to his hotel room. He'd done it. He'd gotten Kelly's job back for her, he just knew it. Whether or not she accepted it was another thing. He was sure there'd be some groveling on Bill's part to get her back. Alec would talk to her and make her see the light. They'd work through this together, and if she decided to go back to Lattice Works, it would be on her own terms, not Bill's.

# Chapter Eighteen

A LEC COULDN'T WAIT TO GET back to his hotel room—he knew Alejandro was anxiously awaiting his call. They had a lot riding on this. Not only the successful upgrade at the clinic but, more importantly, Kelly's happiness and future. He walked through the door and threw his suit coat on the bed. Loosening his tie, he opened the bottle of water that he'd purchased on his way back to the hotel. Taking a swallow of the cool water, his mind immediately went to Kelly. How would Bill handle this entire situation? Would he grovel on his hands and knees to re-employ Kelly? Would Ken play into this as well? He wondered just how Bill would work his way through this mess.

Stretching on the bed, Alec closed his eyes momentarily and saw a smiling Kelly looking back at him. She'd been his partner at Angelina and Alejandro's wedding. He'd walked down the aisle after the ceremony, her hand securely holding onto his arm. He remembered that she had such a beautiful expression on her face that day. Her eyes were bright with unshed tears, and the radiant smile that encompassed her face was priceless. He wanted to see her laugh as she had when he caught the garter at the wedding (from what she later told him, his expression had been hilarious.) But most of all, he wanted to see that smile again on her face, and he wanted to be the one to put it there.

Alec dialed Alejandro's cell and waited for him to answer. He knew his brother was working from home since he was preparing another presentation for a conference that he'd be attending in a few weeks. Alejandro was an extremely sought-after speaker for many of the conferences that dealt with organ transplants. Since marrying Angelina, he'd cut back on his appearances, but lately those that he'd scheduled to attend were back to back. Alec wasn't sure if his brother did this on purpose since the anniversary of Tammy's death was upon them. He wondered if he just wanted to be alone during this time and not upset Angelina with any possible mood shifts that he may endure due to his loss.

It took Alejandro several rings before he answered, "Sorry about that. I was in the middle of a thought and needed to get it down. How was your meeting?"

"I think my plan worked like clockwork. He bought it— hook, line, and sinker." Alec went on to explain Bill's behavior. "He was terrified that I'd pull the contract. I wish you could have seen his face when I told him Kelly was Angelina's sister. He started singing her praises almost immediately, acting as though she were still employed at Lattice. I wanted to jump him and demand what he did to her. It was enough that I had to keep my temper in check."

"So what happened after he went on about her job performance?"

"I told him I wanted to know who would be performing the testing and training at the office. I told him I wanted the person's name written specifically into the contract."

"What did he say?"

"That is was an unusual request. I wish you could have seen him squirming in his chair. When I told him that I wanted Kelly to perform the testing, his entire body stiffened up—he almost looked like a statue. He was gripping his pen so tightly, I thought it would snap in two."

"Well, I'd say you hit a nerve with him."

"Definitely. I told him Kelly was it and, if he didn't assign her to the project, then I wasn't going to sign the contract. I informed him that I was leaving tomorrow with or without a signed deal. If he didn't comply with my request, then I was going to go somewhere else."

"How did he react to that?"

"He wasn't happy. He knows that I can make his world come crashing down around him if he doesn't do as I ask. He knows I'll tell all of my friends to not install his upgrade. He has his company to look after, so I think he's going to do anything and everything in his power to rehire Kelly. Now we just have to worry about whether or not Kelly will accept his offer. But I know now that Kelly was not fired for job performance, at least not in Bill's eyes… unless he's a good actor. But I don't think Bill was acting. I have to wonder about her boss, Ken Jones."

"I'll have to ask Angelina about him. I remember her talking about him, but I'm not sure what she said. Sorry, I just remember the name."

"I'm going to try and catch up on my sleep and also look into this Ken. I can't wait to hear what he says to Kelly to get her back. Hopefully she'll accept his offer, or we'll have to go back to the start line and attack this from a different angle." Alec paused and added, "Alejandro, I just hope she doesn't discover what I've done. She won't be able to forgive me, I just know it."

"Get some rest. I know you haven't slept much in the last few days. I'll keep my ears to the ground and hear if Kelly gets that call. Alec, don't worry about Kelly finding out about your role in this. If she does, we'll all deal with the fallout. You're just the spokesperson for us. We're all behind this."

"I hear what you're saying. I know we're doing what's best for her. At least, I hope we are. It's in Bill's best interest to meet the terms of my demands."

"It is," Alejandro said as he watched his wife enter the room. "I'm going to give Angelina a heads up just in case Kelly comes to her for advice."

"That's a good idea, but I already knew you'd tell her since you can't keep anything from her."

"That's true, I can't." Alejandro chuckled as he hung up the phone.

Angelina sat down beside her husband and looked at him questioningly, "Who were you on the phone with, and why were you talking about me and Kelly?"

"Alec. He's in Knoxville."

"He's where?" Angelina asked incredulously.

"He just had a meeting with Bill Lattice."

Angelina was shocked.

"Alec strongly believes there is more to this whole Kelly firing. He confronted Bill and basically threatened him. I think his plan worked."

"Please explain."

"Well, he showed up at Lattice Works without an appointment and made Bill drop everything to meet with him. He made him go through the contract in explicit detail. There's one section of the contract that deals with the installation of the software. Bill told Alec that they'd be sending an employee from the IT department up here to see the process through. Then Alec threw in that Kelly was your sister, knowing full well that she'd worked for that department. Bill had nothing but good things to say about her, acting as though she was still employed by Lattice."

"That's interesting considering he was the one that fired her."

"It surely is, and when Alec demanded that she be the person responsible for the implementation, he almost had a nervous breakdown. Alec said he got all anxious and fidgety. Alec told Bill that he wanted Kelly—no ifs, ands, or buts. He wanted her name written into the contract and, if he couldn't abide by his wishes, then he was going elsewhere."

"Wow, I never thought Alec had it in him."

"Alec only gets this way when someone he cares for is hurt. Angelina, I know my little brother, and I think he's falling for your sister."

"I had no idea Alec was like this."

"Well, he is, and I know he's going to do everything in his power to right the wrong. He wants to find the answers, the reasons for whatever was behind her firing. Alec will not go forward with this deal unless Kelly is taken care of. In all honesty, the clinic really doesn't need this upgrade right now, but they decided to stay ahead of the software improvements that are constantly being made. It won't hurt the clinic if they hold off, but Bill doesn't know that, and that's Alec's wild card."

"When will we know if it worked?"

"Alec told him he was leaving town tomorrow with or without a deal. I would presume that he's doing some fast talking with Ken, and I would expect that Kelly is going to be receiving a call soon."

Angelina wrung her hands together. "I can't wait. This is better than a soap opera," she said as she stood up. "I'll let you know if I hear anything from Kelly."

Alejandro watched as Angelina left the room. He was thankful that she was a part of his life. He loved her so much. He just hoped that Alec could find that, too. Maybe he'd find his happiness with Kelly.

❧

Kelly offered to pick up Matthew from school that day. Angel had been extremely fussy all afternoon, and Alejandro had to go into the hospital for a meeting.

Angelina thanked her, "I'm so thankful that you're staying with us. I don't know what Angel's problem is, but I've come to the conclusion that if Alejandro works from home, she throws a fit when he has to go in. If he's gone into the hospital before she wakes up, it's not a problem. It's almost like separation anxiety with her. Hopefully, she'll outgrow it."

"He's so good with her. I can see why she misses her daddy."

"Yeah, but it's not like he's holding her the entire time he's home. He generally is locked in his office working."

"I know, but I guess she feels his presence."

Angelina shrugged and thanked Kelly again. "It's getting late, so more than likely you'll find Matthew in Gabriella's classroom. He goes there after school and waits for me. He just loves her."

"Thanks for the heads-up. I'll park the car and go inside. How do I get to her classroom?"

Angelina told Kelly that she needed to check in at the office with Mary Flynn, the principal, prior to going to Gabriella's classroom. "I'll call Mary and let her know you're picking him up. She'll take you to Gabriella's room."

Kelly left and shortly thereafter Angelina phoned Mary. Mary was still on the phone with Angelina when she saw Kelly walking up the front walk. "Your sister's here now, so I'll take her down to Gabriella's room. Come by soon with Angel—everyone would love to see you both."

"Thanks, Mary. We'll come by one day for lunch."

Mary hung up the phone just as Kelly walked through the office doors. Mary escorted her down the long hallway to Gabriella's classroom.

Matthew was the first to see Kelly, and ran to the door shouting her name. Gabriella turned to see both Kelly and Mary standing in the doorway.

"I take it your excited to see your Aunt?" Mary asked Matthew.

"I am. Did you know she's living with us?"

"No, I didn't." Mary smiled at Matthew. She turned to the two ladies, wished them a good evening, and headed back to her office.

"So what brings you by?" asked Gabriella. "I expected to see Angelina today."

Kelly explained what had happened and that she'd offered to pick Matthew up. "That little niece of ours is spoiled rotten. She hates it when Alejandro leaves her."

"I know. He's a good dad. He always knows just what to do to calm her. I hope she's good while Alejandro's on his trip. If not, I guess Angelina will have to call in Alec. I hear he's got the magic touch, too."

Kelly and Matthew said their goodbyes and walked out to the car. Kelly made sure Matthew got settled into his seat, then got in herself. She looked over her shoulder and said, "Ice cream?"

Matthew was beside himself. "Yes," he practically screamed back at Kelly.

Kelly turned into the local ice creamery. Thankfully, they had a drive thru. "Let's do drive thru, and then we can eat in the car."

Kelly asked him what he wanted and then placed their order. Matthew waited in anticipation for his scoop of Superman ice cream. Kelly had chosen a scoop of strawberry.

"Aunt Kelly, you need to try something different. You always have strawberry."

"I do, don't I?"

"Yep, you and Uncle Alec always get the same thing. Strawberry."

"Really? That's nice to know."

They sat enjoying their ice cream when Matthew asked, "My dad's going out of town again, isn't he?"

"I believe he is. Why?"

"I don't know. He's just seemed kind of sad lately. I've seen him looking out the window a lot. He always looks sad. I hope that when he comes home, he feels better."

"I'm sure he has a lot on his mind. He's been really busy with work and all, but he's been traveling more than usual, hasn't he?"

"He has, but it's something else, Aunt Kelly. I can't say what it is, but… Oops, my ice cream is melting."

"Well you'd better lick that all up. We don't want your mother getting wind of any ice cream drippings on you. This is our secret, right?"

"Uh huh," he said as he caught another drip getting ready to slide off his cone.

They finished their ice cream and headed home. She was going to think long and hard as to whether she would share Matthew's comment with Angelina. *Maybe I'll keep it to myself,* she thought. Kelly didn't want to worry Angelina about her husband any more than she already was. She had enough on her plate with Alejandro going out of town lately. If she saw it affecting Matthew, then she'd speak with her sister. Otherwise, it was her and Matthew's secret.

❦

Kelly's phone had rung several times while she was in St.

Margaret's, but she'd missed the calls since she'd left her purse in the car. The caller had left one message and had tried back several more times, but there was no answer. It was almost five o'clock and he needed more time if he was going to convince her to return to Lattice Works, and Bill didn't want to have to call Alec to ask for more time. He hoped and prayed that he could reach her within the next half hour. If not, he'd have to convince Alec that he needed to extend the deadline.

# Chapter Nineteen

A FTER ALEC GOT OFF THE phone with Alejandro, he tried taking a nap but sleep just wouldn't come. His mind kept replaying the meeting that he'd had with Bill over and over again. He wondered if his threats would pan out. Would Bill rehire Kelly? He had no idea what she would do if he decided to rehire her. He just hoped that, in the end, he could discover what truly happened with her firing. It had come as a complete surprise that Bill couldn't say enough positive things about Kelly's job performance. He'd seemed sincere as he openly praised her accomplishments. He wondered if he truly believed that there were issues with Kelly's performance. Did he fire her based on someone else's word? More than likely the answer to that question was yes, and more importantly he wondered if Ken was involved in this. Was Ken the one that had the issues? Alec felt assured that the answers were forthcoming and were just around the corner.

Based upon his meeting with Bill, Alec decided he needed to do some additional investigation. Since he couldn't sleep, he decided to call Jonas Sounds. Jonas was a friend of his that had helped him out with background checks and other investigative work in the past. He knew Jonas would find the answers that he was searching for, namely why Kelly was fired and why she'd changed. Jonas wasn't in his office, so Alec left a message for him to return his call.

Alec began pacing and began to feel like he was turning into Alejandro. He kept watching the clock. Alec blinked, and the clock read five o'clock. His phone had yet to ring. Alec began to fidget.

At five fifteen, his phone rang. The caller ID indicated it was Bill. Alec let his cell ring a few times before answering. Alec didn't want to act too eager when taking his call. He answered on the fifth ring, right before his phone went to voicemail.

He could hear the apprehension in Bill's voice when he answered, "Alec?"

"Yes?"

"This is Bill Lattice."

"I know." Pausing, he made Bill hold momentarily. He then added, "Do you have my answer? Is Kelly going to be your representative?"

Bill didn't know how he was going to break the news to Alec. How would he explain that he hadn't had the opportunity to speak with her yet? She was supposed to be working for him. Then, he came up with a quick reply. "Ah, Kelly's on vacation right now. I've tried her cell phone several times, and she hasn't answered."

"Vacation? Huh," Alec said. "Shouldn't you have known that when we talked earlier?"

"I believe it was a last-minute personal day," he said.

*Last-minute personal day? Yeah, I believe that one.* Personal day in that she was currently living with his brother and sister-in-law.

"As I said, I've left her several messages. I hope she'll return my call shortly. Since I've reached out to her, I'd like to extend my time frame until eight o'clock tomorrow morning. And since you originally gave me until tomorrow, I hope you are a man of your word and will allow that."

Alec agreed to the revised time frame. "I expect to hear from you by eight. That's when I expect to check out of here tomorrow. If I don't hear from you, then be advised that I am terminating any relations I have with Lattice Works, and I will find another vendor to perform my upgrade."

"Understood," Bill said.

Alec disconnected the call and rang Alejandro. Alejandro's phone went straight to voicemail, so he assumed that he was busy. He called Angelina next. She knew what was going on and hopefully knew if Bill was actually telling the truth about trying to reach Kelly.

Angelina answered on the first ring. She was still home waiting for Kelly to return with Matthew from school. "Alec, hi there. What's up?"

"Is Kelly home?"

"No, she picked up Matthew from school for me. Angel was fussy, and since your brother isn't here to calm her, I needed to focus my efforts on her."

"Shouldn't they be home by now? Isn't school out at like three thirty?"

"It is, but Kelly probably chatted with Gabriella for a while before taking him out for an ice cream. She has a sweet tooth and knows just how to spoil Matthew. Any news?"

"I just spoke with Bill. Supposedly he's left several messages for Kelly, and she hasn't returned any of his calls."

"Well, I don't know anything about that. More than likely she left her purse in the car when she went in to get Matthew. She might not even be aware of the messages." Pausing, she said, "Hold on a second. I think they just got home."

Matthew walked in sporting a huge smile.

"How was the ice cream?" Angelina asked him.

His eyes quickly shifted to Kelly, then back to his mom. "How did you know?"

"Moms always know. Now, go do your homework. Your father should be home soon, and then we'll have dinner."

"Okay," he said as he started from the room. Talking to himself, he said, "How did she know? I don't have any ice cream on me."

Angelina and Kelly both laughed as he left the room. For a second, Angelina forgot that she had Alec holding.

Kelly pointed at the phone in Angelina's hand. "Is there someone on the phone?"

"Oh, yeah," she said. "I'm talking with Alec."

Kelly left her alone to finish her conversation.

"I'll think of a way for her to check her phone." Angelina was just about to hang up when she heard Kelly running down the hall, "Hold on a second. I think I hear Kelly."

"Angelina! You're never going to believe this."

"What?" she asked, acting as perplexed as she could.

"Bill left me a voicemail. He wants me to come back to Lattice."

"That's such a surprise!" Angelina said. "What are you going to do?"

"I don't know. I guess I'll hear him out. See what he has to say."

"That's good news, Kelly. Let me know what you decide."

Alec heard her entire conversation with Kelly. At least he knew Bill had been good for his word—he had reached out to Kelly. Now, he'd just sit back and see what happened. "Let me know what happens, Angelina. I'll be waiting." Alec felt like his plan had worked. Bill was going to rehire Kelly, if she wanted it.

❦

Bill sat in his office. He couldn't stop tapping his pen against his desk. He was nervous as he waited for the phone to ring. He hoped and prayed that Kelly would return his call sooner rather than later. He'd left not only his office number, but also cell phone numbers on her voicemail.

It was almost six, and he was just getting ready to leave his office when his office line rang. He took a deep breath and answered the call. He let out a relieved breath when he heard Kelly's voice on the other end.

"Bill, this is Kelly Samuels. I'm returning your call."

"Oh yes, Kelly, thank you for getting back to me so quickly." In the back of his mind, he wished her call had come earlier, but he'd already dealt with Alec and hopefully he'd be able to return his call with the news that she agreed to return to work at Lattice.

"So, what is it exactly that you wanted? After all, you did fire me a few short months ago."

"About that… I think I was wrong to fire you."

"Wrong?" she practically screamed into the phone. "You told me I was being fired for poor job performance. I still wonder where that excuse came from. How could I have exhibited poor job performance when I was promoted, mind you, three times in just over a year?"

"I need to apologize for that. I went over your file again and realized we made a horrible mistake. I hope that you will entertain the idea of coming back to work here in light of my discoveries. I'm offering a pay increase and additional vacation time, if you will consider it. I'm also talking to Ken about giving you more responsibility and maybe having you start to travel more for the company, helping to perform the installs at our clients' offices. You would have an expense account and have additional responsibilities, like on-the-job training for our clients. You will be the liaison between our company and the client, handling any and all issues that may arise out of the upgrades. I think you would be the perfect person for this job. You helped with the testing and fully understand the intricate workings of the program. You have excellent people skills, and I just think you'd be the perfect fit for this job."

Kelly was silent on the other end.

"I hope that you think I'm sincere with the apology. I wish I would have been a little more involved in the process of your departure, but from everything I've heard and saw from our HR department, I was sure we'd made the right decision. Now that I look back on it, I know we failed both you and the company. We need your expertise, and I hope you will truly consider this offer. I am being honest when I say we miss you at Lattice and hope that you will return."

"Bill, I am a little surprised by this call. I'm going to have to think about this offer. In fact, I'd like it in writing before I make my decision."

Bill asked for her email address and informed her that she'd receive his offer within the next half hour.

"I'll have to get back with you after I review everything."

"Ah, when do you think this may be?"

"Do I have to know immediately?"

"Ah…"

"I'm sorry Bill, but you've taken me totally by surprise. I'm going to have to think about it, and I'll get back with you soon."

"Soon?"

"Yes, soon. If you can't wait for my decision, then I'm going to have to say no. I don't want to be pressured into this. You ruined my life when you fired me, so I think I should be given some time to decide if I want to return to Lattice Works."

Bill couldn't speed up her decision. He knew she needed to do what was right for her. In fact, he was telling the truth when he told her they'd made a terrible mistake in firing her. He'd spoken with Ken and discovered that Ken had overacted and shouldn't have recommended her firing.

Bill replayed in his mind his conversation with Ken. In fact, he'd caught Ken off guard which had made the conversation even more interesting.

As soon as Alec had departed, Bill had immediately made his way to Ken's office. It had been approaching noon, and Ken's office door stood open. Ken was sitting at his desk with his back to the doorway.

Bill walked through the door unannounced and slammed the door closed. Ken spun around so quickly in his chair that, if his desk wasn't there, Bill was sure he'd have flown right out of his chair.

Bill approached Ken's desk, pointing his finger angrily at him. "Don't say a word," Bill said as he stood in front of Ken.

"But?"

"Not one word."

Ken sat silently in his chair, waiting for Bill to continue his tirade.

"Why the hell did you recommend the firing of Kelly Samuels?"

"Well, Bill I—"

"Stop, just stop! I reviewed her file backwards and forwards. Do you realize she had three promotions in her short tenure here?"

"I—"

Bill glared at Ken. He wanted to finish his speech before Ken could say another word.

"Ken, don't say another word until I tell you to speak. As I said, I went through Kelly's file. Three promotions and not one, not two, but three glowing performance reviews by whom?" Bill stared at Ken. "Who else? You. Ken, you not only rated her exemplary, but you recommended two of the three promotions. So tell me—Wait. Wait until I ask. How could you have recommended her firing?" Pausing Bill added, "Now, you may speak."

Ken took a deep breath and loudly swallowed before speaking. Bill immediately picked up on Ken's obvious nervousness.

"I g-guess I made a mistake?"

"A mistake?" Bill yelled. "A mistake? You made more than a mistake."

"I realize now that I overreacted to a situation and, before I could correct it, you'd already dismissed her."

Bill was furious with him. He wanted to fire Ken instead, but knew that he couldn't—he had no one that could replace Ken on staff currently, especially with how close they were to rolling out the new software. Bill decided then that he was going to work towards finding a replacement. "What I should have done was fire you instead." Ken sat there, totally surprised by Bill's declaration. "I am placing you on corrective action, and we will revisit this whole situation as to why you recommended Kelly's firing. To rectify your error, I've offered Kelly her job back. And, if she accepts my offer, she will have additional benefits added to her job. One of those will be as a liaison to our clients, additional vacation time, along with a sizeable pay increase. I can't believe your stupidity, and now I have to question any and all of your decisions. Realize this, Ken—you are under the microscope. One wrong move, and you will be out the door faster than I can say, you're fired. Do you understand me?"

"Yes sir, I do."

"And you will welcome Kelly back with open arms. Get

it?"

Ken nodded and with that, Bill opened the door with such force that it slammed against the wall.

The last thing Bill had said to Ken was, "You need to walk the straight and narrow, or you're going to be the next one watching the door slam behind you as you're escorted out of the offices."

Ken was stunned by Bill's comments. He'd never seen him this upset. And now, not only did he have to welcome Kelly back as though her firing had never happened, he was the one on the outs.

Corrective action for a misfiring... If he were eventually fired for this , he didn't think that would stand-up in a court of law since both Bill and HR had signed off on Kelly's dismissal. Ken was sure he had the law on his side. But he'd be careful and hope that this storm passed by with no additional issues raised.

&

Bill knew that a mistake had been made. Unfortunately, a potential client had brought it to his attention. He was going to be more involved with Ken's department. If something was awry, he would discover it.

Bill didn't think twice before he picked up the phone to call Alec. It was the second time he'd phoned Alec in an hour, and he wasn't sure how he would react with his news. But he couldn't make the decision for Kelly. He could only hope for the best.

&

Alec was surprised to see Bill's number pop up on his phone so soon after their conversation.

"Alec, it's Bill again. I wanted to give you an update to our earlier conversation."

"Did you speak with Kelly?"

"I did." Pausing momentarily, he added, "She has to think about my offer, so I wanted to let you know that the ball's in her court, and I can't control what her decision will be. I've offered her a substantial pay increase, along with additional vacation. I've enhanced her job responsibilities, offering her the job of client liaison. She will, however, continue to work for the IT department since they manage the client installations."

"So I suppose the reason for your call is to get me to extend my timeframe for walking away from Lattice Works?"

"It is."

"Well, since neither you nor I can control Kelly's decision-making process, I will wait for Kelly to make her decision. We will go from there."

"Thank you, Alec. I appreciate this. I will prove to you that you won't be disappointed for putting your trust in our company. I'll get back to you as soon as I hear from Kelly."

Their call ended, and Alec decided then that he was going to return home—he had no reason to remain in Knoxville. The sooner he got home, the sooner he could meet with Kelly and see what she had to say. He was running on nervous energy and wasn't tired. He decided that if he got woozy while driving home, he'd pull over at a truck stop and take a power nap. He quickly packed his bag and checked out of his room. He hoped to be home in the early hours of the morning. He'd run by Alejandro's first thing the next morning and see what Kelly had to say.

# Chapter Twenty

KELLY WAS MORE THAN SURPRISED when she opened Bill's email. She was totally taken aback by his offer. The pay increase alone was amazing—something that she never would have expected. Add to it the additional bonuses that he was throwing in… It was a dream employment package. It would be crazy for her to turn it down. She waited for the kids to be put to bed for the night and then sought out Alejandro and Angelina. She needed their opinions on what she should do.

"Can I talk to you both for a second?"

"Sure," said Alejandro. "Have a seat."

Kelly sat in the chair opposite the sofa where Angelina and Alejandro sat.

"What's up?" Alejandro asked like he didn't already know. He'd received a phone call from Alec while driving home from the hospital, detailing the conversation he'd had with Bill. Alec told him that Bill was basically offering her the moon to return to Lattice Works. Alec also believed that Bill was sincere in his offer, and that Bill had done some research and obtained some additional information regarding Kelly's firing. In the mean-time, Angelina had informed Alejandro of her earlier conversation with Kelly. She was just waiting to hear what Kelly's decision was regarding Bill's offer.

"I got the strangest call today."

"From whom?" asked Alejandro. Angelina kept her mouth shut—Kelly had already told her about the call.

"Bill Lattice."

"Bill? Really?"

"Yep, the one and only. And you'll never guess what he wanted."

"What?" Alejandro asked again.

"He wants to rehire me! He offered me a salary increase, additional vacation, and even added responsibilities. He wants to make me a client liaison."

"Really? What are you going to do?" asked Angelina.

"I don't know. That's why I'm coming to the two of you. He seemed sincere with his offer. He said it had been his mistake for not looking into the reasons behind my firing. He went with HR's recommendation and didn't question them. The only problem I have is that I still need to work for Ken."

"Why is that a problem?" asked Alejandro. He grabbed Angelina's hand and squeezed it. He thought she was about to reveal what had really happened to her at Lattice.

"He doesn't manage his staff, he looks the other way when there are personnel issues, and he doesn't like anyone finding problems with the programs. He expects perfection and doesn't like to hear it when someone finds an issue—he lives by deadlines and doesn't care if there is a problem that may cause the deadline to be missed, and he only cares about looking good in Bill's eyes by always making his deadlines, no matter what suffers in the process."

Angelina's eyes widened, "That's a lot. Is this something you can possibly share with Bill when you decide what to do? I'm sure he can replace him if he has enough complaints."

"That's the problem—no one complains. I've thought

about going to HR, but he's the golden boy and I don't think they'd believe me. I've tried to raise problems with Ken before, and look where that got me. I was fired."

"Huh," said Alejandro. "Kelly, you're the only one that can make this decision. If you enjoy the job for the most part, maybe you can overlook some of the short-comings. Better yet, maybe you could transfer departments after you return."

"Yeah, I know. The problem is that I really liked what I'd been doing—I just didn't see eye-to-eye with a few people. I realize I'm the only one that can make this decision. After all, Bill's the one crawling back wanting to rehire me. In fact, I probably could sue him for firing me without cause, especially since he admitted they'd made a mistake in firing me in the first place. But that could backfire on me, and I just don't want to ruin my reputation any more than he already has. I think I'll sleep on it, maybe wait a few days to make my decision. Thanks for the help, though."

Kelly stood and went over to both of them. She placed a kiss on Alejandro's cheek and turned to her sister who jumped up from the couch. Angelina pulled her into a tight hug and whispered, "Take your time. If he wants you badly enough, he can wait for your decision. I love you, Kelly." She kissed her sister's cheek.

"I love you, too, Angelina. Thanks for everything." Kelly turned and walked out the door. She had a lot of thinking ahead of her.

❧

Alec somehow made it home without incident. He pulled into his driveway around three in the morning. He dragged himself through the door and, when he later woke, he found himself lying on the couch in the family room. He didn't remember even sitting down—the last thing that he remembered was walking into the house and looking at the clock, thinking that morning was right around the corner.

Alec had thankfully slept soundly for about four hours. He scrubbed his hands across his face and pulled himself up from the couch. He made his way to his bedroom where he took a shower and lay back down for what he told himself would be only a few minutes. The next thing he knew, it was almost nine o'clock and his cell phone loudly announced that Alejandro was calling.

"Where are you?" he asked.

"I'm home. Got in around three this morning."

"You didn't tell me you were coming home last night."

"I know. I thought I'd be around this morning so I could talk with Kelly. Did she decide what she's going to do?"

"Not that I'm aware of. She's having a tough time with this. We talked last night, and I'm not sure which way she's leaning. She thinks Bill is being sincere with his offer, but she still has issues with her direct boss, though. Ken seems like an interesting chap. I'm wondering if he's her problem. She did complain that he doesn't seem to manage personnel issues."

"Yeah. I realized when I talked to Bill yesterday that she'd still be reporting directly to him, so I called Jonas Sounds."

"You did?"

"Uh huh. I'm still waiting for a call back, but I think I'm going to hire him to look into his background. According to Bill, Ken's worked for him for a while, but he definitely hasn't made a career out of working at Lattice—he worked somewhere else before. I'm just going to do a little check into his background, that's all."

"I'm glad you thought about that. By the way, I wanted to remind you that I'm heading out of town tomorrow. Just a heads-up in case Angel needs your magic fingers."

"Yeah, yeah, yeah," Alec said as he yawned into the phone.

"I'd better get some caffeine in me before I head over to your house. I don't want to fall asleep while I'm there."

They said their goodbyes and Alec headed to the kitchen. He had two cups of coffee before he felt he was awake enough to visit Kelly. He was going to act like he didn't know what she was talking about when they talked about her job. He knew she'd open up to him, he just knew it.

Alec arrived later than he expected at Angelina's. By the time he'd had his coffee, unpacked, and done a load of laundry, it was past noon. He rang the doorbell and was greeted with Kelly and a crying baby.

"I swear all she does is cry lately," Kelly said as she pushed the baby onto Alec. "I'm glad you're here. Please work your magic."

Alec reached for little Angel and followed Kelly into the kitchen.

"You just missed Angelina—she went out to run a few errands leaving Angel with me. I was getting ready to eat lunch when she woke up crying. I changed her and was just getting ready to give her a bottle."

"Here, let me feed her. You get your lunch."

Kelly handed Alec the bottle and he fed his niece for the first time. She was hungry and chugged down her bottle. "I guess she was hungry. Look, she's already finished her bottle." Alec placed Angel on his shoulder to burp her.

Kelly looked back at him. He looked so comfortable holding Angel while he stroked her back. "What is it between you and your brother? You're miracle workers when it comes to this little girl." Smiling at him, she couldn't control where her thoughts were taking her. He'd make a perfect husband. He wasn't afraid of holding a little one like most men were. He seemed like he was in pure heaven holding his niece. "You'd make the perfect father."

"Why do you say that?"

"Well, look at you…"

"I am a pediatrician."

"Like that matters."

"I think it does. I love kids and I don't mind holding a baby. Actually, I enjoy it. The babies are so innocent. They trust everyone and are content just to be held. They don't talk back…"

"Uh huh, yeah right."

"Well, except when they cry. Usually that's because they're hungry, wet, or have an upset stomach. If you can figure out what's troubling them…" he said, watching Angel yawn her head away. Her eyes were drooping and then she was fast asleep in his arms. They both watched her, then Alec carried her to the nursery where he put her down for her nap.

Alec returned to the kitchen where Kelly was starting to eat her lunch. "I'm being rude. Can I offer you something to eat?"

"No, I'm good. I ate a late breakfast."

Alec washed up the dishes while Kelly ate her lunch. She joined him in the family room when she was finished. He was sitting on the couch with his eyes closed. She couldn't tell if he was asleep or not. She sat down beside him and watched his chest as he breathed in and out. Something caught her eye and she looked up into his face. He was staring at her. He reached out to touch her cheek, but she pulled away.

*There she goes again*, he thought. He watched her until she decided to speak.

"Alec, I got a call from Bill last night."

"You did? What did he want?"

"To rehire me."

"You've got to be kidding. Where did that come from?"

"I haven't the foggiest idea. He said that he reviewed my file and determined that he fired me in error. He wants to rehire me with added benefits and additional job responsibilities. What do you think I should do? I just don't know."

"Tell me about your conversation. What did he say?"

Kelly went through the specifics with him.

"Are you okay with staying in the same department?"

For a moment, he thought he saw something like fear cross her face. She collected herself and said, "I loved my job. What I didn't love was my boss."

"Who was your boss?"

"His name is Ken Jones. He's worked for Lattice for about seven years, I think. He came from a company called Trexor."

"I'm familiar with Trexor. I think Alejandro has a patent pending with them. He developed some type of instrument that they're producing for him."

"Really? It's certainly a small world, isn't it?" Kelly said.

This was great intel that Jonas Sounds could use, and they'd definitely have no issues speaking with the owners of Trexor since Alejandro was close friends with Albert Trexor, the owner. They'd gone to medical school together, but Albert used his degree to help develop tools that would aid the medical profession. Albert's father had turned the company over to him right after he'd graduated from medical school.

"Why don't you like Ken?" Alec thought that by prodding her along, she'd open up a little.

Kelly just clammed up even more though. "Let's just say he's not a people person and leave it at that."

"Okay, then. What are you going to do?"

"I don't know. I'm going to sit on it for a few days. I think I may talk it over with my dad. He manages people and he may have some insight on how I can handle him."

"That's a good idea. I want you to know that I'm always

here for you in case you want to bounce an idea off of me."

"Thanks, Alec. I appreciate that."

They talked a little while longer when Alec asked her, "What are you doing tonight?" They still hadn't gone out for their dinner. They'd had dessert, but dinner would be a more formal affair.

"Sitting here trying to decide what to do. Why?"

"Come out with me. I still owe you that dinner I promised. We can talk about your job offer, if you'd like."

She stared at him.

"Or not," he chuckled.

"You know, I think I'll take you up on it. Alejandro leaves for his conference tomorrow, and I'd like to give him and Angelina some alone time. That is, as alone as they can be with two kids."

At that moment, Angelina walked in the front door, interrupting their conversation.

Angelina looked at Alec in surprise. "I didn't know you were home."

"What do you mean by home?" Kelly turned to Alec in confusion, "Did you go somewhere?"

"No, I didn't," he said, narrowing his eyes at Angelina who had realized her mistake at that point. "I just took the day off. You know, trying to catch up on a few things. I haven't had much down time at the clinic, and I needed to finish writing an article for a publication."

He was in fact writing an article, but he'd already completed it and had emailed it to the editor a few days ago. Alec quickly changed the subject, "Alejandro leaves tomorrow for his conference, doesn't he?"

"Yes, he does. Now, you know you're on-call for Angel, right?" she chuckled.

"I know," he said, rolling his eyes. "I just thought you and

Alejandro would like some alone time before he goes out of town. I asked Kelly to dinner."

"Alone time? With two kids in tow?"

"Well, you know what I mean."

"I do," she said. "And I—rather, we—appreciate it. Now, where are the two of you going?"

Kelly made an exasperated huff, "He just asked me, Angelina. Right before you came through the door."

"My apologies for interrupting," Angelina said. "Maybe I should walk right back out that door so you can decide."

Angelina started to stand, but Alec stopped her, "Don't leave. After all, this is your home."

"Well, I don't want to stand in the way of you two deciding where to go on your first date." Angelina said raising her fingers making quotation marks around "first."

Kelly narrowed her eyes. "What first date? Angelina, this is not a date. It's just two friends going out for a bite to eat, that's all."

"Yeah, sure it is. You know it's a date. Isn't it Alec?"

"Let's just say it is what it is… Friends having dinner," Alec said, shrugging.

"Sure, if that's what you call it," Angelina said as she left the room.

"Date? Alec, this is not a date. Get that word out of your vocabulary. We are not going on a date."

"Okay, okay settle down. It's not a date. Now, what time should I pick you up for our not-a-date?" he teased her, smiling. Alec considered it a date, but if she didn't want to refer to it in those terms then that was fine with him. As far as he was concerned, he was just happy to have one-on-one quality time with her.

Kelly rolled her eyes. "How about seven? I can get Matthew to bed for Angelina so all she'll have to worry about is

Angel."

"Sounds like a plan. I'll make reservations and surprise you, if that's okay."

"Fine. You can choose the restaurant as long as you don't refer to this as a date."

"You bet. This is not a date," he laughed as he walked out the door.

Alec knew this was a date. If he was a betting man, she also believed it was a date, but just didn't want to admit it. He'd take it one day, or one "date," at a time. He was going to go out with her and he was going to have a relationship with her. He had feelings for her that he wasn't going to let go of—he wasn't going to give up without trying. It would require some work to get past whatever was going on with her, but Alec would be by her side guiding her every step of the way.

# Chapter Twenty-One

ALEJANDRO WAS SURPRISED TO SEE Alec's car in the driveway when he arrived home. He strolled through the door and was greeted by Alec who was dressed for an evening out. He had on a dark suit, white dress shirt, and a fabulous purple tie.

"What's this all about?" Alejandro said, pointing to Alec's clothes.

"I'm taking Kelly out on a date." Getting close to Alejandro, he whispered, "Don't tell her it's a date."

"Huh? Why not?"

"She doesn't see it as a date. It's friends going out with friends."

"Okay, whatever," Alejandro said, shaking his head. "Has she made a decision?"

"When I talked with her earlier, she hadn't." Alec straightened his tie and changed subjects, "So how long are you going to be out of town this time? Ya know I need to be prepared for daddy duty. I got here today and Kelly practically threw your daughter into my arms."

"She was crying?"

"Yep. I fed her a bottle and she was asleep in no time."

"I'm not sure what's going on with her. She's been awfully

fussy lately. Maybe she's getting ready to cut her first tooth. We'll have to watch her a little more closely. So where's your date?"

Alec hit his brother and made a shushing noise, "Not so loud. She may appear and decide not to go if she hears it called a date. She's really touchy with that reference."

"That she is," Alejandro nodded, looking behind Alec. His eyes widened and Alec whipped around. Kelly walked into the room and seemed to not have heard their conversation.

"Wow, Kelly. You look fabulous." Alec couldn't take his eyes off of her. Her hair hung in long tresses that curled about her face. She had on a knee-length purple dress that fitted across her chest and gathered at her waist. The skirt flowed openly around her legs. It perfectly matched his tie.

"Did you two coordinate your outfits or what?" Alejandro asked as he pointed at Alec's tie.

"Definitely not."

"It just seems that way. You're both wearing the same shade of purple."

Kelly just looked at Alec. It almost looked like she was mad at him. Maybe she *had* heard Alejandro's comment about this being a date.

Suddenly, her face broke into a smile. "You'd think we did coordinate," Kelly laughed.

Alec smiled, relieved, "Ready to go?"

"Yeah, just let me grab my coat."

Kelly left the room and Alejandro just smiled at his brother. Alec was sinking deeper. He knew that look on his face and knew what he was feeling.

"I don't know what you're smiling at, but you can wipe that smirk off your face," Alec said as he walked from the room.

Kelly was standing in the living room when Alec met up

with her. Alec placed his hand on Kelly's back and guided her out the door. Alec called back over his shoulder, "Oh, Alejandro. If I don't see you before you leave, have a good trip."

"Thanks, I will. By the way, to answer your question, I'll be gone for five days. So…"

"I know, I'll be prepared for that call," he laughed as he led Kelly out the door and to his car.

Alec helped her settle into the car and he moved into the driver's seat. "So, what are you in the mood for?"

"I thought you made reservations."

"I did," he said, grinning. "I chose a wonderful place that has fabulous steaks, pasta, and just about anything. Have you ever been to Miss Kelly's?"

"Really? Miss Kelly's?"

"Yep, that's the name. And it's just perfect for you, Miss Kelly," he laughed as he pulled away from the house.

Miss Kelly's was in mid-town. Alec pulled up to the valet and hurried from the car. He reached Kelly just as the attendant reached for her hand. "I'll get that," Alec said. He held his hand out and Kelly grabbed ahold of it. Stepping from the car, she glanced up into his eyes. She'd never noticed the gold flecks that peppered his brown eyes. They were almost glowing. Alec wound her arm through his as he escorted her into the restaurant.

Miss Kelly's didn't seem too crowded and, as they approached the hostess, they were greeted by a beautiful, young woman with blonde hair.

"Dr. Alvarez, it's good to see you again."

Alec smiled at her, "Amy, this is Kelly Samuels. Kelly, this is the owner's daughter, Amy Favor. The restaurant is named after her mother, Kelly."

"Wow, what a coincidence that your date is also named Kelly, Doc," Amy said, smiling at the couple. "Let me show you to your table. My mom's in back, and I'll tell her you've arrived. Enjoy your date." Amy laid the menus on the table and returned to the front of the restaurant.

Alec looked at Kelly and chuckled at her scowl. "I know it's not a date," he said as he held her chair for her. Alec sat down and passed Kelly her menu. He buried his head in the wine menu and said, "Would you care for a glass of wine?"

"That sounds nice," she said.

"Any preferences?"

"No, you can just choose one for me."

*Date, not a date*, he thought. Alec ordered a bottle of the specialty white wine that Miss Kelly's highly recommended. He knew Kelly preferred white over red.

As they perused the menu, Alec heard his name being called and looked up. A woman was walking over to their table, and she was smiling at Alec. Alec rose and pulled the woman into an embrace.

"Doc, how are you? It's been a while."

"It has. I've been pretty busy between the clinic and a few other things. How's Bryce?"

"He's doing great. After that last bout of strep, he's been well. No reason for us to come see you until his annual check-up."

"Not that I don't enjoy seeing you."

"I know." The woman turned to Kelly, "So who's this lovely lady? Looks like you're on date."

Kelly smiled at the proprietor of the restaurant. She wasn't going to deny they were on a date. She'd deal with that after Miss Kelly left the table.

Alec introduced Kelly as Angelina's sister.

"I haven't seen either Angelina or Alejandro in here in about six months, maybe longer. How are they?"

"They're great. They just had a baby girl a few months

ago—she keeps them pretty busy. She's got Alejandro wrapped around her little finger."

"I'm sure she does. Well, it was great meeting you, Kelly. Give my best to Angelina and Alejandro, and I'll let you get back to your date now. Enjoy your dinner."

After Kelly Favor left their table, Kelly glared at Alec. "Why didn't you deny that we were on a date? This is NOT a date."

"I know that, Kelly. Just calm down a little."

At that moment, their wine was delivered. The sommelier presented the bottle of wine for Alec's inspection, then opened it and poured a sampling for Alec to try.

"That's really good, Fred," Alec said as Fred poured Kelly's glass and topped off Alec's. Alec took a sip of his wine and looked at Kelly over the rim of his glass. She was staring intently at the menu.

"Do you know what you'd like?"

"Everything sounds so good, I can't choose. Since you're so familiar with the entrées, why don't you order for me?"

"You're sure about that?"

Kelly nodded.

"Okay, then."

Alec placed their order. He ordered several of his favorites, including chicken Florentine, a blackened tuna steak, mixed vegetables, and Caesar salads. He also wanted to order dessert. If she agreed to it, he'd ask for it to-go and they'd feast on it at his home.

Alec had a hard time keeping the conversation going. "So, how have you been spending your days?"

"Oh, you know. Helping Angelina with the kids."

"Do you take Matthew to school?"

"Sometimes, but Alejandro chips in if he's headed into the hospital."

Silence.

"You like to jog?"

"I do when the weather permits. I've only gone out once since I've been here—you know the day."

*Well at least I got more than one sentence. I need to think of a safe subject. Definitely not her mother.* She seemed unsure of herself, so he brought up Colleen and Wyatt. She smiled and finally opened up—she couldn't stop praising them.

"Have you seen Colleen and Wyatt since you've been in town?"

"I have. The day I told my parents about my job."

"I'm sure they're excited to have you home."

"They are. In fact, I'm going to one of Wyatt's hockey games this week. I can't wait to see him play. It's been some time since I was in town during hockey season. I bet he's going to get a full scholarship to college to play hockey—he's that good."

"I wasn't aware of that."

"He's already being scouted, and he's only in middle school."

"Wow! That's something. I didn't think kids were scouted until their junior, senior year's in high school."

"I know. And Colleen—I think she's received five maybe six scholarships for field hockey."

"I knew she was good, but after her injury I didn't think she'd continue."

"It didn't stop her that's for sure. She's careful and wears some protective gear. She was injured on a fluke of a play. She happened to turn the wrong way. I'm proud of her because I don't know if I could have continued." She went on and on about Colleen's accomplishments and Wyatt's hockey season. He was thankful that he'd found a subject that she was comfortable discussing.

They enjoyed their dinners and equally shared them. The

waiter came by and asked if they were interested in dessert. Kelly's eyes brightened—he could tell she was interested.

"I'd love dessert, but I'm a little full right now. How about we get it to-go and take it back to my house?" he asked.

"I'm a sweets freak. Yes, that sounds like a great idea."

"Since I ordered dinner, you choose dessert."

Kelly's smile lit up her entire face. She decided on a German chocolate cheesecake and tiramisu.

"Add a piece of key lime pie to that."

Kelly smiled at him.

"I always have that here. It's the best I've ever eaten."

The waiter brought them their desserts, and Alec paid the bill. "You ready?" he asked.

"I am," she said. Alec grabbed the bag containing their desserts and helped Kelly from her chair. He placed his arm around her waist and led her from the restaurant.

"Enjoy the remainder of your date," Amy said as they walked out the door. Surprisingly, Kelly let the comment pass. Alec took that as a good sign and pulled her close as they waited for the valet. She started to shiver a little, and he asked if she was cold.

"A little," she said as she snuggled closer to him.

"I'll make a fire when we get home. That should warm you up."

She nodded and smiled, "And we can enjoy these sugary treats in front of the fire."

The valet appeared with his car and Alec helped her inside. As he walked to the driver's side, he had a huge smile on his face. This not-a-date was going just as he planned.

It was almost ten o'clock when Alec pulled into his garage. Before he could help her from her seat, she met him in front of the car. He led her inside the house and reached for her coat. His hand brushed hers and, for a second time, she didn't flinch. Maybe she was becoming more comfortable around him.

He started the fire as she looked on. The wood started to crackle and the flames danced around the log as the fire took. Kelly was seated on the sofa, watching the flames leap about, when he sat down beside her with their desserts and two forks.

"No plates?"

"I thought we could just eat out of the boxes." Alec placed the desserts on the coffee table in front of them. He opened the boxes and immediately forked a bite from the key lime pie. "Mmm, mmm," he said as he took another bite. "This is better than I remember." He reached down a third time and spiked another bite onto his fork. "Here, try this. You'll love it as much as I do." He held the fork in front of her mouth.

She seemed apprehensive, but took the bite. She closed her eyes and smiled as she chewed. "Heaven, absolutely heaven," she said. "Let's try the cheesecake." She reached her fork in and took a sampling. "Wow," she said. "Here you try." She fed him a bite of cheesecake and he agreed that it was pretty fantastic.

"I've never seen the cheesecake on the menu. I think it's new. I have to say that it rivals the key lime pie."

She opened the tiramisu and fed him a bite before taking one for herself. As he watched her eat the tiramisu, he realized that this had been an excellent idea. She'd relaxed so much since arriving at his house.

As the fire continued to crackle around them, they finished the last of their desserts. "Do you mind if I sit on the floor?" she asked. "I love to sit on the floor to watch the fire as it burns." She placed her fork inside one of the dessert boxes and slid to the floor.

Alec decided to follow her lead. He lowered himself to

the floor and put his arm around her. They sat in silence, watching the flames change colors in front of them.

He decided then that he wasn't going to ask her if she'd made a decision about her job. He knew she would share it with him when she was ready. He tightened his arm around her, and she looked at him and smiled. The warmth of the room lured both of them to sleep.

Alec woke to Kelly mumbling in her sleep, but he couldn't make out what she was saying. He tightened his hold on her when he noticed a change in her breathing, and then she woke with a start. She pulled away from him and quickly rose from the floor.

"Kelly, what's wrong. Are you okay?" She looked like she was afraid. It took her a moment to recognize her surroundings and then she took a deep breath.

"Yeah, I'm okay. Would you please take me home?"

"Sure. Let's get your coat." He retrieved her coat and asked again, "You sure everything's alright?"

"Yeah, I just want to go home. I'm tired, and it's getting late." Kelly slipped her arms into her coat. "I had a good time tonight, Alec. Thank you."

They drove to Angelina's in silence. Alec pulled up the driveway and started to get out of the car when Kelly opened her door, turned back towards him, and thanked him for the evening. "You don't have to show me to the door. I've got it… Thanks again, Alec."

"Not a problem."

Alec watched her as she stood. Turning back she said, "I'm going to dream about that cheesecake and that pie and that tiramisu. They were wonderful. I'll have to go back and try the remaining desserts off the menu."

"Anytime," he said as she closed the car door. He watched her as she opened the door to the house. She waved at him and closed the door.

As he pulled away, he wondered what she'd been dreaming about at his house—it definitely hadn't been the luscious desserts. He hoped one day he'd discover who'd hurt her. He felt that she was more comfortable with him, but for only a few moments at a time and then she closed off again, not wanting to be touched and not wanting to really be in the moment. She kept shying away from him and, for the life of him, he didn't know why. He thought their "date" had gone well, but something had freaked her out. He just hoped that, if he wasn't the one to right the wrong that happened to her, someone would be able to bring the happy-go-lucky Kelly back to the real world.

# Chapter Twenty-Two

A LEJANDRO HAD BEEN GONE FOR only two days when all hell broke loose. Matthew woke up with a high fever and sore throat, while Angel was just as fussy as ever. Angelina refrained from calling Alec—she wanted to be able to calm her own daughter.

She called the clinic to make an appointment for Matthew, only to discover that Ashton was scheduled to be out of the office. Both Alec and Joe were in, though, so he'd be able to see one of his uncles in the early afternoon.

When it was time for Angelina to take Matthew into the clinic, Angel started crying for the third time since waking up. Anything that Angelina did for her didn't work. She thought for a minute and decided to ask Kelly if she'd take Matthew to his appointment. Before Angelina could even ask Kelly for the favor, Kelly offered to take Matthew—clearly she could tell that Angelina was ready to lose her mind between Matthew's whining and Angel's screaming.

"Thanks, Kelly. I'll call ahead and let them know you're bringing him in."

Kelly hadn't been gone for more than five minutes when Angel settled down to sleep. Angelina wondered what that was all about, but happily thought it was Angel's way of getting Kelly and Alec back in the same room. Angelina had asked Kelly about their dinner at Miss Kelly's, and she'd told Angelina that she'd had a good time, but she didn't seem that happy. It seemed as though Kelly was just saying what she thought Angelina wanted to hear. Angelina hadn't had a chance to talk with Alec yet, so she wasn't sure what had really happened.

☾

Kelly and Matthew were greeted by Sadie. "Didn't we just see you in here?" she asked Matthew. Anyone who looked at him could tell he wasn't feeling well.

Kelly placed her hand on his shoulder when Matthew didn't say anything and said, "Aren't you going to answer Nurse Sadie?"

"Yes, I was," Matthew softly replied.

Nurse Sadie led them to an examination room where she took his temperature and vital signs, informing them that the doctor would be right with them. Before they knew it, there was a knock on the door. They both looked up and watched Alec walk in.

"Uncle Alec," Matthew said. "I'm glad it's you. I don't like Dr. Holder."

"You don't, do you?" Alec remembered that Matthew had complained the last time he'd seen Ashton.

"No, I don't," he said adamantly.

"Well, why not?"

"He got really mean with Mom about Dad. He doesn't like Dad."

"Oh, that's not true, Matthew."

"Yes, it is. He doesn't understand that Dad gets sad sometimes and he's been sad again." Alec looked up and caught Kelly's eye.

"You think your dad's sad?" asked Alec.

"Yeah, he is. I saw him looking at a picture of Tammy and Michael the other day. I thought he was crying, and then when I said something to him, he put the picture away. When he looked at me, he seemed okay. Uncle Alec, is Dad ever going to be happy again?"

"Well, he's happy right now. He has you and Angel and your mother. He loves you *this* much," Alec said as he spread his arms out as far as he could. "Now, let's take a look at that throat of yours. I hear it's pretty sore."

Matthew nodded his head.

Alec confirmed that Matthew did in fact have strep throat. He called in the prescription for him and then told Matthew he'd come by to check on him later. Matthew walked out of the examination room and started down the hall when Alec placed his hand on Kelly's forearm, stopping her from leaving the room.

"How are you?" he asked her as she tried to get past him.

"I'm fine. I need to catch up with Matthew."

"Oh, he's fine. Sadie will take care of him." Alec placed his hand above her head on the doorframe and leaned in close. "What do think about what Matthew had to say about Alejandro?"

"I have to agree with Matthew. Ashton was a little abrasive when we were here last time. I don't think he likes Alejandro's involvement. I think he may feel threatened by it."

"Maybe," Alec said. "I'll see you later tonight. I'm going to come by and check on him."

"Maybe you could look at Angel while you're there, too. She's been…"

"Cranky, I get it." Alec placed his hand on her shoulder as he started to walk away. Squeezing it slightly, he added, "Tonight."

She wondered what he really meant by that, but didn't give it a second thought since she needed to catch up with Matthew. He was just where Alec said he'd be, talking to Sadie near the front desk.

"Let's get going, Matthew. Your prescription should be ready, so we'll pick it up on the way home."

"And ice cream, too?"

"Yes, ice cream, too," Kelly said as she waved goodbye to Sadie, walking out the door.

☾

Alec finished up his day and sought out Joe. He was in his office reading a medical journal. Alec sat down and waited while Joe finished reading whatever he was reading.

"Interesting article?"

"Yeah, it is. What's up? I saw Matthew in here earlier. Is he sick?"

"Strep."

"Huh." Joe watched Alec. "And?"

"And, Matthew said he doesn't like Ashton and Ashton doesn't like our brother."

"Why does he say that?"

"When I walked into the room, he was thrilled to see that it was me and not Ashton examining him. He said he doesn't like Ashton."

"Really… How come?" It wasn't as though Matthew's reasoning had changed.

"According to Matthew, he doesn't like Alejandro. He said Ashton wasn't too kind the last time he was in regarding Alejandro. Kelly confirmed it, too. Remember, she was with them because Alejandro was out of town."

"I remember, and I also remember Matthew complaining about Ashton then, too." Joe said as he ran his hand across his cheek. "Maybe we need to sit Ashton down again and talk to him. He needs to understand what Alejandro has gone through these last few years, and he also needs to work on his bedside manner."

"Yeah, but there's more." Alec threw his head back and sighed. "Matthew also said that Alejandro's been sad lately. I'm a little worried that an eight year old can pick up on that. I think we also need to speak with our brother. I don't want him upsetting Matthew. He needs to be aware of his moods."

"He does, but again I can understand his sadness."

"I'm going by the house to check on him and Angel tonight. I think I'll say something to Angelina." Alec stood and went to leave the room. "Let's sit down with Ashton maybe tomorrow and talk to him about this."

Joe agreed and watched Alec walk out the door. Joe wasn't going to allow his colleague to speak ill of his brother, especially in front of his son.

❧

Kelly picked up Matthew's prescription at the pharmacy, along with plenty of ice cream and popsicles. When they got home, Kelly was surprised when they walked into a quiet house. There was no crying baby, and she found her sister wrapped up in a blanket on the couch, sleeping. Matthew took his medicine, ate a popsicle to soothe his sore throat, and then went right to bed—he was exhausted. Kelly checked on the baby and then headed off to the kitchen to start dinner.

She was in the middle of peeling potatoes when she heard a soft knock on the kitchen door. Before she could get to the door, Alec was opening it. She placed her finger to her lips so that he wouldn't talk too loudly. Not that the baby or Angelina could hear them from the kitchen, but she wanted him to know that they still needed to be quiet.

He shook his head, not quite understanding, and she whispered, "I am declaring this a quiet zone."

"I'm not following you."

"I have two sleeping children, along with a sleeping parent who needs her rest. I don't want anyone waking up."

"Gotcha," he whispered back.

She returned to her place at the kitchen sink and continued peeling the potatoes.

"Mashed potatoes?" he asked.

She nodded her head in affirmation. "With Matthew's sore throat, he shouldn't have any problem eating these. What are you doing here?"

"I wanted to check on everyone. And then, if Angelina's up to it, I want to talk to her about what Matthew said concerning Alejandro."

Kelly looked at him out of the corner of her eye. Smiling at him, she said, "We all understand the grief that your brother carries around on his shoulders. We all realize how it can still consume someone, even out of the blue, after all of this time. What I think you should do is talk to your hot shot physician and explain everything to him. If he has problems with your brother, then he needs to either address it with him directly or to you and Joe. That's just my two cents."

"No, I agree with you. I spoke with Joe before I left tonight and we are going to talk to Ashton tomorrow."

"Glad to hear that. Now, would you like to stay for dinner?"

"Sure, if you're okay with it."

"I wouldn't be asking if I weren't." Kelly finished up the potatoes and moved on to preparing the chicken for baking. "We won't eat for another couple of hours."

"That's fine. I've got some reading material in the car that I can catch up on, or maybe you and I can sit and have a conversation."

"Whatever," she said as she slid the chicken into the oven for baking. She washed her hands and left him standing alone in the kitchen.

He found her sitting in Alejandro's office, staring out the window. Alec could tell something was on her mind. He wondered if she'd made a decision on whether she was going to take Bill up on his job offer.

"I think this room has a side effect."

"Huh?"

"It seems like it's a requirement for anyone who sits in here alone to stare out that window."

Smiling at him she said, "Oh, yeah. You got me there."

"Something on your mind?"

"You know there is."

"Do you want to talk about it?" Alec sat beside her on the couch. He threw his arm across the back and turned towards her. "What's keeping you from making a decision?"

"I don't know. I wonder if I have it in me to go back. I wonder if I should just move on. I wonder if I was ever cut out for that job. Maybe I need to just—"

"Sounds like you're having a little issue with your self-confidence."

"You could be right…"

"The way I look at it, Bill wouldn't have offered you the compensation package that he did if he didn't believe in you. Is there maybe another reason why you're hesitant?"

Her hands were clasped in her lap and he noticed how tightly they gripped one another. She wouldn't look him in the eye. Alec placed his hand on her shoulder and squeezed it lightly, letting her know that he was there for her. They sat in silence a little longer when Angelina interrupted them.

"Alec, what are you doing here? Is it Matthew?"

"He's fine except for a good case of strep throat. I came by to see how Angel was doing and also to see you. And Kelly even invited me to stay for dinner."

Angelina smiled at her sister.

"On that note, I'd better check on the chicken." Kelly jumped up from the couch and left them alone.

Angelina looked after her sister, "So what's that about?"

"Not sure. I was asking her if she'd decided on what she was going to do about her job. I think she has a confidence problem going on right now and maybe something else. I can't quite put my finger on it, but I will. Now, about Matthew—he has strep. It's going around right now. I called in a prescription which I'm sure Kelly picked up. He should be feeling better in the next twenty-four hours or so."

"I'm glad to hear that."

"I actually wanted to talk to you about something he said in my office."

Angelina raised her eyebrows at him.

He put his hand up to hold off her questions. "First of all, Matthew does not like Ashton."

"I know that. And I know Ashton doesn't care too much for my husband, either."

"Matthew told me what happened at his last visit. He also told me he thinks Alejandro is sad."

"Yeah, I know he thinks that. We talked about it just yesterday. Did he tell you about Alejandro and the picture?"

"He did."

"Matthew caught Alejandro with their picture the day before he left. Matthew told me about their exchange, and I know that it bothers him. We talked about it and I think he understands…"

"I know he understands. He's just worrying about his dad, that's all. Joe and I are going to speak with Ashton, and when

Alejandro returns we're both going to talk to him as well. Maybe he just needs to talk it through again."

Angelina hugged Alec, thanking him.

"Joe and I aren't going to take this lightly with Ashton. He shouldn't be questioning our patients' needs. Alejandro wants these specific tests run for whatever reason, and since he's the expert in this field, no one should question it. We will deal with him. Got it?"

"Thanks, Alec. I just want you to know it's getting harder and harder to take Matthew in to see him. He really puts up a fight and he never used to. That little boy's been through an awful lot in his eight years. We need to do whatever we can to make sure he remains comfortable with any and all doctors. He never had any issues before, so you know it's a problem. I didn't want to say anything to you, but Alejandro knew about Ashton and I know he dealt with him directly."

"Don't worry, I'll take care of it." Alec clapped his hands together, "I'm starved. Let's see how long it's going to be before dinner's served." He grabbed her hand and led her to the kitchen.

Alec thoroughly enjoyed his dinner, helping himself to two servings of everything.

"Kelly, that was fantastic."

"Thank you. I wouldn't have known since you had two helpings of everything," she laughed as he reached to take a third helping of mashed potatoes.

"I'm going to check on the kids, and then I think I'm going to bed," said Angelina. "I hope and pray Angel sleeps tonight. She misses her daddy."

"I'm sure she does. Alejandro has always had a way with the wee ones."

"Just like you do," said Kelly.

"Well, I am a—"

"Pediatrician, yeah, yeah, yeah. Like I haven't heard that song before."

They all laughed as Angelina headed off.

Kelly started to reach for the dishes and leftovers when Alec stilled her hand. "Let me get this. You cooked—I'll clean up the kitchen."

Kelly smiled at him, thanking him. She was watching Alec methodically clean up the kitchen when her cell phone chimed. She viewed the text and couldn't believe her eyes— Ariel Layton wanted to talk to her.

Kelly got up and said, "Excuse me while I make a phone call."

She went to her room while Alec finished up the kitchen. Kelly dialed Ariel's number. She didn't want to speculate on what she wanted.

Ariel must have been waiting for her call—she answered immediately. "Kelly, I'm so glad that you called me."

"Hi, Ariel. What did you want?" Kelly wasn't being too friendly. The last time she'd seen Ariel, she'd pretty much thrown her under the bus by her not taking the blame for the testing issue that she missed.

"Kelly, I've missed you."

"Sure you have. That's why you've waited weeks to call me and see how I'm doing."

"No, Kelly, I do miss you. I overheard a conversation that I probably shouldn't have heard… Is it true? Are you coming back?"

Kelly didn't know what to say to Ariel. Kelly believed that she lost her job because of Ariel refusing to take the blame for missing a programming flaw that would impact the upgrade.

"Kelly? Are you?"

Kelly didn't say anything.

"Kelly you have to come back. It's a mess here. Ken still

wants to go through with the upgrade, even knowing about the flaw you found. You're the only one that can fix it. You know what to do. Think of our clients."

And then Alec's smiling face appeared before her eyes... The clients. She did have a vested interest in the program since Alec was planning on upgrading with it. She couldn't let that happen. It would affect her family and not in a positive way. She decided then and there that she'd do it, if only for a short period of time. She'd use this to get her confidence back. She'd use it to strike the black mark from her résumé. But one thing was for sure, she'd negotiate a letter of recommendation from Bill before she agreed to return. That way, if it all fell apart again, at least she'd have the letter and could walk away on her own terms without feeling like she was a complete failure.

"You know, Ariel, I can't confirm what you're talking about. I'm not even sure that I can still call you my friend."

"Kelly, I'm sorry. I had to do it. Ken made me. He made me lie."

Kelly's eyes widened, "He what?"

"I can't go into it any further, but just know I didn't have a choice in the matter."

"Everyone has a choice, Ariel."

"Not this time. Please, if you were my friend for only a minute, you'll come back and right this wrong. There's too much to lose here. Please think about it."

"Thanks for calling, Ariel," Kelly said as she disconnected the call—she didn't want to listen to Ariel's pleas any longer. She'd made up her mind.

Kelly found Alec sitting in the family room. His eyes were closed and his head was resting against the back of the sofa. She wasn't sure if he were asleep or not. She walked over to him and placed her hand on his forearm, startling him.

"Sorry, I didn't mean to scare you."

"You didn't. I was just resting my eyes."

"Sure you were," she said as she sat down beside him. She eased herself close to him and placed her head on his shoulder. He placed his arm around her shoulders and pulled her as close as she'd let him.

"Talk to me," he said. "Who was on the phone?"

"Ariel Layton."

"Who's she?"

"Well, I thought she was my friend until she turned on me right before I got fired."

"What happened?"

Kelly told him the story about finding the flaw in the program and going to Ken regarding the issue. "I tried not to blame her, but when I did, she turned the tables on me and said that I was responsible for missing the error in the program. One thing led to another, and the next thing I knew I was being escorted out the door, carrying a box that held my few personal belongings."

"What did she want?"

"She said she overheard a conversation that I was returning to Lattice. She pleaded with me to return to fix the problem that hadn't yet been fixed."

"Well, what are you going to do?" he said, looking directly in her eyes.

"She said I have to think about the clients."

"What did you decide?"

"Alec, I can't let you go through with an upgrade that contains a major flaw. It wouldn't be right if I let that happen. You and Joe are family. I feel like everyone at the clinic is family."

"So?" he said as he raised his hand to her face, cupping her jaw. He took his thumb and rubbed it against her lips. "What are you going to do?"

"First of all, I've decided that if I return I'm going to ask Bill for a letter of recommendation. That way, if it all falls apart again, I can be the one to walk away this time. I will have expunged the black mark from my résumé and will have a glowing letter of recommendation to boot."

"Smart girl," he said as he stroked her jaw with his hand.

"If I can get that letter, and if he still agrees to give me all of the compensation, then yes. Yes, I will return. I have to do what's right. I wouldn't feel comfortable with myself if I let Lattice Works sell an upgrade to clients that wasn't right. I can't do that to you, Alec." She started to chew on her bottom lip. "Am I doing the right thing?"

"Only you can make that decision. But I think it's a good move for you. Make sure you have everything you want and need. I think the letter of recommendation is a brilliant idea. I wouldn't have thought of that."

"Alec, thank you for letting me talk this through with you. It means the world to me. So, yes, I will return to Lattice Works. At least for the time being."

Alec smiled at her and moved closer to her. Her eyes got big—she knew he was going to kiss her. He briefly brushed his lips against hers. She seemed to enjoy the kiss at first, but then abruptly pulled away and jumped from the sofa.

This was too much for her. Alec was wonderful, caring… but she just couldn't get involved with anyone right now. She couldn't let anyone close. She just couldn't.

"Okay, then," Alec said. "Well, I guess I'd better get out of here. I have an early morning tomorrow. I'll see you soon."

Yes, Alec was deeply affected by Kelly's withdrawal. He wanted her, and he believed she wanted him, too.

Alec walked from the room and she heard the front door close. He was gone. What had she done? He was everything that she'd ever wanted in a man. Smart, tall, dark, handsome… What was wrong with her? Why couldn't she get over the past and move on? She would use this time at Lattice Works to heal, to move on from what happened and find the man of her dreams. Hopefully he would still be waiting for her when she finally found the courage to deal with her past.

# Chapter Twenty-Three

THE NEXT MORNING, KELLY CALLED Bill. "Bill, I've gone through your job offer, but I have one request that will be a deal breaker for me if you can't fulfill it."

Bill wasn't sure what she was going to say and continued to listen.

"Before I agree to come back to Lattice Works, in addition to everything you laid out in your job offer, I expect a letter of recommendation from you. I expect this letter in my box today with a signed copy sent to me as well. If this is done, then I will agree to return to Lattice Works."

Bill didn't think twice. He needed her to return or else Alec would pull out of the deal and take everyone else that he'd recommended to Lattice Works with him. "Agreed," he said. "I will email it to you this afternoon."

"Fine. I'll get back to you tomorrow then." She couldn't believe how easy that had been. While she'd lain in bed during the night, contemplating how she would approach Bill, she decided that she also needed to speak with Alec again. She needed to address their kiss.

❧

Alec and Joe sat in Alec's office, waiting for Ashton to arrive. Joe had called Ashton the evening before, leaving him a message that they wanted to have a meeting first thing the following morning.

"I spoke with Angelina last night and she wants to make sure we remind Ashton about Matthew's background—about the loss of his parents, their adoption of him, and of course the transplant. We need to make sure that it's none of his business concerning Alejandro's past. As long as his behavior is not causing damage to Matthew, then Ashton needs to stay out of it. I don't want to alienate him—I really think he's added a lot to the practice. We just have to reel him in, and make sure that, if he's got a problem with something, he needs to run it past us before speaking out like he has with Angelina and Matthew."

"I know what you're saying. Let's see how the conversation goes. Now about Alejandro," Joe paused, "he comes home tomorrow?"

"I believe he does."

"Let's try and meet up with him for breakfast Saturday morning. I'll leave him a voicemail letting him know that we want to discuss Ashton with him. That way he'll definitely make time for us."

"Yeah, I'm sure he'll want to speak with us considering what came out of Matthew's appointment yesterday. Angelina was troubled by it, and I'm sure she's passed that along to our brother."

"Yep, I'm glad we're meeting with Ashton today so we can pass along the outcome to Alejandro. More than likely he'll be calling for his head."

"I'm sure of that since he's already questioned our decision to hire him."

They heard a knock on the door and Ashton walked in. Alec reached for his coffee—he needed the caffeine to deal with not only Ashton, but also the sleepless night he had thinking about Kelly and their kiss.

Ashton sat down next to Joe and placed his coffee cup on the desk.   "I can't believe all the paperwork that's involved with buying a house. I felt like I was signing documents for hours. I have a cleaning company coming by today and, if all goes as planned, I'll be living in my house tomorrow."

"Well, I'm glad that it went smoothly.  It's a process as I recall," Alec said.  "I don't remember all of the paperwork signing per se since it's been awhile for me, but I'm glad that it's all worked out."

Joe and Alec looked at one another. Joe took the lead with the meeting.  "Ashton, the reason why we're meeting today is we became aware of a situation that concerns both of us."

Ashton looked back and forth between the two men, confused.

"Yesterday, Alec saw our nephew, Matthew.  He was in for strep throat."

"That is going around," Ashton commented.

"Yes, it is," Alec said.  "And I've never seen anyone so happy to see me as Matthew was."

"Makes sense.  He is your nephew.  Think about it—he was at the doctor's office.  Don't most kids hate doctors?"

"Matthew hasn't until now."

"I don't understand what you're trying to say."

"Matthew was so happy I walked through the door because I wasn't you."

Ashton drew his eyebrows close, "Why do you say that?"

"I think the main reason is that he knows you don't like Alejandro."

"That's not true."

"That's not what I heard from Angelina.  Ashton, I think we need to share a few things with you, and then maybe you will change your opinion of our brother."

Ashton took his coffee cup from the desk and held it between his hands.

Joe stood up from his chair and walked behind Alec's desk—he couldn't sit still any longer. He wasn't comfortable with Ashton's attitude and decided to make his point clear. "I think you need to listen closely to what we have to say because I do not want to have this conversation again," Joe said as he leaned against the credenza to the side of Alec's desk. He'd rested his hand on his cheek, gripping his elbow in his other hand, and stared intently at Ashton.

"Alejandro was Matthew's doctor while he was waiting in the hospital for a kidney transplant."

"I'm well aware of that."

"Were you also aware that his parents were killed in a car accident while he was in the hospital?"

"No, I wasn't. I just knew that your brother adopted him."

"Okay, well this little boy not only lost his parents, but also went through an extensive stay in the hospital. He's been around doctors since he was four. He's never been afraid of any of his doctors until you. He really hates you as his doctor."

"I don't understand why."

"Well, let's see," said Alec. "You complained about Alejandro in front Matthew and Angelina. You do not do that in front of a patient. If you have a problem, especially with our brother, you need to take it to one of us. He is well respected, and if he has a reason to have a specific test run, we need to honor his request and not question it. It would be different if we were dealing with a layman here, but Alejandro was Matthew's doctor and would probably still be his physician in some aspect if his parents hadn't died. He had a phenomenal rapport with Matthew and his family. Never once have there been any problems with Matthew's perception of a physician until you came into the picture. If you can't make things right with them, then maybe you don't belong in this practice." Alec looked at his brother for additional support.

Ashton was shocked by Alec's words. He did his best to keep his emotions from displaying across his face and hoped that he did. He thought he had been doing a stellar job and had been fitting well into the practice, but maybe not.

"Ashton, we believe you've added a lot to the practice, but I can't be having my nephew afraid of visiting a physician. You're aware of his physical issues, and we can't have him missing any appointments because of how you've acted towards his father." Alec took a swig of his coffee and continued. "Next, you need to understand a little bit more about our brother." He explained in detail about Tammy and Michael's deaths.

"I'm well aware that he lost his son and wife in a flash flood."

"Were you also aware that she'd just discovered that she was pregnant?"

Ashton shook his head.

"Were you also aware of everything that he and Angelina went through before they got married?"

Ashton said he knew something about her infertility.

"Well, not only did she deal with that, she also was the donor in a liver transplant with her sister. She experienced complications from that as well."

The color drained from Ashton's face. "No, I wasn't aware of all of that. I knew some, but..."

"Okay, there you go," said Joe. "Alejandro is very protective of those he loves. He carries around some guilt with all of this, too, even though he shouldn't. Yes, he is sad at times, but who wouldn't be under his circumstances. He's human. Aren't we all?"

"Now listen to me carefully," said Alec. "I do not, and I want to stress *do not*, want you accusing Alejandro of being a poor father because he sometimes shows emotions. That makes him who he is. Matthew is aware of what his father has endured—he's fully aware of everything. Does he understand it all? I'm not sure, but it's not up to you to question Alejandro's protectiveness of his family. His family means the world to him. Yes, this time of year is hard on him, but his family is here to support him. Do you understand what I am saying? You either get on the train and accept him for how he is, or you get off. It's just that simple."

Ashton knew he wasn't standing in the best light with Alec and Joe. He put his coffee cup back on the desk and nodded. "I understand. I apologize for any issues I've caused. I wasn't aware that Matthew disliked me so much, and I also wasn't aware of the death of his parents. I can understand now why they are so protective of him. I will do my best to make amends with everyone."

"That's what we wanted to hear, Ashton." said Joe. "We want this to work out. As Alec said, you've added a lot to this practice. We hope this is just a blip on the radar."

"I understand. Thank you for bringing this to my attention. I'll contact Alejandro and apologize."

"That's a good place to start, but you also need to apologize to Angelina and, more importantly, Matthew. He needs to understand that you don't dislike his father. Alejandro means the world to him. They have a special relationship stemming all the way back to when he was his physician."

"I understand." Ashton rose and grabbed his cup. "I'd like to stay on the train. I hope I don't have to get off of it anytime soon." He smiled at the men, turned, and opened the door. "I have patients to see, gentlemen." He walked from the room.

"I think he gets it. At least, I hope he does," said Joe. "I'd hate to lose him. I'll leave Alejandro a voicemail. Plan on breakfast tomorrow unless you hear from me."

Joe stood and saluted his brother as he left the office. Alec raked his hand through his hair. He was glad that was over. Now he had to get through the day. This had surely been a week from hell between dealing with the debacle with Ashton and all of the sick children. He couldn't wait for it to be over. Hopefully, he'd be able to catch up on some much needed sleep.

❦

Kelly checked her email late in the afternoon and, true to his word, there was a glowing recommendation from Bill. In part, it read: *Kelly Samuels is a dedicated employee. She is extremely thorough and accurate. She is a team player and hard worker that does whatever it takes to get the job done. She never hesitates to help her co-workers whenever the need arises. Ms. Samuels is focused and offers suggestions to improve upon a process. She is a good role-model...*

Kelly was shocked with everything Bill had to say about her. Then, she noticed a second attachment. There was a second letter from Ken. She was taken aback but wouldn't complain. She assumed Ken recognized his wrong and realized that he needed Kelly and her expertise. She was thrilled and couldn't wait to tell Alec.

❦

Angelina couldn't wait for her husband to return home. Matthew's temperature had broken the night before and he was feeling much better. Angel had been an angel—so peaceful since her crabbiness the day before. Kelly had discovered that Angel was indeed cutting her first tooth and that's what Angelina attributed all of the crabbiness to.

Kelly was helping Matthew with his homework—Gabriella had picked it up for him from school.

Angelina stood with Gabriella in the kitchen, enjoying drinks. Angelina told her about Matthew's conversation with Alec the day before.

"See, I told you so. There's something about him…"

Angelina told Gabriella that her brothers were handling the situation.

"Well, good. Matthew doesn't need to be scared of doctors right now."

"I didn't tell Alejandro about what happened. Actually, I went to bed early and missed his call. I think your brothers got to him because he left me another message when he was getting on the plane today, wanting to know why your brothers needed to meet him for breakfast tomorrow."

"I feel sorry for you. When do you expect Alejandro home?"

"Soon—for dinner."

"Well, on that note, I'm out of here. Call me if you need to vent." She hugged Angelina and headed out the door. "Call me," Gabriella called back over her shoulder as she made her way to her car.

"I will," Angelina said as she watched her friend leave. *I'm going to need all the help I can get dealing with Alejandro, especially if he knows about Ashton,* she thought to herself. Alec and Joe should have waited until he returned home to set up their breakfast meeting.

Alejandro walked through the door a few minutes later—he was earlier than Angelina expected. He walked in with a huge smile on his face, dropped his bag inside the door, and pulled Angelina into his arms, kissing her. She knew he hated traveling and was always happy to come home to his family. "I missed you," he said.

"I missed you, too." Angelina kissed her husband and pulled away. "Oh, by the way, you were right."

He looked at her, eyebrows raised. "About what?"

"Your daughter. She's cutting her first tooth."

"It all makes sense—she's normally pretty laid back. I guess this has been working on her for the last few weeks." Alejandro paused as he reached for her hand. "Now, do you know what's going on with my brothers? They want to have a breakfast meeting tomorrow."

"I do," she sighed. "How about a glass of wine first?"

"It's that bad, huh?"

She nodded and led him into the family room where she poured him his drink and explained the events from the last few days. "I know they had a meeting with Ashton this morning. I'm not sure how it went, though."

"I think I'll wait to hear all about it tomorrow." Alejandro got up from the couch. "I'm going to change and say hi to the kids before dinner."

He didn't seem upset by what she'd told him—he was taking it much better than expected. He seemed at ease, better than he'd been before leaving on his trip.

Kelly joined them for dinner and then told Angelina that she needed to run an errand. She needed to see Alec, to tell him about what transpired with Lattice Works and to talk to him about their kiss.

Since Alec's house was only a short drive from Alejandro's, she got there before she could plan exactly what she wanted to say to him. The front lights were on and she hoped that meant he was home. She also noticed a dim light shining through the curtains in the front windows. *Well, here goes it,* she thought to herself. She reached for her purse in the dark and knocked it off the seat. Reaching over, she picked up the contents, stuffing everything back into its places, making sure her cell phone wasn't missed. She was really nervous. Taking a deep breath, she exited the car and made her way to the front door. She took another deep breath and rang the doorbell. She hoped she was doing the right thing by coming to see him. She thought she was, but realized she could always second guess herself.

It took a few moments and then he turned on the foyer light and opened the door.

He seemed surprised. "Ah, Kelly, come in. What are you doing here?" he asked, reaching for her jacket. The days were getting longer as they entered spring, yet the nights still had a chill in the air. She took off her light-weight jacket and handed it to him. He turned towards a chair and draped her jacket over the back.

"Come on in. I was just sitting in my office doing some paperwork."

"Oh, I'm sorry. I shouldn't have come over without calling in advance. I'll leave and let you get back to—"

"Oh no you don't. Think of it as rescuing me from another headache." He laughed and reached for her hand. "Come on back. Would you care for something to drink? I was just enjoying a glass of wine."

"That sounds good."

Alec led her back to his office. On the way, he grabbed another glass and poured her some wine. He led her to the sofa and handed her the glass of wine. He walked over to his desk and grabbed his own glass.

"Would you care for a fire? I was thinking about lighting one earlier and then got sidetracked."

"That sounds nice." She felt herself calming. Between the wine and the fire, along with Alec's delight at her presence, she knew she'd made the right decision in coming. She felt herself relaxing as she watched Alec.

He leaned into the fireplace and lit the fire starter that was already laid out—he'd prepared for the fire earlier. When he was sure the fire had caught, he sat beside her on the couch. His leg brushed hers as he settled himself.

"Did Alejandro make it home?"

"He did, and I overheard him tell Angelina that you were getting together for breakfast tomorrow."

"Yep, we are. I haven't heard from him to confirm, but I'm sure he'll call later after the kids get to bed." He took a sip of his wine and set his glass on the end table. Turning back to her, he said, "So to what do I owe the pleasure of this visit?"

"I wanted to thank you."

"Thank me for what?"

"Our conversation last night. Actually, our last several conversations. I called Bill today."

"Really? And?"

"He sent me not one, but two letters of recommendation. One from him, and one from my boss, Ken that I was totally surprised by."

"That's fantastic. When do you start back?"

"I'm not sure. I have to call him back tomorrow. I realize it's Saturday, but oh well. I told him he needed to email me his letter by this afternoon, and then I'd get back to him. I'm letting him stew right now. I'll call him first thing tomorrow morning. I need to check with Angelina to make sure she's okay with me leaving this week."

"Why wouldn't she be? She was doing okay before you moved in."

"I know, but they've been so good to me. I want to make sure that she doesn't need me, that's all."

"That's kind of you, but I'm sure she's happy for you."

"I'm sure she is, too."

Alec sensed a change in her. She turned towards him and

looked at him directly. She was chewing on her lip which was a sign that she was nervous about something. He reached for her hands and held them between his. He squeezed them slightly, then reached a hand out and cupped her face. "Sweetheart, what's wrong?"

She scrunched her face up and then looked him directly in the eyes. "I have something to say to you, and I'm not really sure how to go about it."

"Don't worry about that. Just say what's on your mind."

"Okay," she said, glancing away and taking another deep breath. She was getting pretty good at taking deep breaths. "I wanted to say that I'm sorry about last night."

"Sorry about what?" He knew what she was apologizing for but didn't want to let on. He wanted her to feel comfortable with him and be able to tell him what was on her mind. He wanted to hear what she had to say. He moved his hand underneath her chin and lifted it so she was looking him directly in the eyes. "Go on, I won't bite," he chuckled.

"Alec, I don't know where to start."

"Then start at the beginning."

She started to chew on her lip again. He didn't know what to do to put her at ease.

She looked down at her hand clasped in his. It felt right to her, being this close to him. "Alec, I like you a lot. I really do."

"I like you, too."

"No, I mean, I… what I'm trying to say is… That kiss was really nice last night."

He wouldn't have known given how quickly she'd jumped out of his arms, but he wasn't going to broach that with her. He smiled at her and waited for her to go on. As long as she was in control of the situation, she was fine. As soon as he took control and advanced, though, she got scared and withdrew.

"I'm sorry I ran away. It's just that—"

"Kelly, it's alright. Don't worry about it."

"But I do, Alec. I really like you and would love to go on another date with you. But with me moving back to Knox-ville…"

"We can work through that. I can come down there, and we can see one another when you're home." Little did she know, she'd be in St. Louis soon performing the installation and testing at his clinic. "We can take it one day at a time. Kelly, I like you too, and I'd love to take you out again."

He started to move in and kiss her, but she pulled away again. He looked at her, his eyebrows raised. She'd just ba-sically declared that she wanted to date him, but what was it with the kissing? Kissing was a part of dating.

Kelly was having a difficult time with the idea of dating Alec. She liked him, but to think of him—them—in those terms… she couldn't deal with it. There was just way too much pressure. And then she remembered what had hap-pened, and she couldn't begin to think of seeing anyone. Now, or maybe ever.

She didn't want to lose her friendship with Alec. But if he discovered what had happened to her… she didn't know how he would perceive her. Could he accept it? Could she ever put it aside and get on with her life? It was still too soon for her.

It would be better for them not to "date" because dating involved so much more—kissing, cuddling and more… way more. Right now she wasn't ready for any physical relation-ship. Going out as friends was all she could handle.

"Alec, I'm sorry. I don't want you to get the wrong im-pression of me. I really want to date you, I do. And maybe, in time, even have a true relationship. It's just that something happened to me, and I need to work through it. Please just give me some time."

"I'll be here for you every step of the way. I don't know what happened to you, but know that if you ever—and I mean ever—want to talk about it, just call me. Anytime of the day or night, and I'll be there for you."

She moved closer and put her arms around his neck.

"It'll be okay."

She nodded into his neck and held onto him. He had known something had happened to her all along. Kelly had definitely been changed when she returned home, and now he knew he wasn't imagining it. He'd be there for her every step of the way, getting the Kelly that everyone knew and loved back.

# Chapter Twenty-Four

A LEJANDRO MET HIS BROTHERS AT Pedals for break-fast. Joe had arrived first and had secured a booth in the back, far away from any other patrons. Alec and Alejandro arrived at the same time. They joined Joe and placed their orders without needing to look at a menu—this was a favorite restaurant of theirs and they knew the menu well. Right after Alejandro moved back to St. Louis, they had made it a point to meet there every Saturday morning for breakfast. Married life sometimes got in the way for Alejandro, but they still tried to meet several times a month.

"How was your trip?" asked Joe.

"It was good. I left a screaming daughter behind and came home to an angel, no pun intended."

"What happened?"

"Angelina discovered that she's cutting her first tooth."

"That makes sense," both Alec and Joe said in unison. They looked at each other and laughed.

"So what's this I hear about you having a meeting with Ashton? That it had something to do with Matthew's visit?"

Joe and Alec told Alejandro everything. "We told him a little more about Matthew's background, along with Angelina's transplant. We didn't go into any details or break any confidences—we only told him about her donating her liver to Colleen. Since this is pretty much common knowledge, we didn't think she'd mind."

"No, I'm sure she's fine with that. So what did he say?"

"He apologized. We also talked to him about how protective you are of your family. Although, Matthew did tell me that he thought you were sad."

"Yeah, I know. He caught me at a bad moment. I was looking at a picture of them."

"Alejandro, we want you to know that we're here for you. I know we sound like a broken record, but you need to know it."

"I know that, and I realize that you care about me. This time of year is a little rough, but I think I'm past the worst part. My trip really helped me, and I'm seeing things more clearly."

"I'm glad to hear that," said Joe. As the waitress brought them their meals, he added, "Now, let's enjoy our breakfast." Alejandro had chosen pancakes, while Joe and Alec always chose an omelet.

They ate in silence for a few minutes, enjoying their food, when Alec broke the quiet. "Kelly came by last night."

"She did? I thought she was running errands."

"Well, I guess I was that errand then." Taking a bite of his omelet, Alec said, "She's going to return to Lattice Works."

"She is?" Joe said, sounding surprised. "I didn't think she'd go through with it."

"Well, she is. And I also discovered that something *did* happen to her. She wouldn't tell me anything other than she had to work something out."

"I wonder what it is," Joe said as he took a bite of his omelet.

"What brought that up?" Alejandro asked as he sipped his

coffee.

Clearing his throat, Alec took a swallow of his coffee and said, "She wants to date me."

"I knew it," said Alejandro. "Congratulations."

"Yeah, well all I can say is something big must have happened to her. I tried to kiss her the other night, and she literally ran away. Anytime I try and hold her, she pulls away. If she initiates the contact, she seems to be okay. But if I try and start something, she runs. I hope that she finds herself soon. Whatever happened to her has really mixed her up."

"Now that we know something actually happened to her, we all should be more aware of her moods—see what sets her off. I know she's going to go back to Knoxville, but what she doesn't know is that she'll be temporarily relocating to St. Louis to run the testing and installation of the software at the clinic soon. She's going to be our client liaison," Alec said.

"I wasn't aware that that was the deal you worked out," commented Joe.

"I had to do a little fast talking and act like I didn't know she'd been fired. If she doesn't work through what she needs to in Knoxville, maybe she'll be able to once she comes back here."

Alejandro clasped his brother's shoulder, "Good work, man. Good work."

They finished their breakfast and were discussing the clinic when Alejandro's cell phone rang. It was Angelina—she wanted to know how much longer he'd be since Kelly wanted to talk to the two of them.

"I'll be home within the hour," he said as he reached for the check and paid for their breakfasts. He hung up the phone and said, "It's on me. Thanks for watching out for my family. It means a hell of a lot to me."

Alejandro left the two of them at the table once the bill

had been paid.

"He seems much more relaxed, doesn't he?" asked Alec.

"He does," said Joe. "Maybe the worst is behind him for the year.

☾

Alejandro arrived home well within the hour time frame that he'd given Angelina. He strolled through the door with a box of cinnamon rolls that he'd purchased after he'd left the diner.

Angelina was delighted with the treat. "Oh, I love these," she said as she reached up and placed a kiss on his cheek. "Thanks. Kelly's waiting for us in your office. Angel's napping and Matthew's in his room playing."

Alejandro smiled at her and reached for her hand. He set the box of rolls on the counter as they headed off to meet with Kelly.

Kelly was anxiously awaiting Alejandro and Angelina. As she paced around the room, she hoped that they would be happy for her. She thought she might finally be seeing the light at the end of the tunnel—it felt that way, at least.

"Hey, Kelly. Are you okay?"

Alejandro's voice snapped her out of her trance. She smiled at him and asked how breakfast was.

He grinned back at her as he sensed her nervousness. "It was great. They told me about their meeting with Ashton, and hopefully all of that is behind us now. So, what did you want to talk to us about?"

They all sat down, Alejandro and Angelina on the sofa and Kelly in the chair adjacent to the sofa. Angelina wasn't sure what she wanted to talk to them about. Kelly played with her hair, curling a strand around her finger. Angelina took that as a sign that she was nervous about whatever she wanted to tell them.

Clearing her throat, Kelly told them about returning to Lattice Works. "I wanted you to be one of the first to know that I've decided to return to Lattice Works. Bill offered me a compensation package that I couldn't turn down, and he's also giving me additional responsibilities. I'm going to be a client liaison for the upgrades, interfacing directly with the clients and dealing with any issues that arise with the upgrades."

"Wow, that's fabulous, Kelly. But are you sure going back to Lattice is the right thing for you, especially with everything that happened?" Angelina asked as she looked at Alejandro.

"I am. In fact, I told Bill that one condition for my return would be that I expected a letter of recommendation from him before I agreed to the deal. That way, if things don't work out, I could leave on my own terms with a recommendation. I know everyone's concerned about me. But I have to do this. I have to find my own way and if this isn't it, at least I have two letters of recommendation and I'll feel better about moving on "

"That was smart of you, Kelly. When do you return to Knoxville?" Alejandro asked as he looked back at Angelina.

"That's what I wanted to talk to you both about."

"Don't be worried about me, Kelly. I'll be fine," Angelina chimed in. "It's you I'm worried about. You haven't been the same since you lost your job. I hope that you can find yourself again and work through whatever happened. I know you were shocked, and I know I would have been upset if I were in your shoes." Reaching for Alejandro's hand, she squeezed it and added, "We only want you to be happy. If it doesn't work out, know that you have a home with us again. We appreciate all that you've done while you were here. You were a godsend with Angel and Matthew—I know they'll both miss your terribly."

"Kelly, I want you to remember what I said when I married your sister. You're my family, too. If you ever feel that you need someone to talk to besides your sister, know that I am here for you as well. I'd do anything for you and your family. You all mean the world to me, and I don't want you to forget that."

"Thank you, Alejandro. I remember. That's one of the reasons I came here when I lost my job. I needed somewhere to go besides Mom and Dad's, and I thank you for opening your home to me, especially after just having Angel. I know you're still getting your feet under you, Angelina, and I want you to know I think you're doing a fantastic job with the kids. I know it can be overwhelming at times, but you just roll with the punches. I really admire you."

Alejandro drew his wife closely and placed a kiss on her forehead.

"Now, I have one more thing that I want to share with you."

Angelina looked at Alejandro, then back at her sister.

"Since I first got home on that god-awful day where I almost hit a deer, Alec has been there every step of the way with me. He took care of me when I needed to get pulled out of the ditch, he helped me through that migraine, and he's been my sounding board as I worked through this with Bill. I want you to know that we're going to try to start dat—"

Before Kelly could even finish her sentence, Angelina screamed and jumped off the couch. She ran to Kelly and pulled her from her chair and threw her arms around her. "I can't believe this!" she said as she tried to jump up and down with Kelly in her arms.

Kelly was shocked, to say the least, by Angelina's response.

"I had that feeling all along. You're perfect for one anoth-

er. I'm so happy for you. The best thing I ever did was have
that photographer at the wedding capture your picture with
Alec. I knew by the looks on both of your faces that this day
was coming."

"Really, now?" Alejandro said, "I couldn't tell." He chuck-
led as he too stood to give Kelly a hug. "That's terrific news,
Kelly. I'm glad to hear this. Alec has been alone way too long.
He needs someone like you in his life."

Pulling away, Kelly smiled at both of them. "We both
know it's going to be difficult with me moving back to Knoxville, but we're going to give it a try. That's all I can say."

"Have you told Mom and Dad yet?"

"About Lattice Works?"

"No, about you and Alec. Mom's going to be thrilled."

Kelly laughed, "No, I haven't spoken to them. I was going
to talk to Dad about the offer, but I spoke with Alec. They
have no idea that I was even in negotiations. I guess I'll have
to head over there after I talk to Bill. I need to call him today
and tell him I've decided to accept his offer."

"Kelly, I am so happy for you. Everything's going to work
out. Between your job and Alec... I see very good things
in your future," Angelina said. "Now let's go dig into those
cinnamon rolls."

"What did you say? Cinnamon rolls?"

"Yep, Alejandro brought them home from the diner."
Turning to her husband, she smiled and said, "This certainly is the best way to celebrate the good news, isn't it?" She
reached for her sister's hand as they headed off towards the
kitchen. Now it all made sense. Alejandro had known exactly
what Kelly had to share with them. He'd wanted to make it
a special moment, and he did.

Angelina and Kelly were sitting around the kitchen table
enjoying their treat when they heard a knock on the door.

Alejandro was pouring himself a cup of coffee, so he went to open the door.

It was Alec, and he walked in with a huge smile on his face. Before Kelly could even react, Angelina shouted, jumped up from her seat, and ran over to Alec, throwing her arms around him. He wasn't prepared for the force behind her jubilation, and she almost knocked him over.

Chuckling, he righted himself and hugged her back. "What's this for?"

Angelina just couldn't contain herself and Alejandro roared with laughter as he looked on. Alec looked over Angelina's shoulder and smiled at Kelly. She, too, had an enormous smile on her face.

"Okay, now. Please tell me why I deserve this welcome."

Angelina pulled away and looked back at her sister. She hadn't seen her smile that warmly at anyone in a long, long time. She had a sparkle in her eye as she looked at Alec. Yes, she did believe that her sister had found her man. "Well, what do you think I'm so excited about? My cinnamon rolls?"

"Ooh, those look good," he said as he walked over to the table, snatching a sampling.

Alejandro smirked, "Hey, didn't you just have an omelet for breakfast, along with potatoes and biscuits and—"

"So what if I did. These are fabulous. I should have had one of these, too," he said as he winked at Kelly. "So go on now, Angelina. Share with us why you're so overjoyed."

She looked back and forth between them, then leaned up and placed a kiss on Alec's cheek. Jubilantly she spoke, "I think you make a wonderful couple. I wish you the best. I just knew you two were meant for each other."

"Well, don't go there now. We're not a couple yet either. We're going to give it a try and see where it goes. It may not go anywhere, but we're going to try," Alec said as he leaned over and placed a kiss on Kelly's cheek. She smiled up at him, quickly blinking tears from her eyes.

Kelly was happy. Happier than she'd been in a long, long time. She loved how well Angelina got along with Alec. The ease between them caused her heart to flutter and filled her with such emotion.

"So what brings you by, Alec? Didn't I just leave you?" Alejandro asked.

"You did. I thought I'd come by and check on Matthew."

"Yeah, excuses, excuses. You just wanted to see my sister," Angelina joked.

"And what if I did?"

"Even better. Now, Alejandro and I have to check on the kids." Grabbing his hand, she pulled Alejandro from the room.

"She couldn't be any more obvious, could she?" Kelly said as Alec took the chair beside her.

Alec laughed and asked, "How are you this morning?"

"Good. I just told them about my job and us."

"Like I didn't figure that one out? I think your sister is more excited about us than she is about your job."

"Well, you know Angelina. I just told them that I need to tell my parents. Would you like to come with me?"

"Sure, if that's what you want."

"Yes, I do. That's what I want," she leaned over and placed a soft kiss on his lips.

&

Kelly had called her parents in advance to make sure they'd be home, and Ben wondered what her visit could be all about. Normally Kelly just showed up without notification. If they weren't home, she'd just leave a note saying she'd been there. When Ben told Jackie about Kelly's visit, she'd looked concerned. She knew her daughter was having difficulties dealing with her job loss, she just hoped that everything was okay with her.

Kelly and Alec pulled up at her parents' house promptly at two o'clock. He came around to the passenger's side and helped her out. He gazed into her eyes and stopped her before he closed the car door. "I just want to say that you look absolutely beautiful today. Thank you for including me."

Kelly smiled, "Thanks. I'm just glad you showed up. I was planning on calling you, but you just made it easier for me. I wouldn't be here today without your help and guidance."

He closed the door and put his hand on the small of her back, guiding her to the door.

Kelly rang the doorbell and anxiously waited for the door to open. She nervously chewed on her lip, catching Alec's eye out of the corner of her own and reached for his hand. He smiled at her encouragingly.

Her father opened the door, looking surprised when his eyes fell on their clasped hands. "Oh—Alec, hi. It's good to see you. Come on in." Ben kissed his daughter on the cheek and shook Alec's hand as he led them to the living room. He called for Jackie, letting her know that Kelly was there. If her dad had been shocked to see Alec with his daughter, her mom was going to be even more shocked. Neither one of them knew that there was more than a friendship between the two of them.

They were all seated when Jackie appeared through the doorway. As soon as Alec saw her, he stood. She couldn't even get Alec's name out before he approached her and gave her a warm hug. "It's great to see you, Jackie."

Jackie quickly got over the shock of seeing Alec when Kelly appeared at his side and also hugged her mother. "Mom, it's great to see you."

Jackie caught her husband's eye and then glanced back to the couple standing before her. "Sit, please sit," Jackie said as she sat in one of the wing-backed chairs in front of the sofa. Alec and Kelly sat down on the sofa together. Jackie noticed how closely they were sitting. "So, how are you Alec?"

"I'm good. I've been pretty busy as of late—strep throat's been going around, so we've seen quite a few cases of that. In fact, Matthew's just getting over it himself." He looked at Kelly and smiled.

"So Kelly, what brings you by today?" her father asked. "We haven't seen you very much since you've been in town."

"I've been helping Angelina. She's had her hands full with the kids, and Alejandro's been traveling a lot lately. Did she tell you that Angel's cutting her first tooth?"

"She called and told me. I knew that's why she's been so fussy lately. When you were a baby, I hardly slept when you were cutting your teeth."

Jackie wasn't paying attention to the conversation—her eyes kept darting back and forth between them. Alec looked warmly at Kelly and smiled. She reached for his hand and smiled back at him. Jackie anxiously looked at her husband, then again at her daughter.

Kelly picked up on her mother's anxiousness and decided to just jump in on why she was there, "Mom, Dad, the reason why I came by today is—"

"P-please tell me you're not pregnant," Jackie stuttered.

Kelly looked at her mom in shock. "Ah, no Mom. I'm definitely not pregnant."

"Then why are you here with Alec?"

"He came as my friend."

Kelly's father interrupted, "Just tell us what you need to tell us, honey. As you can see, your mother's overactive mind is at it again. I'm sure you can remember when Angelina and

Alejandro were dating."

"I am well aware, so I'm just going to tell you that I've found a job."

"You have? That's wonderful!" her father said. "Where are you going to work?"

Kelly caught Alec's eye and took a deep breath. She knew how her mother would react, but she just had to get this over with. "I'm going back to Lattice Works."

"You're what?" her mother was shocked. "How could you go back to that company? Especially with how they treated you?"

Kelly could see her father put his business perspective head on and he said, "I thought they were downsizing. How can they suddenly have the budget to rehire you?"

She hadn't thought this all the way through. She'd forgotten that she'd told her parents she lost her job due to downsizing.

"Ben, they've had an influx of clients lately," Alec interceded, squeezing her hand. "Joe and I are going to upgrade with their new software. I've spoken with many of my peers and they're going to sign on as clients, too. I guess they've just had a lot of new orders, and they feel they can rehire those they had to let go."

"Huh, I guess that makes sense. Kelly, you should feel honored that they came back to you."

"I do," she said. Unfortunately there was a lot more going on than they could ever know.

"When do you start?" asked Jackie.

"I have to work that out with Bill. I'm thinking in the next week or so. I'll let you know when I'm going back to Knoxville."

"You'd better. I want to have a celebration." Jackie smiled at her daughter. "So what else is new in your life?"

Clearly her mother picked up that she had more news to share. Kelly smiled up at Alec and patted his thigh. She knew her mother was waiting with bated breath to know why Alec had accompanied her daughter to their house, and she'd already asked the most pressing question on her mind.

Alec smiled at her and looked back at her mother. He reached back and put his arm along the back of the couch. He laid his hand along her shoulder and gave it a slight squeeze.

"How are Colleen and Wyatt? I haven't seen them in a while," Kelly said, delaying the inevitable. "Didn't Colleen have an appointment with you recently, Alec?"

"She did, and she's fine."

Her mother kept looking on, not sure what was really happening.

Alec looked at Kelly and said, "Ben, Jackie, the other reason why we're here is because—"

Kelly squeezed his thigh, stopping him in thought. She appreciated what he was doing, but it needed to be her that told her parents.

"Mom, Dad, what Alec was just about to say was… Well, Alec and I are seeing one another."

Jackie gasped.

"We're going to date and maybe, in time, we'll see if we can have a long-distance relationship. We both know it's not going to be easy, but we're going to try." She glanced over at Alec, smiled, and reached for his hand, squeezing it tightly said, "Mom, Alec means the world to me, and I don't want to give up on something that is so real just because I'm moving back to Knoxville."

Alec winked at her as she spoke. She hadn't openly declared how she felt to Alec, but now that she had, it felt pretty good.

Alec jumped in, "We've become quite close with what

Kelly's going through with this job upheaval. I've always liked Kelly, but I didn't realize until recently that we could have a relationship. I know it's going to be difficult, but if we can make it work long-distance, then that bodes well for us."

Jackie stood and walked over to Alec. She reached down and kissed him on the cheek. "I'm glad you're in our daughter's life. She needs someone just like you, Alec, to look after her. I hope it works out. You know I'm going to be on the sidelines cheering away. Congratulations, dear," she added as she gave her daughter a peck on the cheek.

"So how long has this been going on?" Ben asked as Jackie returned to her chair.

"Pretty much since the day Kelly returned, and I found her in the ditch."

"What?" Jackie raised her eyebrows, "Now I've got to hear this story. I thought it might have begun at the wedding."

Alec looked at Kelly and laughed. Both Alejandro and Angelina kept throwing the reception in their faces. Maybe there was some truth to that photograph. Kelly made a mental note to look at it again when she went home. Maybe she'd missed that special look that they had talked about.

Alec proceeded to tell them how he found her on the side of the road after she'd just missed hitting a deer. "I was shocked to see that it was Kelly. I got a tow truck and had her pulled out. I guess you could say we've been growing closer, especially since she's been living at Alejandro's. I'm over there all the time checking up on the kids. It was bound to happen." He squeezed her shoulder again, and she smiled affectionately at him. His touch was comforting to her—she was happy that it no longer sent a jolt of panic down her spine.

They spent the remainder of the afternoon at her parents. Colleen and Wyatt showed up and so they decided to have dinner with her family. Kelly wanted some alone time with

Alec after and decided to say goodbye to her parents.

"Thanks for everything, Mom. I think we're going to head on out."

Alec stood and reached for her hand, helping her from the couch. He put his arm around her waist and leaned forward to shake her father's hand. Jackie hugged both of them goodbye as they walked towards the door.

"Thanks again for dinner. It was another fabulous meal. I still remember how you pulled that Christmas buffet together at a moment's notice a couple of years ago."

"Oh that, yes that was fun. I really enjoyed having your family here. Come by anytime, Alec. You're always welcome."

"Thank you," he said as they started out the door.

Jackie turned to Ben as she closed the door. "Well, that was quite a surprise. I didn't see that one coming."

"Neither did I," Ben said. "I hope they can make it work. Long distance is difficult."

"It is, but if I know Alec like I think I do, he'll make sure it does. He loves our daughter. I could see it in his eyes."

Ben nodded his head in agreement. "I'd have to agree with you, honey. He has the same look that his brother did when he fell for Angelina."

☾

"Well that wasn't so bad," Alec said as he opened the car door for Kelly.

"No, it wasn't. Thank you for stepping in."

"I didn't tell them, you did."

"Well, it took me long enough to get there. I had to bring Colleen and Wyatt into the conversation before I had the nerve to tell them about us."

"It doesn't matter. You told them, and that's all that counts. Now, let's go home."

"Home?"

"Yeah, to my house. We have some planning to do." Alec closed her car door and walked around the back of the car. He noticed the drapes moving in the front window. Yes, Jackie was it at again. Alec remembered Alejandro telling him how she'd watched their every move when he had been dating Angelina. She had always been observing them when they came and went from the house, always sneaking a peak through the drapes. And today she didn't fail. Shaking his head, he slid into the car.

"What's wrong?"

"Your mother, that's all," he laughed as he backed out of the driveway and pointed the car in the direction of his home.

# Chapter Twenty-Five

A LEC PULLED INTO THE GARAGE at his house and looked at Kelly sitting beside him. He couldn't believe his eyes. She was his, at least for the time being, and was sitting beside him without being apprehensive. He smiled and jumped out of the car. He reached her side before she could exit the car. He extended his hand, and she gladly accepted his. She walked beside him as he entered the house. Never in his wildest dreams did he think this would be happening to him. A few days ago, he thought his attraction to her was only one-sided. But she wanted to be with him—he just needed to go slow. He was fine with that as long as they could be together.

He led her into the family room and turned on the stereo. An instrumental piece played softly in the background. "Would you care for something to drink? A glass of wine?"

"That sounds nice," she said as she sat down on the sofa. Alec headed to the bar and poured two glasses of wine.

He handed her a glass and said, "To us."

She raised her glass in salute and clinked his glass. "To us," she said.

They each took a swallow and then he reached for her hand. "Would you care to dance?"

Kelly hadn't danced in a long time. She loved to slow dance and jumped at the chance. "I'd love to," she said as she stood.

Alec pulled her into his arms. She pulled away slightly but then settled back into his arms. They swayed to the music. No words were needed. She put her arms around his neck and leaned into him, placing her head on his shoulder. It felt nice to be in his arms.

"This is nice," she said as she swayed with him in time to the music.

He turned his head towards hers and placed a soft, gentle kiss against her brow. He didn't want to scare her, but felt that he needed to let her know that this was an important step for them.

"I've missed dancing. I love this."

"Well, we're going to have to do this more often then," he said as he nuzzled her cheek with his.

They danced for a long time, and then he led her to the couch. They had come to his house to have a conversation, and they were going to have it. They sat down and he drew her close, putting his arm around her shoulders. She laid her head on his shoulder. "This has been a really nice day. Thank you for including me."

She took a sip of wine and smiled at him.

"I couldn't believe your mother, though, asking if you were pregnant."

"That's my mom. In fact, she asked me the same thing when I came home. Today, I can certainly say she was pretty much speechless. We definitely caught her off guard."

"You could say that. Alejandro told me how she was when he and Angelina were dating. She wanted to know everything."

"She did. In fact, Angelina even threatened to move out.

Mom settled down then. But I also think Alejandro asked her to marry him shortly after that, so she had no cause to worry. She'd gotten her way. She knew they were a couple way before they admitted it to themselves. They tried just being friends, but we know how that went."

He reached for her glass and set it on the table in front of them. He turned slightly and cupped her cheek. "I hope we can be more than friends, Kelly," he said as he leaned in to place a soft kiss on her lips. *Okay*, he thought to himself, *she's okay with this. I'm going to try again.* He pulled her closer and tried kissing her a second time, but she tensed and pulled away.

She looked away from him and pursed her lips. "I'm sorry, Alec. I just can't." She tried to pull out of his arms, but he wouldn't let her. She started to push against his arms, and he finally released her. She scooted out of his arms and reached for her glass again. Taking a long gulp, she fingered the rim of her glass. "I need time. Please give me time."

"Sweetheart, you've got all the time you need. Just know that I am here if you ever need an ear."

"Thank you, I know that. I just need to work through this. I'll be fine, in time," she said.

He wondered what had happened to her, but he really didn't have any idea. He believed that whatever happened had to be of the physical nature, he just wasn't sure what it was or who was involved. He cared about her, and that summed it all up. He was falling under her spell. He just prayed that she could deal with these demons that troubled her.

He took a sip of his wine and set the glass back on the table. "So, when do you want to go out on a real date?"

"Haven't we already been on one already?"

"I don't think so," he chided her. "It was a date for me, but you refused to call it that. Don't you remember?" he teased her.

"Yes, I remember," she replied shyly, securing a lock of hair behind her ear.

"Let's have that first date one night this week. I'm sure you'll be going back to Knoxville by the end of the week, and I'd like to say we had our first official date before you ran off on me."

Kelly smacked his arm, "Hey! I don't want you spreading rumors that your girlfriend ran off and left you."

Alec stopped laughing, "I would never do that. You should know that. In fact, let's plan our second date, too. I'll come to Knoxville the day you start your job, and we can celebrate."

"You'd do that for me? Wow. I think I've met my man," she said, laughing. "No seriously, you would come down just for a date with me?"

"In a heartbeat. I wouldn't have suggested it if I didn't want to."

"Wow, I do feel special."

"Well, you are."

They sat talking for a little longer when Kelly began to yawn. She tried to sneak her yawns behind her hand, but Alec caught on pretty quickly. Reaching for her hand, he pulled her from the couch. "I think it's time I got you home."

Alec drove her home and walked her to the door.

"Do you want to come in?"

"No, I'm sure Alejandro and Angelina are in bed, and you're pretty tired. We'll talk tomorrow?"

"Yes, definitely." She leaned up and placed a kiss on his cheek. "Thanks for today. I'll never forget it."

He started to turn away, then leaned back and kissed her softly on the lips—he knew she couldn't run far since she was home.

She watched him as he walked down the sidewalk and got

into his car. She waved as he pulled away. "I've got to get myself together," she said as his taillights disappeared around the corner. "He won't wait for me," she whispered to herself as she entered the house.

❦

The next few days passed in a blur. Kelly was scheduled to return to Knoxville the next day. After speaking with Angelina about her return to Knoxville, she called Bill. They'd set her return for the following week. Alec had been pretty busy at the clinic, so they hadn't been able to schedule their first official date until earlier that day. She was nervous to say the least. She'd tried on several different outfits and finally decided on a fuchsia dress with a deep v-neck. It fit her like a glove, accentuating her slim waist. She finished the dress off with a strand of pearls and pearl-dropped earrings. She'd pulled her hair up into a French twist with wisps of hair framing her face. For once in a long time, she felt beautiful. Looking back on it, she hadn't felt beautiful since that horrible night. But she wasn't going to go there now. She was going to enjoy her date with Alec. Tomorrow, she was returning to Knoxville to restart her career. She was nervous, but excited, too. She'd give it some time, but if things didn't work out she was prepared to walk away. Thankfully, she had two recommendations in hand.

Alec surprised her with a bouquet of flowers. She couldn't believe how thoughtful he was. She raised the flowers to her nose as soon as he handed them to her and inhaled. "I love fresh flowers," she said. "Thank you. Let me get them in water and then we can go."

He followed her into the kitchen and was greeted by Angelina.

"Well, don't you two look lovely. Here, I'll put those in

water," she said as she reached for the flowers. "Go, enjoy yourselves. Time's a wasting."

That statement was definitely truer-than-not since she was leaving the next day. "Thanks, Angelina," Kelly said as she turned back to Alec.

"Have a good time," Angelina said "Don't do anything I wouldn't do," she laughed as they walked from the room.

He took her to a well-known Italian restaurant not far from his house. Mama Zia's was known for its romantic setting, and it didn't fail. When they were seated, she was presented with a red, long-stemmed rose.

Smiling at Alec, she said, "Did you arrange this?"

"Would I have bought you that bouquet if I thought you'd get more flowers at dinner?" he teased. "Seriously though, I had no idea they'd give you a rose."

Alec ordered a bottle of wine while they looked over the menu. "What looks good?" he asked.

"I think I'm going to have the lasagna. I haven't had that in ages. What about you?"

"I think I'm going to have Mama Zia's specialty pasta. That sounds delicious, especially with the melted provel on top. How can I pass that up?"

The waiter poured their wine and took their orders, then brought them each a salad and basket of bread. "This is definitely my downfall. I love this bread." He broke her off a piece and handed it to her.

"This is good," she said as she slowly chewed it, watching him intently. She didn't want to forget a moment of this date. She was going to burn it into her memory so she could pull it up at a moment's notice whenever she missed him. And she *would* miss him. She no longer had any close friends in Knoxville since Ariel had pretty much turned her back on her. If Ariel thought she'd give her a second chance, she had another thought coming. She was not going to have a friendship with her any longer.

"Where'd you just go?"

"Huh?"

"I was talking to you, and you just sat there with that smile on your face."

"I was just burning this image into my mind. I don't want to forget a minute of tonight. When I'm alone in Knoxville, I'll be able to call up my memories and smile, thinking how happy I was tonight."

"Well, I'll make sure you have memories to cherish until we meet again. By the way, do you know when you're starting at Lattice yet? I need to let Dad know so he can fill in for me."

"What are you talking about?"

"I told you that I was going to take you on our second date the day you start your job. I talked to my dad and he's going to fill in for me so I can come down to Knoxville."

"I didn't think you were serious about that. I thought you were just joking."

"Well, I'm not. So, when do you start?"

"I'm not going to start until next Monday—I wanted to give myself a few days before I went back. I need to do some serious cleaning. My condo is filthy, I'm sure, since I pretty much fled the city the night I was fired. I have no idea what condition I left it in."

"That's even better. I'll come down Saturday and we can spend the weekend together, if that's alright with you."

A weekend together? She felt her breath quicken and a nervous sweat break out across her forehead.

"I plan on getting a hotel room, so don't worry about that," he said, looking at her carefully.

"You can stay with me," Kelly said nervously, defiantly.

"No, I don't want to put you out or cause you undue stress. A hotel is fine, just let me know which one is closet to your house. That's all I need to know."

"Are you sure?"

"I am. I'd like to arrange a meeting with Bill, too, so it works out just fine."

They enjoyed the rest of their meal. They had been going to forego dessert, but somehow their waiter discovered it was their first date and so Mama Zia's provided dessert on the house.

"Oh my, that tiramisu was fabulous!" Kelly said as they walked to the car. "I think it's the best I've ever had."

"We'll have to remember that for next time." He smiled as he opened the car door for her. She hated that it was time to call it an evening, but it was getting late and she wanted to get an early start in the morning.

"What time are you leaving?"

"The earlier, the better. It's a longer drive than you realize, and I don't want to be too tired when I get home since I can't remember how I left my condo. I'm sure I'll be up late cleaning."

They arrived at Alejandro's, and he put the car in park. He turned in his seat towards her. "I'm really going to miss you, Kelly. I had a fantastic time this evening and I can't wait until the weekend when we can do this all over again. Decide on a restaurant you'd like to go to Monday night and make reservations, okay?"

She nodded.

"I'm going to kiss you, if that's alright with you?"

She nodded again. He leaned forward and kissed her soft lips. He pulled back and then leaned in a second time and she allowed the second kiss. He pulled away and smiled at her. "That was a perfect ending to our evening."

"It was. I plan on remembering every minute detail. Thank you for a fabulous evening. I will never ever forget it." She turned to open the door.

"No wait, let me get it." He hurried from the car and opened her door. He helped her from the car and raised his hand to caress her cheek. He leaned in again and took another kiss. He pulled away and brushed his thumb across her lips. "Drive safely, sweetheart. Please call me when you arrive."

She nodded in agreement. She was mesmerized by his kisses. She threw her arms around him and hugged him tightly. She didn't want to let him go. "I'm going to miss you so much."

"The weekend's just around the corner. I promise we'll sit down and figure something out. I can't go weeks on end without seeing you, Kelly."

"I can't either, Alec. I'm…" Tears started to gather in the corners of her eyes. She didn't want Alec to see her crying, so she pulled away and ran for the door, closing it behind her. She made her way to her bedroom where she sat on the bed and softly cried. She knew she was falling in love with him, but she also knew that she had to resolve what had happened to her before she could fully commit to Alec.

Alec watched her run away from him again. He knew she was starting to cry and attributed it to that. He decided in that moment that he was going to surprise her the following morning before she left. Maybe she'd feel a little better about leaving knowing that she'd be seeing him in a few short days.

*❧*

Kelly slept terribly that night. She tossed and turned between the happy images of Alec and the heart-pounding ones of Ken. She awoke at four in the morning and her heart was racing wildly—it felt like it would jump out of her chest.

She knew that she wouldn't get anymore sleep, so she got up, dressed, and finished her last minute packing. As quietly as possible, she packed her car and waited patiently for Alejandro and Angelina to wake. She was on her third cup of coffee when Alejandro appeared dressed for work. He was just as handsome as Alec, especially when he was dressed in a suit and tie.

"What are you doing up so early?" he asked.

"I couldn't sleep, so I thought I'd get an early start. Is Angelina awake yet?"

Reaching for a mug, he said, "She is and is in the shower."

"That's good."

"Aren't you going to say goodbye to Matthew?"

"I already did. He was using the bathroom when I first got up. I'll look in on Angel when I get ready to leave. I don't want to wake her."

Alejandro poured his coffee and sat down beside her, "Kelly, are you sure you're doing the right thing here? You don't have to go back to Lattice. With your talent, you could have easily found a job."

"I'm not so sure about that. How would I explain my firing?" Shaking her head, she added, "Thank you for the compliment. That was kind of you."

"I mean it. Kelly, you are good at what you do. Don't think otherwise. I know this firing was a blow to your self-confidence, but you need to know that, between me and my brothers, we would have helped you find a job."

"See, that's the point. I needed to do this on my own... Without intervention from family or friends. This is about me finding my way, and only I can do that."

"Okay then" he said. He hoped and prayed she didn't find out what part Alec had played in helping her secure her job. She'd never forgive him.

Angelina walked into the kitchen. "Are you leaving already?"

"I thought I'd get an early start. Try to beat the traffic."

"But you need to say goodbye to the kids."

"I already said goodbye to Matthew, and I'll look in on Angel right before I go."

Alejandro quickly gulped down his coffee. "I gotta go. I have an early surgery." He went over to Kelly and pulled her into an embrace. "We'll miss you, Kelly. Don't be a stranger. Remember what I told you—if you ever want to come back, just say the word. The door's always open for you."

"I know. Thank you, Alejandro. I really appreciate what you and Angelina have done for me."

"No thanks are necessary—I know how much you helped Angelina with the kids. Take care, and drive safely," he said. He gave Angelina a kiss and then hurried out the door.

Kelly and Angelina shared one last cup of coffee—it was almost six thirty, and she wanted to get on the road. She took one last peak at her niece, kissed her fingertips, and softly applied a kiss to Angel's forehead. "I'll miss you little one," she said.

Kelly and Angelina embraced one more time before she headed out the door. Matthew was stirring, so Angelina needed to get him up and going for school. "Drive safely, call when you get home... I love you, Kelly."

"I love you, too, Angelina," Kelly said as she got into her car. Kelly waved goodbye to her sister and watched the front door close. As she watched the door close, she thought, *One door closes and another opens.* She guessed her rehiring was a door opening for her. She started the car, brushed aside a tear that had escaped her eye, and put her car in drive. She had just started down the driveway when a set of headlights pulled up beside her. She stopped her car and Alec came rushing up to her door.

Kelly was surprised to say the least—they'd said their goodbyes the night before. He tore open the door, reached in, and released her seatbelt. Pulling her from the car and into his arms, he said, "I couldn't let you go without this." He pulled her so close that she would have broken in two if she were a piece of china and kissed her.

"I had to see you one more time."

Kelly was taken aback, "I'll see you this weekend."

"I know, but I just needed to say goodbye one more time." Pulling away from her, he dropped his arms and let her go. "Drive safely."

"I will," she said as she returned to the car and closed her door. *He can't see me cry*, she thought. *He just can't*. She put on a stiff upper lip, smiled, and started the car. Luckily the driveway was wide enough for her car to pass his.

He stood and watched what he was beginning to think of as the love of his life drive off. He hoped and prayed this would work out for her, but if it didn't, he'd be there with her to help pick up the pieces.

The next thing Alec heard was Angelina's voice. "Is that you, Alec?"

"Yeah, it's me."

"Did you get to say goodbye?"

"I did, but I almost missed her. I didn't think she was leaving for another couple of hours."

"She surprised both of us this morning. When I got up, she had already packed her car and was saying her goodbyes to Alejandro. I guess I'm lucky she waited for me."

"She would have never left without saying goodbye to you."

"I'm not so sure about that. She was in a strange mood this morning, that's all I can say."

"Maybe she's questioning her decision."

"I guess time will tell," Angelina said as she turned back to the house. "Are you coming in?"

"No, I need to run by the hospital before I go into the office. I'll talk to you later."

"Alec?" He turned back to her. "She'll be okay. And if she isn't, she'll come back. She cares for you, I know she does."

He swiped his hand across his jaw and looked back at Angelina. "I guess we'll see about that," he said as he ambled slowly down the driveway to his car. It was sure going to be a long day until he heard her voice again. And even longer until he saw her in person.

# *Chapter Twenty-Six*

K ELLY'S DRIVE BACK HOME TO Knoxville took longer than she expected. She hit rush hour traffic leaving
St. Louis and then encountered several construction delays.
The normal seven hour drive took almost ten hours. It was
after five o'clock and she was more than exhausted when she
pulled into her garage. She hauled herself out of the car and
unlocked her condo. As soon as she walked in the door, she
smelled the stale air from being locked up for so long. She
decided it was too late to tackle the cleaning that she'd anticipated doing. Focusing on the cleaning was a way to keep
her mind off of missing Alec so much. She sat down for a
moment to clear her head and recharge from the long drive.
She closed her eyes momentarily, and then the next thing she
became aware of was the ringing of her phone. She reached
for the handset that was next to her. She'd forgotten to call
her mom, Angelina, and Alec. She'd been too tired when she
first walked through the door.

She barely got a hello out when Alec was practically coming through the phone at her. "Why didn't you call? Where
have you been?" he paused momentarily and added, "I was
worried. I've been trying you off and on."

She let him ramble and waited until he was finished. "Sorry, I was exhausted when I got in. I sat down for a few seconds and must have dozed off. Traffic was hell! I lost count of the number of construction zones that I went through. They weren't there when I left, but I guess they're all out in force since spring is here."

"I'm just so glad to hear your voice. I was worried all day, especially with how you tore out of Alejandro's this morning."

"I didn't tear out of there—I just needed to get on the road."

"I talked with my dad and he wants to fill in for me longer than I expected. He misses the office and thinks I need a little vacation... I know this is short notice, and I realize that you just got home, but I'd like to come down tomorrow night. I thought I'd work a half-day and leave from the office." Alec started rambling, clearly nervous about her reaction, "That is, if you're comfortable with seeing me so soon. I can help you clean or whatever you need to do before you go back to work on Monday. I'm pretty proficient at using a vacuum cleaner—"

She was getting more tired as she listened to him ramble on. "Alec, would you just stop for a minute?"

He started laughing.

"You don't have to ask if you can come—you're more than welcome. No, I do not expect you to help me clean. And lastly, I wish you'd stop rambling. You're making me tired just listening to you."

Alec roared with laughter. "I guess I was rambling. Sorry about that. I was worried about you and all. I'd heard about an accident outside of Nashville where there were several deaths, and when I didn't hear from you, I got anxious. When I get nervous, I do tend to ramble, so I will try and watch out for that in the future and not let it happen again."

"Alec, I was just kidding. Thank you for worrying about

me. Now, since you woke me, I need to call my mom and Angelina and let them know I got here safely."

Before he ended the call, he told her he'd call when he was on the road. "Oh, by the way I wanted to tell you I set up a meeting with Bill while I'm in town. Just to touch base—"

"Okay, Alec. Thanks for calling and checking on me. I was going to call you, I promise."

"I know that, sweetheart. I'll let you go so you can make your phone calls. Sleep well, and I'll talk to you tomorrow."

"Bye, Alec. See you tomorrow," she said as she hung up the phone. She was looking forward to his visit. The sooner, the better. Taking a deep breath to clear her mind, she called her mother and sister to let them know she'd made it home safely. They were glad to hear from her. Neither her mother nor Angelina was upset with her for not calling sooner. They knew of the road construction delays and expected her drive to take longer than she'd anticipated.

She was tired and decided to head off to bed. Tomorrow was another day and she'd run to the store to restock her refrigerator and clean. Her condo wasn't in too bad of shape— nothing a little dusting and vacuuming couldn't take care of.

Angelina slept for a few hours when she had another terrifying dream. She woke up drenched in sweat and her heart pounding. This was the second night in a row. She sat up in bed and wiped the sweat off of her forehead, pushing her damp hair out of her eyes. Her nightshirt was soaking wet and she was developing a chill. Slowly, she eased off the side of the bed and made her way to her dresser where she pulled out a clean t-shirt and threw it over her head. She looked at the clock and it was only eleven thirty. She needed to talk to someone. Alec said she could call anytime, and anytime was right now.

Alec answered on the third ring. "Hey there, sweetheart.

Miss me already?"

His voice had a calming effect on her and she focused on that.

"Hey, are you there or is this a prank call?" he chuckled.

"No, I'm here," she whispered.

"Hey, are you okay?"

She couldn't find her voice.

"Kelly, are you still there? What's wrong? Kelly?"

She found her voice and started talking. "No, I'm here. I just… I just…"

"What?" he asked.

"Wanted to hear your voice, that's all."

"Are you sure that's all?"

She couldn't say anything else.

"Kelly, honey, what's wrong? Did something happen to you? You know what, I'm coming down there. I'll call my dad and leave now. I can be there first thing in the morning. My dad will be—"

"Alec, I'm fine. I just wanted to hear your voice, really."

Alec didn't say anything. She knew he was worried about her, so she continued, "Alec, come as planned. Tomorrow evening. I'll be fine until you get here. I just miss you."

Alec made up his mind when he heard the quiver and the uncertainty in her voice. He was leaving first thing in the morning. He knew his father would still be up so, as soon as he was done talking to Kelly, he'd call his dad and move up his expected arrival at the clinic from early afternoon to first thing in the morning. Something had happened in the few short hours since he last talked to her.

"Alec, are you still there?"

"Honey, I'm still here. Hey, you never told me the name of the closest hotel."

"I want you to stay here. Please. I need you."

"Okay, whatever you want. I'll be there before you know it. Are you going to be okay now?"

"Yeah, I'm fine," she said as she finally felt her heart slow to its normal pace. That dream had really scared her. She couldn't remember the entire thing, but knew it had been about that night. "Okay. I guess I'll see you tomorrow."

"Tomorrow," he said as he hung up the phone. He quickly dialed his father and arranged for him to cover for him at the clinic first thing in the morning. Alec stopped what he'd been doing, pulled out his suitcase, and threw in whatever he could get his hands on—he'd finish reading his article at another time. He grabbed his laptop and copy of the Lattice Works contract and threw it into his briefcase. He called Joe and told him that their father would be covering for him since he was leaving earlier than expected. The last thing he did before leaving was phone Alejandro. He wanted him to be aware of what had happened. Something had spooked her and Alec felt Alejandro should know, too.

"Hey, it's me."

"Hi, me," said Alejandro. "What's up?"

Alec proceeded to tell Alejandro about his short conversation with Kelly.

"What do you think happened?"

"I don't know. Last I knew, I thought she was going to call her family and then clean. She seemed fine."

"I know Angelina spoke with her and she had no concerns. She'd even told her that you were coming in late tomorrow night."

"Well, plans have changed. I'm leaving now. Dad's going to cover for me first thing. I just wanted you to know. I'll call you and let you know if something's seriously wrong or if she just misses me," he chuckled.

"I doubt that she misses you already."

"One can hope," he said as he ended the call.

ℭ

Kelly didn't sleep the remainder of the night. Every time she closed her eyes, she saw him… Coming towards her. She couldn't deal with the images, so she got up for good at three o'clock and started cleaning. She vacuumed and dusted, changed the sheets on the bed in the guest room, laid out clean towels, cleaned bathrooms, wiped out her refrigerator, mopped the floors throughout. She was just getting ready to wash the windows inside and out, but since it was still dark outside, she decided to sit down for a few minutes.

She'd just poured herself a glass of iced tea when she heard a knock at her door. She wasn't sure if she was hearing things or not—it was just a little after six. She sat and listened, and she heard it again. She wasn't sure whether she should check into it or not when her phone rang. She reached for the phone, answering with an unsure, "Hello?"

"I'm glad you're awake. Open up, it's me."

"What are you talking about?"

"Open your front door, please, and you'll see."

How did he get here so quickly? She'd only just talked to him a little over six hours ago. She practically ran to the door, looked through the peephole, and confirmed it was him. She threw open the door and found herself in his arms before she could take a breath. He held her as tightly as he could. He pulled away slightly and looked into eyes. Deep, dark circles surrounded her eyes; she was pale and looked exhausted as she stood in front of him. What had happened to her in the twenty-four hours that it had been since he last laid eyes on her?

She pulled out of his arms and reached for his hand, dragging him into her condo. She led him into the kitchen and sat down at her kitchen table. She covered her face with her hands, took a deep breath, and scrubbed her eyes with her fists. "Am I seeing things? What are you doing here at the crack of dawn? I didn't think you were coming until late this evening."

"Before I answer your question, what the hell happened since I last saw you?"

She knew she looked slightly disheveled, but didn't think she looked that bad.

"Have you even slept tonight?"

Looking up at him, she stifled a yawn and shook her head, "I've been cleaning."

"I thought you were going to do that today."

"I changed my mind," she said as she reached for her glass of tea. She took a sip, which should have energized her even more, but she just grew wearier. He was here. He would protect her from the bad. "I was just getting ready to wash the windows but realized it was still dark outside so I decided to take a break."

"A break? I think you need more than that. Let's put you to bed."

"No, I'm fine."

"Well, I'm tired and I'd like to take a little snooze. Come on now," he said as he reached for her hand, pulling her to her feet. "Show me to my room. I've been up for twenty-four hours straight and I could—"

She had a look on her face. She looked terrified. He reached up and placed his hand on her cheek. "Sweetheart, what's wrong? You look terrified. I can go get a hotel room. I don't need to stay here. Please tell me what you're thinking."

She couldn't make eye contact with him. She tried to look down at the floor, but his grip on her face prevented it. She looked over his shoulder at absolutely anything else so she wouldn't have to look him in the eye. She didn't want him to see the fear in her eyes. She didn't want him to feel that she was shaking, but she was.

He placed his hand on her shoulder and lowered his head so he was the one looking her directly in the eyes. "Honey, you're shaking. Are you ill?"

She shook her head no.

"Then, what is it?"

She wrinkled her forehead, chewed on her lower lip, and tried to prevent herself from crying. But she finally found her nerve, reached for his hand, and drew him down the hallway towards her bedroom.

He was confused. Was she leading him to her bedroom? He put the brakes on their advance right outside her bedroom. He reached up cupped her face again and said, "Kelly, what's going on here? Just show me to my bedroom." He could tell that she was holding back tears. Her eyes glistened.

"Please hold me. Hold me so I can sleep." She turned away and headed into her bedroom. He could tell that she'd been in bed at some point during the night since her sheets were rumpled. She crawled up onto the bed and looked down at her hands clasped tightly in her lap. "Please?" she said.

Alec sat down on the edge, reached down, and removed his shoes. She scooted over to the other side of the bed when he stretched out, fully clothed. She looked scared but also seemed relieved. He reached for her and she moved into his arms. She laid her head on his chest and wrapped her arm around him. He could tell she'd taken a deep breath, and then she sighed.

She felt like she'd come home. She was protected, and that's all she cared about. She believed his presence would protect her from the horrid dreams she'd been having the last several days.

Alec kissed the top of her head as she settled deeper into his arms. Before he knew it, she'd fallen asleep. He could tell by her even breathing. He watched her for a long time before he was finally consumed by his own tiredness and fell asleep.

He felt like he'd just fallen asleep when he was woken by Kelly. She was getting restless in his arms. When he realized she was in the throes of a dream, he talked softly to her and tightened his arms around her. "Kelly, I'm here. It's okay," he murmured against her forehead. As soon as he tightened his hold on her, she settled down and returned to a peaceful slumber.

Alec laid there with her in his arms. He'd only had about forty-five minutes of sleep when she'd woken him. His mind went into overdrive. All he could think about was what her dreams were about. Was this the reason why she couldn't sleep and had decided to clean? He'd see if she remembered her dreams in the morning.

He became mesmerized listening to her breathing in and out, and the next thing he became aware of was her pulling herself out his arms and getting out of bed.

"Where are you going?" he asked groggily.

She turned back towards him, surprised that he was awake. "I'm going to the bathroom. Then, I'm going to fix a pot of coffee."

"Come back to bed instead. I just want to hold you and talk. Talk about last night."

"Talk about what?" she said as she walked through the bathroom door, closing it behind her. Alec waited for her to return to bed, but she was in there longer than he expected. He was so tired that sleep overcame him again. He woke up to the ringing of a phone, then silence. He looked at his watch and it was almost two.

He pulled himself up from the bed and headed off to the bathroom. He then proceeded down the hallway towards the kitchen. He found Kelly sitting at the kitchen table with the phone to her ear and a mug of coffee sitting in front of her. As soon as she saw him, she stood and poured coffee into another mug. He sat down in the chair while she continued her conversation. He could tell that she was on the phone with Angelina just by the questions she was asking and answering.

"Yep, he made it. Actually, he surprised me coming way earlier than I expected."

Alec watched her as he sipped his coffee.

"I couldn't sleep, so I cleaned."

The back and forth continued and Alec zoned out. The next thing he knew, Kelly was staring at him with the phone at her side.

"Angelina?"

"She wanted to make sure you got here safely. Alejandro told her that you'd left earlier than expected, and she wanted to know why."

He just looked at her.

"What did you tell him?"

Alec looked guilty. "I told him I was worried about you after our call last night and that I had to get to you and make sure you were alright."

She jumped up from the table and went to pour herself another cup of coffee. He shot up from his chair and went to her side. He put his arm around her waist. "I'm here now. Please tell me what's troubling you. I could see it as soon as I walked in here earlier, I could feel it as you slept. Something's happened since you left me yesterday. You're tense, afraid of something or someone. Did something happen to you when you got home?"

She shook her head.

"Then what is it?"

She turned, wound her arms around his waist and held on. She didn't say a word—it was if she were in her own world. Then, she pulled away, filled her coffee cup, and returned to sit at the table. "When's your appointment with Bill?" she asked like nothing had happened and nothing was wrong.

"Where did that come from?" he asked as he returned to his chair. He took a sip of his coffee and tried to stare her down, but she kept looking at her hands clasped in her lap. "Kelly?"

"I'm fine. Really. I just missed you, that's all. It was quiet. I was lonely after being around so many people for so long. I miss the kids. That's all it was. I'm fine now."

He narrowed his eyes at her. He didn't believe a word she was saying.

"Now, I need to get to the store. I have nothing to serve you. After all, I didn't expect you until later—and I mean much later—today," she said as she smiled at him. "If you care to eat, let's get going because I'm starved." She stood and poured the dregs of her coffee down the drain. She turned back to him. "Are you ready or not?"

Alec stood and poured almost an entire cup of coffee down the drain. He followed her as she grabbed her purse and opened the front door. *Wow,* he thought. That was a complete about-face. He wasn't sure what had just happened, but he was going to find out.

# Chapter Twenty-Seven

KELLY TOOK HIM OUT TO breakfast and then they headed off to the grocery store. By the time they got home, she was exhausted. They unpacked and put away the groceries, then Alec grabbed her hand and led her down the hallway to her bedroom.

"Rest, doctor's order," he sternly said with a smile. "I need to make a few calls." He pushed her into her room, turned, and walked away. He knew how tired she was—she'd barely made it through the grocery store without collapsing.

Kelly didn't question his motives. She glanced over her shoulder as she made her way to her bed, mouthing, "Thank you," as she lay down. If he thought she should rest, she would. She was pretty exhausted.

Over the years, Alec had learned to take power naps, and that's how he planned to deal with his lack of sleep from the night before. He'd take a nap once he touched base with Joe and made contact with Bill. He planned on meeting with Bill to set up the details of when Kelly would be returning to St. Louis for the installation of the software. Alec preferred a face-to-face meeting rather than doing it my email.

Alec set up his "office" in Kelly's living room and dialed his brother.

"You need to come home now," Joe said. "Dad is driving me crazy. I don't know how we worked for him all of these years," Joe said, laughing. "He's spending way too much time with the patients. He's making balloon animals, handing out suckers instead of stickers… He's going to kill me."

"He's having fun, Joe. That's how he ran the practice for years."

"Yeah, but suckers?" Joe laughed. "I realize why we have the practice we have today. It's all because of Dad's bedside manner. All of his patients loved Dr. A."

"They did, and we need to continue with his antics. That's why we're liked, too."

"I know. I'm just frustrated that we ran late all day long. I know we don't abide by time constraints, but after today…"

"I'm sure you guys will figure something out. Now, the reason for my call. I'm going to meet with Bill while I'm in Knoxville, and I wondered if you have any concerns?"

"Not with Bill directly. How's Kelly?"

Alec filled him in on why he'd left so suddenly. "She seemed really stressed this morning and then she was fine. I'm not sure what that was all about, but maybe I'll figure it out in time. I'm going to call Bill now, and I'll let you know if I have any issues. I'm hoping we'll have an idea when Kelly will be back in St. Louis."

"Sounds like you've got it all under control, Alec. I've got to go—I think I hear Dad in the hallway making another one of those balloon animals." Alec laughed as Joe hung up the phone.

Alec's next call was to Bill, but he had to leave a message for him to return his call. After Alec hung up the phone, he walked around Kelly's condo. She had a cute place. He loved how she'd filled it with photographs of her family. She also loved throw pillows—they covered all the chairs and sofa, and were in all different sizes and colors. He was looking out the patio doors when he saw a squirrel scamper by in the yard. He opened the door and walked outside. It was a beautiful spring day and he sat down on one of the patio chairs. He watched the birds fly through the yard. It was a peaceful setting. He closed his eyes and drifted off into one of his power naps.

He woke when he felt her hand on his shoulder. He opened his eyes and looked over his shoulder at her. She looked somewhat rested. At least, she looked better than when he'd first arrived.

"Your cell phone was ringing. Sorry, but I couldn't get to it fast enough." She handed it to him and then sat down in the chair directly across from him. "I hope you didn't miss an important call." He glanced at his missed calls and saw that Bill had returned his call. He had a new voicemail, so he assumed it was from him.

"I think it was Bill, and I believe he left a message. I'll check it later." He reached across the table for her hand. "You look rested. Feel better?"

"Yeah, I do. What were you up to while I napped?"

"I spoke with Joe. My dad's driving him absolutely crazy."

She laughed as he explained the antics his dad went through. "You seem to forget that he was my pediatrician, too."

They watched the birds feed at the feeder Kelly had filled that morning.

"So what shall we have for dinner?" Kelly suggested an easy chicken dish that she loved to make where she marinated chicken breasts in a mixture of salad dressings and then rolled them in a bread crumb-parmesan cheese mixture. "I'm also dying for my tomato and pepper dish that I top off with balsamic vinegar. It's also simple and easy to prepare."

"I love chicken and absolutely love both tomatoes and peppers."

They quickly decided on dinner and, while Kelly went inside to begin fixing it, Alec checked his voicemail and returned Bill's call.

Alec's call was screened and, almost as soon as he told Bill's assistant who it was, Bill was answering his call.

"Alec, it's good to hear from you. What can I do for you?"

"I'm in town a little earlier than I expected and was wondering if I could come by and see you tomorrow morning, say ten o'clock? Does that work for you?"

Bill didn't have to think about it and agreed right away.

When Alec was done with his call, he phoned Alejandro at the hospital. Suzie, Alejandro's assistant, answered his line and told him that he was in surgery and would be for the next few hours. "Just leave a message for him that I called. It's nothing urgent. If he doesn't have time today, tomorrow's fine, too."

Alec ran his hand through his hair. *What next*, he thought? He'd spoken with Joe and Bill, left a message with Alejandro... He guessed he'd check in with Kelly and see how she was doing with dinner.

Kelly was standing at the counter making a salad while the chicken was already in the oven. "We've got about forty-five minutes until dinner's ready," she said as she moved to stir the peppers that were cooking on the stove.

"Anything I can do?"

"You can set the table." She pointed to the various cabinets and drawers that contained the plates and silverware.

When he'd finished setting the table, his phone rang again. He stepped outside and looked at the caller ID. It was Ashton. *What does he want?* he thought.

Alec answered. "Ashton, what's up?"

"Hi, Alec. I didn't want you to think I'd blown off our

conversation from the other day."

Alec had no idea what he was talking about, and then it clicked. Alejandro.

"Since I'm off tomorrow, I called Alejandro and we're going to have lunch and discuss everything."

"Oh, that's good. I'm glad that you took our talk seriously and you're making the time to clear the air."

"I appreciate the meeting you and Joe had with me. I knew some of Matthew's background but not everything. Next time, before I react, I'll ask questions."

"You're learning and that's important."

"Now, about your dad..."

"I've heard." Alec said.

They discussed the antics of his father until Ashton's other line rang and he took the call. They'd made a good call when they hired Ashton. He was able to take the criticism and use it to right a wrong. He would work out.

Alec and Kelly enjoyed their dinner and then sat on the couch watching TV the remainder of the night. They channel surfed until it was time to go to bed, and Alec insisted on sleeping in his own room. Kelly seemed fine with it and, when he walked her to her room, he pulled her into his arms and kissed her on the lips. She pulled away and smiled at him as she said goodnight and walked into her room, slowly closing the door behind her.

He turned towards his room, turned on the light as he crossed the threshold, and partially closed the door behind him. He wanted to hear her in case she had another nightmare. He wasn't tired, so he decided to stay up and read one of the journals he brought along on the trip. A nice, comfortable-looking chair sat in the corner, so he grabbed his cell phone and journal and made himself at home. He sat down in the chair and gazed about the room. He couldn't get over the change in Kelly. She was back to her old self. She seemed happy and relaxed.

While Alec waited for Alejandro to call, he finished reading his medical journal. Alejandro must have had a long night in surgery since he didn't return Alec's call. Alec guessed he'd talk to him after his meeting with Bill. He grew tired of waiting on Alejandro and decided to go to bed at around two in the morning.

*C*

Alec slept well and woke at dawn. He decided to go for a run, so he pulled on his shorts, shirt, and running shoes. He left Kelly a note on the kitchen counter.

*Kel,*
*Good morning! I hope you slept well. I'm headed off on a run.*
*I won't be gone long.*
*Alec*

Alec walked out of the house, stretched his legs, and headed off down the street. It felt good to get out and let loose. The sun was just getting ready to rise. He stopped for a moment, jogging in place, and watched as the sun crested the horizon, casting a one-of-a-kind display of color. The orange and pink hues spread across the sky like fingers, and then the orange orb appeared on the horizon. When he ran, he always tried to stop and take in the moment of a sunrise or sunset. It was one of the highlights of his day.

By the time he made it back to Kelly's, the sun was well on its way to crossing the sky. He opened the door and was immediately greeted by the smell of coffee. Kelly was up and waiting for him in the kitchen. He briefly greeted her, placing a chaste kiss on her cheek, and headed off for the shower.

"I'll be right back. I need a shower."

She smiled at him and watched him head down the hall to his bedroom. She loved having him staying with her.

Before she knew it, Alec was walking into the kitchen dressed in a suit and tie.

"Where are you going?" she asked as he poured himself a cup of coffee.

"I have my meeting with Bill at ten. I thought we could enjoy a breakfast on the town first before I have to deal with your boss," he chuckled as he took a sip of his coffee. "The last time I met with him was a meeting I will never forget. So go get dressed—breakfast is on me."

Kelly quickly showered, dressed, and met Alec in the family room. He was on the phone. She signaled to him that she was ready and returned to the kitchen where she rinsed their coffee cups and cleaned out the coffee pot. While she was rinsing, he handed her his cell phone. She looked at him, unsure who was on the other end, when he mouthed, "Angelina."

Smiling, she took the phone and spoke with her sister. Angelina wanted to know how she was and what their plans were for the weekend. "We haven't planned anything yet. I guess we'll talk about it over breakfast." At that moment, the baby started crying in the background.

"I'll talk to you later," Angelina said, promptly ending the call.

Kelly looked at the phone in her hand, scrunched up her face, and said, "She hung up on me."

Alec roared with laughter. She scowled and practically threw his phone at him. He reached for her and pulled her into his arms.

"I guess she needed to go."

"She did, but she didn't need to hang up on me," she giggled. "That's my sister. That's all I can say."

He kissed her forehead and asked if she was ready. She nodded and he grabbed her hand, pulling her from the room. He reached for his briefcase while she grabbed her purse and they headed out the door. They decided to take two cars in case their breakfast went long because he didn't want to be late for his ten o'clock meeting.

They ate breakfast at a restaurant that was directly across the street from Lattice Works. Alec chose his usual—an omelet—while Kelly had waffles. They talked about anything and everything and decided they'd make plans for their weekend that evening over dinner.

He hadn't realized how late it had gotten when he paid the bill and looked at his watch. It was nine forty-five. He had fifteen minutes to get across the street for his meeting. He was glad they'd decided on this restaurant. He kissed Kelly goodbye, jumped into his car, and made it to Lattice Works with a few minutes to spare.

Bill cordially greeted Alec. Instead of meeting in the conference room like they had the last time, they met in his office, just the two of them.

"So, what brings you to Knoxville this fine day?"

"I came to visit a friend and thought I'd stop in to firm up that date for our install."

"Well, Kelly doesn't—" Bill stopped himself. He was about to say that Kelly doesn't start back until Monday. He thought for a moment, then restarted his thought. "Sorry about that, I'm going to have to check with Ken to see if he's firmed up his schedule."

Alec was pretty sure what Bill was about to say—that Kelly didn't start back until Monday. He played along with Bill.

"Why don't you call Ken down here so we can see what he has planned?"

"I'm not sure he's in today."

"Well, why don't we see?   Better yet, maybe we can take a stroll down to his office and meet with him there."

"O-okay," Bill kind of stuttered.  He hadn't alerted Ken that Alec was visiting today.  Alec reached for his briefcase and stood, indicating that he wanted to meet with Ken right then.  Bill stood, grabbed a pad of paper, and led Alec out of his office.  He escorted him down several long hallways and through a set of glass doors marked *IT Department* and directly to Ken Jones's office.  Ken was sitting behind his desk looking at some type of report when Bill knocked on the door.

Ken looked up, surprised to see Bill along with another man dressed in a suit and tie.  Lattice Works operated in a relaxed work environment.  The managers mainly wore khakis and polo shirts, while the worker bees tended to dress casually in jeans.  Ken wasn't sure what was going on.  Rarely did Bill visit him in his office, and never did he bring a visitor with him.  Ken knew he needed to be on his best behavior especially with being on corrective action.  Ken stood to greet Bill.

"Ken this is Dr. Alec Alvarez.  His clinic is one of the first that will receive the new software.  He's trying to set his schedules and wants to know when Kelly Samuels will be available for the upgrade."

Ken wasn't following Bill completely since Kelly wasn't scheduled to start until Monday.  Bill then added, "Kelly Samuels's sister is married to Dr. Alvarez's brother."

Now Ken knew how he should respond.  He wasn't aware of this little piece of information.  He understood the importance of the relationship and knew he shouldn't say anything that would make Alec suspicious about Kelly's return.  As far as he was concerned, Alec knew nothing about her firing.

He stuck out his hand to shake Alec's, and then motioned

for Bill and Alec to be seated in the two chairs that stood in front of his desk. At first, Ken looked Alec directly in the eyes and told him that they were finishing up their testing in the next couple of weeks and were then running a series of regression tests that would take another few weeks. "I would think she'd be available in six to eight weeks?"

"I didn't think it would be that long. What's the delay?"

When Alec questioned him, he seemed nervous and had difficulties keeping eye contact. "There is no delay. We are on target to meet our deadlines. We always do, no matter what is thrown at us."

Well, there was that attitude he'd heard about. "I need to know so I can schedule things on my side. Just when will you know for sure?"

"I think we'll have a better handle on it in the next two weeks." That gave him time to get Kelly back up to speed since she'd been gone for so long. "I'll let Bill know in the next week or so, and he can pass the schedule on to you."

"If that's what it's got to be, then that's what it is. Please keep me updated, though. In fact, I think we should have conference calls at least twice a week so I can stay updated on the progress. And I expect Kelly to be present on these calls as well."

"You are the client," Bill said. "We'll do anything to make sure you're comfortable."

*You'll do that, especially since I wrote specific guidelines into the contract. We'll walk away otherwise,* thought Alec.

Alec walked away from his meetings at Lattice unsure of exactly how he was feeling. He was a little more comfortable with Bill, but there was an undercurrent that he felt with Ken. Maybe it was his posturing or what, he couldn't say. He was going to have to watch what he said to Ken. He was also going to stay attuned to Kelly as she began interacting more with him. He didn't get a good impression of Ken and wondered if he was the true cause for Kelly's job loss. Time would tell.

❦

"Alejandro, I'm glad you could meet me on such short notice," Ashton said as he shook Alejandro's hand. They'd agreed to have lunch at one of the restaurants across the street from the hospital. Ashton had chosen the American Grille as it offered a variety of sandwiches and entrées.

They were shown to a table that overlooked a retention pond. Several Canadian geese swam about the waters. It was a clear and sunny day in St. Louis, and Ashton hoped that feeling would carry through to their lunch meeting. Ashton wanted it to remain a friendly affair, so he immediately started talking about Alec and his decision to visit Knoxville. "I talked to Alec yesterday, and he's in Knoxville."

"Yeah, Alec decided that he needed a little time away from the office since he's been working nonstop, so he's taking the time since my dad was available to cover for him."

"But Knoxville? Does that have anything to do with Kelly?"

Alejandro smiled at Ashton and started laughing.

"It does, doesn't it? Are they dating?"

Alejandro just looked at him and continued smiling.

"Okay, I get the picture. I'll stay out of it."

"Good choice. Alec's my brother and I love Kelly to death, but they have to be the ones to decide what's going on between them. Not me, Angelina, or her mother—only them. When Angelina and I were just starting to date, her mother interfered one too many times and it almost caused a problem between us. It all worked out in the end, but I think Jackie learned her lesson to stay out of her kids' love lives. Angelina and I plan on doing the same thing with Alec. Whatever happens, happens. I know Angelina would like to see them together in a relationship, but either way, we'll be happy for them."

The waiter came by with their drink orders and asked if they were ready to order. They placed their food orders and the waiter left them to their discussion.

Alejandro squeezed lemon into his tea, looked Ashton directly in the eyes, and said, "So what's the real reason behind our lunch? I know you don't want to just talk about Alec and Kelly…"

Ashton took a gulp from his iced tea and then played with the silverware in front of him. Swallowing, he tipped his chin upward, looking unsure. "I wanted to talk to you about Matthew, and how I've acted towards you."

Alejandro nodded, waiting for Ashton to continue.

"First of all, I want to apologize. I should have done a little more research into Matthew's background. I wasn't aware that his parents were killed in a car accident. I also wasn't completely aware of the part you played as his doctor before this happened. I definitely have egg on my face."

Alejandro chuckled.

"No seriously, please accept my apology."

"I do, Ashton. But what I want you to understand is that even though Matthew is now my son, I have a vested interest in his care as a doctor. I am more up to date on some of the tests that I feel should be run on his behalf, and I don't think you should question my motives."

"Duly noted, and I won't question you again. I also want to apologize for the comments I made in front of Matthew about your protectiveness. He was concerned about it, and I guess I fueled it as well. Again, I didn't have all the facts surrounding your wife's death and the problems you encoun-

tered with Angelina. I can understand why you are as protective of your family as you are." Ashton looked down at his
silverware again and started rearranging it. "I have a lot to
learn about your family. One thing I have to say, though, is
your dad's a hoot."

Alejandro roared with laughter. "That he is," he said as the
waiter brought their food.

Both enjoyed their sandwiches. Their conversation
switched to the upgrade of the software at the clinic and the
upcoming christening of Angel. Family meant the world to
Alejandro, and Ashton realized just how important it was to
him. Ashton paid the bill and both men exited the restaurant.
Alejandro stopped Ashton as they approached the hospital. "I
know that took a lot to apologize, Ashton, and I appreciate
the sincerity that you showed. I'm going to consider this
water under the bridge, and I'm sure we can move forward."

"Thanks, Alejandro. I also want to do something for Matthew as well. I know Angelina was concerned about him
being fearful of doctors. I'd like to have a chat with him and
hopefully change his opinion of me."

Alejandro slapped him across the back, "That may take
some doing, but we'll all help Matthew work through it. I'm
sure he'll be fine with it. I'll speak with Angelina and we'll
work something out. Maybe at Angel's christening you can
speak with him outside of the setting of the clinic. He'll see
you as more than a doctor."

"Well, we'll give it a shot."

"I'll make sure Angelina invites you to the christening and
party afterwards. I've got to run—I have office hours that
start in the next fifteen minutes."

"Thanks again, Alejandro. I'll talk to you soon." The men
shook hands and Alejandro jogged off in the direction of the
hospital while Ashton returned to his car.

*That went better than I expected*, he thought. *Now I have to convince an eight-year-old that I'm not the monster he believes me to be*. He chuckled as he started the car.

# Chapter Twenty-Eight

A LEC FOUND A PARK AND decided to follow up with his private investigator Jonas Sounds before returning to Kelly's condo. He hadn't spoken to him recently and wanted to see where he was in his investigation. He found a bench and sat down, dialing Jonas's phone number. He answered on the second ring.

"Jonas, hey. It's Alec here."

"Oh hi, Alec. Before you say anything, I want you to know that I haven't gotten very far in this investigation. I've hit a few road blocks."

"Well, I can share some additional information with you that may help."

"Okay, shoot."

"I know that Ken formerly worked for Trexor. He left there seven or eight years ago. In fact, Alejandro has an in there—he knows Albert Trexor, so if we need to use that, we can. I really feel that there's something not right with him. I'm not sure what it is, but my instincts tell me he has a past that needs investigating. I just don't get a good feeling about him. I just met him for the first time today and, to be truthful, I didn't like what I saw."

Alec had watched Ken closely when they met. He seemed

reluctant when Bill introduced him. Then, when he realized Kelly was related to him by marriage, he opened up. But then when Alec challenged the timeframe, he had difficulties looking directly at him. Ken's eyes shifted back and forth and Alec felt he was looking over his shoulder often during their short meeting. He also picked up on a nervousness about him—like he was hiding something. Ken definitely wasn't personable as far as Alec was concerned.

"Alec, I've known you for a long time. You aren't judgmental, so if you feel something's not right with this Ken Jones, then something must be up. I appreciate the additional information. I'll get right on this, and I'll get back to you as soon as I know something."

Alec disconnected the call and seconds later his phone rang. He thought it might be Jonas calling him back, but it was Alejandro.

"Alec, how's it going?"

"I just met with Bill and Kelly's boss, Ken Jones. Do you really want to know?"

"Of course I do."

Alec gave Alejandro a detailed description of his first encounter with Kelly's boss.

"I just got off the phone with Jonas, and he's going to run with my Trexor connection. I told him to call you directly if he needed your help. But to top it all off, we shouldn't expect to see Kelly for six to eight weeks."

"It's going to take that long?"

"I asked the same question. I think they had both forgotten that I shouldn't know about her firing. They both slipped and caught themselves. I acted like I didn't know anything to see how they would react. Ken made excuses about testing and regression testing, and I just let him go on about it. I'll be honest with you—I didn't get a warm and fuzzy feeling with this Ken."

"Huh," responded Alejandro.

"So I told them I expected twice-weekly conference calls with Kelly in attendance, and Bill's reaction was basically 'You're the client.' What the client wants, the client gets."

"Maybe we need to rethink this."

"No, Kelly's made her decision, and I think I've written enough into the contract that we'll be able to pull it if we need to without repercussion. Let's just see where this goes."

"That's fine. So the real reason why I called…"

"Yeah?"

"I had a little conversation with Ashton today."

"Well, that's good. And?"

"I think we worked out everything. I invited—or better yet told—him to be at Angel's christening where he can turn Matthew around."

"How did he take that?"

"You know, I think everything will work out just fine. We all got off on the wrong foot, and he's made the steps of clearing the air. I think he may be an asset and not the liability that I first thought."

"Coming from you, that's good to hear."

They talked a few minutes longer when Alejandro needed to end the call because he was being paged. "Enjoy your time with Kelly."

"I will," Alec said as he smiled, ending his call.

He walked the remainder of the trail in the park. He needed to clear his head from the meetings—he didn't want his frustration with Lattice to come through the remainder of his time in Knoxville. He wanted Kelly back in St. Louis sooner than the six to eight weeks that he'd been quoted. He also wanted to enjoy what little time he had left with Kelly and not worry about the future. He had to let things unfold at their own pace and deal with them as they came to light.

He didn't understand why they had wavered back and forth on the installation date. Between regression testing being thrown at him and not knowing when Kelly could come home... he was frustrated and worried about her and what she was still working through. She needed to be close to him so he could take care of her and help her come to grips with whatever happened. His feelings for Kelly had grown even stronger since coming to Knoxville. He'd never felt this way before.

&#x1D302;

Kelly wondered where Alec was. She glanced at her watch—it was nearing four o'clock. She was just thinking that his meeting should have been over hours ago when she heard a knock at her door. She walked to the door and looked through the peephole and saw a bunch of flowers staring back at her. She opened the door and Alec presented her with a bouquet. He leaned in, kissed her on the cheek, and pulled her back inside the condo.

"Wow, thanks for the flowers," she said, sniffing them. "Where have you been? I was getting worried."

He pulled her into the family room and sat down with her on the couch. She laid the flowers on the end table while she listened to how he spent his day.

"I had an interesting meeting."

"Really?"

"I met your boss."

"Ken Jones?"

"In the flesh. And I didn't get a warm, cushy feeling either."

She frowned at him.

"He definitely has a high opinion of himself, doesn't he?"

"He does."

"Well, I met with Bill and wanted to get the ins and outs of how the installation would proceed, and that's how I met your boss." Alec didn't want to tell her exactly why he met him, or that she'd be the one to work on his project. If she found out the part he played with her rehiring, she'd never forgive him and that was something that he never wanted to have to deal with.

Kelly jumped off the couch, "Oh, I forgot."

"Forgot what?"

"About my flowers. I was going to get a vase for them," she said as she hurried into the kitchen to fill a vase with water.

He got up and stood in the doorway, watching her. She was beautiful, especially when she had a smile on her face. He walked over to her while she arranged the flowers in the vase. He encircled her waist with his arms, leaning in to kiss the side of her neck.

"What's this for?"

"Just because. I was watching you, realizing how much I'm going to miss you when I go back home."

"You're not going home until Tuesday. We have plenty of time to make memories before you go home. And it's not like it's the last time we'll see one another. I'll be home for Angel's christening. We'll just need to sit down and map out when we're going to see one another. You know there is Skype, too."

"I know. This is all so new to us. I'm just going to miss times like this when I can pull you into my arms and hold you for no reason at all. I'm going to miss seeing the sparkle in your eyes when you're excited about something. I'm going to miss seeing you first thing in the morning and saying goodnight to you every night. I know we've only experienced this a few times, but to me it seems like forever."

"We can still have that, it will just be long distance. We'll work through this. Also Alec, you need to remember that I need to go about this slowly."

"I know that, sweetheart. But I want you to also know that you mean the world to me." He turned her in his arms and kissed her softly on the lips. "Always remember that, no matter what happens." The role he played in her rehiring would always be in the back of his mind. In the event she discovered his part, he hoped she'd remember what she meant to him.

She didn't understand the last part of his comment, but she let it pass. She was enjoying just being in his arms and feeling loved.

❧

Alec and Kelly enjoyed their weekend together. They went on long walks and even went jogging together one evening. As they neared the end of their latest walk, the sun began to set. They stood, wrapped in one another's arms, watching the end to a beautiful day. They were expecting storms later that evening and, as the sun set, it presented a display of color that neither one of them would forget. The clouds in the distance were illuminated. It was a breathtaking scene. "What a way to end the day," she said as she hugged his waist.

He leaned down and kissed her on the forehead.

"It was a beautiful day, and I think it's an omen for new beginnings. I'm really excited for tomorrow."

"I'm glad to hear, and I hope it goes as well as you expect."

They walked arm-and-arm the remainder of the way to her condo. "I'll make reservations for dinner tomorrow night. Shall I surprise you?"

"Yeah, why don't you." As they approached her condo, she

told him she needed to lay out her clothes for the next day. "I need to look perfect, professional. I'm so excited," she said as she opened the door to her condo. "I know its crazy feeling this way, especially with what happened—being fired and all. But to me, this is all about new beginnings. I loved my job. Outside of all the overtime, I looked forward to writing test scripts and seeing if what I expected to happen, happened. If I didn't achieve the result I was looking for, I was able to analyze the issue and recommend how to fix what failed."

He wanted to comment on her dress attire but didn't. From what he saw, everyone dressed casually. He wondered if she really fit into the culture at Lattice especially if she dressed up every day.

While Kelly decided on what to wear, Alec caught up on his email. He laughed when he read the subject line on Joe's latest email: "Come home… I need you." He knew he was making light of their father's presence at the clinic, but this time Joe was bothered by it for whatever reason, or at least seemed like he was bothered. They normally both loved it when their dad filled in. Joe was probably razzing him for taking off without notice. Joe told Alec that they needed to have a word with their father if he continued to fill in for one of them. Joe's rant went on for over a page.

"What are you laughing at? I could hear you all the way into my closet."

"Joe. He's not too happy with my dad right now."

"What did he do now?"

"Ah, nothing out of the ordinary. Dad's just being Dad, that's all.

Alec closed his laptop and turned his attention to Kelly. "Well, are you ready for tomorrow?"

"I am. And I want you to know that I am going into this with my eyes wide open. If I don't like how things are going,

I'm out of there."

"I'm glad to hear that. I want you to know that if this doesn't work out for you this time, I'll help you find something closer to home."

"I don't need your help. If I decide to leave Lattice, I will do it on my own and I will find a job myself—without your or Alejandro's help. Got it? I'm the only one that can take care of myself right now." She needed to prove to everyone that she could stand on her own two feet. She was successful in school and would also be successful in her job. She stopped and looked at him—he looked worried. "I'm sorry. I didn't mean to sound like I'm ungrateful for your support these last few months. I appreciate you being by my side. I just need to be the one in charge here."

"I understand," he said.

"On that note, I'm going to head in for the night. I need to get a good night's sleep since I have to get up so early. I'll see you in the morning."

"Of course. In fact, I'll make you breakfast."

"What, cereal?" she teased as she kissed him on the cheek and headed off to bed.

As he watched her head down the hallway and the door close to her bedroom, he prayed that she never found out about what he'd done. She'd never forgive Alejandro or Angelina and, most importantly, she'd end their relationship. He just knew it.

❦

Alec woke up at four in the morning and couldn't go back to sleep, so he decided to go for a run. He didn't bother to leave a note for Kelly since he didn't plan on being gone too long. He knew she planned on getting up at six, so he'd be back in plenty of time to pour her cereal for her. It was their joke, and he was going to send her off with it playing in the back of her mind.

True to his word, he was waiting for her with an empty bowl and glass of milk when she strolled into the kitchen. He was standing in the kitchen with her apron and chef's hat on, and she burst out laughing. Colleen had given her the chef's hat as a joke at Christmas. In one hand he held the cereal box, and in the other he held a spoon. She sat while he poured the cereal, giggling the whole time. It was just what she needed. She was a tad nervous and Alec put an end to that.

He sat at the table holding his chin in his palm with a huge smile on his face, watching her eat every morsel of her cereal. He loved listening to her laugh.

"I love your laugh," he said.

Smiling at him, she shoved another spoonful of cereal into her mouth.

"What time do you think you'll be home? I want to make reservations for dinner. Make it early since this is my last night, and I want to spend every minute enjoying your presence."

"I'll try and be home by six."

"You call that early? It's your first day."

"Alec."

"Alright, alright. I'll plan on seven."

She stood up and placed her bowl in the sink. She started to wash it, but he stopped her. "Leave it, I'll get it later."

She returned to his side, reached down to grab his hands, and pulled him into her arms.

"Thank you. Thank you for making my first morning a memorable one. Before I leave, I need to get a photo of you in that chef's hat." She went to grab her phone and quickly took his picture, even with a bowl and spoon in his hand. "I'd better be off, wish me luck."

"I don't need to wish you luck. You're going to shine." He opened the door for her and kissed her on the cheek. "You look beautiful, sweetheart. Enjoy your day. Call if you need anything. I'll see you at six."

He watched her walk down the walkway. He prayed that her day went well and that her second tour of duty at Lattice Works would go much better than her first. She was an exemplary employee and should be recognized for all of her efforts.

Alec wanted to do something special for Kelly, so he spent his day shopping. The first thing he did was order a bouquet of spring flowers to be delivered to her office. He wanted her to know that he supported her decision to return to Lattice. Next, he went to the jewelry store and bought her a necklace. He knew this was a first step in showing her how much she meant to him. Indeed, he was falling fast and hard for her.

He chose an eagle charm that had diamonds set into its wings. He wanted her to soar with her new beginnings—he knew she'd shine amongst all of her peers. He researched local restaurants and discovered an Italian place that was family-owned and reminded him of Miss Kelly's.

℃

Kelly was late. Late by his standards, at least. It was six thirty when she walked through the door.

"Sorry," is all she said as she headed into her bedroom. He followed her and stood in the doorway with his hand resting on the doorframe. She threw off her blazer—she'd worn a suit for her first day. He wasn't sure he liked the expression on her face, but didn't say anything as he watched her. She sighed and took a deep breath. She stopped for a second and looked at him. She walked over to him and put her arms around his neck.

"Sorry I rushed right past you. Thank you. Thank you for the beautiful flower arrangement. It made my day. I decided to leave it at work so I can enjoy it and think of you as I work." She leaned up and kissed him. She took the initiative, and he let her. He was really enjoying himself when she pulled away. "I tried to be home early, but I just couldn't get away. I tried, really I did."

"Kelly, don't worry about it. Our reservations aren't until seven and the restaurant is ten minutes away. Why don't you change, and I'll wait for you."

Alec was dressed casually for himself in navy pants and white shirt. He'd elected not to wear a tie, but did wear his signature cuff links. She figured she could get by with a nice pantsuit. When she walked into the family room five minutes later, he held out his hand and drew her close. "Rough day?"

"Yeah, I had to go through orientation again, and I absolutely hated that. Then I got stuck listening to Ken ramble on and couldn't get away. But I just kept thinking about you this morning, and nothing he said got under my skin." She took a deep breath and said, "I'm starved, let's go."

Alec pulled up at Little Italy. They had a valet service which he was thankful for as the parking lot appeared to be full. He jumped out of the car and met Kelly as the valet helped her exit the car. She draped her arm through his and he escorted her through the front door. They were greeted by a cheerful hostess who welcomed them. He gave her his name and she commented on the fact that it was a special evening for them.

"Indeed it is," he said as they followed the hostess to their table. Alec pulled out Kelly's chair while she seated herself. He brushed a soft kiss on her head and then made his way to his seat. Unlike when she walked through the front door only moments ago, she was now glowing. He reached across the table and grabbed ahold of her fingers. "Happy?" he asked.

She nodded and, before she could utter a word, the waiter appeared with their menus.

Alec ordered a bottle of wine to celebrate. The waiter returned and poured a sampling that Alec approved. He watched as Kelly swirled her wine in her glass before taking a sip.

"Fantastic choice," she said as she continued to scan the menu. She shook her head in disappointment.

"What's wrong?"

"No key lime pie or German chocolate cheesecake on the menu."

"That gives us more reason to return to Miss Kelly's."

"It does," she smiled at him and kept perusing the menu. She was starving—it seemed like forever since she'd had lunch with Bill and Ken. She knew Alec wouldn't be happy with her since she really hadn't eaten much of her lunch, on top of getting home late. She wondered what kind of hours she'd work when he went back home. She wasn't going to tell him, that was for sure.

She decided on the lasagna while Alec chose shrimp fettucine. He held her hand while they waited for their salads.

"So how was the first day? Be honest."

"Busy. It felt like I never left. Ariel's on vacation, so at least I didn't have to be graced with her presence."

"Do you think you'll ever be friends again?"

"Not in this lifetime, as far as I'm concerned. I'll be civil to her, but I will never trust her again."

Their salads and entrées were served. They both enjoyed them. "This was good but not quite as good as Miss Kelly's. Next time I'm home, we're going," Kelly said.

"For sure," he said. "Dessert?" he asked as he saw the waiter returning with the dessert tray. She was chewing on her lip, deciding whether or not to have dessert, when he said, "We'll have the tiramisu and two forks."

The waiter nodded and headed off to the kitchen to get their dessert. Alec held her hand until he returned with two desserts that he placed in the center of the table. "I heard this was a special occasion, so I also chose a piece of our famous lemon cheesecake. It's light and fantastic. Enjoy."

"That was kind of him," Kelly said as she tried the cheesecake. "He's right—it is light. Really good," she said as she dug in for another bite.

Alec watched her sample the tiramisu. She looked absolutely beautiful tonight, and she really seemed to be enjoying herself. They finished their dessert when Alec reached into the inside pocket of his jacket and withdrew a jewelry box. He reached again for her hand.

"I want you to remember this day. Remember that I was here with you and we celebrated your new beginning. I want you to always carry with you the happiness you had this morning when you saw me in that chef's hat."

She chuckled.

"No, seriously. I want you to know how much you mean to me. I want you to have something special to mark this day." He handed her the jeweler's box.

She picked up the box lightly and looked at it for a minute. She had tears in her eyes.

"No tears now. This is a happy day."

Smiling, she opened the box. She gasped when she saw the diamond-studded eagle resting on a bed of blue velvet. She smiled at him. "It's gorgeous, Alec. I love it. Will you put it on me?"

He stood, moved her hair aside, and clasped the necklace around her neck. He placed a kiss on the side of her neck and moved her hair back. Leaning down, he kissed her on the lips.

"It looks even lovelier on you."

She picked up the eagle delicately and looked at it.

"I want you to soar like the eagle. Always have faith in yourself and, when you look at it, know that I believe in you and whatever choices you make. You mean everything to me, Kelly and somehow, someway, we are going to make this relationship work."

Kelly didn't know what to say or how she should react to Alec. The necklace was beautiful and his words—wow. *I really had no idea. He wants to make this work and he doesn't even know what happened. What will he think when he knows?* She decided she wasn't going to let her mind go there. She was going to enjoy the rest of the evening.

They left Little Italy and returned to Kelly's condo. Hand-in-hand, they walked through the door. He could tell that her first day had taken a toll on her. Going from not working to working in an environment like Lattice would take some getting used to.

"Go get ready for bed. I'm going to check my phone and email. We'll talk when you're done."

She smiled at him and then raised her necklace to look at the eagle again. "Thank you again for this. It's beautiful." She turned and headed off to her bedroom. She hung up her suit from the day and selected her outfit for the next day. She took off her makeup and dressed in her pajamas. She put on a robe and returned to find Alec shaking his head while reading his email.

"I'm not even going to ask. I would presume by the look on your face that Joe's complaining about your dad again."

"Bingo," is all he said. He moved his laptop aside and raised his hand to Kelly. She grabbed ahold of it and sat beside Alec. He drew her into his arms and held her tightly as she placed her head against his shoulder. "I'm going to miss this."

She nodded into his shoulder.

"Kelly, I'm going to sit down with Joe and my dad and see what we can work out. I will do my best to see if my dad can cover for me at least once, maybe even twice, a month. I figure I could come down late on Thursdays and we'd have the whole weekend together. I'd return first thing in the morning on Monday and miss only my morning appointments. In fact, I think I'm going to try and reschedule some of my appointments so I can spend even more time with you."

"I don't want you to rearrange everything or put your family out for me. You have a job, too. We have so much going for us. We can email, talk, skype. If this relationship means as much to you as it does to me, we'll make it work." She smiled up at him. "We'll figure it out, but we don't have to do it tonight. Tonight, I want you to hold me like you did the night you arrived. I want to carve these memories in stone and remember the way I feel right now. I've never felt this way about anyone, Alec. I know this has pretty much happened overnight, but that's how I feel. I know I have some issues that I need to overcome, but with you by my side…"

"Let's not think about the negatives now. Let's think about how happy we are right this very minute."

She tried to suppress a yawn, but he noticed. "Let's get you to bed."

She agreed and reached for his hand.

"I'll be there in a few minutes. I have a little more to pack. I want to leave when you do tomorrow."

She nodded and left for her room.

By the time he finished packing and joined her, she was sound asleep. He slid into bed next to her and pulled her into his arms. She immediately laid her head on his chest. She felt safe in his arms and, in her sleep, moved as closely as she could.

When Kelly woke the next morning, she realized she'd had one of the best night's sleep she'd had in a long time. Alec had already showered and was waiting for her in the kitchen. His car was packed, and he was ready to head out when she left for the day. He greeted her with the silly chef's hat on and a bowl of cereal in his hand.

"You know, I think I'm going to share that photo of you with your brother."

"You wouldn't."

"Hmm, I think I would," she said as she laughed at him. "I'm going to skip breakfast today—I'm still a little full from last night's wonderful meal."

His eyebrows knitted together.

"Don't worry about me. I'll be fine. Let's go, I'm running late." She didn't want to leave, but she had to. She couldn't be late on her second day and have Ken on her back again. She was going to try her hardest to stay under his radar.

Alec put his arm around her waist as they walked out the door. He could feel her body tense up the further they made their way down the walk. When she opened her car door, he saw tears in the corners of her eyes. "Sweetheart, no tears," he said.

She smiled at him.

"I'll see you at the christening, or maybe even sooner," he said as he pulled her into his arms. She held on for dear life. He put his hands on either side of her face and placed his forehead against hers. "Remember this moment. Remember our time together, and know that these moments are just right around the corner again." He leaned in, kissed her, and didn't want to release his lips from hers. He was going to miss her more than she ever knew. "I'm going miss you, sweetheart. Call me tonight when you get in, okay?"

She nodded her head.

He wanted to tell her he loved her, but didn't think it was the right time. Alejandro had seen it coming well before he'd ever thought about it. He hadn't even been aware that he was developing feelings for her until his brother pointed it out to him and he'd begun to acknowledge it himself. And yes, those feelings had practically blossomed overnight. For him to be thinking that he was in love? Well, that was a minor miracle in and of itself since he'd pretty much declared himself a career-minded bachelor. He hadn't been looking for a girlfriend, and definitely wasn't looking for love, but it had snuck up on him.

When he thought back to Alejandro's wedding, he guessed that's where it all began—from that photograph. Even though he hadn't seen Kelly in some time, he realized now that's when he truly became aware of her. He'd grown to love her as a sister back then, but somewhere along the way his feelings changed from love of a sister to love of a woman who could someday be his wife. He, the confirmed bachelor, never thought his thoughts would drift down this path. Times had certainly changed. He'd seen how happy Alejandro and Angelina were, and now he wanted that for himself—a wife and children and a family that he could call his own.

He hugged her once more and released her from his arms. She got in the car and he closed her door behind her, waiting for her to start the car. She waved at him as she drove away.

She didn't know when she'd fallen in love, but she knew she was in love with him. She hoped he'd give her the time she needed to work through her problems. He didn't see it, but tears were cascading down her cheeks. "I love you, Alec," she said to herself as she pulled away from him.

He knew she was upset with his leaving, but he couldn't help it—he recalled the words that she'd said to him just minutes before. Those words would stick with him his entire drive home. "I'll be fine," she'd said, and he hoped she was right.

# Chapter Twenty-Nine

TRAFFIC FOR A TUESDAY WAS practically non-existent and Kelly arrived at work early. She was shocked when she pulled into the parking lot to only a handful of cars. She glanced at her watch and discovered that she was almost a half-hour early.

Instead of going straight inside, she sat in her car and re-played her first day back at Lattice. She still laughed thinking about Alec standing in the middle of her kitchen in her chef's hat. She pulled out her phone and started searching for a chef's hat online. She was definitely buying him that and an apron for Christmas.

Kelly then moved on to how she felt crossing the threshold of Lattice's front door. She recalled the last time she walked through the door, hearing the security guard's last words: "Don't ever come back here." Well, here she was—actually invited back by the owner of the company. A wave of nerves overcame her when she'd reached the security desk and asked for Bill Lattice.

Kelly hadn't even had the chance to sit down when Bill rushed to greet her. He'd actually pulled her into a hug wel-coming her back.

Bill had led her to HR where she spent the first half of the day attending orientation. She'd hated every minute of it and wished that she could have spent more time with Alec that morning. Her mind had drifted off and she recalled wondering what he was doing and where he was planning on taking her to dinner. Little Italy turned out to be a fantastic choice.

Lunch time arrived and Bill met her in HR at the conclusion of orientation. He insisted on taking her to lunch and escorted her to the IT department where she'd been greeted by Alec's beautiful flower arrangement. The flowers had been sitting in the middle of the desk in the office assigned to her.

Bill had given her a few moments and then returned with Ken. He'd also invited him to join them for lunch.

Bill had already made reservations at the restaurant just around the corner from work. Haynes BBQ was a popular hangout for the lunch crowd. It was almost impossible to get a table without a reservation, especially at lunch time.

They had been shown to their table where Ken had held her chair for her to her surprise. They had a nice lunch enjoying the daily special: burnt ends, french fries and cole slaw. Bill briefly discussed work, but tried to keep the focus of lunch on how good it was that she'd agreed to come back.

Ken had just sat listening to the two of them talk, interjecting only occasionally. They'd wrapped up their lunch and returned to the offices just after one. Kelly thanked Bill for the lunch and headed off towards her office. She'd barely sat down when Ken had come through the office door, closing it behind him.

"I'd like to fill you in on what's happened since you left. I'd like to look at the schedule, so we can plan out a few things. Is that okay with you?"

"Sure, Ken. That sounds great. Do you mind if we open the door? I think it's a little stuffy in here."

Ken had a funny look on his face when he turned to open

her door. Kelly grabbed a pad of paper and glanced at her watch. It was close to one-thirty when Ken started the meeting. She'd been so enthralled with his review on the project that she'd lost track of time. She'd noticed several people stream past her office and glanced at her watch. It was after five at that point, and she'd promised Alec she'd be home by six. Even if she'd left right then, she still wouldn't have made it in time.

Politely, she'd reminded Ken of the time and he'd stopped mid-sentence and apologized. "I'm sorry. You know how I can get when I start talking about a project. I lost track of the time. The last time I looked at my watch it was only four." He'd jumped up from his chair, indicating they'd pick up their conversation the following day. Ken's apology shocked her. Kelly wondered if, in fact, he'd changed since her firing.

By the time Kelly had grabbed her things and said her goodnights, it had been almost five forty-five. She'd made much better time driving home than she expected and rushed through the door at six-thirty.

She recalled the homey feeling she felt knowing Alec had been waiting to greet her. Coming home to him, she felt a sense of hope—a sense of belonging to someone. They were building a relationship together and she was excited that he'd chosen her to travel down that road with him. He was someone she could spend the rest of her life with, and she hoped he felt the same way, too.

Yes, it was still early for them, but she'd known of several friends who'd met, fallen in love, and married within only a few months. She wasn't looking for the wedding bells right now, but she just hoped she and Alec could forge a future together. She still had to get past what happened, but with Alec by her side, along with his patience, she knew they had a chance of finding their happily ever after.

Kelly heard a car door close and glanced at the time. She still had fifteen minutes, but by the time she grabbed a cup of coffee it would be right about the time to start her day.

*C*

Kelly's second day didn't go well at all. She didn't get home until nine, and she was exhausted. Her answering machine was beeping, and she knew who'd called. Alec. He'd called not once, but three times. He'd even left messages on her cell, but she'd turned it off while at work. She didn't want her phone being a distraction especially on her second day back. In his last message, his voice quaked a little. He indicated that he was worried about her and expected her to call him as soon as she got home.

Kelly grabbed a quick peanut butter and jelly sandwich and a glass of milk. She'd just taken one bite of her sandwich when the phone rang. The shrill scared her, causing her to jump and spill milk all over herself. She grabbed a napkin to wipe off her shirt and answered the phone.

"Where the hell have you been? I've been worried."

Tiredly, she sighed into the phone. "I just got home five minutes ago. I had enough time to make myself a sandwich and pour myself a glass of milk, which I just spilled all over myself."

"But where were you? I left messages on your cell, too, but I imagine your phone was turned off."

"I'm just getting home from work, and yes, my phone was off."

"Kelly."

"Kelly what?" she asked.

"Please do one thing for me."

"I can't do it if you don't tell me what you want me to do."

"Please do not, and I mean do not, run yourself into the

ground for this job. It's not worth it."

"Alec, I'm fine. I'm just trying to get back up to speed. A few things have changed and I'm trying to understand. Give me this week, and I promise you I won't work so hard." She started to clean herself up. "Changing subjects, how was your drive home?"

"I had the drive that you had going back to Knoxville. It was hell, and the highway was at a dead-stop at one point because of road construction. Maybe next time, I'll just fly."

"Only you can make that call," she said shortly.

He thought for a minute and said, "Kelly, I'm glad you got home okay. I know you're tired, so I'm going to let you go. You call me when you have some time."

"Alec?"

"I'll talk to you later," he said as he hung up the phone. He hated to be that way with her, but he didn't feel he could talk to her when she was in this frame of mind. He was sure she was starving and just wanted to go to bed.

"Alec?" she said into a dead line. He was gone. He'd hung up on her. This upset her. She'd tried to get home so she could talk to him, but every time she'd tried to gather her things to leave, Ken came by with another request. She lost her appetite and placed her plate on the coffee table in front of her. She curled up in a ball on the couch and tried not to cry. The more she thought about Alec, the more up-set she became. Their relationship was still so new. Add the long distance to the equation, and she didn't want him to fall through her fingers. He was a good thing for her and she'd do everything in her power not to lose him.

Before she knew it, one tear escaped her eyes and trailed down her face, followed closely by another. She reached for a tissue, wiped her face, and clutched it tightly in her hand. Before she knew it, she fell asleep.

She woke with a start, feeling like she was falling. She sat up quickly and shouted, clutching her chest. When she became aware of her surroundings, she realized she was lying on the couch with all of the lights on. Her heart was beating rapidly, and she couldn't catch her breath. She pulled herself up on the couch and covered her face with her hands. *I need to get in control*, she thought. *I need Alec.* She picked up her necklace and concentrated on it. She hadn't taken it off since Alec had given it to her the night before. As she rubbed her fingers across the eagle, she noticed that the diamonds were sparkling up at her. She thought they were sending her a message.

It was one in the morning. She hated to do it, but she had to hear his voice. The phone rang four times before he picked up. She could tell he'd been asleep. She could barely hear his voice when he answered.

"Alec?"

"Kelly, is that you?"

"Uh huh."

"Sweetheart, what's wrong?"

She started crying. "I'm… I'm sorry about earlier."

"It's okay. Why are you crying?"

"You're upset with me."

"I'm not upset—I was worried. There's a difference."

"I guess."

"What's wrong?"

She told him that she didn't know what was wrong. "I woke up and couldn't catch my breath. My heart was beating so fast I thought…"

"Did you have a dream? A dream that frightened you?"

"I don't know. I think I remember falling, and then I woke up. I thought I'd find myself on the floor, but I was still lying here on the couch."

"You mean you're not in bed?"

"I know, I know. When I got off the phone with you I was upset and just curled up on the couch. I fell asleep here."

"You're not going to like what I have to say, but you've only been working for two days, and it seems like you're right back where you left off."

"What do you mean?"

"Kelly, you need to take care of yourself. Angelina told me about the hours you used to keep. You can't do that again. You're going to burn out and—"

"I hear what you're saying. I really do. Just give me this one week, and I'll cut back. I promise."

"Only you can do it, Kelly. Only you."

"I know. Thanks for talking to me. You've settled me down. Good night," she said, hanging up. She didn't give him a chance to say anything.

Alec lay awake until he finally fell back to sleep at dawn. He'd only been gone for two days, and she was starting to fall apart. What was it with this job? He just added another item to his list of things to discuss with Jonas Sounds.

❦

Kelly was busier than ever, working late into the evening every day, and Alec found himself in the same boat. Several of his young patients had been hospitalized and he ended most of his days at the hospital late into the night. He didn't want to wake Kelly, so he often texted her a goodnight message well after midnight. More often than not, though, she had just gotten home when Alec's text came through.

A week passed in which they didn't speak directly to one another. Every night, Alec ended his texts with, "I'll talk to you tomorrow," but tomorrow came and went without either of them picking up the phone.

Kelly found herself exhausted at the end of her second week back at work. Thankfully Friday had finally rolled around, and she made up her mind that she was going to leave early for the weekend. Early for her was normally six o'clock.

As the day wore on, though, Kelly became more and more fatigued. She looked at her watch. It was four o'clock, the time she was *supposed* to be able to go home. She didn't hesitate. She grabbed her briefcase, threw in some test scripts that she needed to review over the weekend, shut down her computer, and grabbed her purse. Just as she was standing with briefcase and purse in hand, Ken walked unannounced into her office.

"Where do you think you're going?"

"Home."

"Your day's not over. You still have another five or six hours ahead of you."

Kelly looked at her watch and glanced up at him. "According to my watch, it's four o'clock and time to go home."

"I think not," he said as he walked right up to her. "Where did you get the idea that four o'clock was quitting time?"

"Ken, my eight hour work day begins at seven thirty and ends at four. I haven't worked an eight hour day the entire time I've been back. I don't have to work more than that, but I choose to. And today, I've decided to go home. Now, if you'll excuse me."

Ken reached out and grabbed her upper arm. "Don't think you will get away talking to me like that. I am your boss, and you will do what I say. If I tell you to work until midnight, you will."

Kelly glared at him, then looked at his hand clutched around her arm. "Let go of me."

"I'll let go of you when you say you'll do exactly what I tell you to do." Ken's grip on her arm tightened.

Kelly tried to pull away, but that only caused Ken to tighten his hold even more, pulling her closer to him. She started to struggle to get away from Ken. A voice in the hallway broke his concentration enough for her to pull away from him. She didn't think twice—she turned and ran out of her office, leaving Ken to watch her run from the room. Several of Kelly's coworkers watched as she ran down the hallway towards the elevators. None of them tried to stop her to see if she was alright.

The next thing Kelly was cognizant of was walking in her front door. Her skin felt tight from the dried tears. She threw herself down onto the couch. *What just happened?* she thought. She was bone tired and just wanted to not work overtime on a Friday night. She recounted her conversation with Ken over and over again in her head. She wanted to call Alec, but she couldn't. She hadn't told anyone about Ken and his treatment of her. No one would believe her—he was Lattice's golden boy.

She curled up on the couch and drifted off to sleep. The memories assaulted her from every direction.

She didn't know how long she'd slept when she was awakened by her chiming doorbell. She thought she was hearing things, but then she heard a soft rap on her door. Pulling herself off the couch, she rubbed her face clean of the dried tears, brushed her hair back from her face, and went to the door. She knew it was late since her apartment was fairly dark— only the light over the kitchen sink illuminated the room. She flipped the light switch on in her foyer and stopped to check who was at her door before she opened it. She glanced through her peep hole but couldn't make out who was at her door. All she could tell was that it was a male figure. She thought of ignoring the visitor, but realized they knew someone was home since she'd turned on the foyer light. Just as she was ready to walk away from the door, the man turned towards the door. As he reached for the doorbell again, she recognized her visitor. She didn't think twice as she threw open the door and ran into his arms. Alec.

"Kelly," he said as he pulled away far enough to kiss her. He could tell right away that something was wrong from the way she held onto him. He pulled away again and looked at her. He could tell she'd been crying—he saw the streaks of dried tears on her face, and her eyes were bloodshot.

"Are you okay? You've been crying," he said as he pulled her closer again. She laid her head on his chest and hugged him tightly.

"Kelly, come on. Let's go inside." He led her inside, closing the door behind him, and headed towards the couch. Never once did she let go of him as they sat down—she practically crawled into his lap. Alec recognized the unusual behavior and smoothed her hair back from her face. Looking her directly in the eyes, he asked her again what was wrong. She drew closer to him but didn't say anything.

It took her a few moments to realize that Alec was truly sitting beside her. She'd needed him desperately, and he had magically appeared out of nowhere. She broke the embrace and then settled herself in the corner of the couch. "I can't believe it. Alec, you're here. Really here."

"That I am," he said. "I hoped to make this visit a surprise, and I can tell I did surprise you… but maybe not in a good way."

"No, I am so happy that you're here. I can't believe that you're sitting here beside me. Why didn't you tell me you were coming? I would have prepared. I would have—"

"Kelly, stop for a second. I want to know what's upset you. I can tell you've been crying."

Kelly didn't want to tell him about Ken—she would work

through that on her own. She knew she could and would. If it got worse, she'd go to Bill. She didn't want to complain, she just wanted to do her job to the best of her abilities. Today, she didn't know what had triggered his reaction to her leaving early.

"Alec, I fell asleep on the couch and had an awful dream. I really can't remember what it was about, just that it upset me. You woke me up when you rang the bell. I'm fine, really. I am." She leaned over and kissed his cheek. "Now, about this surprise… I can't believe you're here. Why the visit? How long can you stay?"

Alec knew Kelly well enough to know that she wasn't being totally honest with him. He decided to let it go for now. In time, he'd find out what upset her. "I decided at the last minute that I wanted to see you. I've missed you. I had a horrible week and, when I got off a little early today, I looked to see if there was a flight available. There was, and here I am." He reached over and drew her back into his arms. "I just wanted to spend a little time with my girl. I missed you so much, especially since we only had time for a few texts this week. I wanted to see you, hear your voice, and just relax with you in my arms."

"That sounds nice. I've had a rough week, too. In fact, I came home early today."

"What time did you get off?"

"Four."

"Four? That's considered early?"

"Indeed, it is. I wasn't feeling my best and decided to take off, especially with it being the weekend. I thought I'd rest tonight and go over a few things tomorrow. I don't know why, but I am just exhausted. I hope I'm not coming down with something."

"You're working too much. I bet you haven't come home

before six o'clock all week."

"Try ten, on average, and you'd be close."

"Kelly."

"I know. I tried to leave on time tonight and Ken had a fit. He thought I should be working until midnight."

"He what?"

Kelly opened her mouth and then closed it again—she hadn't wanted Alec to know about Ken. She must be tired to have accidentally let that slip. She didn't want Alec getting any more suspicious of Ken than he already was.

"Kelly, you can't keep up this pace. You just can't."

"I know. That's why I left early tonight." She laced her fingers through Alec's and squeezed his hand. "I know you think I work too hard. I promise that I will work on cutting my hours back. If I need to work late, I'll start bringing my work home. At least I'll be in the comfort of my own home then."

Alec listened intently to Kelly. He heard what she was saying, but he also heard what she wasn't saying. She was having issues with Ken and she was also falling back into the trap of working an endless amount of hours.

They sat together on the couch, holding hands, when Alec turned to her and said, "Are you feeling any better since you've come home?"

She looked down at their clasped hands. Her hair had fallen back into her eyes. He turned slightly on the couch, raised his right hand to her face, and brushed her hair out of her eyes, securing the wisps of hair behind her ear. He stroked her jaw and tried to look her directly in the eyes, but she wasn't looking at him. He nudged her jaw upward and their eyes finally met. Immediately, he could tell she wasn't herself. "Have you eaten today?" She looked down again. "Kelly, honey, have you had anything to eat today?" He knew what her answer was going to be, so he answered for her. "You haven't, have you? Breakfast maybe, but that's all. Am I right?"

A few seconds passed before she nodded.

"Kelly, that's one of the reasons why you're not feeling well." Alec reached for his cell and scrolled through a list of contacts before he pressed a button.

She wasn't focusing on his conversation until she heard him giving out her address. Then she saw him place his cell on the coffee table.

"I don't know about you, but I am starved. Actually, I have to believe that you are, too. Dinner's on its way. It's going to be about an hour. Go take a shower, put on your pj's, and by the time you're done, dinner will be served." He leaned over, brushed a kiss across her forehead, and stood up, pulling her into his arms. Hugging her tightly, he could feel her weariness. "Go on. Take your shower, and I'll be here waiting for you with my chef hat and apron on." He thought he'd get a chuckle out her, but she just stood there in his embrace. He tightened his hold, then released her and guided her to the hallway that led to her bedroom. He hoped that she wasn't getting sick. That was the last thing she needed.

While Kelly took her shower, Alec decided to set the table for dinner. He went into the kitchen. It appeared as immaculate as always. He grabbed the plates and silverware from the cabinets and set the table. He even found cloth napkins in a drawer. He'd give this meal the feel of being in a restaurant. He located the wine glasses and decided to look in the refrigerator to see if the bottle of wine that he'd purchased the last time he was in town was still there. He pulled open the refrigerator door and stared at the contents. What sat on the shelves of the refrigerator was definitely not what he expected. A loaf of bread, a gallon of milk that had seen better days, and take out container after take out container filled with meals that were barely eaten. He braced his hand along the top of the freezer, closing his eyes and swearing to himself.

*Damn it, what have I done*? He'd practically forced her into taking this job and, by the looks of things, it was running her into the ground. He moved the carryout containers around until he located the wine. Taking a deep breath, he grabbed the bottle and closed the door.

Alec didn't know how to approach her with this. He stood with his back to the entryway, just staring into space. He had to do something. What, he didn't know, but he couldn't let the woman he loved do this to herself. He still didn't know how it happened, but he loved her. Yes, he had to say that he was definitely in love. Why else would he have flown to Knoxville on a whim? He'd been worried about her since he'd returned to St. Louis. He knew she was working herself to death, and he was going to try to put a stop to it.

He wanted to see her smiling up at him with that Kelly-sparkle in her eyes, enjoying life to the fullest. But what he'd seen when she'd answered the door was the same Kelly he'd discovered when her car went off the road: the unhappiness, the tiredness, and yes, the sense that she wasn't herself. She wasn't the Kelly that he'd left just weeks ago. She seemed almost reserved, like she was detaching herself from him and everyone that cared about her. Even Angelina had made the comment to him earlier in the week that she didn't seem herself—she hadn't been able to put her finger on it, but she knew something wasn't right with her sister.

Angelina had found her conversations with Kelly to be one-sided. Normally Kelly asked her questions about the kids, Alejandro, her parents and even herself. Now, it was just Angelina speaking with little input from Kelly. Angelina wondered if Kelly even listened to her because she often asked the same questions over again. Angelina had relayed this to Alec, and that was one of the reasons why he'd hopped on a plane, without thought, to come see her. Yes, he was worried about her.

He didn't realize he'd been standing there for as long as he had until he felt her hand on his forearm. He turned and saw the expression on her face—she was exhausted. She'd removed her makeup while taking a shower and, by doing so, revealed just how tired she really was. Deep, dark circles were under her eyes. Her face was drawn. Lines that he hadn't seen before had formed under her eyes. What had happened to her since he last saw her?

## Chapter Thirty

"KELLY, WHAT'S HAPPENED TO YOU?" he asked as he reached up to brush his fingertips beneath her eyes.

She looked away from him and walked away. She retraced her steps and soon found herself sitting on the couch in the family room. He followed close behind and crouched down in front of her. Placing both hands on her face, he drew her near, looking her closely in the eyes. She couldn't look at him—she knew how she looked. When she'd taken her shower and was drying her hair, she'd really looked at herself. She also wondered what had happened to herself in the last two weeks. She noticed the dark circles beneath her eyes, the fine lines forming out of nowhere. All she knew was that she could barely hold her head up. After her afternoon with Ken, she really started to question her decision to return to Lattice Works, but the only things she had going for her were Alec and those letters of recommendation. She was determined to see the project through, and then she'd make a decision whether to stay or go.

"Sweetheart," he said as he brushed her cheeks with his fingertips. "Talk to me, tell me what's happened. What's troubling you?"

She couldn't form her words. She wanted to look him in

the eyes, but couldn't. She knew he'd figure out what had happened to her eventually.

And then, he looked down. Taking in a sharp breath, he reached for her arm. He'd seen her bruises. "Who did this to you?"

She pulled her arm away and withdrew to the corner of the couch. She didn't want him touching her any longer.

Alec didn't like what he saw. Kelly was withdrawing, pulling herself into a ball in the corner of the couch. He brushed his hand across his jaw. He was still crouched on the floor beside the couch and he raised his arm to touch her, but she pulled even further away from his touch, withdrawing even more. Before he could say another word, the doorbell chimed, breaking his concentration. He watched her for a few more seconds before he stood and headed for the door. His thoughts were all over the place. He had no idea what had happened to her. He was thankful that the doorbell rang when it did—it allowed him to walk away from her before he said something he would regret.

Alec paid the deliveryman for their food and placed it on the counter in the kitchen. When he went to get Kelly, she was gone. He walked down the hallway towards her bedroom. Her door stood open. He rapped his knuckles on the doorframe, announcing his presence. "Kelly," he called out. No answer. He called her name again and received the same nonresponse. He walked into her room. Nothing seemed out of the ordinary. Her bathroom door stood open and he didn't see her. He called her name again and then he heard a faint noise. He started to leave the room, but heard it again. It sounded like she was crying.

The door to Kelly's closet stood ajar. He pulled it open and looked down. There sitting on the floor, hiding behind her clothes amongst her shoes, was Kelly. Alec dropped down in front of her. Her hands covered her face and the streaming tears. He wanted to pull her into his arms, but he didn't know how she would react. He watched her for a few moments before he could no longer stay in this position. He eased himself down beside her, pulling his knees up in front of him. He wrapped his arms around his legs, fearful that he'd upset her more if he embraced her. *What the hell is going on here?* He wanted to scream at her.

He sat with her until she seemed to calm a bit. He reached over and took her hand—it seemed so small in comparison to his. At first, she was tentative holding his hand, but then she was squeezing his hand for dear life. They sat in her closet, holding hands and not saying anything for at least fifteen minutes when she released his hand and tried to stand. She lost her footing and fell into him.

"Damn shoes," was the only thing she said as she made her way to her bathroom. She closed the door, and leaned against it. She didn't understand what was wrong with her. She felt like she was falling apart. On unsteady legs, she made her way to the counter and turned the hot water on. Reaching for a washcloth, she placed it under the stream of water, waiting as it warmed. The warmth of the water as she wrung the washcloth out seemed to bring her back to life. She moved the washcloth along her arms, and then moved it to her face, washing away the remnants of her tears. She turned off the water and looked at herself. She knew that Alec knew something was wrong with her, especially after he saw the bruise on her arm. She couldn't tell him what happened. Just couldn't.

Kelly hung the washcloth up to dry and opened the bathroom door. Alec stood with his hand on the doorframe, blocking her exit. She didn't say a word but just wrapped her arms around his waist and held onto him. He, in turn, held her. They stood in one another's arms until her stomach started growling. Reaching down, he tipped her head up-wards so she was looking him directly in the eyes.

"I think it's time to eat," is all he said as he reached for her hand and led her to the kitchen. He held her chair for her while she sat, and then he pulled the containers from the take-out bag. "I hope Chinese is okay."

"Perfect," she said as she watched him spoon fried rice onto her plate. She reached for a second container that con-tained her favorite dish, Mongolian beef, while Alec topped his rice with cashew chicken. She reached across the table and grabbed the bag that contained crab rangoon and egg rolls. Grabbing one of each, she passed the bag to him. The air was filled with tension. Neither knew what to say or how to act.

Alec tried to eat, but each bite he took made him more nauseous. He stared at his plate for several minutes before pushing it aside. He watched her eat, one bite and then an-other. Thankfully, she was eating something. He had to won-der when the last time she truly ate was.

He was pleased when he saw that she'd eaten half of the food off of her plate. Groaning, she pushed her plate to the center of the table. "I can't eat another bite."

He just looked at her. She'd barely eaten anything as far as he was concerned.

"I can't, really I can't," she said as she stood and reached for her plate.

Alec couldn't formulate a thought. Words just escaped him. Kelly dropped her plate in the sink and that finally brought him out of his trance. He saw her carrying on like nothing had happened since his arrival. She walked over and grabbed his plate from the table, along with the reminder of the food. She placed everything in reusable containers and moved towards the refrigerator.

"I think you need to clean a few things out of there before you can find room for these leftovers," he said, his voice flat.

She glanced at him over her shoulder. She didn't know what to say in response. She walked away from the refrigerator and braced herself against the counter. Lowering her head, she looked at her hands as she clenched the sides of the countertop.

Standing, Alec made his way to her. He stood directly behind her and loosely placed his arms around her waist. Lowering his head, he placed his chin on her shoulder. "I'm sorry. I don't know where that came from."

They stood like this for several minutes when he finally felt her relax. She placed her hands on the tops of his and breathed a sigh. Their moment was interrupted with the ringing of his cell phone. He pulled away and headed to the family room where he'd left it earlier.

Kelly took a deep breath when Alec left the room. *I can do this,* she thought to herself as she grabbed the leftovers and made room for them in the refrigerator.

She'd just finished washing up the dishes when he rejoined her. He grabbed the bottle of wine that he'd gotten out earlier and reached for the wine opener. He didn't know if she wanted a glass, but he certainly did. He popped the cork and turned to get his glass when Kelly lifted two glasses in hand. He poured their wine and looked her directly in the eyes. While on the phone with his father, he decided that she was going to have to be the one to make the first move. She was troubled and he didn't want to scare her. In fact, maybe he shouldn't have surprised her with his visit. But then again, he was glad that he was here. If he'd been home, more than likely he wouldn't have witnessed her mood change. He wouldn't have seen the fear in her eyes, nor seen her shyness as she cowered in the closet. In fact, he wondered what drove her to that. The doctor in him was working overtime trying to diagnose everything that he'd witnessed since she opened the front door. And lastly, he wouldn't have seen the bruise on her arm, the bruise where he could clearly see the markings from fingers. Who had done this to her and why? Should he or shouldn't he ask her what happened? He didn't know what to do. What he did know was that he needed to take things slowly. She'd been working through things before she'd even gone back to Lattice. He wondered if the reason for tonight's behavior was the same reason for the ongoing pain that she was still trying to work through.

She turned and made her way back to the family room. She sat down on the couch and drew her knees up under her. Taking a sip of her wine, she sighed and ran her fingertips through her hair. He knew this was a nervous habit of hers. He chose to sit in the recliner that was adjacent to the couch. Releasing the lever, he raised his legs. He also took a sip of his wine, then placed the glass on the end table beside his chair. She lowered her head and stared into her glass of wine.

Alec broke the silence. "My dad says hello."

She nodded.

"Kelly, please look at me."

She raised her eyes.

"You know, maybe my surprise visit wasn't such a good idea after all. I'm going to call the airline and see if I can get on a return flight tonight."

"No, please don't do that."

"Kelly, I don't know what to do. Someone has hurt you, and I wish you'd tell me what happened. I also know that you are working yourself to death. I have to wonder if going back to Lattice Works was in your best interest. You look like you haven't slept in days. I have to believe by the contents of your refrigerator that you're not eating either."

She didn't say anything.

Alec lowered the leg rest and got out of the chair. "Please talk to me. I want to help you, but I can't if you don't let me in." He could feel her slipping away from him. He'd just come to terms with the fact that he was falling in love with her, and now she was backing away from him again.

He turned his back on her and reached for his glass of wine. The next thing he knew, he felt her hand brush his forearm and reach for his hand. She entwined her fingers with his and squeezed his hand. This was the first move that she'd made towards him and it was a good sign. He turned and looked her in the eye.

Tears were forming in the corners of her eyes and she said, "Don't go. Please don't go. I need you."

Alec moved his wine glass to the coffee table and sat down beside her. She wrapped her arms around his neck and laid her head on his shoulder.

"Just know that I am here for you, Kelly."

"I know, and I appreciate your surprise visit. You just caught me at a weak moment. I don't know what's going on with me. I'm just so emotional today."

"I'm sure it's the exhaustion setting in. You're burning the candle at both ends. You're not eating, and—"

"Alec, we don't need to talk about it. I'm fine physically. What I need from you is what you're doing right now. You're here with me, and that's what I need."

They sat on the couch, drinking their wine, and he listened to her talk about her week. Ariel had returned to the office and it affected Kelly more than she thought it would. Ariel had been her friend, or so she thought, until she'd betrayed her. Ariel thought it was all behind them and wanted to be friends again, but Kelly couldn't forgive her for what she'd done. Her life had blown up in front of her and the only good thing that came out of it was Alec and their relationship.

Alec played with her hair while she described what she'd been facing at the office. Late hours, but also some jealousy from her coworkers when they discovered that she'd been re-hired, and what her new position was slated to be. He hadn't thought this whole thing through, how it would affect her in the long run. Maybe he'd done the wrong thing seeking out Bill.

Kelly started yawning, and Alec took that as his cue that it was time for her to go to bed. "Come on sleepyhead. Time for bed." He stood and pulled her up beside him. He'd already moved his duffle bag into the spare bedroom. He led her down the hallway past his bedroom.

When she reached the threshold, she turned to him saying. "Alec, I don't know why I cowered in the closet, but all I can say is thank you for showing up at my door. I don't know what would have happened without you here tonight." She reached up and placed a soft kiss on his cheek. Pulling back, she told him good night, and he watched as she closed the door behind her.

As he approached his bedroom, the reason for her mood change became all too clear. He hoped he was wrong, but the doctor in him said all signs were pointing to his diagnosis.

☾

Kelly was awakened at three a.m. Her head was pounding. She felt like a set of drums were playing around in her head. As she rose and headed towards the kitchen, she lost her balance, and ran directly into her doorframe calling out an expletive as she made her way down the hallway. As the pain intensified, she clutched the side of her head slowly ambling towards the kitchen. She realized she must have awakened Alec when she knocked into him. He groggily stood in the hallway running his hand through his hair. She somehow noticed, through her pain, that his pajamas were riding low on his hips as he greeted her. She grabbed him around the waist discovering that he was bare-chested and wearing only a pair of bottoms.

"Migraine?" he asked as she leaned into him.

"Yeah. I should have known with how I was acting last night."

"I had a feeling you might be getting one. Come on, let's get your medicine and you can go back to bed."

She leaned against his doorway while he retrieved her a glass of water.

"Where are your pills?"

"My room," she said.

He wrapped his arm around her waist and led her back to her room where he located her pills. She reached for the glass of water that he offered her, took her pills, and settled back into bed. "Stay with me," she said as she covered herself. "Please?"

He couldn't turn her down. He turned off the light in the hallway and made his way to the other side of her bed where he slid in beside her. He reached for her in the dark. She curled up next to him and went to sleep. He hoped that this migraine wasn't as bad as the one he'd witnessed back in St. Louis. He attributed some of her behavior the night before to the beginnings of her migraine, but not all. And there was still the bruise on her arm. He was sure everything that she'd been experiencing the last two weeks, on top of whatever caused the bruise, had led to her migraine.

*C*

Alec woke at six with Kelly wrapped in his arms. He eased his way out of bed and went back to his bedroom where he showered and dressed for the day. He knew she had nothing in her kitchen for breakfast, so he headed off to the corner market to get breakfast makings and a cup of coffee for himself. He'd left her a note but didn't expect her to wake in time to read it before he returned. He knew how the medicine affected her and expected her to sleep well into the early afternoon.

He returned home and made himself something to eat. While he enjoyed his coffee, he texted Alejandro that he was visiting Kelly and that she'd had another migraine.

Alejandro texted back, *You're in Knoxville?*

*I am,* Alec texted. *I'll call you when I get home. Can't talk.*

*Okay,* Alejandro replied.

Alec checked on Kelly several times before she woke around one o'clock. Alec just happened to be leaving her room when she woke.

"You're leaving?"

"I thought you were still asleep. Sorry if I woke you."

"No, you didn't. Hey, you're dressed."

"I am, sleepyhead. It's after one."

"One… one in the afternoon?"

"Yep, sure is."

"Oh my. I'm sorry I slept so late."

Alec approached her and sat down on the side of the bed. He reached out and stroked her cheek. "Feeling better?"

"I am. I still have a little nagging pain, but it's so much better." She reached up and stroked his cheek. "I'm sorry."

"Sorry for what?"

"My behavior last night. I don't know what came over me…" She stilled her hand on his jaw. "Yes, I do. My headache. Oh, Alec, I acted so badly. I'm embarrassed by my behavior."

"There's nothing to be embarrassed about. The only real

concern that I have is this." Alec stroked the bruise on her arm. "I'd like to know where this came from."

She looked down at his hand and made an excuse about running into the door. Alec didn't press her because he knew she wasn't feeling well. He knew the signs of abuse, and someone had abused her. He was sure of it.

# Chapter Thirty-One

KELLY SPENT THE REMAINDER OF Saturday getting over the after-effects of her migraine while Alec caught up on the medical journals he always seemed to be carrying around in his briefcase.

Kelly woke from another nap to discover Alec milling about in the kitchen with her chef's hat and apron on. He got the reaction he'd been hoping for—hysterical laughter on her part.

"I know what I'm getting you for Christmas," she said when she entered the kitchen. He stood with a spoon in one hand and fork in the other. "Did you make dinner?"

"Don't be so surprised. I can cook."

"I know you can, and so can your brother. In fact, Alejandro's probably a better cook than Angelina."

Alec laughed—Angelina had been known to burn a few things.

"Everything's ready, if you are." Alec went to the refrigerator, which he'd cleaned out earlier that morning, and retrieved a bottle of sparkling water. "No alcohol for you tonight," he said as he uncapped the water, pouring them both a glass. He seated her at the table and returned to the refrigerator where he pulled out two fresh garden salads. The greens looked exquisite. He'd topped the salad with tomato, mushroom, and feta cheese. He grabbed a bottle of salad dressing and set it on the table.

"What, you didn't make the vinaigrette, too?"

"Sorry, didn't have time," he said, laughing.

They had renewed their comfort level between the two of them. The tension had flown out the window when she'd awoken with her migraine. Alec had been so kind and caring when he discovered her in the hallway looking for a glass of water. He'd held her as she slept. She knew he had feelings for her or he wouldn't have appeared out of nowhere Friday evening. When she thought about his reaction to the bruise on her arm, she knew that his feelings were more intense than she'd first thought. Alec didn't put into words what he thought, but the look on his face and the way he clenched his jaw told her everything she needed to know about what he was feeling. If she told him about Ken, she worried that he would go to him directly or even seek out Bill. And if he did that in an accusatory way, who knew where she would be? Unemployed again? She couldn't take that. If she was unemployed, it would be because she walked away, not because she was fired.

As they enjoyed their salads, Alec brought up Angel's baptism. "You're still planning on coming home for the baptism, aren't you?"

"Of course I am." Raising her fork and pointing it at him, she added, "We are the godparents." She laughed at the expression he had on his face. "You were asked, weren't you?"

"I was. I just wanted to see what you'd say, that's all. I can't wait to become Angel's godfather. I act in the absence of her father as it is anyway."

"That you do," Kelly said, laughing. "I don't know what's up with you two, but between you and Alejandro I've never

seen a male calm a crying infant as quickly as the two of you."
She lifted a forkful of salad into her mouth, but some of the
vinaigrette missed and trickled down her chin. Alec reached
over the table and used his thumb to sweep the dressing aside.

"Mmm," he said, sucking the dressing from his thumb.
"Yours taste even better than mine." Reaching across the
table again, he swept his finger back over her chin, pulled her
in closely, and kissed her lips. "Yep, yours is definitely better
than mine." Winking at her, he grabbed a forkful of greens
and started chewing. "Now, about the baptism. When do
plan on coming to town?"

"I hope to come home for a week."

"A week?" Alec said. "I'm surprised that you'll be able to
get the time off."

"That's what I'm hoping for, at least. I still have to clear it
with my boss, but that's the plan."

Smiling at her, he rested his chin on his hand and just
looked at her.

"Something wrong?" she asked.

"No, nothing at all. I'm just reviewing the vacation schedule in my head. I don't think either Ashton or Joe have any
time scheduled off. When you know your schedule, let me
know and I'll arrange to take vacation, too."

She reached her hand across the table, grabbing ahold of
his fingertips. "You'd do that for me?"

"Of course I would. I want to spend as much time with
you as I can. What better way than to take advantage of your
time home? I have so much time built up that I can't begin
to use it all. Anyway, it's time for me to unleash Dad on Joe
again. It's been a few weeks. I think it's time Dad drove him
crazy again with his balloon animals and suckers. What do
you think?"

Kelly broke out in laughter. Joe would complain to Alec

nonstop the entire time his father was substituting for him.

Things were back to normal between them and their conversation flowed easily. Alec served the remainder of their
meal—baked chicken, roasted potatoes, green beans, and even
cheesecake for dessert. "I know this cheesecake isn't nearly as
good as Miss Kelly's, but it will do."

"You're right. This is good cheesecake, but nothing will
compare to Miss Kelly's German chocolate cheesecake. Will
you promise me one thing, Alec?"

"Sure, if I can."

"Will you take me on another date to Miss Kelly's so I
can savor another slice of it? I've been dreaming about her
desserts since you took me there."

Alec chuckled again. She loved it when he did that.

"Will you?"

"I don't know." Smirking, he said, "I think you need to
do something for me in return."

"I do?"

"Yes, you do." With that, Alec stood and reached for her
hand. He pulled her from her seat and into his arms. She
wasn't sure what he expected from her. A kiss maybe? And
then he led her into the family room where he pressed play
on the stereo and the room filled with soft music. "May I
have this dance?" he asked as he started swaying with her to
the music.

"That's all you want from me? A dance?"

"I'll start with that," he said as he pulled her closely.

They spent the remainder of the evening in one another's arms, swaying to the music. Every once in a while, Alec
would sneak a kiss. It was a fabulous way to spend their evening, especially after the evening before. The remnants of her
headache had all but disappeared. She was back to her old
self, feeling rested and relaxed.

Sunday passed in a blur and, before she knew it, Alec was preparing for a late-night flight back to St. Louis. "I can't believe you're leaving me already," she said, frowning as he finished putting the last of his clothes into his duffle bag. The room was quiet. All she heard was the zipper closing as he secured his bag. "I don't know what I am going to do without you. I miss you so much when you're not here."

Alec turned and pulled her into his arms.

"I can always get back on track when you're around."

Brushing her hair behind her ear, he said, "Kelly, I don't want to sound like I am ordering you around, but you need to take charge of your life. Don't let Ken walk all over you. You shouldn't feel like you have to work these ungodly hours because you're new again. Who did the work when you weren't there? Someone did, and I'm sure they didn't put in as much time as you do. I know you want to do a good job, but please, don't run yourself into the ground." Moving his hand up to her jaw, he continued. "Kelly, you've come to mean so much to me," he said, stroking her jaw. "I don't like seeing you in the condition you were when I first arrived. No job is worth it. Remember, you've got those letters of recommendation. If you need to walk away, if only for your health, then do it. I'm just concerned that you are starting to develop your migraines again. From what Angelina told me, you didn't have them for a long time and now you're starting to again. I have to wonder why."

Alec rubbed his thumb across her lips, leaned in, and softly kissed her. "Kelly, please think about what I've said."

"I will."

"And, don't forget to let me know when you're coming in for Angel's baptism."

"I plan on talking with Ken tomorrow. I don't think it

will be an issue since I have all of this vacation time."

Alec glanced at his watch and noticed that the time had slipped away from him. "I need to get on the road or I'm going to miss my plane."

Kelly wrapped her arms around Alec. She didn't want to let him go.

"Hey, I'll call you as soon as I land."

She nodded.

"Look at me, Kelly."

She raised her head, looking him squarely in the eyes.

"I will do everything in my power to talk to you on a daily basis. No more texts. I need to hear your voice."

She nodded her head again.

"Got it?"

"I agree. Now, let's get you on the road." Squeezing him as tightly as she could, she added, "Thank you for my surprise. Somehow you knew I needed you... I'll let you know to-morrow about my vacation. I'm sure it won't be a problem." Kelly took the initiative. She leaned in and kissed Alec. "I'll miss you," she whispered against his lips. Pulling away, she reached for his hand while he reached for his bag and brief-case.

"I'll talk to you in a little while." Alec gave her one last hug before heading out the door. He felt good about how he was leaving her, but he was still bothered by the bruise on her arm—he wasn't going to let that go. He'd find out who did that to her, and they would pay for it. No one hurt Kelly. And no one would get by with abusing another person.

☾

Kelly woke Monday morning with the nagging signs of another headache. Alec had texted her the night before that his plane had been delayed and he wouldn't be getting in until very late. He wouldn't call her as he didn't want to wake her. Kelly had worried about him last night. She assumed he'd made it home since she hadn't heard of any plane crashes. She lay in bed a little longer than usual, hoping her oncoming headache would wane. Just as she was ready to get up, her phone rang. Blindly, she reached for it on her nightstand. Maybe if she kept her eyes closed she'd be able to trick herself into believing that her headache was just a figment of her imagination. It didn't work of course.

Almost groaning into the phone she said, "Hello?"

Alec could tell by the tone of her voice that something was wrong. He didn't want to sound alarmed, so he said, "Sweetheart, good morning. Although by the sound of your voice it doesn't sound like a good morning."

"Alec, it's not. I can't believe this but I have another headache. I don't get it. I felt really good yesterday."

"Are you going into work?"

"I'm going to give it a try. If I don't feel any better by lunch, I'm going to have to come home. You know how my medicine affects me." Kelly didn't let Alec reply. "But enough about me, what time did you get in last night?"

"Late. I got home around one."

"You're up early then."

"Yeah. Joe called me last night before I got on the plane. He was at the hospital with one of our patients. I told him that I'd cover for him first thing so he could sleep in a little this morning. So, I'm up early. I'll call you later to see how you're feeling, but please do me a favor. If you do stay all day, come home at your normal time. You don't need to be a superstar. Your body's telling you that you need to take it easy."

"I know that. I promise that if I don't feel any better, I will come home."

Alec paused. "Sorry, sweetheart, I've gotta go. I have another call coming in. I'll talk to you later. Please, no heroics."

They said their goodbyes and Kelly lay there for a few moments longer before she forced her feet to the floor. She said a silent prayer to herself, hoping that she wouldn't end up with another migraine.

Kelly dressed for work and barely made it there before her start time. She'd just sat down at her desk when Ariel came rushing through the door. *I do not need this today,* Kelly thought to herself. Ariel was completely engrossed in herself, going on and on about what a wonderful weekend she'd had. Never once did she inquire as to what Kelly had done.

Finally, Kelly had heard enough. Her head was starting to throb listening to Ariel. "Ariel, don't you think we need to get to work? I know I do."

Ariel frowned and stopped talking. She turned sharply, walking out the door. Kelly breathed a sigh of relief. She looked at the time and it was only seven forty-five. She didn't know how she'd make it through the day, much less make it to lunchtime.

Kelly drafted her memo to Ken, asking for time off. She was giving him almost a month's notice. When she was re-hired, human resources told her that her probationary time was being waived and that she could take vacation time at her boss's discretion. She didn't think she'd have problems getting the time off. She'd checked the vacation calendar and no one in the department was scheduled off.

Kelly had barely hit send on her email when she received a reply.

*My office now*, was Ken's response.

All she could think of on her walk to his office was, *I really don't need this today.*

Kelly knocked on Ken's office door and waited for his approval to enter. She was greeted with a terse, "Sit down." Ken looked angry. His face was red and blotchy. His eyes were pointing lasers at her as she moved to the open chair in front of his desk. She knew she was seriously in trouble, but what for? Her email?

Kelly slinked into the office chair. She hadn't expected this reaction to her vacation request. He began the conversation with no pleasantries and dove right in. "The next time you walk out of this office ignoring my request to work overtime will be the last time that you cross Lattice Works' threshold. Do you understand?"

She didn't know what to say at first and then she remembered Alec's comment about standing up for herself and taking charge of her life. "Ken, I have worked non-stop since I came back, often working until ten or eleven o'clock at night. I wasn't feeling well, so I left. I didn't take sick time, didn't leave early. I left at my appointed quitting time like everyone else. If you have a problem with that, then I will have to consult HR."

She watched him as she spoke. Ken didn't like what she said. He was clasping a pencil in his hand, and she watched as his knuckles grew whiter by the second as he tightened his grip. She thought for sure it would snap in his hands.

She continued, "Now, about my vacation time… I reviewed the vacation schedule and no one is scheduled off the week that I've requested. Also, we are not in a critical phase of testing. So, are you approving my time off or not?"

Ken stared at her. "You will not get away with this."

"What? Taking vacation?"

"You know what I mean."

"I actually don't. Are you approving my time off or not?"

In the end, Ken approved her time. She took a deep breath leaving his office. He certainly had it out for her. She had no clue why he was so upset with her. As far as she was concerned her leaving on Friday was a nonissue. If he kept up this nastiness, she wasn't going to hold back. She'd go to HR and lodge a complaint.

Kelly didn't know how, but she made it through the day and left at four o'clock. By the time she got home, her head was pounding almost as bad as the headache she had in St. Louis. She texted Alec that she was lying down and that she'd phone him when she woke up.

Groggily, she woke at around eleven o'clock and realized that she hadn't called Alec yet. She reached for her cell. She had no missed calls. Surprisingly, he hadn't tried to call her. She selected Alec's number and waited for Alec to answer. He answered on the first ring.

"Honey, how are you feeling?"

"I've been better. I took your advice today and stood up to Ken."

"You did? Tell me about it."

Kelly recounted her conversation with Ken and how she'd stood up to him. "And, I even threatened human resources on him."

"I'm proud of you. Did you get the time off?"

"I did." Kelly rubbed her eyes, "Alec, I think I am going to stay home tomorrow. I need to get rid of this headache, and I think a day of rest will work wonders."

"I'm glad you're listening to yourself. I think you've finally realized that you need to slow down. I'll let you go for now—I'll call you tomorrow."

"Thanks, Alec."

"For what?"

"For believing in me and for giving me the strength to stand up for myself." She wished him a good night and hung up the phone.

Alec came to a definite conclusion while on the phone

with Kelly. He did not like, nor did he trust, Ken. First thing in the morning, he was contacting Jonas Sounds to see if he'd obtained any information on him. Alec did not like how Ken treated her and wondered if he was the one that put the bruise on her arm.

❧

Tuesday dawned in Knoxville with heavy rains. Kelly assumed this was the reason for her headache that still hadn't gone away. It wasn't debilitating, but she was at the point that she needed to stay home. She called Ken's office and thankfully he hadn't arrived in the office yet, so she left a voicemail. She'd already fallen back to sleep when Ken returned her call, leaving a harassing message on her cell phone—she planned on keeping it in the event she had future problems with him. It would be evidence for HR as to how he treated his direct employees. Many thought Ken walked on water since he never missed a deadline but, if needed, she would prove to the powers that be what Ken was truly like.

❧

Alec woke bright and early, and the first thing he did was phone Jonas Sounds. Jonas didn't answer so he left him a message. Alec wanted to know if he'd uncovered anything with Ken's employment with Trexor.

Next, he phoned Kelly. She didn't answer her phone either. He wondered if she was feeling better and had gone into work. He was worried about her—she was getting way too many headaches.

He was zero for two. He hoped his day improved. Alec dressed and stopped by Alejandro's. Both had a scheduled day off. He rang the doorbell and was surprised when his brother actually answered the door.

"Alec, what brings you by today?"

"I knew you had a day off and thought maybe, if you have time, we could do breakfast?"

"That sounds like a great idea. Come on in and let me tell Angelina that I'm going to be going out."

Alejandro disappeared inside and, a few minutes later, Angelina came through the door with Angel in her arms. "Here, you can hold your goddaughter while I get her bottle."

Alec followed Angelina into the kitchen and watched while she prepared Angel's bottle.

"So, I hear you were in Knoxville for the weekend. How was my sister?"

Alec played with Angel's feet, and she giggled at him. The more he played with her feet the more she giggled. "I just love listening to her giggle."

"Are you avoiding my question?"

Alec looked up at Angelina.

"Alec, how is she?"

"You really want to know?"

Angelina frowned, and Alec gestured for her to sit down. "Angelina, I have to wonder if I did the right thing in securing her job for her."

"Why do you say that?"

Alec went on to tell her about her migraine and all of the take-out containers that filled her fridge.

"That's not like her at all. When I talk to her, she's always cooking, or at least she says she is. Maybe her cooking is warming up that take-out."

"I know. I have to be honest with you—I'm worried about her. I talked to her yesterday morning and she had another headache. Maybe she never really was over the one from Saturday, but I don't know. Something's just not right."

"Alec," Alejandro said, joining them in the kitchen. "Did I just hear you say that Kelly's suffering migraines again?"

"Yeah. I have something else to tell you even though I probably shouldn't." Taking a deep breath, he went on, "Please don't let her know that I told you this, and do not—and I stress do not—tell your parents."

Angelina looked at her husband, her eyes wide. Alec stood and handed Angel to her mother. He walked over to the kitchen sink. With his back to them, he took a deep breath. He turned back to them and ran his hand through his hair.

"Out with it, Alec," snapped Angelina. "What happened to my sister?"

Alec started from the beginning. "We hadn't talked all week—only text messages. I was working late and she was too. I got off early Friday and decided to surprise her. I wasn't sure if she was home when I first rang the doorbell since I didn't see any lights on in the house. When she finally answered the door, it was like we hadn't seen one another in years with the way she grabbed onto me. She looked exhausted. One thing led to another, and that's when I saw it."

"Saw what?" asked Angelina.

"The bruises."

"Bruises?" asked Alejandro.

"Yeah, bruises. It looked like someone had grabbed her arms. They were fresh, and I could make out where the fingers wrapped around her arm."

"Oh my," Angelina stuttered as she reached for Alejandro's hand. "What happened to her?"

"She wouldn't tell me. I had ordered take-out when I discovered them. When I returned from paying the deliveryman, she wasn't in the room. You'll never believe where I found her."

Neither Alejandro nor Angelina could formulate the words to ask.

"She was sitting on the floor of her closet, wrapped in a

ball and crying."

"Oh my God, Alejandro. Kelly…" was all Angelina could say before Alejandro interrupted.

"Shh, Angelina. Let's listen to what Alec has to say."

Alec went on to describe what happened in full detail. "I have no idea who hurt her, but I will find out. No one treats anyone that way, especially Kelly."

Angelina looked at Alec. She was surprised with how he spoke of her sister—the utter emotion that came through every time he said her name.

"She almost seemed like a broken doll, and I won't let her feel that way. If I have to, I will go to Bill and break this wide open."

"What are you thinking, Alec?" asked Alejandro.

"I can't be sure. That's why I contacted Jonas Sounds again today. I want to know if he's uncovered anything about Ken and his prior employment with Trexor. From what Kelly described to me, I have to believe he is harassing her to some degree. Do you know that he expected her to work until midnight Friday? Midnight! When she tried to leave early on Friday, or rather at her normal quitting time, he had a fit." Scrubbing his hand across his face, he looked at Angelina. "I wish I wouldn't have contacted Bill. Angelina, it's my fault that she's going through this…"

"Alec, don't say that. Maybe it's just growing pains going back to Lattice and trying to get back up to speed. You know what a perfectionist Kelly is. Maybe it's all her and not Ken."

"I don't know, Angelina. You should have seen her. She was a shell of herself. I didn't know her. I don't normally jump to conclusions, but you should have seen her. I don't want to upset you, it's just that…"

"You love her," Angelina said.

Alec jerked his head up and stared at her. He didn't say

anything.

"You love my sister that's what it all comes down to. Alec, you wouldn't be this upset if you didn't love her."

Alec didn't say a word.

"Alec, neither Alejandro nor I will say anything to anyone. Kelly's smart. She'll figure it out, and if Lattice Works isn't meant for her, she will walk away. After all, she was smart enough to secure those letters of recommendation."

Alec nodded.

"Now little brother, didn't you come by for a breakfast outing?"

"Yes, I did."

"Then let's go."

Alec started to walk out of the kitchen, but Angelina placed her arm on his, stopping him in his tracks.

"She's lucky to have you in her life, Alec. And, if I was a guessing woman, I'd say she loves you, too."

Alec reached out and pulled Angelina into a hug.

"Thanks for being you, Angelina. My brother was pretty lucky when you walked into his life." Alec kissed Angelina's cheek and walked from the room. Alejandro met him at the front door. As they walked down the sidewalk to his car, Alec thought Alejandro was a lucky man when he'd found Angelina. He believed he was pretty lucky in finding Kelly, too. He hoped she had the same feelings for him that he had for her.

# Chapter Thirty-Two

K ELLY SOMEHOW MADE IT THROUGH the week, and late Friday afternoon she was called into Ken's office. She'd seen Bill enter the department and make his way to Ken's office earlier that day. Bill rarely was seen outside of the executive wing, and she wondered what his visit had been about.

Kelly knocked on Ken's closed door. A few seconds later, the door was opened by none other than Bill Lattice himself.

"Hi there, Kelly. Come on in."

Kelly was taken aback when Bill opened the door. *Now what have I done,* she thought to herself.

"Have a seat," Bill said as he pulled a chair away from the table that was situated in the corner of Ken's office. "How are you feeling? I heard that you were out the other day."

Kelly thought it was strange that he was asking her about her health. How did he know she'd been out?

"I wanted to meet with you on Tuesday, but Ken told me you'd called in sick. I had to go out of town, so this is the first chance I've had since then to meet with both of you."

Kelly sat at the table with her hands clasped in front of her. She didn't want to seem closed off to either of them, but she worried about what they wanted.

"I hope you're feeling better."

"I am, thank you."

"I was wondering how things were going since you've returned to the fold? I guess you've settled in like you never left."

"You could say that," Kelly said, mainly referring to the long hours that she was working.

Ken's phone rang as if on cue. He answered it while Bill continued talking to Kelly. "This call is the reason why we called you in here today. As promised when you returned to Lattice, one of your new responsibilities is acting as a client coordinator. With the beta testing complete and our intent to roll-out the new software in the next few weeks, I am assigning you to the first client that will be installing the software. I'm sure that you are quite familiar with him and his clinic."

Kelly looked at him, unsure of who he was talking about.

"Ken, is that him?"

"Yes," Ken said. He'd placed the caller on hold while Bill spoke with Kelly.

"Okay, then. Kelly, you are the expert when it comes to this software, and you come highly recommended by Ken and all of your colleagues. We'll talk further after this call, but I am placing you in charge of our first installation." Turning to Ken, Bill said, "Why don't you bring him on the line. Kelly, you are going to be in charge of bringing Alec Alvarez's clinic on line."

Kelly's eyes widened. She had no idea that Alec was still considering the upgrade with Lattice Works. She knew that they'd met but since Alec hadn't talked about it lately, she assumed it had been taken off the table. Before she could say a word, she heard Alec's voice coming across the line.

"Alec, are you there?" asked Bill.

"I am."

"We've finally gotten to the stage where we can start the pre-installation work. I have our client coordinator on the line with us." Bill didn't want Kelly to know that he was aware of the familial relationship between her and Alec. He didn't want her to think she gotten the job based solely on that. In fact, more than likely, if he'd come up with this plan himself, he would have put her in the position based solely on her performance and job knowledge. He and Alec had previously decided that Alec would act surprised that Kelly was going to be his liaison. Bill hoped Alec could pull it off—he didn't want Kelly to know about Alec's request of her assignment to the project. She could never know that he was behind it.

Bill wanted Kelly to believe he'd been the one to discover the err in her firing. Bill knew Alec didn't want her to know his involvement, and when he looked at the situation wanted Kelly to believe it had been his idea-not anyone else's that kept him looking good in her eyes.

"Alec, I have Kelly Samuels here with us. We have assigned her to your team."

"Kelly, hi there."

"Alec?" Kelly was flabbergasted and didn't know what to say or how to react. Did Bill know that they were in-laws? What she did know was she and Alec would have a talk about these latest developments.

Bill led the discussion. "Kelly, we've chosen you to lead this install because of your proven abilities, but also because it will give you the chance to be home for an extended period of time."

She looked at Bill, not quite following him.

"Kelly, you will relocate back to St. Louis for several months. Alec has elected to have you do all of the pre-installation work at his office. He also wants you to perform all of the on-site training. You will also be tasked with making sure the upgrade performs flawlessly. Based on the success of this install, we will begin to schedule the remaining clients for their upgrade."

Kelly didn't know what to say. The only thing that came to her was, "When do I start?"

Both Bill and Alec laughed while Ken just stared at her.

Alec came back on the line saying he had an emergency and had to cut their talk short.

"We'll talk soon," Bill said to Alec as the call ended.

Ken turned to Kelly and said, "Don't think you're being given preferential treatment here just because your sister is married to an Alvarez."

Both she and Bill were shocked by his comment. Bill made a mental note to speak with him about it. He didn't want Kelly knowing that they knew about her familial association with the Alvarez's. In fact, she'd never disclosed anything about her family except that she was from St. Louis. Bill wouldn't have known about the affiliation if it weren't for Alec pointing it out to him. Bill was afraid she'd figure out why she'd been rehired. Bill had come to know just how valuable Kelly was to their organization and he couldn't lose her or her experience.

Ken continued his rant. "I will be making regular visits to make sure you are staying on task and meeting all of the deadlines that we establish."

"I understand."

"I also expect you to work your same schedule. No slacking because family is involved."

Kelly looked at both men. "Ken, I want you both to know that I had no idea the clinic planned on using Lattice Works' software. I just learned of this relationship on this call, so don't think that I did anything to earn this assignment."

Ken sneered at her, *Yeah, I'm sure you knew nothing about this relationship… That's the only reason you got your damn job back.*

"Kelly, I never thought that," said Bill. "I'm just glad that I can give you the opportunity to spend some quality time with your family outside of work."

"Yes, it means a lot," she said. "Now, when does this assignment begin?"

Ken sat back while Bill made the arrangements with Kelly. In no uncertain terms did he like these plans. In fact, he didn't like the fact that Bill had rehired her at the insistence of Alec to begin with.

Bill told Kelly that he expected her to leave for St. Louis the following week. "It's up to you when you leave. In fact, I'll leave it up to you and Ken to work out the details. I guess the next time I see you will be in St. Louis when we perform the install. I want to be onsite when this baby goes live for the first time. I have all the confidence that this will be flawless. Have a good weekend and safe trip back home." Bill stood to leave and reached out to shake her hand. "I know we've chosen the right person for this."

"Thank you, sir. And thank you for your confidence. I won't let you down."

Bill exited the room and closed the door behind him, leaving Ken and Kelly alone in Ken's office for the first time since he threatened her earlier in the week.

"Don't think you're going to have an easy go of this. I will be watching everything you say and do. One slip up, and you're out of here. This whole idea of you being a client coordinator was Bill's, and since you report to me, I can make or break it for you. Got it?"

Kelly did not like Ken, but she wasn't going to stoop to his level. "If that's all then, I've got to set about making plans for next week. I hope you'll be comfortable with me leaving by next Friday. Sooner, if I can get everything together that I need."

"You can head out of here whenever you want. Just remember, I will be keeping tabs on you."

"Understood," Kelly said succinctly as she stood and left the office. She made up her mind then that she'd move heaven and earth to get to St. Louis sooner rather than later. She'd work all hours of the day and night if it meant her temporary freedom from Ken would come sooner.

Not five minutes after Kelly left Ken's office, his office line rang.

"I am not pleased with your behavior and the way you spoke with Kelly Samuels. I do not, and I mean do not, want her knowing what part Alec Alvarez played in her re-hiring."

Ken's grasp on the pencil in his hand tightened.

"And don't you forget that your ass is on the line. One wrong move by you and you will find yourself walking out of Lattice Works for the last time. Don't think your term of corrective action is over in the next month. You will remain on it until I say you're off it. Understood?"

"Yes, I do," Ken said as he snapped the pencil in his hand and heard the dial tone on the other end of the line. He had had enough of little miss goody-two-shoes... If he was going down, so was she. And he'd definitely make her ride to the bottom an eventful one.

☙

Kelly went back to her desk and started making lists. One was work-related and the other was personal. She needed to make sure she brought everything and anything she needed from the office to make this project go smoothly. The more smoothly everything ran, the less likely Ken would come and visit her. And, if she knew Alec, he wouldn't put up with any of his antics. She worked well past eight. Even though it was a Friday night, she wanted to get out of Knoxville and return to St. Louis by Tuesday, if possible.

Her back was to the doorway of her office, and she didn't hear a noise until she felt a hand come around her face and close over her mouth. She was about to scream when her chair was spun around. Standing in front of her was Ken. He got right up into her face and whispered, "If you think I'm going to let you go, think again. I will make sure that we end what started earlier this year. Don't think that I won't." He leaned in and growled in her face. "Watch your back."

In the blink of an eye, he was gone. If she didn't know better, she'd think his visit was a figment of her imagination. She needed her job, but under what conditions should she remain? She should tell Bill about Ken's harassment, but thought better of it. She wanted to see this project through. She wanted the clinic to receive top notch service and, in her opinion, she was the person to provide it. She wasn't going to let him intimidate her. She'd get through this with Alec's help.

She waited half an hour before she left the offices. She asked for the security guard to walk her to her car in case Ken was lurking in the wings. She was nervous driving home, and she couldn't wait to get inside her house. She nervously looked about her street, looking for unusual cars as she drove up to her house. She didn't see any and thought everything was clear. She hurried from her garage into her house, swiftly locking the door behind her. Blowing out a deep breath, she finally felt safe for the first time in the last hour. Now she had to call Alec. She needed to know what he knew about her becoming his liaison.

Water. She needed a glass of water first. All of a sudden

she was parched. She attributed it to her nerves. She walked into her kitchen and took a glass over to the fridge. She jumped at the sound of the ice dispensing into her glass. She needed to get ahold of herself. She hoped Alec was home. She needed to hear his voice.

❧

Alec's day had gone downhill after he had spoken with Kelly. One of his patients had an asthma attack and had been rushed to the hospital. He'd met the ambulance at the emergency room and treated the little girl, staying until she became stable. He'd admitted her to the hospital for observation to be sure the treatment that he'd ordered had been successful. He hated dealing with asthma attacks, especially when the child hadn't had any signs of asthma before ending up in the emergency room. The look of panic on the child's face brought him to his knees every time. Luckily the father knew the warning signs and had called 911 at the outset of the attack.

By the time Alec got home, he was wiped out and had even forgotten about the conference call he'd had earlier with Kelly. He'd just sat down when his home phone rang. Wiping his hand across his brow, he reached over the end table to answer the call—he really wasn't in the mood to talk with anyone.

He growled a hello into the phone.

"Alec?" said Kelly.

He regretted his tone immediately when he heard Kelly's voice. "Kel, is that you?"

"Yeah. Why did you answer the phone like that? You growled at me."

"Sorry about that. I had a rough afternoon. I had a six-year-old admitted to the hospital with an asthma attack. I met the ambulance and treated her."

Kelly knew the reason why Angelina had fallen in love with Alejandro—his patients meant the world to him. And listening to Alec, she knew he was the same. In fact, their father had made house calls when she was sick as a child. Dr. A would stop by on his way home and examine not only her, but also her other siblings to make sure they weren't coming down with whatever she had. All three of his children, that were doctors, had inherited his bedside manner. She was proud to know each of them.

"Alec, you are just like your dad. He had, and still has, the best bedside manner ever. Joe can attest to that, can't he?" Kelly laughed. Between the balloon animals and suckers, everyone loved him, including his sons.

"Thanks for thinking so highly of me."

"It's true. And I can attest to it, too. You took care of me both times that I had migraines. It wasn't that you felt you needed to—it was because you wanted to. It just comes naturally to you, Alec. And that's one of the things that I lo— like best about you." No, she wasn't going to tell him that she loved him. Not now.

"Are you just getting home?"

"Yeah, I am. After our conference call, Bill told me I was free to leave for St. Louis whenever I was ready. And after dealing with Ken this evening, I can't wait to be out of his hair."

"What happened?"

She didn't want to tell him about how he pretty much attacked her right before she'd left. If Alec knew, he'd go crazy. She just knew it. She had to keep that to herself, at least for the time being. If it got worse, she promised herself that she would go straight to Bill and make him see what kind of employee he had in Ken.

"Ah, nothing. I can deal with him for the meantime. So

I stayed late and made my lists."

"Lists?"

"Yeah, lists. So I don't forget anything. I'm going to get all of my personal stuff together this weekend—put my temporary forwarding order in place at the post office, stop my newspaper, and pack so that as soon as I'm ready, I can come home."

"And when do you anticipate that?"

"Tuesday. I am going to do everything in my power to leave directly from work. And that will be four o'clock at the latest. I'm hoping to finagle a mid-afternoon departure time with Bill."

"Bill? What about Ken?"

"Yeah, I meant Ken," she said. She was going to Bill for this one—if it was up to Ken, he'd have her there until midnight.

"Is there anything I can do to help you? That is, can I have things here for you that you won't have to worry about transporting?"

"No, I'm just bringing my computer, various files, and test scripts—nothing that you can provide. I do have a question for you, though."

"Okay, shoot."

"You didn't have anything to do with me being assigned for your install, did you?"

"Why would you think that?"

"I don't know. Just wondering."

He knew he needed to change the subject, so he did. "Have you called Angelina to tell her the good news?"

"Not yet. I just got home and needed to hear your voice, so I called you first."

"Well, now that you've heard my voice, don't you think you should call her and your parents?"

"I'll call them tomorrow morning. It's getting late and she has the kids to worry about. Mom and Dad are probably out since it's Friday night."

"Okay, then. I better let you go. Oh, I forgot to ask—do you know where you're staying?"

"Bill told me that I could stay with my family if I wanted to. And, of course, I jumped on that. I hope Angelina will let me stay with her. I miss seeing the kids."

"Or… you could stay with me."

"Alec, I'd love to, but I can't. Remember, I need to take this slow. And Bill can't know that we're involved, at least not yet. Just being able to be near you for a few months is a gift. It's the next best thing that I could ask for. We can see one another whenever we want to. No long distance planning needed."

"True. Okay, I agree with everything you just said. Hey, I've got another call coming in. We'll talk tomorrow."

"Yep, sounds good. I miss you."

"I miss you, too." Alec said, hanging up the phone.

He'd lied to her—he didn't have a call on the line. What he'd gotten was a text message from Jonas Sounds. *I'm working on a lead, but I have to go out of the country, unrelated to Ken. Just wanted you to know. I'll call when I return.*

Alec was glad that he was looking into something, but what? He decided he wasn't going to bother Jonas. Kelly was on her way home out of Ken's hands, at least for the time being.

# Chapter Thirty-Three

KELLY GOT UP EARLY SATURDAY morning. She'd had problems sleeping because her mind kept spinning out of control with mental lists of what she needed to do, on top of the paper lists she'd already made. She worried about failing in her assignment, but on the flip side she knew she was the best person for the job. She was excited to be able to spend uninterrupted time with Alec. They didn't have to worry about the long distance commuting between cities— they could focus their efforts on their relationship. She hoped that she could overcome her fears and make their relationship work. She really wanted to, but it seemed like whenever she was walking on the straight and narrow path, she fell off. Her demons always seemed to catch up to her. Her only real worry was Ken, but he would be hundreds of miles away from her. She wondered how often he would come visit her. More than likely he'd harass her with emails, voicemails and text messages. She didn't expect to see him much. It was more a vailed threat than anything else. She was sure of it.

Kelly had pretty much packed everything that she was taking from home by eight o'clock that morning. She was surprised that she was working that efficiently with as little sleep as she'd actually had. She decided to phone her parents first.

She hadn't treated them right when she went home after losing her job. This time, they'd be the first to know that she was coming home for an extended period of time.

Her mom answered the phone as usual—her dad rarely answered. She told her mother about her job assignment, and her mom was thrilled not only for her own selfish reasons, but also for the fact that her daughter would be able to spend time with her beau.

Jackie knew Alec was the one for Kelly just like she'd known Alejandro was Angelina's love match. She wasn't going to press the issue—she'd learned her lesson with Angelina. Time would tell and, for once, Kelly would have time on her side.

Kelly hung up the phone with her mother and immediately dialed Angelina. Surprisingly, Alejandro answered the house phone. "Alejandro, hey. It's Kelly. How are you?"

"Well, and yourself?" Before she could answer, he added, "Any more headaches?"

"I had one earlier in the week, but I'm better now. I have some good news."

"You do?" Alejandro said, like he didn't already know—Alec had called him the evening before with the news.

"I'm coming home."

"Yeah, for Angel's baptism."

"No, I mean I'm coming home for an extended stay. Bill has assigned me to perform the install at the clinic."

"Well congratulations are in order. I guess it paid for you to return to Lattice Works."

"Yeah, I guess so. But the best part is that I'll be home for a couple of months."

"That is good news. Where are you staying? I hope with us."

"Well, that's what I was calling for. I can stay in a hotel, or

I have the chance to stay with family. If it's okay with you, I'd love to stay with you, Angelina, and the kids. I miss them so much."

"Well, they miss their Aunt Kelly, too. I'd love for you to stay, and I know Angelina will be thrilled with the news. She's grocery shopping right now. Do you want me to have her call you?"

"No, I'll call back later. Let this be our little secret until I can speak with her."

"Sounds like a plan. Hey, does Alec know your good news?"

"He certainly does. He was on the call when I found out about my assignment."

"I'm sure he's tickled pink about it. I know he worries about you."

"I know he does. He certainly surprised me last weekend with his trip. I don't know how he knew, but I really needed him. He always seems to know when I'm getting a migraine and he's right there taking care of me. I told him that you all learned your bedside manners from your dad."

"Yeah, he's one of the best. Hey, I'll talk to you later—Angel's crying and we can't have that."

"No, you certainly can't. Get those magic fingers working."

Laughing, he said, "You know I will," and hung up the phone.

☾

Kelly ran some errands and even went into the office. If she could get everything done this weekend, there should be no questions with her leaving Tuesday.

She got home late Saturday afternoon and phoned Angelina. She answered and was thrilled with Kelly's news.

"Now, you are going to stay with us, right?"

"I was hoping you'd be okay with that. I miss you and the kids so much. Oh, and Alejandro, too."

Angelina laughed.

"Just so you know, I've already cleared it with your husband."

"You mean he already knew you were coming home?"

"Yep, but don't get mad at him. I wanted it to be my surprise."

They talked a little longer, and Kelly told Angelina she'd call when she knew the exact day of her arrival. "I can't wait to see you, Angelina."

"Hey, I'm going to make this a surprise for Matthew. He'll get a kick out of seeing you when he comes home from school. That is, if you get here before he comes home."

"I'll let you know when I leave. I promise."

&#x2767;

Kelly got everything accomplished that she needed to, so when she went into work on Monday morning, she was prepared to have a fight on her hands. She wanted to leave bright and early Tuesday morning for St. Louis. She left for the office at six o'clock which was earlier than normal for Kelly. She wanted to get a little bit of work under her belt before having to talk to Ken about her plans since he normally arrived around eight. As she drove into work, she prayed this would be the last day she had to face Ken for a little while.

Kelly pulled into the parking lot at six thirty and was surprised that Ken's car was already there. Groaning, she exited her car. She did not want to have to face him this early. By the look of things, theirs were the only two cars in the lot. As she approached the lobby doors, she wondered if she had made the right decision in coming in early for the day. She'd avoided being alone in the office with him since her return, although he had snuck back in and surprised her Friday night. He'd unnerved her then. She wanted to forget that confrontation, and she was counting the minutes until she didn't have to be in his company. Taking a deep breath, she entered the building and made her way to her office. She thought she could sneak in the back way so she could avoid walking past his office door.

The best laid plans did not go her way. She went around the back, sneaking around the cubicles, practically crawling on her hands and knees to make her way to her office. Just as she was settling into her chair, she heard her office door close. Spinning around in her chair, she was greeted by Ken in all of his glory.

"Are you trying to avoid me? Sneaking in the back way won't get you anywhere. If you didn't want me to know you were here, you shouldn't have worn that luscious perfume that you always do. It's like a bee to honey. It will always draw me in."

He'd never spoken to her that way before. She became extremely nervous. She didn't know what to do—as far as she knew, they were alone in the office. She had to get his mind off of her. "Yeah, I came in early because I want this to be my last day before I head off to St. Louis." Yes, that's right. She'd be all business around him. She'd ignore his comments. "I came in over the weekend and got all of my stuff together, so…"

Ken approached Kelly. He slithered in next to her desk. "Now Kelly, I just don't understand why you want to leave me so soon. I thought we'd have a little more time before you headed off. You know, I can make things a whole lot better for you if you'd just do what I say." Ken eased around the side of her desk. As he neared her chair, he reached for the arms of her chair, roughly pulling her towards him. He'd trapped her. Kelly didn't know what to do. She started trembling. He reached towards her, smoothing her hair along her jawline, grabbing her chin. Her lips started to tremble. She was alone with him, and she didn't know what he was going to do to her.

"Kelly, are you afraid of me? Don't be afraid. I won't hurt you as long as you do what I say. Remember last fall? You shouldn't have run away from me. And what happened next? You paid the price."

Kelly tried to push her chair away from him, but she was trapped by her desk. Before she could react any further, they heard voices from the hallway. Ken whipped his head around. Looking out her office window, he noticed several employees were making their way to their desks. He got down in her face and sneered at her. "Just because you're going out of town for a while doesn't mean you've stopped me. I will have you, Kelly Samuels, and you won't be able to do anything about it. Don't forget, I hold all the cards." And with that, he pulled away. Standing upright, he walked towards the door. Opening the door, he spoke loud enough so the other employees could hear him. In a sickeningly sweet sort of way he said, "Kelly, I can't believe you've gotten everything accomplished so quickly. Why don't you finish up this morning and head out early. You might even be able to leave for St. Louis this evening."

Kelly couldn't believe her ears. He was putting a show on for her peers. He acted as though everything was hunky dory. She was scared… Scared about what he expected of her, and what he would do if she didn't comply. She was thankful that she wasn't going to be in his company for some time. She needed to do something. She should tell Bill, but she didn't want to ruin her chances of going home. She wanted to be successful. She knew she needed to report Ken's behavior, but she didn't want to destroy her career. It meant too much to her. She'd get through this. She would. He wasn't going to harass her. He just wasn't.

As soon as Ken left her office, she stood and closed her door. She spun her chair around so no one could see her through her office window. She needed to calm herself. Taking deep, cleansing breaths, she tried to calm down, but her heart continued to pound in her chest. She worried she was going to begin hyperventilating. And then, her cell phone rang.

Kelly knew who was calling her—he always called this time of the morning, right before she left for the office. He must have tried her home phone before calling her cell. She wanted to answer the phone but decided against it. She let it go to voicemail. If she answered and Alec heard the trembling in her voice, he'd know right away that something was wrong. She needed to avoid him for the time being. He couldn't discover that she was being harassed. He just couldn't.

Kelly was so thankful that she'd come into the office over the weekend. Her preparedness enabled her to leave at lunch time. She packed up her car while Ken was at lunch and left the office. She sent him an email and then said her goodbyes to everyone. Before leaving, Ariel stopped her in the ladies room.

"Kelly, I hear you're going back to St. Louis to run the project for the first install."

"I am." Kelly still hadn't fully recovered from her confrontation with Ken, and Ariel could tell something was bothering her.

"Kelly, are you alright? Is something bothering you?"

Kelly looked at Ariel. Once, she might have shared her encounter with Ken. She often wondered if she was the only one that he targeted with his sexual innuendos. She must be the only one though since he was still employed and no one else seemed to have issues with him.

"You seem upset, not yourself."

"I'm fine. I've just been working really hard to get ready to leave town. In fact, I'm heading out right now, and I won't be back for a while."

"Kelly, I'll miss you. I know you're still upset with me, but I hope you'll be able to forgive me someday. I miss our friendship."

Kelly watched Ariel in the mirror.

"I hope you still have my number. Maybe, if you get lonely while in St. Louis, you can give me a call. We can chat. I can fill you in on all of the office gossip.

"I doubt that I'll be lonely since I'll be with my family." Kelly dried her hands, turned, and opened the door, ending their one-sided conversation.

Kelly hurried to her office, grabbed her purse, and ran out the door, never once looking back. She made it home in record time. It was just after one when she walked through the door. She changed her clothes, threw her suitcases in the car, and fled for St. Louis, forgetting to call Angelina in the process. It had taken her almost an hour to get out the door. After she'd been on the road for almost two hours, she realized she hadn't called. It would take her at least seven hours without stopping to get home. Add in construction traffic and stopping for food, she wouldn't get in until nearly ten o'clock if she were lucky. And, due to her spontaneity with leaving, she'd arrive in St. Louis way too late to disturb Angelina and her family. She thought she could stop mid-way and stay in a motel or drive straight through and hope that she got there at a reasonable time.

Kelly elected to drive straight through, but she got stopped just outside of St. Louis. An accident had all the lanes of traffic tied up on both sides of the interstate. She sat for a little over two hours before she was able to start up again. When she finally pulled into town, it was almost one in the morning. She didn't know what to do. She could sleep in her car... Because of the hour, she knew she couldn't go to her parents or to Angelina's. Without another thought, she pointed her car in the direction of Alec's house. She was almost positive that he would still be up since he was a night owl. She pulled into his driveway and noticed that there were a few lights on in the front of the house. Breathing a sigh of relief, she unfolded herself from her car and made her way to his door. She rang the doorbell and waited, but there was no answer. *Where could he be,* she asked herself. She rang the bell again and still no answer.

Kelly was simply exhausted. It was well after one in the morning now. She was too tired to drive so she got in her car, locked the doors, and drifted off to sleep. The next thing she knew, she heard a tapping on her window. She pried open her eyes and saw Alec staring back at her. Quickly she sat up and unlocked her car door. Alec opened her door and squatted down in front of her. "Kelly what are you doing here? Why didn't you call?"

Kelly flung herself into his outstretched arms. "Oh God, Alec, I am so glad to see you."

"How long have you been camping out in my driveway?"

"What time is it?"

"Almost three."

"Oh, I don't know... A couple of hours maybe."

"Come on now, let's get you inside. Why didn't you call before you came? Or better yet, why didn't you write," he said sarcastically as he helped her into the house.

He led her to the kitchen table where he pulled out a chair

for her. Then he turned and grabbed a couple of glasses. He filled them with ice and water from the fridge. He placed her glass in front of her while he took a swallow of his water and waited for her answer. "Kelly, I didn't expect you tonight. And I don't think Angelina did, either. In fact, I was with both her and Alejandro earlier this evening before I got called into the hospital."

"I forgot to call her."

"You forgot? I can't believe that."

"Well, I did. And then after I'd been on the road for a while, I realized it would be too late to stay with her or my parents. I was going to stay in a motel but decided against it. I certainly thought I would have arrived sooner that I did but then I got stopped in traffic on the highway. An accident had everything backed up."

"You could have at least called me." He looked her directly in the eyes. He could tell something wasn't right again. She looked sad and her face was drawn. For someone who couldn't wait to get home, he couldn't understand why she wasn't thrilled right now.

Alec reached for her hand and squeezed if ever so softly, "Sweetheart, is something wrong? You look sad and, for someone who's been pretty much given a vacation at home, you don't look particularly happy." He pulled her in and gave her a hug. She placed her head on his shoulder and just let him hold her. Pulling back, he brushed his hand on her cheek and said, "Tell me what happened."

Alec knew her too well. She couldn't tell him what happened, so instead she elected to tell him about Ariel. "Can you believe after everything that happened Ariel still wants to be my friend?"

"Yeah, I can."

Kelly glowered at him.

"Well, I can. But tell me, is that what's troubling you or is it something else."

"No, that's it," she said as she reached for her glass of water. He watched her, not believing a word that came from her mouth. He decided to just leave it for the night. He wasn't in the mood for any type of argument. They both needed their sleep.

"Come on now, let's get you to bed. You know where the spare bedroom is, I'll go get you something to sleep in. It's definitely too late to get your suitcase out of the car." She nodded in agreement and headed off to the bedroom she used when he rescued her from the snowbank.

Kelly sat down on the bed, waiting for Alec to return. She didn't want to be alone. What she really wanted to do was settle herself in Alec's welcoming arms and go to sleep. She lay back against the pillows and closed her eyes.

And that's where Alec found her. Sound asleep. He didn't want to wake her. He went to the closet and retrieved a blanket. Carefully, he covered her. Alec didn't want to leave her alone, so he settled in the corner chair and watched her sleep.

As he sat there watching her, he realized that the Kelly he knew would have called someone before she came home, especially since everyone was expecting her. Something wasn't sitting right with him. He decided he wasn't going to interrogate her. In time, he believed she would open up to him, and he would be there waiting for her.

# *Chapter Thirty-Four*

KELLY WOKE UP AROUND FIVE o'clock that morning. She'd only been asleep for two hours when a noise coming from the corner of her room caught her attention. She turned her head and saw Alec sound asleep. His elbow was resting on the arm of his chair while his chin was nestled in the palm of his hand, uncomfortably holding his head in place. She was sure he was going to have a stiff neck. She crawled out of bed and went over to him. She didn't want to startle him awake, so she rubbed her hand across his back. Her gentle touch woke him from his sleep.

"Alec, you can't sleep like that in that chair. Come to bed." She reached out her hand to him. He clasped it and stood. He followed her to the bed where she lay down and moved to the center of it. He crawled in next to her, reached over, and pulled her to his side. She curled up next to him, placing her head on his shoulder and her hand across his chest. In a matter of seconds, he was back asleep. She attributed his ability to fall asleep quickly to the many power naps that he took while he had been in med school. He'd told her he could fall asleep in a matter of seconds and, true to his word, he did.

Kelly wasn't able to follow his lead quite so easily. She lay there, listening to him breathe as he slept. She realized how lucky she was that he'd rescued her that day when she'd slid off the road. From that moment on, they'd developed a closeness that she'd never had with anyone else. Yes, she'd had her fair share of boyfriends, but this was different. Alec got her. He understood what drove her to the extremes with her job. Did he like it? No, and she thought that if it were up to him, she would walk away from Lattice once and for all. For some reason that she couldn't explain to herself, this tour of duty with Lattice was killing her. She was working the same number of hours as before, but for some reason she was having a hell of a time with the demands of the job. She didn't understand why. And, for some reason, she was getting migraines again.

Her migraines had come out of left field. She hadn't had one in almost a year when she got that first one while she was home after losing her job. And since her return to Lattice, she'd had two more within two weeks of her re-hire. The stress of the job was going to kill her. No, it wasn't the stress so much as it was the anxiety she had when she thought about Ken, what he did and what he could do to her. She believed that if she could get through Alec's software installation, she'd be able to walk away with the job experience and the two letters of recommendation in hand. She wouldn't disappoint anyone this time. She was the one in charge controlling her destiny.

Kelly finally fell asleep just as it was time for Alec to wake up. He didn't want to disturb her as she was safely nestled in his arms. He watched her as she slept. Dark circles were again prominently displayed on her face. She looked tired even in her sleep. Something was up with her. He couldn't quite put his finger on it, but he had his own opinion as to what was troubling her. If he was a betting man, he was sure he'd win the lottery. Most assuredly, Ken was somehow involved. He didn't know to what to extent, but he was sure Ken was behind her problems. He'd give it some time and hope that Jonas Sounds would come through with the valuable information he needed.

He was thankful that Bill had encouraged Kelly to arrange her own schedule for her temporary relocation. If it were up to Ken, Alec was sure that he would have kept her tied to her desk in Knoxville. He was happy with himself for pushing Bill so hard with the contract, making him put in writing that Kelly would be his liaison. He'd put himself in control, at least temporarily, of her schedule. He'd make sure that she didn't work herself to death. She'd keep realistic hours and get the necessary rest she needed.

Alec knew he was falling deeper for her by the second. He was constantly worrying about her—she was always on his mind. He needed to guide her down a path that would have her seeing a future. Their future.

Alec looked at the clock. It was almost six and he needed to get up, get dressed and call both Joe and Alejandro. He didn't want to leave Kelly until she woke and had her feet under her. He eased his arms from around her and gently moved her aside as he edged out of bed. He covered her with a blanket and took another look at her before heading off to his shower. He hoped that she would find her way while she was home—decide what was best for her, whether it be Lattice Works or not. But he had to help her see that this way of life was wrong for her. Working non-stop did not prove anything. Yes, she'd moved up the ranks at the company, but at what cost? She was still the capable, skilled woman that had graduated at the top of her class. She didn't need to prove her intelligence to anyone, especially him. Everyone was proud of her accomplishments. She had to see it with her own eyes, believe in herself and take charge of her life again. She'd develop the confidence she once had before what happened at Lattice had damaged her psyche.

Alec quickly showered and phoned Joe.

"What now, Alec?  Please tell me you're coming into the office today."

"About that…"

"Oh no you don't.  Don't sic Dad on me again.  Please tell me that you're not."

"No, I'm not.   But I will be in a little late." Alec went on to tell Joe about his evening and discovering Kelly sleeping in his driveway.

"At least she got home safely," he said.

"I'm waiting for her to wake up, then I'm going to follow her over to Alejandro's and help her get settled.  I'll be in after that."

"Thank God.  I was worried there for a second."  Pausing, Joe added, "How is she?"

"I'm not sure.  She seemed disturbed by something.  She blamed it on a friend of hers, but I'm not sure she was telling me the entire truth.  Joe, I have to be honest with you—I'm worried about her.  I just left her a little over a week ago, and she looks worse than when I left her. She even went through the throes of another migraine.  Something's got to give with her, or I'm afraid she's going to crash."

"Take all of the time you need—Ashton and I will hold down the fort and, if needed, I'll call in reinforcements."

"You mean Dad?"

"What do you think?" Joe chuckled as he hung up the phone.

Next, Alec phoned Alejandro on his cell phone.  It was almost seven and he figured Alejandro was just getting ready to head out the door.  Alejandro answered almost immediately.

"What's up Alec?  This is pretty early for you on a school

day. Normally, you don't call me until seven thirty." Alejandro laughed at his brother. "Only kidding."

"I just wanted to give you a head's up that Kelly showed up here last night."

Alejandro was surprised by his statement.

"I found her asleep in her car around three this morning."

"How did that happen?"

"When I left your house, I got a call from the hospital and went in. When I got home, I found her locked in her car sound asleep. She said she forgot to call Angelina to let her know she was on her way."

"That seems odd, especially with how much they talk."

"Yeah, I know. I tried to call her out on it, but she blamed it on Ariel Layton. You know, that friend of hers that threw her under the bus before she was fired."

"Yeah, I know the name. And?"

"And, what?"

"I sense there's something else."

"I think there is, but I'm not sure. I just told Joe that she looks worse than when I left her. Alejandro, something's just not right here. I can smell it. I hope Jonas uncovers something about her boss. I sense all of her problems stem from him. He's not a very likable character."

"I think I'm going to try and speed this investigation up. If you think something went down while he was employed at Trexor, then I'm going to contact Albert and see if he can shed some light on it."

"Thanks, Alejandro."

"I know she's important to you—" Before he could say any more, he was interrupted by Angelina. "Here, let me put Angelina on and you can fill her in."

Alec spoke briefly with Angelina. She was also surprised that Kelly hadn't called her before leaving.

"Angelina, I think Kelly's awake. I'm going to go check on her. What time should I bring her by?"

"Anytime. I'll be waiting." Angelina hung up the phone and turned to her husband. "Alejandro?"

"I know, I know. I'll talk to her while she's here. Maybe between Alec and I, we can figure out what's going on in that head of hers."

"Thank you," she said as she reached up and kissed her husband on the cheek. "I'd better go finish getting Kelly's room ready. I had planned on doing that after Matthew went to school."

"You know what? You go ahead and take your time. I'm free this morning. I'll take him to school. It will give me a chance to see Mary and maybe even Gabriella."

"Thanks, honey," she said as she headed off to Kelly's room.

❧

Alec was getting ready to make a cup of coffee when Kelly entered the room. "Morning," he said as he went about preparing his cup of coffee.

"Thanks."

"For what?"

"For letting me spend the night here."

Alec turned and walked towards her. He pulled her into his arms. "You don't have to thank me. You're welcome here any time. I just wish you would've waited until today to come up. Driving that late at night…"

"Okay, I got your point. I should have called before I came." She pulled away from him and took a mug out of the cabinet. She handed her cup to him as he prepared the coffee maker for her. Kelly sat down at the table waiting for her cup of coffee. Alec joined her and watched her as she played with the handle on her cup. "When do you want me to come into the office? I can probably be there by nine or so."

"I don't think so."

"Huh?"

"You are first going to take a shower, and then I am going to follow you over to your sister's. You're going to take your time unpacking and then rest."

"But Alec, I need to work. We need to start preparing for—"

"Stop. Listen to yourself. Work, work, work. That's all you seem to think about. What about you, Kelly? What about you?"

"I don't know what you mean."

Alec had heard enough. "I'll be in my office. Come get me when you're ready to go to Angelina's."

She didn't know what she'd done to make him angry with her. Maybe he was just tired after coming home so late and getting up as early as he had. She watched him as he grabbed his cup of coffee and left the kitchen. She stared blankly at her cup for a few minutes, and then finally decided she needed to get moving. She had work to do. She wasn't on vacation. She still had a job. Did Alec forget about that?

Twenty minutes later, Kelly approached Alec in his office. His head was buried in a medical journal. He didn't hear her enter the room until she cleared her throat.

"Ready?" he said tersely. He didn't even glance up from his journal.

"Yes, I am." She left his office, grabbed her purse, and stalked out the door. *What the hell is wrong with him?* she thought as she slammed her car door. She decided not to wait for him. She revved her engine, threw her car in drive, and headed off to her sister's house. Hopefully Angelina would be glad to see her.

Alec didn't know how to compartmentalize his emotions.

Because of that, he didn't even know how to talk to her right now. He heard her zooming down the driveway. He'd give her a head start. Maybe by the time he got to Alejandro's, he'd have a better head about himself.

He was really worried about her. He knew she was so focused on her job that she couldn't see what it was doing to her both physically and emotionally. It wasn't normal for her to fly off the handle like she just did. He loved her and was trying to protect her from herself and the demons she was carrying on her shoulders. Maybe he was totally wrong in going to Bill in the first place. Maybe he should have left well enough alone and let her find her own job. He couldn't dwell on that.

Right now he was too emotional. He needed to take a deep breath and back away, give her some time to settle in at the office. Maybe he'd even speak with his dad—maybe he could shed some light on what she was going through.

His father had known Kelly since she was a baby. It was possible his father might know how to deal with her. Kelly had had the drive to succeed while in school, and she still maintained that drive in business. Alec was too close to the situation right now. Maybe his dad, Joe or even Alejandro could shed some light on what to do—give him the advice he needed. Right now, he should remain open to any and all suggestions on ways to get through to her.

By the time Alec made his way over to Alejandro's, Kelly had already moved all of her things into her room. Angelina greeted him at the door, looking at him questioningly.

"What did you do now?"

"Nothing. Why?"

"Because she came in here all hot and bothered." Shaking her head, she led him to the kitchen. "Alec, why is she so upset?"

"I have no idea. All I said was that she should have waited until daylight to drive up here, and that she should have called someone first. Then I told her she needed to get settled in here and rest before she came into the office. But Kelly didn't like that since she's a workaholic—she wanted to come into work this morning."

"I see," Angelina said. She turned her back on Alec and reached for a dampened sponge, wiping down the countertop.

"What? Now you're mad at me, too?"

"No, I'm not. Just thinking. If that's really all you said, then I don't know why she's acting this way. I have to agree with what you told Alejandro this morning. There is something else going on here." Before either of them could say another word, Kelly walked into the room.

Kelly immediately walked over to Alec and put her arms around him. "I'm sorry. You were right. I should have waited until today to leave, and I should have called someone before leaving. I'm sorry I upset you."

He hugged her back. Sweeping a kiss across her brow, he pulled away. He grabbed her hand and led her to the table where all three of them sat down.

"I just wanted to get home. I got off early, and thought I could make it here at a decent hour. Unfortunately, construction traffic and that car accident delayed me. I'll think before I act next time." She squeezed his fingertips and smiled at him. "Are you happy now?" She thought about how she reacted to Alec on her drive over to Alejandro's. She was wrong with how she treated him. He didn't deserve it—he was just trying to protect her.

He smiled at her. "It's not that I'm not happy—you're exhausted, and driving at that late of an hour without anyone knowing that you were on the road… It could have been you in that accident and we wouldn't have been the wiser."

"I know. I realize that now." She looked at Angelina and smiled at her. "Sorry I didn't call."

"I'm just glad you arrived safely."

Alec gave Kelly another quick kiss and said, "I'd better head off to the clinic. I'm sure Joe's just about ready to kill me. I hope he didn't call in reinforcements yet."

"You mean your dad," said Angelina.

"Yeah. I've heard enough of Joe's complaints lately about dad that I don't think I could stomach another one today." He laughed as he stood and pressed a soft kiss to Kelly's lips.

"Can I come by for lunch at least? My treat."

"Only if you come to eat and not work. Got it?"

"Yeah, I got it. See you at around one."

Alec turned and kissed Angelina on the cheek. Both Angelina and Kelly watched him leave via the back door. "You shouldn't be mad at him, Kelly. He has your best interest at heart."

"I know."

"Then what else is going on? There's something else going on here or you would've called me before you left. What spooked you?"

"Nothing. Why?"

"Kelly, I know you better than that. Alec does, too."

"I'm fine, really I am. I just wanted to get home and see everyone."

"Okay then, if that's really the reason. But I have to believe there's something else." The Kelly Angelina knew and loved would have phoned before leaving Knoxville. Angelina believed her departure was compulsive and not well planned, not that she was already packed and ready to go. Kelly hadn't thought—only reacted to something. What? Angelina wasn't sure. She just knew this behavior was atypical of her sister.

Angel chose that moment to start crying. Angelina left

Kelly sitting at the kitchen table while she went to get the baby. Kelly knew she shouldn't have left when she did—Alec was right. It could have been her in that accident.

# Chapter Thirty-Five

A LEC DECIDED THE MORNING AFTER Kelly's late-night return to phone Bill. Deep down, he had a feeling that Bill knew absolutely nothing about how Ken ran his department. He felt almost sure that Bill was clueless to the demands Ken made of his employees. He wanted Bill to be aware of Ken's standards. He didn't care how long it took Lattice to work through the software installation—he was not going to allow Kelly to work the demanding hours that she did back in Knoxville to make some arbitrary date that Ken or Bill had established. Working these ungodly hours benefitted whom? The bottom line of the company? Alec thought Bill would want to take their time and make sure all of the programs worked correctly by not running his employees into the ground. One would think Kelly's health would mean something to Bill.

Alec didn't hesitate. He picked up the phone and called Bill. He decided to tell Bill everything, from the state of Kelly's health all the way through to their relationship and knowing about her firing. It may make matters worse, but he'd find a way to make Bill understand. They'd both made mistakes: he not being totally upfront with Bill, but Bill also firing Kelly without cause. Bill was a rational businessman, and Alec knew Bill would work through it without too much repercussion.

Alec was put through to Bill right away. He told Bill about Kelly's condition due to her long hours, and he asked that she be given some time off in order to ease herself into work at the clinic. Bill seemed surprised by the hours that she'd been working.

"I had no idea Kelly was working that hard. I thought she put in some overtime here and there, but nothing like you've described to me."

"Bill, I am going to be honest with you. Here's just one example, of what I'm sure are many instances, where Ken has pushed her. From what I understand, Kelly wasn't feeling well one evening and wanted to leave at her normal quitting time. Ken expected her to work until midnight, if needed, to accomplish some task. Mind you, this was a Friday night. He will do anything and everything to make sure he meets his deadlines at the expense of your employees. Kelly was in the throes of a migraine, and I can tell you this because I witnessed it."

"You did?"

"Yeah, Bill. Kelly and I are dating. We have been for some time."

"So, that's why you pushed for me to re-hire her? Because she's your girlfriend?" Alec could hear the growing fury in his voice.

"At the time we were negotiating the contract, she wasn't. And to let you in on something else, I had already known you'd fired her."

Silence ensued on Bill's part.

"And just so you know, I believe you were forced into your decision to fire her by something someone told you. Be realistic here. How could you fire someone for job performance when they've received three promotions in a year and a half? Doesn't pass the smell test, does it?"

"You've got something there. I am looking into that whole debacle. I'm just glad Kelly's back in my employ."

"Not for long if she keeps the candle burning at both ends."

"See to it that she doesn't. I had no idea she was putting in those kinds of hours. Ken shouldn't have expected or allowed it. I will look into that."

"Please don't let Kelly know that I told you any of this. I feel like you and I are on good terms now. I want this installation to be a success, but I also want to see Kelly well and not run-down."

"Thank you for filling me in on what's happening in my own company, Alec. I don't like that you kept this from me, but I can see why you did what you did. I will get to the bottom of this. I promise."

Kelly listened to Alec, slowly easing herself into working at the clinic. In a matter of days, Alec could see an improvement in her appearance. The dark circles underneath her eyes were fading, and she seemed more like the Kelly that he knew and loved—the Kelly he grew to know when Gabriella and Angelina were in college. The Kelly that always had a smile on her face, who easily laughed at anything he said.

☙

One of the conditions to the agreement between Alec and Lattice Works was that there would be conference calls with all of the parties involved on a regular basis. They had originally been scheduled two per week, but they'd been reduced to one a week with Kelly's relocation. Generally, Ken and Bill would contact Alec and Kelly, and they would discuss the progression of the project plan. Kelly would let them know if she was having any problems with the conversion of data or the training, and Ken would often fill her in on the final phases of the rollout.

Normally these calls were held on Wednesday mornings right after Alec got into the office so that they could discuss what had been completed the week before, and then they could go over the plans for the following week.

Alec joined Kelly in the conference room, sat down, and waited for the call from Lattice Works. Alec's back was to the door while Kelly sat opposite him, facing the door. Kelly had just raised her coffee cup to her lips when they heard a knock on the door. Alec was reviewing the project plan and called out for the person to come in. The next thing Alec heard was Kelly's coffee cup crashing to the table, spilling its contents all over her and her work. Alec quickly looked at her, and shock passed across her face.

It had been three weeks since she'd last seen Ken when he'd harassed her in her office. She didn't move while her spilled coffee began to soak into her paper and clothes.

Alec jumped up and turned around to see Ken Jones standing in their conference room. Alec looked quickly from Ken to Kelly, then rushed to grab paper napkins to clean up the mess. Kelly finally reacted to her spill and rushed from the room to wash the coffee from her clothes.

Alec took a long look at Ken while Kelly was out of the room. He was shocked to say the least. Neither he nor Kelly knew that he planned on visiting the office. Ken glanced about the room, taking in his surroundings. He wore the same look on his face that Alec had seen the first time he'd met him in Knoxville. Then, Ken had been surprised to see him, yet this time he and Kelly were the one's surprised.

Alec still didn't have a good feeling in Ken's presence. He carried himself authoritatively—like he was the one who was in charge. Alec didn't like him then and liked him even less now. Alec didn't take well to surprises, and he was definitely surprised today.

"Sorry if I disturbed you," Ken said to Alec as he walked into the room. "I thought you were waiting for our meeting."

"We were. We just didn't expect you in person, that's all." Alec finished wiping off the table as Ken took a seat. A few tense minutes elapsed before Kelly rejoined them. Just as she closed the door, the phone rang and Bill was on the other end.

"Good morning, Bill. Ken just joined us. I had no idea he was going to be here in person."

"I thought I told you that he was. I apologize." Bill was under the impression that Ken had advised Alec of his on-site presence that week. Ken and Bill had discussed a visit, but Bill wasn't aware that he'd actually gone to St. Louis. Bill took the blame for Ken not forewarning Alec of his visit. Now he had another issue to add to the many that kept Ken on corrective action.

Alec looked over at Kelly. She was visibly agitated by Ken's appearance. Her hands were shaking, and she didn't look at him once.

Ken advised them that he was in town for the remainder of the week and would be checking in on Kelly's progress while he was there. Alec didn't like Ken's demeanor and spoke up immediately. "Just so you know, Ken, this office is only open from nine to five. Don't expect to find us here outside of those hours."

"But we need to make sure we stay on track—"

"We are on track, and I don't need you telling me how to run my business. Quite frankly, if you don't like it, you can go back to Knoxville. We were doing fine before your graced us with your presence."

Ken stared at him, his features settling into a glare. They quickly went through the project plan ending the call in less than fifteen minutes.

"Now, I need to go and get back to my patients. Kelly, can you show Ken where you're working?"

She nodded and stood, grabbing her things. She led Ken down the hallway, away from the conference room and Alec's office.

Once they were in her office, Ken closed the door.

"What was that all about? You work for Lattice Works, not Alec Alvarez. We pay you. You will do as I say. You will put in the time that I say you will. This will be installed on-time and without delay. Got it?"

Kelly shied away from him and sat down in her chair. What she really wanted to do was run and put her arms around Alec—he'd make her feel safe. Thankfully Ken's cell rang and he needed to phone a client.

"I'll be back tomorrow, and you better have made progress on these tasks." Ken turned and walked out the door, closing it behind him.

She was shaking and mentally exhausted from his visit. She was shocked to say the least. She had been just as surprised as Alec when Ken stood in the doorway. She'd been feeling really good of late. She knew she looked better—her dark circles had faded from underneath her eyes. She was calmer and was enjoying her job. Then, Ken appeared and she felt the acid start to churn in her stomach. She'd become nervous and felt her heart rate accelerate. Thankfully, Alec had been present, so he couldn't pull any shenanigans. That was, until she was alone with him and then he started in with the deadlines and working late again. She could almost feel the dark circles reappearing beneath her eyes. Her worst nightmare had reappeared, and she didn't know how she could get away from him. She'd left Knoxville for her safe haven of St. Louis, but now he was here and she had nowhere to escape.

☾

Twenty minutes later, Alec went to her office. His patient had cancelled and he had a few moments free. He knocked on her office door and didn't wait for her to respond—he'd seen Ken leave the building, so he knew she was alone. What he found hurt him to the core. Kelly was sitting in her chair with her head in her hands. He rushed to her side. "Sweetheart, what's wrong? What happened?"

"Nothing. I'm fine."

"No, you're not. What did he do to you?"

"Nothing. I'm okay. I just needed a minute before I got back to work."

Alec noticed her hands. No matter how hard she tried to hide it, her hands were still trembling. She couldn't look him in the eye. She automatically reached for her project plan and started going through it line by line. Alec just watched her. He couldn't take her silence a second longer—he pulled the report out from under her hand. His move startled her and she jumped in her chair.

"What the hell happened here, Kelly? Your hands are trembling. Did he hurt you?"

"No, it's nothing. My hands shake like this until I get my coffee fix for the day."

Alec knelt in front of her chair. He placed his hand on her knee—he didn't want to upset her any more than she already was.

"Really Alec, I'm fine. I'm just a little tired. Angel kept the entire house up last night screaming at the top of her lungs. Even Alejandro's magical fingers couldn't quiet her down," Kelly laughed nervously.

Alec knew she was trying to lighten the mood. "If you say you're alright, then I have to believe you. I'll leave you to your work then." He leaned over and placed a kiss on her temple. "If you need anything, don't hesitate to come find me." He brushed his hand across her cheek, running his finger against her lower lip. Slowly he turned away from her. As he walked out of her office, he glanced back over his shoulder to take one last look at her. She was upset about something Ken had said or done to her. He just knew it.

Alec went directly to his office and called Jonas Sounds. Alejandro, in the meantime, was trying to get ahold of Albert Trexor. Alec knew Jonas had just returned from being out of the country, and Alejandro was waiting on a return call from Albert. Between the two of them, they would find their answers.

☾

The day dragged on as Kelly tried to get some work done. Every time she set her pen down, her mind drifted back to Ken and his threats. Of course she was the only one to hear them. No one would believe her. Everyone loved Ken. If she complained to HR, they would think she was making everything up. They thought he walked on water.

Five o'clock finally came, and Kelly knew she should start making her way to Alec's office. Every evening since she'd started working out of his office, she met him at the end of the day. Sometimes they went out for dinner, other times they went over to Alejandro's or her parents' house. One of his conditions for working in his office was that she didn't take work home. She wasn't allowed any overtime. He'd even cleared it with Bill. She worked hard while she was in the office, but when it was time to quit, she let her hair down. At first, she hadn't known what to do with herself in the evenings. Slowly, though, she was learning to relax and enjoy herself again.

When Kelly didn't meet him as planned, he headed towards her office, first stopping by Joe's. Joe brought up Angel's baptism and reminded Alec about Ashton.

"Remember, Ashton is supposed to make amends with Matthew this weekend. We need to make sure that happens, and that Matthew is happy with the outcome."

"I know, I know. Alejandro reminded me of that just yesterday." Alec looked at his watch. "Wow, look at the time. It's almost six o'clock."

"Yeah, I've got to get out of here. I promised Mom that I'd stop by tonight for dinner. I think Dad's getting on her nerves again. He really did retire a little too early. He still has so much energy. But, if you keep taking time off, he might as well return fulltime."

"Joe, you know you miss him when he's not in the office." Alec stood, laughing. He waved to Joe as he left this office.

Kelly's office door was closed, so he knocked before entering. He didn't hear her answer his knock and wondered if she were still in there, so he opened the door. He found Kelly slumped over her desk. Her head was resting on her forearms. Rushing to her side, he called her name. She raised her head and brushed her hair from her eyes.

"Hey there, were you napping? It's almost six o'clock and you didn't join me in my office." As he neared her, he could tell she wasn't feeling well.

"I'm fine. Just tired that's all. Remember, Angel did keep us all up last night."

"Yeah, I know. It's just that you haven't been the same since Ken was here."

She ignored that, opening her drawer and retrieving her purse. She slung it over her shoulder and stood. She started to move towards him, but she became light-headed and grabbed for her desk. Instantly, he was by her side. He helped her sit back down.

"I'm fine. I just stumbled."

"Stumbled? Try again."

She didn't want to tell him about her latest headache. It hadn't turned into a migraine, but it was pretty intense. "You know what? I just want to go home and go to bed. I am exhausted." She ignored his presence, stood, and moved towards the door. "Coming?" she called over her shoulder.

Alec knew there was more going on with her than she let on. The only common factor between her behavior now and that of three weeks ago was Ken. When he got home that evening, he was going to reach Jonas Sounds. He wanted to know more about Ken's background.

Alec drove Kelly home and stayed over for a little while. Just as he was getting ready to leave, Alejandro came home. Kelly had gone off to bed and Angelina was seeing to Matthew, so when Alejandro arrived, Alec followed him into his office and closed the door.

"Any word from Albert?"

"Yes, I have a breakfast meeting with him tomorrow."

"Thank God. Maybe we'll get some answers here." He sat down while Alejandro got comfortable after his long day in surgery.

Alejandro removed his suit coat and loosened his tie. He grabbed a bottle of water from his mini refrigerator and sank down into his office chair. "You still haven't heard from Jonas?"

"I know he's working on it. I'm phoning him when I get home." Alec went on to describe his encounter with Ken earlier that day. "He appeared out of nowhere. Bill acted like he forgot to tell us he was going to be there, but I think he was taken by surprise that Ken didn't advise us, too. I had a patient I had to see, so I left him and Kelly alone. I saw him leave the office, so I went to check on her. She was a mess. Her hands were shaking and she seemed lost, withdrawn like she was in Knoxville. If I was a betting man here, from all indications I have to believe Ken is her problem. He has to be the one that's harmed her in some way. I don't know how or what he's done to her, but if he's the one…"

"Alec calm down. Let me talk to Albert, and you talk to Jonas. We'll find out about his background. We can't do anything until we hear from our sources or until Kelly tells us what's troubling her. Until then…"

"I know, Alejandro. I just hate seeing her like this. She's become a shell of herself. I don't know how to help her. In fact, I believe she's dealing with another migraine tonight, just by her behavior and knowing that she was stressed around Ken today. She hasn't had a migraine since she came home. I made sure that she was working in a relatively stress-free environment. She's not working any overtime. She seemed better, and then a half hour in his presence and she falls apart again. It has to be him."

"Sounds like it, but we can't do anything until we have our proof."

"I know. Hey, changing subjects, has Ashton RSVP'd for Angel's baptism?"

"He has, and I know where you're going with this conversation. He's not going to renege on his promise. He'll follow through with talking to Matthew. I'm sure of it. I have to be honest with you… my opinion of him is changing, ever so slowly. I think he may have been a good hire. But again, only time will tell."

"You need to tell Gabriella that. She's still out with her opinion. Last time his name came up, I thought she was going to go through the roof. If he changes your mind, maybe you can work on her, too."

Alejandro laughed, "Our Gabriella definitely can hold a grudge. She does have a strong opinion on the subject, especially with how it's affected Matthew's opinion of doctors. I hope he proves us wrong."

"On that note, I think I'll head on out of here. I want to call Jonas before it gets too late. I'll see you later."

"Later, yes, but not later tonight. I've seen enough of you today," Alejandro said as he slapped Alec on the back. He walked him to the door and said, "I'll call you after my breakfast meeting. Maybe we'll have our answers by morning."

Alec didn't wait to get home to call Jonas. As soon as he got in the car, he phoned Jonas and put the call on speaker. Jonas answered just as Alec was turning onto the main road that led to his house.

"Alec, I was just getting ready to phone you. I'm waiting for one of my contacts to get back to me."

"When will that be? I need answers now."

"Hopefully tonight. I actually thought you were him calling."

"Fine. I'll wait for your call. Don't worry about the time. I need answers as soon as you can get them."

"I understand, Alec. I'll call you as soon as I hear something."

Alec drove the rest of the way home on autopilot. He needed answers. Depending on what Jonas and Albert relayed to them, he was prepared to speed dial Bill with his findings. As far as Alec was concerned, Ken Jones was a scumbag and needed to be dealt with sooner rather than later. He wondered how a man as bright as Bill could overlook Ken's shortcomings. He must be a good bullshitter because Alec saw through him immediately. He hadn't gotten through that first meeting before he knew what kind of man Ken was. He was manipulative, cunning, and didn't care how he treated his employees. Alec saw him for what he was and, if he had anything to say about it, Ken wouldn't last much longer at Lattice Works. Alec was going to take him down.

Alec hardly slept waiting for Jonas's call. He finally gave up on him around two o'clock and headed off to bed. He tossed and turned until it was time to get up. His thoughts were never far from Kelly. He hoped and prayed she didn't have a headache, but all signs pointed to the fact that she did. It wouldn't surprise him if she was late for work.

Six o'clock came mighty early when one didn't sleep. Alec was tired and on edge. He needed to hear from Jonas. He was in a fighting mood. He got that way when he was short on sleep. He hoped someone didn't look at him the wrong way—he wasn't sure how he would react.

☾

Alejandro rose early. Albert had worked him into his schedule for the day, and he was scheduled to meet Albert at six thirty at Pedals diner.

Albert had already secured a table in the back of the restaurant. He knew Alejandro was looking for answers and, regrettably, he had them. That was one of the reasons why Albert wanted to meet him face-to-face. What he had to share with his friend wasn't something that he felt comfortable telling him over the phone. He stood and waved to Alejandro as he entered. Albert didn't want to be interrupted once they'd started their meeting, so he asked for a carafe filled with coffee. It arrived just as Alejandro approached the table. Neither of them took a look at the menu as they already knew what they wanted to order. Outside of eating, they were there for one reason and one reason only—Ken Jones. Albert ordered pancakes while Alejandro decided on just toast.

Albert poured their coffees. They got through the pleasantries as they waited for their waitress to return with their breakfasts. Albert asked how Matthew was fairing since his transplant. Alejandro was quick to pull out a fistful of pictures from his wallet that Angelina had insisted he carry. They were for times like this when he could gloat about his family.

Alejandro inquired about Albert's wife and children. Before he could pull out his own photographs, their waitress had arrived with their breakfasts. Alejandro watched Albert as he spread the butter across his pancakes, carefully pouring the syrup across the stack. Albert cut into the stack, and started to raise a bite to his mouth when he stopped and laid his fork down on his plate.

"Alejandro, you wanted to ask me about Ken Jones?"

Alejandro took a sip of this coffee, swallowing, and nodded. "Yes, I had heard that he worked for Trexor a few years back. Is that true?"

"Indeed it is." Albert took a bite and again laid his fork down. "Alejandro, may I ask why you are so interested in his employment with Trexor?"

Alejandro looked Albert squarely in the eyes and said, "My sister-in-law currently works for him. I have some concerns about him and wanted to run a few things by you."

"I'm going to be upfront and honest with you. We go back too far for me not to be. Ken is trouble. Trouble with a capital T. What are you noticing that has you concerned?"

"Kelly, Angelina's sister, was recently fired from Lattice Works for no apparent reason. Although the owner had told her it was for job performance, which doesn't make sense since she's received promotion after promotion since her hiring."

"I see," Albert said, reaching for his coffee cup.

"What I am about to tell you needs to be kept in the strictest confidence."

Albert nodded in understanding.

"When Kelly came home, she was changed. Whether she would admit it or not, she was exhausted after working eons of overtime. The firing really affected her self-confidence, and Alec noticed that she didn't like to be touched. A simple touch by him and she'd pull away. She and Alec are dating and she's told him that she has a few things she needs to work out." Alejandro paused, "Kelly was happy-go-lucky once. Nothing bothered her. Now she gets migraines all of the time. Something happened between the two of them, and I'm just trying to figure out why he may have left Trexor. Was it a career move on his part? I know I'm reaching for answers. I just want the old Kelly back. Alec has a good sixth sense, and for some reason he really dislikes this guy."

"Alec's spot on." Leaning in across the table, Albert said, "You didn't hear this from me."

That quickly got Alejandro's attention.

"If you do your research, which I'm sure you will, you'll uncover what I am about to share with you."

Alejandro leaned back in his chair, listening intently to what Albert had to say.

"About ten years ago, Ken was an up-and-coming executive with us. Over time, we noticed that women in his department were either transferring within the company or resigning at an alarming rate. One day, HR was served with a lawsuit naming Ken in a sexual harassment suit. We discovered that he was requiring excessive amounts of overtime for only the women employees. And to top it off, he was requiring sexual favors in exchange for these women to keep their jobs. Our portion of the suit was dismissed. I'm not sure what happened after that."

"You've got to be kidding me. Now it all makes sense." Alejandro's heart dropped. He could only imagine what Kelly may have been through. He knew about the excessive hours, but what else?

"We gave him the choice. We could fire him or he could resign."

"He took the easy way out and resigned, right?"

Albert nodded.

"I wonder if he's harassing Kelly…" He asked the question aloud, but it was mainly for himself. He didn't want to picture what Kelly may have been forced to experience.

Both men had had enough of their breakfasts. Alejandro was sick with this news. He grabbed the bill and thanked Albert for the information. "I'll be in touch. Thanks for the help."

"Not a problem. I hope your sister-in-law isn't being targeted."

"I hope so, too, but I think that's wishful thinking."

Both men stood. Alejandro turned and reached out his hand to Albert. Shaking it, he said, "Thanks for your time."

Alejandro drove straight home. He wasn't quite sure how he got there safely since he didn't even remember getting into the car. He turned into his driveway and immediately saw Alec's car. He checked his phone as he pulled into the garage and there were no messages or missed calls from him. It was still relatively early, but Alec should've been getting ready to leave for the office. Alejandro wondered if he'd heard from Jonas yet.

Alejandro was greeted by both Alec and Angelina as he entered the kitchen. A look of utter disgust was on Alec's face when Alejandro saw him.

"You, me, in your office, now." Alec said to Alejandro, tension lacing his every word.

Angelina reached out and grabbed ahold of Alejandro's hand. Squeezing it, she leaned in and gave him a quick kiss on the cheek. "He knows," is all she said as Alejandro followed Alec down the hallway into his office. Closing the door behind him, Alejandro made his way to the window that overlooked the backyard. He just stood there waiting for Alec to say something, anything. Then the famous pacing began, but this time it was Alec and not Alejandro.

"If that God-forsaken man has laid a hand on her..."

"Alec, calm down. We don't know if anything physically has happened to her."

"Well, why the hell does she act the way she does? He has to have touched her, maybe even—"

"Don't go there, Alec. Don't think the worst. We need to somehow do our own investigation—get our own answers, maybe without Kelly even knowing." Alejandro made his way to his office chair and sat down. "Is Dad filling in for you?"

"No, I was off today. Joe and I were supposed to go to a conference but I cancelled this morning after I got the news. Alejandro, Jonas has witness statements. He harassed quite a few women before he left Trexor."

"That's what I heard. What about Kelly? Did she go into the office?"

"That's another story. She overslept this morning. She told Angelina that she had another headache but was going to try and make it through the day. She knew I was going to be out today, and she told Angelina that if I knew about her headache I would have made her stay home. We've got to do something."

"I know. Let's go over what Jonas told you, and I'll see if it differs from what Albert shared with me."

Alec and Alejandro spent the morning going over everything that they knew about Ken. They decided to call Bill. He needed to know what they'd discovered about his all-star executive.

Alec dialed Bill directly. He put him on speaker and both he and Alejandro went over not only what they had discovered from their sources, but also went into detail what they knew about Kelly. "I fear that she's been a target, too. Bill, who led the charge in her firing?"

Bill was silent for a few seconds, then said. "Gentlemen, I've been doing my own investigation. An employee, who will remain nameless, contacted me just yesterday about Ken. They were being harassed by him as well."

Alec and Alejandro looked at each other. "Bill, I've got to go. Kelly's alone at the office because Joe and I are both out. I've got to go check on her." Alec rushed out the door, hurrying past Angelina in the hallway.

"What's wrong?" she asked, walking up to her husband. She still had no clue what Alec and Alejandro discovered.

Alejandro didn't want to worry Angelina, so he told her that he had an emergency with a patient and needed to head out. Alejandro drew his wife into his arms. "It's going to be okay. Alec and I will see to it that Kelly's not harmed."

# Chapter Thirty-Six

KELLY DIDN'T ARRIVE AT THE office until ten o'clock. She stopped by Alec's on the way in, but he wasn't home. She guessed that he'd already left for his meeting. She wanted to start her day with his reassurance, but on the flip-side she was glad that she didn't have to deal with him since she had a headache.

The office was pretty much closed for the day. Only a few people were there taking appointments and answering calls. Kelly grabbed a bottle of water and headed off to her office. She approached the door to her office and noticed that it was closed. Kelly was confused—she'd left it open the night before. She guessed the cleaning crew had closed it when they finished cleaning.

Fear washed over her as she placed her hand on the doorknob, but she turned it and opened the door. The light was off. Yes, she thought, the cleaning crew must have closed her door. She walked through the door and reached to turn on the light, but the door quickly closed shut behind her. She was slammed up against the wall, the breath knocked out of her. A hand closed over her throat. She couldn't breathe. Her captor was in the shadows of the room.

Then she heard, "You're late." The hand against her throat

tightened. "I've got you now, and you will do as I say." She recognized the loud voice—Ken. "Yesterday, I told you that you needed to be here on time, and you come in late the very next day. That's another reason why I should have you fired." He released his hold enough so she could speak, but she believed he would tighten it again if she didn't do what he wanted.

"I don't know what you're talking about," she softly uttered.

"It's after ten. You're to be here by nine. And you are not staying current on your tasks. You're behind… I knew Bill shouldn't have agreed to this deal." Ken got louder with every word he spoke.

"What deal?"

"Your boyfriend," he yelled.

"I don't know what you're talking about."

"Dr. Alvarez is your boyfriend, isn't he?"

"Where did you get that idea?"

He removed his hand from around her neck and seemed to relax somewhat as he continued, "Come on now, Kelly. He's the reason why you have your job. He's the reason why you're working at his clinic. What favors did you give him that you couldn't seem to give me, huh? I know how this works."

Kelly was shocked. *What is he talking about? Did Alec bribe Bill to rehire me? No, it can't be.*

Ken leaned in and nibbled at her neck. He tried to kiss her, but she struggled against him, turning her head. She still had a hold on her purse. She tried to hit him with it, but she couldn't move her arms as he'd trapped them against his body. He slapped her across the face, grabbed her head, and roughly turned her head back towards him, slamming it into the wall. He lowered the tone of his voice. "You know I love your perfume. It drives me crazy. The only way that I'm going to allow you to keep your job is if you come with me to my hotel. You know, have some fun with me."

She tried to pull away, but his hold on her face tightened. He moved his hand from her face to her neck, grazing her breast as he made his way to her forearm. "I will have you fired if you don't come with me." He grabbed her hand and tried to pull her out the door. As he reached for the door-knob, she kicked him in the shin and pulled away from him as he shouted in pain. She was momentarily disoriented and somehow made it across the room to the back left corner of her office before Ken advanced on her again.

He had backed her even further into the corner when her office door flew open. As he'd hurried down the hallway to find Kelly, Alec heard Ken yelling at her, telling her how she got her job back. Alec stood there, in the doorway, and saw Kelly against the wall with Ken walking towards her.

Alec rushed towards Ken, grabbing him by the shoulders and pulling him down, away from Kelly. Kelly didn't waste any time fleeing from her office. She needed to get away from Ken.

Thankfully, she still had a hold on her purse. She had to get out of the clinic, away from both Ken and Alec. She ran to her car, started the ignition, and threw it in reverse, almost hitting a passerby. She put her car in drive, screeching the tires as she flew out of the parking lot. *Where should I go?* Kelly knew she had to get out of town. She didn't stop to think, just jumped on the interstate. *The cabin. That's where I'll go. It can be my safe haven. At least for the time being,* she thought.

As she drove, she kept hearing his words as they replayed over and over again. "He's the reason you're working at his clinic." Kelly knew the truth. Alec had lied to her. He should have told her he was behind Bill reaching out to her offering back the job she loved. He was the reason she got her job back. Who could she trust? Did Bill really think she deserved her job back or did Alec threaten to take his business elsewhere if he didn't rehire her? Alec—she thought he was on her side, but now she didn't know what to believe.

While Kelly was driving down the interstate, Ken was being taken into custody at the clinic. Alec watched as Ken was escorted from the clinic in handcuffs. That's when he noticed Kelly was gone, and that's when he remembered what he'd heard as he ran down the hallway towards Kelly.

She'd disappeared. Frantic, he ran around the building calling her name. Sadie rushed to his side.

"Alec, Kelly ran out of here."

Alec was surprised. He'd been so busy dealing with Ken and the police that he thought she'd taken refuge in his office. Alec grabbed his phone out of his pocket. He called her, but his call went straight to voicemail. He tried her again and again with the same response. He was becoming increasingly more worried. He phoned Angelina next.

"Have you heard from Kelly?"

"No, why?"

Alec went on to describe the scene when he entered her office.

"Is she alright?" Angelina was frantic with worry, but she knew she had to keep herself in check for Alec's sake.

"I don't know. I don't know where she is. She's gone."

"Calm down. We'll find her. I'll call my mom and see if she's seen or heard from her."

"Angelina, you should have seen the look on her face when I entered the room. When she looked at me—Angelina she knows."

"She knows what?"

"She knows the truth about what I did. I heard Ken yelling at her. He told her everything."

"What are you talking about?"

"On top of everything that he said and did to her, Ken told her that I was the reason she got her job back. She hates me. The look on her face… The way her eyes pierced mine. It happened so fast, and then after dealing with Ken I realized she was nowhere to be found. Sadie told me she saw her running from the clinic."

"I'm going to call Alejandro and have him meet you at the clinic. I'll call my mom and call you right back. We'll find her, Alec."

❦

Alejandro found Alec in his office. His eyes were bloodshot, like he'd been crying. He looked like someone close to him had recently died.

"She's gone."

"We'll find her."

Shaking his head, Alec didn't agree with Alejandro.

"I'm sure she's not far. She probably just went for a drive."

"You didn't see the look on her face. She hates me."

"I doubt that. Has Jackie heard from her?"

"Angelina was calling her. I haven't heard a word." Alec was drowning in his misery. He knew that he'd lost the only woman he'd ever loved. He hadn't even had the chance to tell her that he loved her.

The phone rang. Alec jumped to answer it, thinking it was Kelly, but it was Bill. Alec and Alejandro spoke with him. He told them about Ariel.

Ariel had gone to Bill and spilled the beans. Ken had been sexually harassing her, too. Her lies had led to Kelly's firing. Ariel had developed a conscious of late. She missed her friend and needed to do something to fix their relationship, so she went to Bill and told him everything about Ken. She was pressing charges and having him arrested for raping her right before he left for St. Louis. She had the evidence—physical evidence and photographs of the beatings she endured at Ken's hands.

❧

Earlier that morning, Ariel sought out Bill. She'd been waiting for him to arrive, and she approached his car before he could even get out. At first, Bill hadn't recognized her—she had a scarf covering her face. She pushed it aside and that's when he saw the black eye and bruising on her face. "Ariel, what happened?"

"Not here. Can we go for a drive? I need to do this away from the office."

"Sure, whatever you need." He jumped out of the car, ran around to the passenger side, and opened the door for her. She slowly eased her body into the car.

Bill drove away from the office and headed towards a nearby park. He pulled up alongside the lake and put the car in park. He left the motor running since there was a chill in the air.

Bill turned to Ariel. "We can sit here as long as you need. You can tell me what happened whenever you're ready."

Ariel just sat there, watching a bird as it flew along the edge of the pond, searching for its morning breakfast. He tried to watch her face, but she turned away from him slightly as she watched the bird take flight. He noticed her hands as they grasped her purse tightly. They sat in silence—a silence Bill had been prepared to endure for as long as needed. Ariel needed to take her time.

After about ten minutes, Ariel cleared her throat and turned to Bill. Tears were forming in the corners of her eyes.

He wasn't sure what he should do. He wanted to reach a hand out to her, but didn't know if she'd be accepting of it.

He decided to try, so he turned and reached his hand palm-side up to her. She drew her lips in and started gnawing on her lower lip. She was doing her best not to cry.

Ariel reached for his hand and as she did, she could no longer contain the flood of tears. The dam was released and she started sobbing. She held tightly onto his hand. And when she was finally able to control and stem the flow of tears, she started telling Bill her story.

Ariel started at the beginning. She told Bill how Ken had targeted her from the moment she'd entered the department.

He made her work late at night, along with practically everyone else in the department. Often times, he'd corner her in her office, making sexual advancements. She'd kept pushing him aside. The stress from everything caused her to start making serious mistakes, mistakes that no one caught until Kelly.

Ariel had threatened to go to HR on him, but he pointed out the err of her ways. He'd protect her if she turned the cards on her friend. So, instead of doing the right thing, she'd lied to Kelly. She made Kelly take the blame for the mistakes she'd made. She'd assumed he'd also been harassing Kelly to a point since she'd also seen Kelly out of sorts after witnessing Ken leaving her office.

Bill sat in utter shock. He had no idea this was going on in his company. Ken was a phenomenal executive. He almost didn't believe her until she went on with her story.

"I don't know what went down between Ken and Kelly before she'd left the other day, but something did. I just know she ran out of here." She paused for a moment to watch a flock of Canadian geese land on the water. "Ken was fine after Kelly was first fired, but then he started back in. Each time

I encountered him, he was rougher. I know I should have come to you, but I was scared. He threatened to fire me like he had done to Kelly if I told anyone, so I kept it to myself."

Turning back to Bill, Ariel dropped the bombshell that he'd been waiting for—how she got the bruises and black eye. "Tuesday night I wasn't feeling well, and at five I went to leave the office. Ken saw me straightening up my desk for the day. He surprised me and came in, closing the door behind him. He immediately began threatening me. I tried to push my way past him, but he stopped me. He pretty much kept me trapped in my own office until everyone had gone home. He made it appear like we were having a closed-door meeting. It wasn't something unusual since he often did this."

Stopping briefly, she fidgeted with her purse. "I tried to call security, but he yanked my phone out of the wall." Ariel was getting more upset.

"Ariel, take your time. We don't have to be anywhere."

"I know, and I appreciate your patience." Another tear fell, and she started to search her purse for a tissue when he reached into his breast pocket and withdrew a handkerchief. He passed it to her. Ariel dried her tears and then finished her story.

"After everyone left, he stood and locked the door." Taking a deep breath, she continued, "I knew I was in trouble when I heard the lock click into place. Before, he'd kissed me, and we'd even had sex a few times, but this time when he approached me he had a crazed look in his eyes. He pulled me from my chair and threw me to the floor. He started punching me in the face and then—then he tore my clothes from my body and raped me. And when it was all over, he stood, straightened his tie, tucked his shirt back into his pants and nonchalantly went to the door. As he unlocked it, he said, 'This never happened, and if you think you're going to do something about it, think again. I'll fire you." Then he left the room, never looking back. He walked out the door."

"Ariel, I'm so sorry this happened. Have you told anyone else?"

"I did. The first thing I did was get myself together. I went directly to the hospital where I was examined and filed a police report. I know the police have gone to his home, but he wasn't there. I have to imagine they're going to come to the office today to arrest him."

Pure panic washed over him. "He's not here. He's in St. Louis. He showed up there yesterday without warning. I had no idea—Kelly," he said, reaching for his phone.

&#x1405;

He hadn't realized what Ken was like until Alec had pointed-ed out a few things to him. Their conversation had caused him to start investigating Ken further. "I wish I would have seen this side of him sooner. I had no idea what happened with him at Trexor. If I did, I'd never have hired him. And now, with him being on corrective action, I'd have fired him as soon as I discovered his past doings at Trexor. I hope you believe me."

"We all have blinders on at some point. It's easy to miss something of this nature, especially if you're not looking for it."

"How's Kelly?"

"We don't know. She ran out of here, and we're not sure where she is."

"Please let me know when you locate her. I owe her an apology. I promise I will make this right."

He sounded remorseful. Bill was a good man who was caught up in making his company successful. If he had stepped back and looked at everything a little more closely, he may have seen the signs. But then again, he may not have. Ken was experienced. He knew how to intimidate his victims and cover his tracks. For once and for all, he wouldn't harass another person. He was going to prison for a long time.

☾

Kelly made it to the cabin in the early afternoon. She'd turned off her cell phone when she'd gotten on the interstate. She removed the battery from her phone when she stopped to get gas right outside of St. Louis. She didn't want anyone tracking her using the GPS from her phone. She fixed herself a cup of tea and sat down on the couch in the family room. Clutching her cup, she replayed the morning's events over and over in her mind. *How could he? Why did he?* Questions kept running amok through her mind. She thought he loved her. She thought she loved him. And then there was Ken. He was a psychopath. He needed to be arrested and locked up for a lifetime.

Then, she realized what the day was. It was Thursday, and Sunday was Angel's baptism. How could she face Angel's godfather and her supposed boyfriend at the christening? Her world was spinning around her. Everything was out of control.

Exhaustion finally took over and she drifted off to sleep. Her sleep was filled of dreams. Dreams of Alec... walking through the park, their date at Miss Kelly's, the look he got on his face when he held Angel.

She awoke with a start and knew what she needed to do. It was almost eight o'clock. If she got in the car and headed out, she could be in Alec's arms in a matter of hours. She had to tell him the truth. She didn't run because of him, she ran because of Ken and what he did to her. She needed Alec.

She had to tell him what had happened all of those months ago. She had to tell him why she got fired. After what happened with Ken, she needed to get everything out in the open. When she thought about what Ken said, she knew Alec. If Alec did what he said, it was because he loved her. He wanted her to be happy doing what she loved. Kelly's decision was made.

She ran from the house with only her keys in hand. She jumped into her car and sped down the driveway towards her future… Towards the love of her life. She needed to tell him that she loved him. After he discovered all that had happened with Ken, he may not want her any longer. He'd never told her he loved her, and maybe he didn't. Maybe he felt obligated because of Angelina to be nice to her. She didn't know how he felt about her because he'd never told her. But she couldn't think along these terms. She just couldn't. She had to get to him and tell him everything.

Now was her time. She was going to open up to him about her feelings. What was the worst-case scenario? He didn't love her and he'd walk away. Well, then she'd move on with her life. Take the lesson for what it was.

Kelly drove until she heard the low fuel warning sound, indicating that she needed gas. It was almost ten. She was still a couple of hours outside of St. Louis. In her excitement to get to Alec, she realized maybe she needed to slow down a little and think through everything that had happened in the last twelve hours. As she approached an exit, she signaled that she was going to get off the highway. That's when she saw it in her headlights—a deer had walked out onto the highway. She applied her brakes, her tires screeching, but she couldn't stop the forward motion of her car fast enough. She understood then the adage "a deer caught in headlights." The deer's eyes were as large as saucers. And then she plowed right into it.

Kelly felt the impact as she hit the deer. She lost control of her car and hit the guardrail that lined the exit ramp. She broke through the barrier, and her car careened into a ditch. Then, everything went black.

# Chapter Thirty-Seven

ALEC WAS A MESS. HE'D finally gone home around seven o'clock. No one had heard from Kelly. They tried tracing her through the GPS on her cell phone, but they were unsuccessful. "Damn it, Kelly, where are you," Alec yelled. He threw himself down in his office chair, covered his face with his hands, and took a deep breath. He needed to get his emotions under control.

He rehashed the events of the day. Where had it gone wrong? From the outset, he guessed. Alejandro's meeting with Albert, his phone conversation with Jonas. And then, his trip to the office—finding Ken trying to grab Kelly, the look of panic on her face, and the realization that he'd lost her. He pounded his fist on his desk in frustration. He had to find her. He had to tell her that he loved her. He didn't know if she would believe him but he had to try.

Alec called Alejandro around nine to see if he had any news on Kelly's whereabouts. No one knew where she was, and Angelina was beside herself with worry. On top of Kelly's disappearance, Angelina was trying to decide what to do about Angel's baptism. The godmother was missing and the godfather was falling apart.

Alec moved to the bar. He grabbed a glass and started to

pour himself a drink. He stared at the bottle that he held in his hand. He watched as the amber liquid sloshed back and forth in the bottle. He was mesmerized by the motion of the liquid. He realized that getting drunk wasn't the answer he was looking for, so he replaced the glass in the cabinet and returned the bourbon to the counter.

He moved to the sofa and sat down. Leaning forward, he placed his elbows on his knees, clasped his hands in front of him, and said a prayer. He prayed for Kelly's safe return and her forgiveness. He then eased himself back onto the couch, laying his head against the back. Closing his eyes, he sat there alone in total silence.

Time passed slowly. Every few minutes he found himself looking at his watch until he was ready to go crazy with worry. His phone rang—it was Alejandro checking in one last time before heading off to bed. Angelina was making herself sick with worry for her sister. There were no new updates, so Alejandro disconnected the call to help his wife.

Alec sat staring at nothing. The silence was killing him. It was almost midnight when he finally started to drift off.

He was startled awake when his house phone rang. He almost fell off the couch rushing to answer the phone. "Kelly?" he said breathlessly into the phone.

"Dr. Alec Alvarez?" the voice said.

"Yes, this is he."

"Dr. Alvarez, this is Officer Carlson." As soon as he heard the word officer, Alec's heart started to beat frantically. "I'm from the Missouri State Highway Patrol."

"Yes," is all Alec could get out.

"I am calling to advise you that someone I believe you may know was involved in a car accident."

Alec's brain started racing. As far as he knew, all of his family members were accounted for, safely in their homes.

"Who could that be? My family is all at home."

"Dr. Alvarez, do you know someone by the name of Kelly Samuels?"

Alec's voice caught. He couldn't speak.

"We checked the car registration, and it's registered to a Kelly Samuels. She was driving without a purse or license, and there was no cell phone in the car. All we found was your business card that had fallen in between the seats."

Stuttering, Alec could barely get out his question. "Is Kelly… is she alive? Was she injured? What happened to her?"

"Yes, Ms. Samuels is alive. She was transported to Jacksonville Hospital where she is being evaluated in the ER. It looks like she hit a deer on the highway. She was lucky that she was decelerating when it happened. It appears as though she was getting off the interstate."

Alec started laughing. "She hit a deer?"

"Yes, she did. Are you alright, sir?"

"I'm just glad that you found her." Alec obtained directions on how to get to the hospital. He quickly phoned her parents before calling Alejandro. Alejandro didn't answer the phone, though—Angelina did.

"Alec?"

"I just got a phone call from the Missouri State Highway Patrol. Kelly was in an accident. She must have been at the cabin. She was on her way home when she hit a deer."

"Did you say she hit a deer?"

"Yeah. I'm headed over to the hospital. I don't know any details other than she's at Jacksonville Hospital and is being evaluated in the ER."

"I want to come with you."

"No, just sit tight at home. I phoned your parents and they're going to meet me there. It's about a two hour drive. I'll call you when I know something."

"Alec, she's going to be alright. Take care of her."

"I will, I promise." Alec ended the call, grabbed his suit coat, and headed out the door. He programmed the hospital's address into his GPS. It looked like he wouldn't get there until just after two o'clock.

℃

Alec arrived at Jacksonville Hospital just after two thirty. He'd received a phone call from Kelly's parents while he was driving—they wanted him to know that it had taken them a little longer to get on the road than they had expected. They wanted to make sure that he was on his way and that he'd watch over Kelly for them until they arrived. Jackie was worried sick about her daughter. He'd done his best not to sound upset, but his voice trembled the entire time he was on the phone with her. He hoped that it hadn't come through over the phone. He didn't want Jackie to worry any more than she already was.

Alec walked through the emergency room entrance at two forty-five. From what he understood from Officer Carlson, Kelly's accident had happened at approximately ten o'clock. A highway patrolman saw the accident happen and immediately called for assistance. She'd arrived at the hospital within minutes. He was confident that she'd been examined by a team of doctors and hoped that they'd already diagnosed her injuries.

Alec stopped at the desk and told the personnel who he was and who he'd come to see. The nurse was expecting him and showed him into the examining room where Kelly was being treated. She was unconscious. Alec tried assessing her external injuries. He noticed a rather large lump had formed on her forehead. She had some bruising on her cheek. A bandage ran across her nose, covering some type of cut. As he glanced down her face to her neck, he noticed the bruising. He walked over the side of her bed and softly touched the bruises that surrounded her neck. It was the exact same bruising that he'd witnessed on her arm when he'd surprised her in Knoxville. He realized who'd hurt her then. "Damn it," he said to himself. How many other times did Ken cause her physical harm?

Alec turned and grabbed a chair that was sitting just inside the doorway. He moved it to Kelly's bedside. He sat down and reached for her hand. He eased it between his and raised it to his lips. Softly, he placed a kiss along her fingers. He leaned in and raised her hand to his cheek and then clasped it between both of his.

He talked to her, "My dear, what happened to you? He's caused you so much pain… I know you can hear me. You've got to wake up. You've got to come back to me. Kelly, I should have told you this a long time ago. I love you… I love you more than I thought I could ever love anyone. You're my world. Come on now, we've got to be there for our god-daughter. Angel's counting on you to get better. I'm counting on you to—"

Alec stopped mid-sentence and just stared at her hand as it laid so still in his. He thought he'd felt her fingers move in his hand. *Sweetheart, that's it. Come back to me. Wake up now. You can do it…* But he must have been mistaken—she gave no reaction. He heard a faint knock at the door and looked up. He was being motioned by a nurse to join someone in the hallway. Alec stood and slowly eased her hand back to her side. He leaned in and softly placed a kiss on her lips. With that, he turned and walked from the room.

☾

Kelly felt like she'd gone through the ringer. Her body

ached from head to toe. She felt her hand being raised and then she could hear a voice. She tried to call out, but her lips wouldn't move. *Alec is that you? I'm fine! Really, I am.* And then, she could hear him talking to her.

"You've got to come back to me. Kelly, I should have told you this a long time ago. I love you… I love you more than I thought I could ever love anyone. You're my world."

*Did I just hear what I think I heard? Alec loves me. Oh my gosh! He just told me that he loves me.*

Then she heard him say, "Come on now, we've got to be there for our goddaughter. Angel's counting on you to get better. I'm counting on you…"

She tried, really she did. But she couldn't move, she couldn't squeeze his hand to let him know that she was going to be alright, and she couldn't speak and tell him the three words that she'd been wanting to tell him for months. Yes, she loved him.

C

Alec went out into the hallway and was greeted by Ben and Jackie, along with the team of doctors that were treating Kelly. Kelly's doctors introduced themselves and led them down the hallway to a small conference room where they discussed her injuries. Kelly had a mild concussion and some lacerations from broken glass. The doctors stressed that when she woke up, outside of a headache, she'd be quite sore from the impact of the crash. She had no internal bleeding and no broken bones. What they were most concerned about was the bruising on her neck and arms. "Do you know what happened to Ms. Samuels that caused such extensive bruising? These bruises did not happen as a result of the accident. She came in with them."

Alec spoke up. Kelly's parents listened as Alec told them

how she got the bruises. "She was attacked this morning in my office in St. Louis. The police have the man under arrest and charges are pending." Her parents looked at him in complete shock.

"In the next few minutes, we're going to take her up to a room." Addressing Ben and Jackie, the doctor said, "If you'd like to visit with your daughter before we move her, feel free. It's going to be a few minutes before her room is available."

Alec, Ben, and Jackie thanked the doctors. Alec shook each of their hands and watched as they escorted Kelly's parents to her room. Alec made his way to the waiting room where he sat down, exhausted. He pulled his cell phone out and texted Kelly's condition to Alejandro. Once the message sent, he powered down his phone. Rarely did he turn off his cell, but he decided that now was the time. He didn't want to talk to anyone, he didn't want to hear a ring tone, and he didn't want to feel a vibration of an incoming call. What he wanted was to hear Kelly's sweet voice… Her voice telling him that she loved him.

Alec sat back in his chair and closed his eyes. The next thing he was aware of was Jackie's soft touch as she placed her hand on his forearm.

"Alec," she whispered. He awakened immediately and shot straight up in his seat. "I didn't want to startle you, but they're moving Kelly to her room. Ben and I are going to take a moment to call the kids to let them know how she's doing. You should follow her up. I'm sure you're the first person she wants to see anyway." Jackie reached down and kissed his cheek. "My daughter has found a winner in you. I hope she sees the love that you have written all over your face for her, because I certainly do."

Before Alec could say a word, Jackie turned her back on him and headed down the hallway with Ben at her side.

"I hope so, too," he said under his breath. He wasn't sure how Kelly felt. After the look he'd witnessed on her face the day before, he wondered if she cared for him at all. Alec was sure she hated him. He'd withheld the part he'd played in her being rehired and he believed she'd never forgive him for it. All he wanted was to see her happy, and he'd thought Lattice was where she needed to be. He was wrong, so wrong. He hoped he could make it up to her because he didn't know what his life would be like without her in it.

Alec felt lost as he made his way down the hospital halls. His senses, for some reason, were on high alert. He felt the sterile environment surround him, he smelled the antiseptic, he heard the beeping of monitors, and he squinted against the intense lighting. In all the years that he'd been in and out of hospitals helping others, never once had he experienced this intensity with his senses. But he'd never been in this situation before either. The love of his life was lying in a hospital bed, injured and in pain, and there was nothing that he could do for her. With all of his medical training, he couldn't recommend a drug to make her wake up. He couldn't do anything except wait for her to wake on her own.

What he could do was say a few prayers and hope that she'd listen to him, listen to why he'd done what he did. And he could be there for her emotionally as she dealt with the pain and after-effects of Ken's attack on her. That is, if she'd let him.

Alec dropped his head as he meandered down the halls to her room. A feeling of malaise overcame him. When he reached the doorway to her room, he leaned his head against the doorframe before entering. A passing nurse stopped to ask if he was alright. Alec nodded and then turned and pushed through the door.

The lights over her bed had been dimmed. He made his

way to her bedside. He glanced at the monitors that kept track of her vitals, and then he sat down in the chair that was positioned in front of the windows. He dropped his head into his hands and let his emotions consume him. Alec couldn't remember the last time that he cried, but he cried for Kelly now. He cried for the choices he'd made, and he cried for the sense of loss that he felt knowing that he'd hurt her as deeply as he had.

Alec wiped the tears from his eyes, stood up, and made his way to her bedside. He moved a second chair to her side. He eased himself into the chair and leaned his head against her bedrail. He watched as she breathed in and out. He reached for her hand and entwined her fingers with his. He wanted her to know that he was by her side. He wanted her to feel his presence and the love he felt for her.

Alec had drifted off to sleep with his head resting on her bedrail. Ben and Jackie quietly entered Kelly's room and noticed him sitting there. Jackie placed her finger to her lips, grabbed Ben's hand, and left the room. "He's exhausted," Jackie said to her husband.

"He is," Ben said as he led his wife down the hallway to a waiting room. "I hope she realizes how much he cares for her."

"I do, too," Jackie said as she sat down next to her husband. "I've seen Alec in a lot of situations, but never have I seen him in this light. He seems helpless, like he's lost his best friend." Jackie laid her head on her husband's shoulder and drifted off to sleep. It was a long night for everyone in the Samuels-Alvarez families.

Time seemed to stand still. Alec woke when he heard a nurse enter Kelly's room. He stood as the nurse approached her bedside. "I'll get out of your way," he said as he watched the nurse begin to check the monitors. Alec left her room when she started taking Kelly's vital signs. He glanced at his watch as he made his way down the hallway, and realized that it was only a little after five. She'd been taken to her room around four. Alec turned the corner and saw Ben and Jackie sitting in the waiting room. Ben caught Alec's eye and gestured for him to join them.

Alec sat down across from them. He brushed his hand across his face and threw his head back, resting it against the wall behind him.

"How's she doing?" asked Kelly's father.

"I don't know. I guess she's doing okay. Her vitals look good. We just need her to wake up." Alec leaned forward in his chair, placing his elbows on his knees and his head in his hands, covering his eyes.

"Alec, I know about what you did for Kelly. I know you helped her regain her job at Lattice Works. Don't blame yourself for what happened with Ken. Kelly knew what she was up against and she's the one that made the decision to return to that environment. I know she loved her job, but what she should have done was go directly to Bill and report Ken for his harassing behavior. Kelly has ownership in this fiasco, too. Don't feel that you should take all of the blame here. It sounds like there's plenty of blame to go around."

Alec scrubbed his hands across his face and looked her father directly in the eyes. "Thank you, sir. I needed to hear that. I blame myself for putting her back in that situation, but yes, she knew what she was getting herself into. What we have to do is forget that and move forward—help her to overcome any of the traumas that she faced today, as well as what she experienced previously. It's not going to be an easy road for her. I think she realizes that herself."

"When do you think she'll wake up, Alec?"

"I don't know. It looks like she had a sizeable bump on her

head, so I guess she hit it pretty hard."

"Did you see the bruising on her neck?"

Alec nodded.

"Ken is responsible for that."

"He is. And I have to be honest with you, Ben—he's responsible for some emotional trauma, too. That's why Kelly acted like she did when she first returned to St. Louis. Kelly never admitted it to me, but I'm sure of it. I just hope she'll be able to find it in herself to trust again."

Alec had just stood and was staring out the window when he saw a nurse's reflection appear in the glass. He turned just as the nurse started to speak.

"Are you're with Ms. Samuels?"

Alec responded immediately, "Yes, we are."

"I just wanted to let you know that I think she's beginning to wake."

Alec looked at Ben who was nudging Jackie awake.

"You go to her, Alec. We'll be waiting."

Alec nodded and followed the nurse to Kelly's room.

"I noticed her moving about in her bed. She was clenching her hands. She opened her eyes momentarily and then closed them again. I do think she's coming around, though. I've alerted the doctors. Why don't you try and talk to her? See how she reacts?"

Alec pulled the chair up to the side of her bed. He eased the bedrail down so he could be closer to her. He sat down and leaned over the side of the bed. He brushed her hair away from her face, cupped her jaw, and leaned in to brush a kiss across her lips.

He whispered to her, "Kelly, sweetheart, wake up. Your mom and dad are here in the waiting room." Alec looked at her face. Even under the cuts and bruising, she was beautiful. She was his for the time being, and he would do anything in his power to make her see the error in his ways.

Alec moved from the chair to her bedside. Sitting on the edge of the bed, he moved to place his hand beside her waist while he used the other to lightly graze his fingers up and down her arm, eventually moving to the side of her face. He leaned in, kissing her brow while avoiding the bump on her head. He moved back and spoke to her from the heart. "Kelly, I'm sorry that I caused you this pain. If I hadn't brought Ken back into your life, you wouldn't be lying here in this bed." Stroking her face, neck, and arm with his hand, he continued, "Sweetheart, I love you. I never thought I'd ever get this involved with someone, but you came home and had to slide off the road into that snowbank. From the moment you opened your car door and I realized it was you, I was lost."

Alec stopped and waited to see if he could detect any more movement from Kelly and then continued pouring out his heart to her. "I never thought I'd fall in love and think about having my own family, but watching your sister and my brother and all the love they share... Add in Angel and Matthew, and it slowly started breaking down my barriers. Then you and I were asked to be Angel's godparents. I saw the way you took to her and how she took to me, and I fell hard and fast with our goddaughter. And then when you agreed to go on our first date that really wasn't a date... I knew I was lost. Kelly, please wake up and come back to me. Come back so we can be the godparents that we're meant to be to Angel. I need you in my life. I love you so much that my heart aches seeing you lying here."

Alec stopped talking. He watched her. And then he saw it—the slightest of movement. Her eyes started fluttering. Alec pressed his hand to the side of her face and waited. He reached for her hand, squeezed it, and waited. He started talking to her again, telling her over and over again how important she was to him, how much he loved her, and how sorry he was... He waited and watched.

Kelly lay there, aware of her surroundings, but she just didn't have the strength to open her eyes. She could feel Alec's presence. She felt his touch, his caresses, his kisses, but she couldn't do anything but listen. *Yes*, she thought to herself. *He loves me, he really does.*

# *Chapter Thirty-Eight*

ALEC SAT AT KELLY'S BEDSIDE until the nurses came through on shift-change, and then he went out to the waiting room. Jackie had woken and was waiting anxiously to hear if her daughter had come around. Alec told them he saw her eyes flutter, but that was it.

"Alec, you've been at Kelly's bedside since arriving. Take a break. Get a cup of coffee. Ben and I will sit with her." She stood and made her way to Alec. She reached up and patted his cheek. She smiled, turned, and headed for Kelly's room. As Ben passed Alec, he reached over and grasped his shoulder, squeezing it in a supportive manner, then followed his wife to his daughter's room.

Alec was running on empty. Between the anxiety he'd felt waiting to speak with Jonas, Alejandro's meeting with Albert, to the events of the day before… Add in little to no sleep, and his gas was running out. He made his way to the cafeteria and got himself something light to eat, as well as coffee for Kelly's parents.

Jackie acknowledged the nurse as she left Kelly's room. Jackie sat beside her daughter and watched her as she slept. Ben stood by his wife's side with his hand on her shoulder. Jackie fidgeted with Kelly's covers, and then she looked up.

And there, staring at her, was Kelly.

Kelly could barely get out a whispered, "*Mom*" but Jackie heard her daughter.

Ben squeezed his wife's shoulder and said, "Kelly, dear. You're awake."

Jackie turned and looked at her husband with tears of happiness forming in the corners of her eyes.

Kelly tried to smile at her mother, but her face hurt too much.

"You're going to be okay, Kelly," Jackie said as she squeezed her daughter's hand. "Oh, Alec! He's been here at your side practically since you arrived. Ben, go find him."

Ben leaned in and kissed Kelly's cheek, then went off in search of Alec.

"Kelly, dear, I'm sorry about everything that's happened. But everything's going to work out. You'll see. Alec, he's a wreck. Please listen to him. Let him explain. Don't judge him for what he did. He had your best interest at heart."

Kelly knew how much he loved her—she'd heard everything that Alec said to her. She wasn't going to let on that she'd heard, though. Deep down, she knew she loved Alec with all of her heart. But in those waking moments right before she hit the deer, she realized that she had to stop running and reevaluate everything that had happened to her. And then, sometime during her sleep-filled fog, she'd decided that she needed to slow down and think this whole situation through. She realized that she needed time—time to heal from her physical injuries, but also time to get over what Ken had done to her. She also had some decisions to make… Decisions that dealt with her job status and their relationship. Time. Yes, time is what she needed.

❦

Ben had barely taken ten steps from Kelly's door when he saw Alec approaching with three cups of coffee and a snack. Immediately, Alec's heart rate increased when he saw Ben walking quickly towards him. "Kelly. She's awake."

Alec stopped. At least one of his prayers had been answered.

"Here, let me take this. You go on in. We'll be waiting for you."

Alec wanted to rush through the door to her, but he held back. He handed Ben the coffee and snacks and slowly pushed open the door. He didn't know what he'd face when he crossed the threshold. Would she be happy to see him or mad? He slowly walked into the room and joined Jackie at Kelly's bedside.

"Alec," Kelly said, her voice hoarse.

*Oh, it's so good to hear your voice,* he thought. Jackie reached up and patted his hand. She stood, smiled at him encouragingly, and walked from the room. Her daughter was in good hands.

Alec chose not to sit in the chair that Jackie had vacated. He sat down directly on Kelly's bed, his thigh brushing her arm as he sat. He reached over and placed his right arm against her leg while using his other hand to brush her hair aside, securing it behind her ear. He moved slowly, making sure she was comfortable with his being near. All indications were she wasn't affected by his nearness.

She could see the emotion reflected in his eyes as he looked directly at her. *He looks like a man in love,* she thought. He looked a sight—his eyes were bloodshot from lack of sleep and worry, dark circles surrounded his eyes, his hair was a mess, standing up on all ends as though he'd been running his hands through it constantly, and he had a five o'clock shadow that was so unlike Alec. When Alec looked at her, he drew his lips in like he was trying to prevent his emotions from spilling out. His eyes became shiny and he licked his lips in a nervous manner before he spoke.

"Sweetheart," he said, leaning in and placing a gentle kiss on her cheek. "Are you in much pain?"

"I have a killer of a headache."

"I would think so with the size of that bump on your forehead."

Kelly reached up and felt her forehead.

"You've also got a cut across your nose. But outside of a little bruising and a mild concussion, you should be fine."

He was being ever-so gentle telling her about her injuries. She smiled up at him and he stared back at her. *Wow, he really does care for me,* she thought. She knew it by the way he was treating her, by his physical state of appearance, the look on his face, and also by his words for her a short time ago. And they only had a few moments before her doctor interrupted them.

Alec leaned over and kissed her brow. "I'm going to phone Alejandro and update him on your condition." He smiled at her as he left the room.

Alec caught up with her parents and phoned Alejandro. Angelina was in the middle of contacting everyone—she was cancelling Angel's baptism and rescheduling it for the following month. Kelly should feel up to celebrating the birth of her goddaughter by then.

Alec returned to Kelly's room where he discovered that she was clear to leave the hospital later that morning. She needed to take it easy, get plenty of rest, not do anything physically challenging, and avoid anything that could potentially lead to another concussion. It was possible she could have some memory problems, and she needed to avoid long amounts of time using her computer. She could slowly return to work, but she wasn't allowed to drive a car until she received clearance from her family doctor. *So many restrictions*, she thought.

Ben had suggested Alec drive her home since she'd be much more comfortable in his luxury vehicle. Jackie went down to the gift shop and purchased a simple dress for Kelly to wear home. Jackie helped her dress right before she and Ben left the hospital. She kissed her daughter goodbye and gave Kelly a knowing look.

For the first time since she'd woken, Alec and Kelly were truly alone. She could tell he was nervous. He started pacing the hospital room, waiting until the nurse returned with her release papers. All of a sudden, he couldn't look at her. She fidgeted with her hair. She'd had enough.

"Alec, will you please sit down. You're making me dizzy with your pacing back and forth."

He stopped pacing, turned, and looked at her, worried that she was experiencing one of the many symptoms of a concussion.

"I'm fine. Just please stop, will you?"

The nurse walked through the door with her release papers and wheelchair. Alec went to get the car while the nurse wheeled Kelly to the front of the hospital.

"Is that your husband?" the nurse asked.

"No, just a friend."

"For a friend, he was quite worried about you. I was working a shift in the ER last night. When he arrived, he was in a panic until he knew you were going to be alright. Whatever you say, that man really cares about you… And he's not bad to look at either."

Kelly laughed. "No, he isn't. Being a doctor, you wouldn't think he'd show such emotion."

"That's because he has feelings for you. I can see it in his eyes and on his face. If I was a betting woman, I'd say he's head over heels in love with you."

"I don't know about that, but yes he is special."

Alec was waiting for them at the front of the hospital. Alec put his hand out to help her from the wheelchair. She grabbed it and slowly stood. He wrapped his arm around her waist and led her to the car. She was quite sore from the crash itself, so he helped her ease down into her seat and secure her seatbelt. Just before closing the door, he leaned down, placing his hand along her jaw and brushed his lips across hers. It was the slightest of touches, but with it she felt a lifetime of promise. She knew they were going to be alright. They'd talk through what happened and make amends.

Alec got into the car, put it in drive, and slowly eased away from the curb. As he got on the highway heading towards home, he reached across the seat for her hand. Grabbing it in his, he squeezed it tightly and glanced at her out of the corner of his eye. They didn't say a word. She saw his love for her in the way he looked at her. He moved her hand and rested it atop his thigh where there hands remained the entire drive home. They were barely on the highway when Kelly drifted off to sleep. She needed her rest to help her recovery. Every few minutes, Alec caught himself glancing Kelly's way. Alec had made his decision when he was on the telephone with Alejandro. He knew Joe would kill him, but he was going to take time off to spend with Kelly as she recuperated.

Kelly slept the entire way to Alejandro's house. Angelina must have been watching for his car, for she ran from the house as soon as he pulled in the driveway. Alejandro wasn't far behind. Before Alec could put the car in park, Alejandro had opened the door and was lifting Kelly into his arms. Kelly woke up just as they crossed the threshold into the house.

"Alejandro what are you doing? Put me down. I didn't break a leg, just my head." She started to laugh, but grabbed the side of her head. She still had a blasted headache that she hoped would go away soon.

Alejandro carried her into the family room and placed her on the sofa. Angelina grabbed a pillow and blanket.

"Will you all please stop! I am not an invalid. I can walk. I can take care of myself," Kelly said as Angelina tried to cover her with the blanket.

Angelina gave her a look that could kill, but relented. "Okay, okay, I'll stop. We were just worried about you after everything that happened."

"I know that, I really do. But I'm fine, really. With just a little rest, I'll be back to normal."

Alec looked at Alejandro and shrugged his shoulders. *If that's the way she wanted it*, he thought.

Alec decided to head on home and get some rest. Kelly was in good hands. Between Angelina and Alejandro, nothing would get past them. "I'm going to head on home for a little while. I'll be back later," Alec said as he leaned down and kissed the top of Kelly's head.

Alejandro walked him out. "Alec you look like hell. You definitely need some rest. Don't worry about Kelly—she'll be fine."

"I know," he said as he walked out the front door.

Alec wasn't sure how he'd made it home, but he did. He went directly to his bedroom where he fell face-first onto his bed. He slept for hours. When he woke, darkness had fallen. He looked at his watch. It was almost ten o'clock. He knew Kelly must be asleep, so he called his brother's and spoke with Angelina. Kelly had gone to bed earlier. She was following doctor's orders and was resting. "I'll come by in the morning, then."

"Alec, she'll be fine. She just needs her rest."

Alec hung up the phone and closed his eyes, going back to

sleep. He dreamed of Kelly—dreamed of a future with her.

Alec woke to a dreary Saturday morning. It was cloudy and rain was expected the entire day. He fixed himself a cup of coffee and spent the morning in his home office planning his future. The first thing he did was check in with Angelina to see how Kelly was doing. Next, he planned on calling Bill. He was going through with the install with or without Kelly—he wasn't even sure if she wanted to stay with the company. Maybe he could convince her to move back to St. Louis. Dream... he could dream all he wanted, but it was ultimately up to Kelly. His future depended on her.

❦

Alec took a week off and spent a good deal of it with Kelly. He didn't want to press her about what happened. He knew she'd eventually talk to him about everything. She hadn't been cleared to drive yet, so he drove her to her parents' and helped wherever he needed to.

First thing Monday morning, Kelly phoned Bill. After speaking with him, she decided maybe she and Ariel could try to have a friendship again. It would take work and forgiveness on her part, but she honestly missed her friend and wanted her back in her life.

Kelly still hadn't had her talk with Alec. She needed to tell him everything, especially since the details would come out at Ken's eventual trial. Kelly was having a particularly good day and she decided now was the time to open up to Alec. That was the only way they could move forward with their relationship.

Kelly asked Angelina if she could help her pack a picnic lunch. Angelina went all out, preparing homemade chicken salad sandwiches with homemade chips, carrots and celery to nibble on, and a mixture of fresh strawberries, grapes, and pineapple for dessert. Angelina had also made lemonade.

Kelly surprised Alec when he came by to pick her up under the ruse that he was taking her to her parents' for a visit. Angelina had snuck the picnic basket into his car while he waited for Kelly. He started in the direction of her parents, but she instead directed him to a nearby park, pretending she decided to go for a walk instead. They had yet to talk about Ken and the events leading up to her accident. He had let things go hoping she'd be the one to open-up. He felt like he'd been walking on egg shells, afraid to broach the subject that was always on his mind. He just hoped they could finally clear the air and make things right between them again. Since she'd returned home from the hospital, things had been tense to say the least.

Alec drove towards the back of the park where he spotted a bench. It was somewhat secluded, so they shouldn't have any interruptions. He exited the car and came around to her side, but she'd already gotten out of the car by the time he'd made his way to her. He grabbed her hand and wrapped it in the crook of his arm.

"Don't forget the picnic basket," she said. "It's in the backseat on the floor."

"We're here for a picnic?" he said, surprised. "I thought you just wanted to talk."

"That, too," she chuckled as she led him towards the bench. "We can eat here."

"You sure?"

"Yep." Kelly sat down and Alec placed the basket on the ground beside his feet. "Eat or talk first?" she asked.

"I'd like to have that talk first. Lately, we've spent a significant amount of time together but mainly we've been with our families. We haven't had that quality time of just you and me." Alec said as he reached for her hand. He raised her hand to his lips and kissed it. "I've missed this… You and me just enjoying ourselves."

He smiled at her and, for the first time since everything fell apart at the clinic, she didn't feel the tension that had hung in the air. Alec looked rested and more himself. It had just taken a few days, knowing that she would make a full recovery, for him to settle down and stop his fretting.

Alec continued holding Kelly's hand. They sat in silence momentarily before either one of them spoke. Alec was the first to speak. "How's your headache? Better?"

"Alec, please. I already told you this morning that it was gone. Please stop worrying. If I have any recurring symptoms, I'll tell you. I'm fine, really."

He nodded. She squeezed his hand and turned slightly on the bench so she was facing him directly.

"I need to tell you something, and I just want you to listen, okay?"

"Sure."

"First of all, you need to know that the night of the accident I was coming home to see you. After the incident in my office, I fled to the cabin because I needed to think. I was furious with you for having gone to Bill behind my back. And then, as I sat in the cabin, I realized that you only had my best interest at heart. So I jumped in the car. And then… well, you know the rest. I hit that damn deer. I can't even think about that."

Kelly looked down at their clasped hands. "What I'm going to tell you, I've wanted to share with you ever since I told you that I wanted to date you, but that I needed to move slowly. Remember that day?"

Alec nodded, listening intently.

"Alec, I need to tell you why I said what I said that day, and why I've backed away from your advances. It's not that

I didn't want to kiss you or get more serious, it's just that I couldn't at the time." Kelly took a breath and looked at Alec—he was looking back at her attentively.

"When I first started working at Lattice, I really enjoyed it. Ariel and I had become the best of friends. I was learning about the corporate world and was slowly making it up the ranks." She paused again and looked at their joined hands. She caught Alec's eye and smiled at him.

"I was there for a few months when I was transferred to Ken's department. I had no choice in the matter, it just happened." She looked away from him then.

Alec noticed her change in demeanor and reached for her. He placed his hand on her face, caressing her jawline. "Take your time," he said as he smiled back at her.

Swallowing deeply, she said, "Alec, I want you to know I didn't encourage his behavior. I'm not promiscuous... I'm me. My focus was my career and not landing a guy." She pulled away from him and his hand dropped from her jaw.

"I'd been working for Ken a couple of weeks when he started expecting the overtime. And overtime for me was not leaving the office until eight o'clock at the earliest. Being new in the corporate world, I thought that my boss could expect those hours of me. I wanted to succeed, so I did what he asked. I'd been doing the overtime for a few weeks when I noticed that he always came into my office. He'd sit down and we'd discuss whatever project we were working on at the time. He tried to get friendly by putting his arm around me, patting my leg—but I didn't encourage him. I just wanted to work—get my job done for the day and go home."

Alec watched as the color started to drain from her face. "One night, he came into my office and there was a change in his demeanor. I hadn't realized what was going on until he came around to my side of the desk and sat down on the edge. He reached for my chair and pulled me closer to him. I was taken off guard. I didn't know what he was doing, and I didn't know what to do. Then, the next thing I knew, he was grabbing me and he tried to kiss me. I slapped him across the face. He just laughed then and stood up, leaving my office. I was in total shock. I wasn't sure what had happened. I grabbed my purse and went home."

Kelly pulled her hand from Alec's and started wringing her hands. "About a week later, I was just getting ready to leave for the night. My back was to the door and he came into my office and closed the door. He surprised me. I turned when I heard the door close, and he grabbed me and threw me against my desk. He tried kissing me, but I fought back. He grabbed my arm and yanked me towards him. Then he took his hand and put it around my throat. I couldn't breathe. He got in my face and told me I'd better give into him or my career would be over at Lattice. I tried to pull away from him, and when I was finally successful, my arm caught him in the nose. I ran for my phone and started to call security when he turned around and started to leave. I'll never forget… He looked back at me and said, 'I will have you, come hell or high water. You will do what I want, and you'll keep your job. If you don't, well then you know the outcome. And if you think someone will believe you, that our little *tête-à-tête* took place here, think not—I walk on water with everyone here, including HR. No one will believe you. They'll think you're just being a promiscuous tramp.'"

Alec inhaled sharply.

"There's more. Everything came to a head when I found the error with the coding of the program. I discovered that the flaw was missed with the initial testing, and I took it to him with a fix. I did all of this research, on my own time, because I wanted this program to work flawlessly. This is when my friendship with Ariel fell apart. When I approached him with the issue, he cornered me in his office and pushed me up against the bookshelves that lined the walls. When I fell against one of the bookcases, several books fell, causing a loud thud. The door to his office was partially ajar, so when the books crashed to the floor, his secretary came running in."

Kelly stopped to take a deep breath. She was having a hard time getting air into her lungs. Alec reached over and placed his hand along her back. He stroked it gently as he listened to her.

"He blamed me for missing the flaw during testing. All along I knew it was Ariel's fault. We had a confrontation—Ken, Ariel, and I. Next, Ken had called me into his office. I just remember him with his sickening laugh, setting that form in front of me. He placed me on corrective action for missing the error in the programming and for not coming into work after I discussed the problem with him."

She looked at Alec then. "I'd had a migraine and couldn't go into work. He didn't think I was sick at all. He thought I was running away from him. I was really stupid back then. I should have realized why I was getting my migraines. I'm sure they were all because of him."

Tears started forming in her eyes. "And then the last straw was… Stupid me, I was alone in the office late at night. I thought he'd gone home, but he must have come back. He surprised me when I was coming out of the ladies room. Before I knew it, he'd pushed me back through the door and had me pinned on the counter. He was crawling all over me. He had his hand around my throat and was trying to kiss me, but I kept fighting back. He reached in and bit my neck. I tried to slap him, but he grabbed my hands and held them over my head. He was trying to get my dress up… I tried, really I did… I kicked him, and he pulled back a little, but then came back at me. I'd just heard the bodice of my dress rip when we heard a noise. The cleaning crew had come down the hall and had started with the men's room. I can still remember him snarling at me and his hot, putrid breath on my face. He pulled away when he realized he was going to be caught. As he left, he reminded me that he was in control of my job. Since I hadn't given him what he wanted, I would pay. Days later, Bill called me into his office and fired me."

Alec pulled her into his arms. The tears were streaming down her face. He held her until she pulled away.

"I felt so dejected. I thought Bill wouldn't believe anything I had to say. Yes, there was physical proof, but it was also my word against his. I know what he did was wrong, and I know I should have done something, but I believed him. I didn't think anyone would believe anything I had to say about their star employee. I was still relatively new, and I thought HR would think I was just trying to cause problems. I know I should have done something… but I can't look back now. Ken's going to pay for what he did to me and Ariel.  I hope he pays for a long time."

Alec pulled her back into his arms and sat back against the bench. She laid her head on his shoulder. Alec knew they needed to discuss his part in her being rehired by Bill. This was the last piece they needed to get out in the open, and then they could get on with their lives.

Alec didn't know how to begin, so he just threw it out there. "Kelly, I'm sorry for what I did." She pulled away and looked at him, unsure where he was going. "I'm sorry for not being truthful with you. I went to Bill and pretty much threatened him to give you your job back. You were so unhappy and seemed to miss the work. If I'd known what I know now, I would have walked away from him quicker than you can say—" Kelly stopped him by placing her hand on his thigh.

"Alec when I discovered the role you played in my rehiring, I was upset. I felt you lied to me about everything. When I ran out of your office, I didn't know who I could trust." She paused and turned towards him, placing her hand on his chest. "But then I sat back and thought about it. You were doing what you thought would make me happy. You had no idea about Ken and what he was doing. All you knew was that I liked my job and wanted it back. What I really wanted was this. Being home with my family and being with you. I didn't know it at first but I certainly do now. Let's forget about your role here. I forgive you, and that's all there is to it."

Kelly wrapped her arms around Alec's waist. Alec continued speaking, "Kelly, thank-you for wanting to forget the role I played. I don't know if I can be so easy on myself. I let this happen here under my own control. I'm so sorry you went through this. I wish you had felt safe going to someone. Alejandro and I only discovered what I'm about to tell you the morning of the incident in your office. I had an investigator look into his background. Ken's previous employer was a good friend of Alejandro's in medical school. We both discovered that Ken had these same issues with another employer. Somehow, he was able to walk away. But this time, I know he won't. We have way too much on him now and since Ariel is charging him for rape—there's evidence in the matter, so I'm sure he'll be doing some serious jail time for that alone."

They sat in one another's arms, watching the birds hop about the open field in front of them. When her stomach growled, they realized that they hadn't eaten yet. Alec retrieved the basket from the ground beside him and pulled out the various dishes Angelina had prepared. "Looks like everything is intact here."

"What do you mean?"

"At least Angelina didn't burn anything."

Kelly snorted, laughing. They'd finally aired out everything that had happened to her and now she was on the road to recovery. Now that he knew what had truly happened to her, he knew he'd be able to help her overcome her memories. He loved her and he was going to show her exactly how much.

Alec drove her downtown after they'd finished their picnic. He loved the riverfront and wanted to walk along through the history of St. Louis with her. He took her to Laclede's Landing and they walked amongst the old buildings. They strolled along the riverfront, taking in the sights and sounds of the city. Alec loved to look at the Eads Bridge. He loved the iron work and arches that spanned the Mississippi River. They ended up at the Arch, the Gateway to the West. It was here, looking up at the arch, that Alec told her he loved her for the second time.

"Kelly, I'm going to say this and I don't' expect you to say anything in return. I just want you to know that I love you."

Kelly knew that he loved her. She reached up, putting both arms around Alec's neck squeezing him tightly. They didn't say anything—they both knew what the other felt. Kelly wasn't prepared to tell Alec that she loved him. Just not yet. She'd do it in her own time.

He squeezed her hand as they continued down the path to the Old Cathedral. They went inside to say a prayer. Alec hoped that one day she'd be able to share the same words with him that he'd shared with her. He believed she would, in time, and knew she'd do it when she was ready.

# Chapter Thirty-Nine

KELLY DECIDED SHE WANTED TO see the project through at the clinic. She would get the experience she wanted running a project of this magnitude, and then she would move on. She was still working on regaining her self-confidence, but she'd come a long way on her road to recovery.

Things were going well for her and Alec. Angel's baptism was the following week and she couldn't wait to be her god-mother. She loved Angel with an intensity she never thought possible. She wondered what it would feel like to have a child of her own. She couldn't begin to imagine the outpouring of love she'd feel for a child of her own flesh and blood.

Alec had worked non-stop since returning to work after Kelly's accident. He felt he needed to make up for the time he missed while Joe and Ashton had covered for him.

They'd spent time together over the last two weeks, but they were always with family. Tonight would be special. Alec finally had a weekend off—in fact, two weekends in a row. He'd been planning a date with Kelly for the last two weeks—one that she wouldn't forget in her lifetime.

❨

Kelly had fully recovered from the accident and was nearing the end of the installation at the clinic. All that remained was some training and the final push of data to the new system. She expected to be done in the next three weeks. She hadn't told anyone yet, about her decision to leave Lattice Works. She needed to move on and put her whole experience behind her. She also couldn't imagine a long distance relationship with Alec any longer. She was spoiled from being with him on a daily basis. She didn't want to give that up, so she was going to take some time off and move back to St. Louis. She learned a huge lesson from what had happened to her—family was the most important thing in the world to her. She didn't want to turn her back on them again, rarely seeing them for only snippets of time. She needed to be around her family. She'd forgotten how much they truly meant to her... And Alec. She knew she wouldn't be able to survive without him nearby.

Kelly was going to share her decision with him when they went on their date. All Alec asked of her was that she dress up. He wanted to take her somewhere special since this was the first time he'd been able to take her out since going back to work.

Kelly decided she owed it to herself, so she splurged on a new dress, shoes, and a purse. She even went to the hair salon and had her hair styled for the evening. She was looking forward to their date because she decided that she was finally going to tell him that she loved him. Neither of them had really outwardly spoken of their feelings since the picnic, and even then it was only Alec sharing. *Now is the time*, she thought. Alec needed to know how much he meant to her. She was leaving her job for two reasons, but mainly because she wanted to be closer to him. He needed to know exactly what he meant to her.

Kelly dressed and met Angelina in the kitchen while she

waited for Alec. Angelina had just finished cleaning up the dinner dishes, Alejandro was reading Matthew a bedtime story before putting him to bed, and Angel was sitting in her bouncy seat, watching her mother put the last of the dishes in the dishwasher.

"Well, how do I look?" asked Kelly as she spun around in a circle before taking a seat at the table. She was wearing a black cocktail dress paired with black heels. She wore a simple, gold, diamond-cut necklace and gold drop earrings that had little diamonds glittering in her ears. Her hair was styled in a French twist.

"You look fabulous. Do you know where Alec's taking you?"

"No, I don't. He just told me to dress up. He wanted to take me somewhere special, saying that we owed it to ourselves after what I'd been through."

"I'm glad that he's treating you to a night on the town. I remember when Alejandro and I used to do that." Angelina got a huge smile on her face. "I remember when Alejandro proposed to me like it was yesterday."

Kelly smiled at her. "Yeah, I know he proposed twice and both times were special."

Angelina became a bit dreamy, "At the Botanical Gardens, it kind of just spilled out. He hadn't intended on asking me to marry him that day, and then we had that special dinner." Sighing, Angelina added, "It was just magical."

"Yeah, and you kept it all to yourselves, too."

"We did, but we wanted to share our news when everyone could be together—a family event. I can still see the look on Mom's face. She was so surprised."

"What? Who was surprised?" asked Alejandro as he walked into the room.

"Mom, when you announced that we were engaged at the

Fourth of July party."

"That was pretty special." Turning to Kelly, Alejandro whistled. "Kelly, you look stunning." Alejandro approached her and kissed her cheek. "My brother is a lucky man."

As if they had called him, Alec knocked on the kitchen door. Alejandro turned and opened the door. "And you cleanup well, too," he said as he led Alec into the room.

One look at Kelly, and Alec was a goner. He was speechless.

"She's stunning, isn't she, little brother?"

She was the most beautiful woman Alec had ever seen. But her dress is what kept his eye. Kelly's dress was elegant and covered in black lace. Alec's eyes went to the V neckline that wasn't cut too low and had three-quarter length sleeves with a black lace overlay. It was a modest length, just coming to her knees. Alec thought she looked spectacular. He loved her hair styled with tendrils of hair framing her face. She glowed. Beautiful was the only word that came to his mind.

Alec approached Kelly, leaned in, and kissed her cheek. "You look beautiful."

Kelly giggled. She was more than ready to go on their date. She grabbed her purse, hooked her hand around his forearm, and smiled at Angelina and Alejandro. "Don't wait up for me," she chuckled as Alec walked her to the door.

"We won't," they said in unison.

Alejandro waited until the door had closed before speaking. "I'll bet tonight's the night."

"For what?"

"If you haven't figured it out by now…"

The light bulb went off for her. Screeching, Angelina said, "Oh, I hope so. They make a beautiful couple."

"Time will tell," Alejandro said as they watched Alec help Kelly into the car. "From the look on his face, he's a goner.

That's for sure."

Alec turned back to the house just as he was ready to shut Kelly's car door. "If it's not your mother, then it's your sister and her husband."

"What are you talking about?"

"Look," he said, pointing to the window.

Kelly started laughing. There stood Angelina and Alejandro, snooping on them just like Jackie had done when Angelina and Alejandro were dating.

"I guess it's in the genes," Kelly said as he shut the door.

Alec drove Kelly out into the country. He was taking her to a special restaurant that was surrounded by a winery. The valet met them as they pulled around the front circle of the restaurant. He opened the door for Kelly, but Alec made his way to her side before the valet could assist her.

"I've got this," Alec said as he helped Kelly from the car. The valet handed Alec his claim check and took off with the car. Alec offered Kelly his arm as he guided her through the doorway into the historic restaurant. Alec had reserved their special dining room. The hostess recognized him—he'd been there earlier in the day, dropping off his surprises for her.

"Dr. Alvarez, it's good to see you. Please, this way," the hostess said as she led them through the restaurant.

"Where are we going?" Kelly asked as they made their way through the main part of the restaurant and headed up a flight of stairs. The hostess led them down a hallway and through a doorway. Kelly was speechless when she saw the room. He had reserved a private dining room with a balcony that overlooked the vineyard.

Alec held her chair out, leaned in, and kissed her cheek. "I hope you like it," he said. With that, their waiter appeared with a bouquet of roses. He handed them to Alec so he could present to her. "Sweetheart, for you," he said as he set the vase on the table.

"Oh, Alec, they're beautiful." Kelly said as she leaned over, smelling them. "And they smell so good. Thank you," she said, reaching over to kiss him. "What's the occasion?"

"I wanted tonight to be special."

Alec had already chosen the wine for the evening. The sommelier entered the room and presented the wine for Alec's approval. He poured a sampling in a glass, and Alec swished the liquid around in the glass, sipped it, and approved. The sommelier filled Kelly's glass, then topped off Alec's. He left the wine chilling in a bucket beside the table. When they were alone again, Alec proposed a toast. "To an evening I hope you will cherish a lifetime." He leaned over and kissed her.

The waiter returned with their menus. Kelly listened to the specials and after the waiter left, she turned to Alec. "Everything sounds so good. I have no idea what I want."

Alec smiled at her.

"Alec this restaurant is gorgeous. I feel like I've been here before, but I know I haven't. The whole setup seems so familiar."

He knew why it seemed so familiar to her, but he wasn't going to share the reason with her until the end of their evening. "How about I order for you?"

"Thank you, I'd love that. I couldn't make a decision even if I had to, and I know I have to if I want to eat," she laughed, putting her menu aside to take in the ambience of the room. Candles were alight all over the room. There was a slight chill in the air and the fireplace was lit, adding a touch of romance.

Alec placed their orders but Kelly wasn't paying attention to what he ordered for her—she was taken in by the beauty surrounding her. A violinist came out of the wings and started playing. Alec stood and reached for Kelly's hand.

"May I have this dance?"

"Certainly," she said as Alec helped her from the chair.

He pulled her into his arms, and they swayed back and forth to the music. He loved having her in his arms. They belonged together always; he just hoped that she saw it that way, too.

They danced until their dinner was served. They started off with Caesar salads. Alec surprised her—he'd ordered grilled salmon with a lemon dill sauce. When the waiter brought it to the table, it looked mouth-watering. It came with roasted new potatoes and wilted spinach. Alec had ordered blackened tuna with the same vegetable combination for himself. He loved tuna fixed practically any way, but blackened was his favorite.

"I knew you loved salmon," he said as the waiter left them alone.

"Oh my gosh, this is fabulous," Kelly said as she took a bite of the salmon. "You know me so well. And the wilted spinach. Not many restaurants serve this on their menu."

"I made sure they had it on hand."

She looked at Alec and realized that she loved him even more than she thought she did. Never would she have thought he would go to these extremes. Roses, wilted spinach…. *Wow, if I wasn't in love before, I sure am now. This is the perfect setting to tell him I love him,* she thought. *Absolutely perfect!*

They ate their dinner. The foremost topic of discussion was their godchild's baptism which was scheduled for the following weekend. "She's getting so big now. I can't believe it. Angelina's such a good mother. And Alejandro…"

"Alejandro is Alejandro. He's a fabulous dad, especially with what he's gone through. I'm just happy we made it past the anniversary of Tammy and Michael's deaths without incident. I know he had some issues right before, but I hope to high heaven that his grief is behind him and he can go on without falling apart every year. It's hard on him, but it's really hard on Angelina. And when Matthew begins to notice it, like he did this year, it makes it even worse. Oh, just so you know, Ashton is supposed to get together with Matthew at the party."

"And do what?"

"Talk to him... Apologize for questioning Alejandro. Put him at ease."

"Really?"

"Yep. Joe and I talked to him, as did Alejandro. I hope he does what he says he's going to do. Matthew doesn't need to be afraid of doctors."

"You're so right." Kelly said as she ate the last bite of her salmon. A winsome smile crossed her face as she swallowed her last bite.

"What's that smile for?" he asked.

"I'm smiling because this is a perfect evening, a perfect choice in restaurant. I loved my dinner and—"

Before she could finish her thought, the waiter returned to take their plates. The violinist was still playing softly in the background. Alec reached for her hand and led her to the dance floor again. If she didn't know better, it looked like the lights in the room had dimmed.

Alec put his arms around her waist and drew her close. Kelly wrapped her arms around his neck and settled her head on his chest, right above his heart. She could hear it beating underneath her ear.

As they danced, Alec squeezed his arms tighter around her. She could hear the thump, thump, thump of his heart increase. She wondered why—they were just swaying to the music. They weren't really moving intensely to cause an increase in his heartrate.

She pulled her head away and looked him in the eye. She noticed a twinkle, but assumed it had something to do with the candles flickering all about the room. Kelly didn't notice that the waiter had returned with their desserts while they had been dancing. He turned her back towards the table and she noticed German chocolate cheesecake and tiramisu were waiting for them on the table.

"Dessert?" she asked as she pulled away from him and made her way to the table. "Is this from Miss Kelly's?"

"Good eye, it is," he said as he helped her with her chair. He sat down and reached under his napkin, hoping that his last surprise was waiting for him.

"I'm shocked that this place allowed you to bring in dessert from another restaurant."

"Well, I told them it was a special night for us, and they were just fine with it."

Looking around the room, Kelly said, "This restaurant, the candles, roses, dessert from Miss Kelly's… what other surprises do you have in store for me tonight?" she asked jokingly. "This has been a night to remember."

Alec turned and reached for her hand, and then he spoke the words he'd never spoken before to anyone. "Kelly, I received a gift the day you slid off the road. I'd been so wrapped up in my career, I had no time for anyone except family. And then you opened your door and there you were. I never expected to have this conversation with anyone, but especially you. You're Angelina's sister—it's not like I didn't know you. And then life threw me a curveball."

Alec reached under his napkin and grabbed the box that had been placed there by the waiter. He slid it into his hand and then dropped down on one knee in front of Kelly.

She gasped, staring at him with wide eyes.

"Sweetheart, I'm sorry you went through what you did, but you losing your job was the best thing that could have happened to me." He squeezed her hand, "I know you lost yourself there for a while, but I hope I helped you find yourself again, too."

She nodded as tears started to fill her eyes.

"Kelly, I know I told you I loved you the other day. I've wanted to tell you that for so long, and then you told me everything, and I thought the time was right. But it wasn't the right time to say what I really wanted to say. I love you. I love you more than I ever thought I could love anyone. When you ran out of the clinic and disappeared, I thought I had lost you. I was going crazy with worry, and then when I got the call from the highway patrol about your accident, I almost lost it. I thought that I had lost the love of my life, and I hadn't had the chance to tell her. But here I am, on bended knee, telling you how much I love you and how much you mean to me.

"And then there's Angel, our goddaughter. I look at you, and the love you have for her shines brightly every time you hold her. And then I think, what would your face look like if you had your own child?"

Kelly was smiling falteringly through her tears, her eyes never leaving his face.

Alec reached up to brush them aside. "Sweetheart, I want to see that special look on your face that you get when holding Angel in your arms, but I want to see that look when you hold our child in your arms. Kelly, what I'm trying to say but not doing a very good job at, is—"

She interrupted him. "You're doing just fine," she said, smiling.

"Kelly, I love you more than you could possibly imagine. Will you do me the honor of becoming my wife? Will you raise a family with me?"

Kelly was doing her best to choke back tears, and said, "Alec, I've loved you from the moment you told me to 'just hit the damn deer' to now. I think we were meant to be together. There's always a reason why events play out the way they do. From the deer, to Ken, and everything that happened in between…"

"Will you please just answer my question?" Alec laughed shakily. "Will you marry me?"

"Yes, Alec. I will marry you. I'd love to have a family with you."

Alec opened the box that he'd kept hidden in his hand. And there before her was a ring like no other. A large oval shaped diamond was the highlight of the ring. Nestled beside it on either side were two smaller heart shaped diamonds mounted at an angle. She'd never seen anything like it before in all of her life.

Alec pulled the ring from the box and reached for her hand. Slowly, he eased it down her finger. It wasn't a perfect fit, but it would do for the night.

"Oh Alec, it's beautiful."

"Almost as beautiful as you are," he said as he leaned in and kissed her with a passion that he'd never felt comfortable giving before. She was healing and moving forward. They'd still work on building her comfort level, one step at a time. Alec returned to his seat and reached for the champagne that the waiter had left. He poured them each a glass. "To love and marriage," he said as she smiled back at him.

"It's finally come to me… Why this restaurant is so familiar. This is where Alejandro proposed to Angelina, isn't it?"

"The second time, yes. It was magical for them, and I thought it would be magical for us, too."

"And it is," she said as she glanced down at her ring. "When are we going to tell our family?"

"I think we should do what Angelina and Alejandro did, but this time announce it at Angel's baptism. All of our family will be there. What better way to spread our good news but on the day our goddaughter is baptized? And besides, I need to get your ring sized."

Kelly laughed.

They ended their meal on a high note, savoring the luscious desserts from Miss Kelly's. It had been a magical night for her. Never in her wildest dreams had she thought she'd end up becoming engaged to Alec Alvarez.

# Epilogue

ONE WEEK LATER, THE FAMILY was gathered to celebrate the baptism of Angelina Maria Alvarez. Her godparents stood proudly on the altar as she was given her name, but Alec couldn't take his eyes off of Kelly. The love she had for Angel just took his breath away. He knew that one day he'd see that look on her face when she was holding their own child in her arms.

The after-party was held at Alejandro's house. It was a beautiful day and everyone had gathered on the patio to celebrate. While Kelly had snuck into the house to help with the finishing touches on the food, Alec snagged Ben and walked with him to the back of the property. He knew he needed his blessing before announcing to everyone their surprise.

"Ben, I need to ask you a question."

Ben knew what the question was going to be from the look he'd witnessed in this very same spot almost three years earlier.

"Yes."

"Yes? I haven't even asked the question yet."

"I know what your question is because Alejandro asked me the same thing in this very same spot. Yes, you may marry my daughter. What is it with you Alvarez boys anyway?

Same spot, and at a family party. How long have you been engaged? I have to believe you've already asked and gotten your answer."

"Yes, I have, and she said yes," he said, grinning.

"You're a good man, Alec. Welcome to the family."

"Thank you, sir. I just want you to know that I love your daughter. I wasn't looking for love, but I'm glad I found it. Kelly's a remarkable woman, and I'm lucky to have her in my life."

Ben clapped him on the back. "Let's get back to the party. I'm anxious to see the look on Jackie's face when you make your announcement. I think she'll be more than surprised."

As Ben and Alec were walking back toward the house, he saw Ashton walking alongside the patio talking to Matthew. Alec couldn't hear what he said, but what he saw put a smile on his face. Matthew reached out his hand to shake Ashton's. Alec guessed that all was well on that front, but then he saw Gabriella approach Ashton. He could hear raised voices and she was pointing her finger at Ashton and then she gestured to Matthew. Something else was said, and she hurried off in a huff. *That's my sister,* he thought. *There's never a dull moment when she's around.*

"What was that all about?" Alec said as he approached Ashton.

"I haven't the faintest idea. One minute I'm putting all of my issues aside with Matthew, and the next Gabriella is yelling at me to stay away from him. All I can say is, women."

Alec laughed as he and Ashton joined everyone on the patio. He knew Gabriella disliked Ashton with a passion, but he knew how he could cheer her up. His and Kelly's announcement would certainly put a smile on her face.

The afternoon proceeded as planned and, just when it was time to cut the cake celebrating Angel's christening, Alec grabbed Kelly's hand and moved to the cake table. Alejandro looked at them with eyebrows raised.

Alec raised his voice so everyone could hear, "I know Angelina and Alejandro are happy that each of you could share in such a special occasion. This is a special day, not only for Angel, but for this family, too." This day was all about family and close friends. Everyone from both sides of the family was in attendance, along with Ashton and Sadie. Alejandro had also invited a few neighbors, along with his assistant Suzie.

Kelly smiled up at Alec, and he reached for her hand. "Kelly and I are honored to be Angel's godparents." Looking towards his brother and sister-in-law, he added, "We hope we won't let you down with our responsibilities—we don't take them lightly. Angel is a special little girl, and we're honored to be here in this capacity... But now to the real reason for me standing up here, blabbering while everyone's waiting for cake."

Jackie reached for her husband's hand. Could this be what she'd prayed for?

"Earlier this year, I was driving home down a country road and, quite frankly, ran into this woman who'd driven off the road to avoid hitting a deer—"

Someone called out from the crowd, "Don't you know you should hit the deer?"

Everyone laughed.

"Well, that day I found a cold and sad-looking woman who had lost her way." He smiled at Kelly. "We've had our ups and downs and, to you in the back, she did end up hitting a deer, just not that one."

Another round of laughter rang out.

"But on a serious note... Kelly came into my life when I least expected it. She's brightened my day every day that she's been here." Alec paused, taking a deep breath. "I'd like everyone to know that I've asked Kelly to be my wife, and she's accepted."

Cheers rang out from the crowd as Kelly beamed at them. Jackie was jumping for joy. Angelina was clapping and grinning for the couple.

Alec turned and pulled Kelly's ring from his pocket. He placed the ring back onto her finger. The jeweler had been able to size her ring and immediately get it back to him so he could share it with their friends and family on this special occasion.

Jackie ran up and hugged and kissed the happy couple. Maria and John were right behind with their well wishes.

Angelina walked up to Kelly, hugging her tightly, "I'm so happy for you two. Who would have guessed that you catching the bouquet, and Alec snagging the garter would lead to this day?"

"I did," chimed in Alejandro. "And what do you know—I was right."

All of them laughed. Yes, he did predict their marriage.

"You know what's kind of ironic about our whole engagement?" said Kelly.

"What?"

"We got engaged at the same restaurant you did. And we're announcing it in the same way you did—a family affair."

"And I asked your father here, too—just like Alejandro did." Alec chimed in.

"You did?"

"According to Ben, the exact same place with the exact same expression on my face."

They all laughed at the irony of the situation.

Alec wrapped his arms around Kelly. Life was good—he'd found the woman of his dreams.

## Author's Note:

Thank you so much for reading Life's Gateway to Happiness, the second book in The Show Me Series. For news and updates from Anne Stone, visit www.AnneStoneAuthor.com where you can subscribe to her newsletter. Here you'll be treated to information about new releases, sneak peeks, giveaways, and bonus material just for signing up.

If you enjoyed reading Life's Gateway to Happiness, please consider leaving a review. Reviews are always appreciated!

*Anne*

# About the Author

Anne Stone has been a fan of romance since reading Katherine by Anya Seton her senior year of high school. In college, she penned her first novel which ended up at the bottom of a desk drawer after being rejected by a publishing house. She's constantly dabbled in drafting stories but her career always seemed to get in the way. Anne decided to take the plunge and self-publish. Self-publishing allows her to write the kind of book that she enjoys reading and doesn't put a limit on her creativity. Originally from St. Louis, Anne currently resides in Wisconsin with her Cavalier King Charles Spaniel.

**Connect with Anne online:**
Visit Anne's website and sign-up for her newsletter:
**www.Annestoneauthor.com**
Follow Anne on Facebook at:
**www.facebook.com/AnneStoneAuthor/**
Join Anne's Facebook Street Team at:
**www.facebook.com/groups/496950213844885/**
Follow Anne on Twitter at:
**@AuthorAnneStone**
Email Anne at:
**Anne@Annestoneauthor.com**

# Also by Anne Stone

**The Show Me Series:**
Life's Second Chances
Life's Gateway to Happiness
Life's Turned Upside Down (Coming soon)
Life's Second Journey (Coming soon)

**Williams & Company:**
Never Lose Hope